It's 1951, and US Air Force Captain Brian Flynn hails from Roswell, New Mexico. He's twenty-six, queer, and back in the closet thanks to his homophobic father. And he's deeply tired of alien jokes. But Brian has bigger worries than his hometown's recent extraterrestrial reputation. Brian's the new security director at a top-secret atomic energy research facility in the sage-dusted plains of Idaho. His job is simple: keep any plutonium from walking out the door, keep the scientists safe from themselves, or, failing that, keep them from killing anyone else.

Nuclear physicist Dr. Aaron Antares is a cowboy in every sense of the word: the boots, the attitude, the homoerotic overtones. But in addition to gleefully violating every security procedure Brian can come up with, he's also keeping a secret.

Brian knows Aaron is dangerous long before he discovers his out-of-this-world secret. The man flirts too freely, laughs too loudly, and can't play straight to save his life. But Aaron's amber eyes and gentle offers of a ride home in the flurrying Idaho snows are wearing down Brian's defenses.

Will these two men find love in the high desert, or will they be kept apart by the cruelties of the Atomic Age?

NUCLEAR SUNRISE

Jo Carthage

A NineStar Press Publication

www.ninestarpress.com

Nuclear Sunrise

© 2023 Jo Carthage

Cover Art © 2023 Jaycee DeLorenzo

Edited by Elizabetta McKay

First Edition, December 2023

ISBN: 978-1-64890-701-2

Also available in eBook, ISBN: 978-1-64890-700-5

CONTENT WARNING:

This book contains sexually explicit content, which may only be suitable for mature readers. Depictions of physical abuse (past, off page), including child abuse, mental abuse by a family member, hate speech, death of a family member, homophobia, murder, institutional regulation against LGBTQ people, racist language, human trafficking/slavery, and workplace harassment.

To M—, who I love with all my heart and A—, who has my heart.

Epigraph

"The new concept was called a breeder reactor and was cooled by liquid metal. Experimental Breeder Reactor I (EBR-I) was designed and built by Argonne and erected in 1950 on a windswept desert plateau in Southeast Idaho. On December 21, 1951, EBR-I became the first nuclear reactor to produce usable amounts of electric power when it lighted four 150-watt light bulbs. Later, it supplied power to the entire facility. Those participating in the experiment on that cold December day chalked their names on the concrete wall of the reactor building to commemorate the event."

—Argonne News, About the People and Programs of Argonne National Laboratory, 1986.

Chapter One: T-100 Days

"It should be borne in mind that even a moderate amount of complaint in a matter of this sort is significant. For a person to make such a complaint in his own case implies that he feels a sense of injustice so great that he is willing to risk publicizing the stigma of having been discharged from the Army under circumstances which savor of disgrace. For each complainant there are many more persons who feel the same sense of injustice but prefer to bury their hurt in as much oblivion as possible."

—History of the Phrase "Discharged Under Conditions Other Than Dishonorable" and Present Discharge Criteria for Three Services. Investigations of the National War Effort: Blue Discharges. United States Committee on Veterans' Affairs, House of Representatives, 1949

September 11, 1951
Experimental Breeder Reactor 1 (19.9 miles outside of Arco, ID)

Captain Brian Flynn slung his duffel bag over his shoulder with a grimace as he stepped out of the air force Jeep, boots crunching in the black volcanic gravel. An older white man in a lab coat hustled out of the massive white cinder block building that nearly glowed in the Idaho twilight. Brian settled his feet a little more firmly in front of the building that would be his home for the next two years as his ride peeled away, heading back east toward the saw-toothed mountains.

"Captain Flynn!"

Brian's attention snapped to the approaching scientist, and he forced a smile; he had to make this posting work. *He had to.*

The man's broad grin made him look a half century younger. Brian felt something lift in his chest. The man's voice was a warm baritone when he said, "Welcome to our little science experiment."

His hand-stitched name tag identified him as Dr. Zinn, the chief scientist of this project. He turned to face the installation, its anonymously industrial architecture stark against a sunset-gilded sea of scrubby sage and dark stone. "It sure is a shitty-looking building."

Brian kept his face stony. "I couldn't say, sir."

Dr. Zinn's gray eyes twinkled, but he kept a straight face. "They picked this site for the Experimental Breeder Reactor number 1—EBT-I to those of us who know and love her—so if we all blow ourselves up tomorrow, it'll be a thousand years of poisoned water for the local cows rather than a real metropolitan area. The fact that they built it to look like a high school gymnasium speaks more to the air force's aesthetics than our mission here."

Brian glanced back across the vast volcanic plain to the mountains, the last of the light shining off their man-eating snowdrifts. "Beautiful mountains though. I've never lived near the Rockies, and with all the sage, it smells like New Mexico." He ground a heel in the gravel beneath his military-issue boots. "The soil here is all volcanic, right? So it's too impermeable for any uranium spill to touch the aquifers of the Snake River Valley? Since they're buried under a thousand square miles of pahoehoe and aa and the intrusive basaltic flows that underpin them?"

Dr. Zinn's eyes widened. "I knew you had a physics background from your commander's letter of introduction, but I didn't know you had an interest in geology as well."

Brian shook his head with a smile. "Only as it relates to atomic energy production. And I had a lot of downtime at my last base and free access to UCLA's library."

"Very good, Captain," Dr. Zinn said. A gust of early fall wind blew around them, and Brian shivered in his thin uniform shirt. Zinn patted his arm, and Brian held back a flinch. "Let's get you inside."

He gestured for Brian to follow him across the parking lot toward the lab. A junior airman opened the door and saluted; Brian returned his salute and stepped inside. He yanked off his hat as the airman swept a Geiger counter over Dr. Zinn's shoes, pants, chest, shoulders, and hands. Brian followed, holding his arms out for his wanding, eyes sweeping from the leaded-glass shielding around a sort of chamber on his left to a thick-walled vault on his right. Above him hung a tangle of tubes covered in a layer of asbestos that would carry liquid metal to the small reactor in the center of the building. Given the pipes' design, Brian figured it would be a sodium-potassium alloy, rather than the light water or graphite the folks at Oak Ridge were experimenting with. Then Brian stepped through the metal detector, glancing up. A high catwalk swept around the three quarters of the building, presumably leading to a few control rooms and labs. And in the middle of everything stood a steel spiral staircase leading up to the nuclear reactor platform. No windows and only one way in or out; *good for avoiding Russki spies, bad in case of a fire.*

Dr. Zinn tapped him on the shoulder. "Captain, you can leave your bag with Junior Airman Freeman. He's on the night shift again, and most of the scientists have headed home already, so he can keep an eye on it while we get acquainted."

Brian nodded and laid the book-heavy duffel with what remained of his earthly possessions down behind the guard's single folding chair. He straightened up, hiding a wince.

"I've got some paperwork for you in my office," Dr. Zinn continued, "then I'll give you the grand tour."

Brian followed him along polished concrete floors to an office the size of a closet. Brian got the distinct impression Dr. Zinn would rather be out in the lab than in this tiny room, but leadership demanded a price from everybody.

"All right, son," he started once he was seated behind his paper-engulfed desk. Brian perched on the edge of the chair and avoided leaning back. "We probably only need to have this conversation once. But this is an Argonne Labs project, and your authority as the incoming security director and as an officer in the air force extends exclusively to the uranium we are working with. The plutonium, too, when we figure out how to make it at scale here. It doesn't mean you can tell my dozen-odd scientists what to do, even if they are pains in the butt. It *doesn't—*"

Brian held up his hand. "Let me stop you there." He tried to think of a diplomatic way to say it, then he just bulled through. "I don't have a lot of ego tied up in this role. If by the end of two years, no uranium or plutonium has been lost or stolen, I'll count that as a win. My commanding officer back at Vandenberg will as well." Brian paused and then asked slowly, "Did he tell you why I requested this role?"

"No, son. He didn't even tell me you requested it. I figured you'd been volun-told—"

"No, I requested it. Just like I requested Vandenberg right out of West Point." He saw the doctor straighten at the name of his alma mater.

"Duty, Honor, Country?"

"Duty, Honor, Country," Brian replied. He looked at the piles of textbooks heaped on the bookcase wedged between two overflowing filing cabinets; several of the spines sported Dr. Zinn's name. "Cards on the table. I requested this posting because I want to be good enough to work here someday. I had the option of Los Alamos, Travis, or Oak Ridge, but I'm not going back home to New Mexico again if I can help it. Travis was straight security, no science. And Oak Ridge is working on weapons projects." He leaned forward, eyes intent. "EBT-I is the only project in the US focused on using atomic energy for peaceful means. That's the work I want to be a part of."

Dr. Zinn sat back, eyes beginning to brighten as he gestured for him to go on.

"I graduated with a degree in physics from West Point in '48, but they didn't want to send me to grad school right away. So I went to help run security at Vandenberg, to get to know the conventional weapons research side. With support of my commander, I applied and had been accepted to UCLA's PhD program, was due to start this week, but"—he took a hard breath—"the air force had other plans. So this is me, doing my service so I can separate honorably in two more years and use my GI Bill to get a physics doctorate. And," he said, lowering his voice with a tiny smile, "I find that when I'm stationed someplace with a lot of physicists, I get to have a lot higher quality coffee break conversations, no matter my actual title. I was hoping it would be the same here."

"And a recommendation letter from a chief scientist for one of the national labs would go a long way to getting back into UCLA or an even better program when your two years is up?"

"I'm not gunning for that, Dr. Zinn. I'm here to do my job. I'm sure we'll butt heads at some point, so I don't want to have that between us. But what I want you to know is that I am here because I believe in your mission—good, reliable energy for millions. Turning a power that killed 210,000 people into a source of life. Helping with that seems worth spending two Idaho winters wanding scientists coming into and out of a cinder block building in the middle of the high desert."

"You said two years. That's how long your assignment is for?"

Brian nodded.

"You know we're a time-bound mission," Dr. Zinn said, folding his hands across his belly. "As soon as we achieve it—breed the plutonium from the uranium, that is—they'll bulldoze this place, and no one will ever know that we did the work."

Brian tilted his head. "But it's not about credit, is it, sir?"

Dr. Zinn's eyes caught his, widening a touch. "No, Captain. It never is." Then he clapped his hands, leaning forward. "All right, it seems we're on the same page. Here is the briefing packet Captain Jerush put together before he caught the bus out of Idaho Falls yesterday." He handed over a black folder. "It has current threats, past incidents. Nothing too thrilling; I promise. You have a six person staff—"

Brian nodded. "That was in the briefing I got before leaving Vandenberg. I used the Greyhound ride from Roswell to plan out the new schedule until the reading lights went out. I'm going to put myself in the rotation with ten-hour shifts. So the rest of the team's shifts will be seven hours of watch duty, which we can extend to eight for training, research, and paperwork if they end up needing it—"

Dr. Zinn gave him a knowing smile. "I do find that as the days get shorter, tempers do, too, so giving those young men a break will probably help everyone's nerves. Can I ask which shift you're planning on taking? Not because I have approval power of any kind, mind. I'm just curious if I'll see you around for some of those 'coffee break conversations.'"

"I'm that rare beast that enjoys nightshifts, so unless one of those under my command has a major preference, I'll take those solo."

Dr. Zinn nodded. "In a few months' time, there's going to be little enough sunlight during the day, so you won't be missing much." He took a breath. "There's really only one of our scientists who uses the lab after eight o'clock." He checked his watch. "We'll probably see him when I show you the reactor. He's a night owl. Honestly, I think it's because he likes talking to the reactor when he's working, and even *he's* realized it scares the nurses. So he's restricted himself to times no one will eyeball him over it."

"I've worked with scientists before," Brian said evenly. "Like I said, to me, that's one of the perks."

Dr. Zinn shook his head, neatening a stack of papers on the edge of his desk, which only threatened to unbalance the whole edifice. "We'll see what you say after six months of dealing with his, shall we say, unorthodox approach to nuclear material management. It's scared airmen off in the past."

Brian frowned, leaning forward in his chair, barely feeling the fresh scabs on his back stretching under his uniform. "As long as the 'unorthodox approach' doesn't lead to it going missing or irradiating anyone, it shouldn't be a problem."

Dr. Zinn rubbed his hand through his sparse hair. "The only person Dr. Aaron Antares has ever put in danger is himself," he said wryly. "Which he does on a regular basis. When he transferred here from the University of Wyoming's post-doctoral research facility, his recommendation letter came with an infraction list about as long as his CV. But since he hasn't fainted or started pissing blood, we're going to continue to let him get on with it."

"Are those the key signs of radiation poisoning? The weapons at my last posting were all pre-nuclear, and my briefing was vague on that point."

Dr. Zinn's warm face turned grim. He leaned over to his bookcase, chair wobbling under his weight, and snagged a sheaf of hand-typed pages, spine bound with duct tape. He slapped it on the desk. The title said, "A layman's guide to nuclear material and security protocols."

"I put it together last year for the other airmen," Dr. Zinn said. "Since evaluating the scientists and staff coming in and out is going to be part of your job, it is going to be important for you to know what the signs and symptoms are."

"Got it." Brian picked up the sheaf and tucked it into his briefing folder.

"Are you ready for the full tour?" Dr. Zinn said, pulling himself to standing. The older man spoke in a professional tone, but there was a vibrating excitement in him.

Brian nodded, a real smile beginning to surface as he followed him out of the office. "Dr. Zinn, I don't know if you're the right person to ask, but where am I sleeping?"

"The airmen assigned to this installation have been staying in the housing units by the two-mile perimeter fence you passed on the way in.

I understand there's heat, space-heaters, hot water, hot plates. It's not homey. Most people go to Arco if they want food or company. I assume you brought a vehicle?"

Brian remembered a crowbar going through the window of his Ford truck, tires slashed and seats immolated. A crumpled Greyhound ticket shoved into his shaking hands.

He shook his head, shoulders tense.

"I see," Dr. Zinn said. "Well, we're a tight-knit community here. I'm sure you'll find someone to get a ride with."

Zinn started walking at what for a smaller man would have been a jogging pace; Brian kept up easily, long legs eating up the hard-polished concrete. Zinn started with the vault Brian had seen next to the entrance. "This is where we store the U-235 pellets. We plan to get the plutonium we need for power generation by enriching uranium. We'll take uranium-235, get some fission going, bombard it with neutrons, and it'll produce uranium-238 *and* plutonium."

Zinn slipped into a lecturing tone appropriate for his tenure at Berkeley. "All the uranium comes in pellets only so big." He measured about an inch with his fingers. "We get them in quarterly shipments from the mines out in Wyoming in these." He pointed to racks of thin steel pipes hung vertically behind the bars, shining and deadly in the dark interior.

Brian ran his hands over the thick bank vault door. *Good quality with a hard-to-pick lock; it would be a pain to force this with explosives.*

Dr. Zinn took him across the way to the leaded-glass-enclosed chamber with a thick metal plating in front of it painted a bright, warning yellow. Brian was careful not to step onto it. "This is where we do some of the initial prep work, to get the material ready for the reactor.

The scientists get their experiments in and out with the tongs." Zinn gestured to leg-length welder's tongs, then waved at the metal plating. "Don't step on that or, if you have to, use the lead dinner plate over there. The whole in-floor storage unit is radioactive—we had to paint the entire thing a few months ago to try to *remind* certain scientists of that."

Brian took note.

As they walked around labs in the back of the building, he saw a row of oversized unlit light bulbs. "What are these?" Brian strode over to where they dangled on a thin wire stapled to the low ceiling, seeming to emerge from one of the labs. "They remind me of the ones on the stage at the Chinese Theatre in downtown LA." He paused for a moment, wondering if he should clarify. "I got to go a few times on my weekends off at Vandenberg."

Dr. Zinn reached out to touch the exaggerated curve of one of them and said, low, "These are my nemeses. These little bastards—excuse my language—have got to light up. Then we'll know we've done it. We've bred plutonium. Son, there'll be a day you'll come in here, and these will be as bright as anything, powered by steam from water heated by fresh-made plutonium."

"And then?"

Zinn tapped a knuckle on the light, letting it swing wildly in the quiet dark. "Then we'll light up this building, then light up Arco, then light up the whole southwest of Idaho. Once we get it to work once, we'll be able to start producing as much plutonium and as much power as we can possibly need. Mark my words, we'll get it done."

Dr. Zinn sped through the rest of the tour: the turbines and a medical office staffed by a rotating crew of seven nurses. They were the only women in the building. Next, a lightless decontamination shower squatted against the wall. Brian figured it was about the size of four regulation shower stalls welded together; on closer inspection, he was pretty sure that was *exactly* what it was. Dr. Zinn then led him to the basement with more leaded-glass-lined chambers, punctured only by long-armed equipment to manipulate the material and secured by large, heavy lead-lined doors.

He turned to Brian, nearly bouncing on his heels. "Ready to see the reactor?"

Brian nodded and followed Dr. Zinn back to the center of the building.

Zinn shooed him up the spiral staircase. "You go first—I've seen it all before."

Brian started up the stairs, and as soon as he was eye-level with the platform, he froze, staring. There was a man. Half in the reactor. Brian looked through the safety railing as the man squirmed deeper inside, legs on the platform, thighs straining. For a brief second, Brian thought, *That is a fantastic ass*, and then came a feeling like a boot to the chest and a belt on his back. Brian clenched his jaw and forced himself to look away, watching his boots as he finished the climb up to the platform with Dr. Zinn following behind.

The man in the reactor dropped what sounded like a heavy wrench and started shouting, echoing out of the chamber. "Cock sucking, god-damned, mother fucking—"

"Dr. Antares!" Zinn said sharply, but the smile he turned to Brian was a little fond. Brian put his hands behind his back as the scientist wiggled his way out of the reactor.

"Dr. Zinn," the man drawled a little breathlessly, his face red. He swiped the mass of out-of-regulation curly hair out of his glinting amber eyes. "How can I help you?"

"You can stop taking the Lord's name in vain, for one," Zinn said evenly, with the sound of a long-stalemated argument. He waved to Brian. "Then you can greet our new Security Director, Captain Brian Flynn."

Brian moved to shake his hand, but Dr. Antares held up his arms, covered in thick, elbow-length, heavy-looking gloves. *Maybe lead-lined?*

"Sorry, I'm a bit irradiated at the moment," Dr. Antares said with a smirk. "Where'd you come to us from?"

"Vandenberg Air Force Base, outside of LA," Brian said. "I handled security around some of the weapons research divisions. A quick trip home, then here."

"Where's home?"

Brian dreaded this question. Growing up, Roswell had been a no-where town nobody had ever heard of, except for his mother's people who had lived nearby since time immemorial; since June 14, 1947, it was still a nowhere town nobody *sane* had ever heard of. But, for a few alien conspiracy theory nut jobs, it was now a place with special significance.

Still, a direct question deserved a direct answer: "Roswell, New Mexico."

Dr. Antares's eyes lit up, and he leaned in conspiratorially as Brian backed up a step and pressed himself against the hip-high railing. "You see any aliens down there?"

Brian tried to sound neutral, but he was certain it came out hostile. "No. That was a stupid air force press officer making a stupid mistake. He issued a correction the next day, but it wasn't good enough for any-body. But I can promise you, there are no more aliens in Roswell than there are aliens at EBT-I."

Dr. Antares looked as if he was ginning himself up to respond when Zinn intervened, stepping between them.

"Dr. Antares has family in New Mexico; he *knows* there's no aliens." He turned to the scientist, continuing severely, "And he knows better than to antagonize the hardworking security staff, just like he knows he's *not supposed to be inside the reactor.*"

Dr. Antares held up his gloves in surrender, stepping back. In a more normal tone of voice, he said, "You get up much to the labs at Livermore while you were in the Golden State? Get into any of that H-bomb stuff?" Brian froze, barely letting his eyes glance to Dr. Zinn.

Zinn made a frustrated sound. "Dr. Antares, you're going to give the poor captain a heart attack." He turned to Brian. "He knows better than to talk like that anywhere other than this building—"

"What am I going to do, tell our national nuclear secrets to the *cows*—"

Dr. Zinn spoke over him calmly as if this was a normal method of communication. "Dr. Antares has spent the last two years working on research protected by the highest level of secrecy, and he is absolutely trustworthy. Just—"

"A bit of a mouthy shit?" Antares grinned and didn't wait for a reply before dropping to his knees—as Brian's breathing hitched—and hunching over to look into the reactor chamber. "I really need to get that lug wrench out of there before I get lunch—dinner? I'll see you around, Airman."

Brian was about to correct him on his rank, but Dr. Zinn was already herding him down the stairs and back to the entrance. He left him with Junior Airman Freeman, waving as he headed back to his office.

Brian turned to Freeman. "I didn't get a chance to introduce myself earlier. I'm Captain Brian Flynn." They shook hands, and Brian asked, "Do you happen to like the night shift? I won't hold it against you if you don't."

Freeman grimaced. "It's hell on my sleep schedule, if you'll pardon the phrase, sir."

Brian smiled a little brighter. "I was thinking of making a new shift schedule. All the airmen would get seven-hour shifts, and I'd take ten-hour overnights."

The airman raised his eyebrows. "That—that would be night and day, for me, for all of us."

"Not starting tonight though," Brian said. "I just got off a fifty-one-hour Greyhound ride from New Mexico, and I need to sleep, preferably horizontally, for at least ten hours before I can be a good human, much less a good commanding officer." He reached down and then heaved his duffel onto his back. "Could you point me in the direction of the barracks?"

*

Brian made the two-mile hike with his duffel over his shoulder, his back and shoulders one unified ache, eyes on the dim lights of the scientist housing and airmen's barracks squatting on either side of the perimeter gate. The sun had set while he'd been inside, the stars now out to keep him company. They were almost as clear here as from his grandmother's backyard on the reservation in New Mexico. Brian hadn't gotten to see the stars much at Vandenberg where they hid behind light pollution from the base or smoke from the summer wildfires or the LA smog. The pure, uncut horizon and the stars that shone above it were the only thing he missed about New Mexico.

The accommodations were as spare as Dr. Zinn had promised. But what his studio apartment lacked in hominess, the barracks gym made up for in thoroughness. A full set of weights and two incline benches filled the room, with a long mirror on the shorter wall. A window gave a view of the winding road back to the installation, and the same beige, found everywhere else in the ten-studio building, covered the cinder block walls.

Brian knew he should be a sensible adult and just go the fuck to sleep. The last bed he'd slept in, he'd been belt-whipped right back out of in the middle of the night two days and three states ago. But he knew from long experience that if he didn't start exercising now, the old scars and new scabs would stiffen, and it would hurt like a son of a bitch to get flexible again.

So Brian went to his studio apartment, unpacked his astronomy and physics textbooks, his back issues of *Astounding* and *New Worlds* and *Comet*, and his small collection of poetry. He shoved his underwear, socks, and workout clothes in the half drawer they took up; he hung his everyday and dress uniforms in the shower after running it hot enough to fill the bathroom with steam to ease out some of the travel wrinkles. Then he changed into his workout clothes. All of his shirts were dark with long sleeves, a necessity if he wanted to avoid staring eyes.

He took a breath and settled his shoulders, then stepped into the hallway and strode toward the gym at the back. A young airman was working out, and Brian introduced himself. The young man's last name was Durbin. He'd been here for a year. They exercised in comfortable silence, Brian feeling the scrapes on his back break open, but he just leaned forward to keep from getting blood on the bench. Durbin went to his unit, and Brian, for the first time in what felt like years, was alone.

He'd grabbed a pair of dumbbells and begun wrist curls when the shape of Dr. Antares's smile flashed across his mind. Brian closed his eyes, twisting his mouth; he wasn't going to do this on this base. He was going to be as sexless as the snow on the mountaintops, as the rocks, as the plutonium they would be breeding with the reactor; he was *not* going to do this again.

Brian headed back up to his studio, took a long hot shower, tended to what he could reach of his back using the first aid kit he found under the kitchen sink, and ate some of the canned soup some kind soul had left in the cupboard. Then he fell onto the stiff, thin mattress. There wasn't really a part of him that wasn't bruised, so he just hoped the long Greyhound ride and the workout would grant him sleep. He'd spend the morning briefing his team, then work through the night and start his upside-down schedule the next day. He'd done it before, and though it ached more than it had a decade ago at eighteen, he could do it again. *I can do this.*

Chapter Two: T-99 Days

"The effect of this upon the fortunes of ex-soldiers with blue discharges is very serious, so serious in fact that such ex-soldiers have been known to ask for an out-and-out dishonorable discharge. That at least is something that can be explained or even perchance explained away. But the ex-soldier, looking for a job and seeking to rehabilitate himself in some civilian sphere of life for which he may be better fitted than for the military service, must approach a prospective employer with a large sheet of striking color in his hand instead of the customary white one. He meets with instantaneous suspicion. It is a vague suspicion of something mysteriously but dreadfully wrong which may be actually more detrimental to the seeker after employment, than something specific which can be discussed. A man might say, "I stole some money," and be given a chance; but if compelled to explain that he had undesirable 'habits and traits of character,' he is damned at the start."

—History of the Phrase "Discharged Under Conditions Other Than Dishonorable" and Present Discharge Criteria for Three Services. Investigations of the National War Effort: Blue Discharges. United States Committee on Veterans' Affairs, House of Representatives, 1949.

September 12, 1951

B rian woke up too early, body aching and head sore from sleeping on the camp bed he'd been issued. He ate whatever came first to hand from the nonperishables in the stocked kitchen, letting the dull September sunlight filter through the small window, not bothering with the electric lights. He knew he needed to figure out who to crib a ride from into Arco for some kind of vegetables or fruit.

He supposed he'd been spoiled at Vandenberg Air Force Base. The fruit and veggies were probably his favorite part of California, better than the beaches where he couldn't take his shirt off, full of men he couldn't look too long at, and women who sometimes sensed he wasn't treating them like prey and so surrounded him. He had some good lady friends back in LA, but realistically, how much were they going to care to keep in contact with one lonely airman? He couldn't even give them his real address, and the PO Box the air force had set up for his official mail in Idaho Falls was never realistically going to get checked.

His single dish washed, Brian peered out the window into the cloudy Idaho sky and then inched his way into his thickest, most water-proof jacket before beginning the walk to the lab.

After a few breaths of crisp morning air, he thought through the shift schedule he'd worked out on the Greyhound ride again, focusing on days off. If he split his team between two seven-hour shifts from 07:00–14:00 and 14:00–21:00, then from here on out, he could work 21:00–07:00. Then on the weekends, they could do a rotation of 07:00 to 19:00 and 19:00 to 07:00, so it would mean everyone could get a full day off once a week. He wanted to protect his team, make sure they were well-rested and able to do their jobs well; this kind of work took a special kind of attention.

At Vandenburg, he'd had to manage some conflict between his men and the scientists they were tasked with protecting when he'd ended up in charge of one of the shift rotations. Watch duty was mind numbing in the best of times, but it was especially soul killing when there was nothing else to do on base. The more time his team here had to fill up their lives in Arco or explore the wilds of the high desert, the less trouble they were going to cause Brian and Dr. Zinn.

Half an hour later, the first thing Brian noticed when he stepped into the lab was how much busier it was. A junior airman was just ending his shift, and Brian caught the exhausted way he saluted. *Hopefully the new schedule will help with that.*

Brian smiled. "At ease, Airman."

The young man relaxed a fraction, keeping a clear eye on his new superior officer. Brian sighed internally. He would have time to earn their trust that he wouldn't bite their heads off for how they stood or, God forbid, if they put their hands in their pockets when speaking with him.

He stuck out his hand. "I'm Captain Flynn."

"Hodgins, sir."

Brian made sure his smile was as warm as his wind-chilled face could make it. "Any trouble last night?"

The young man's entire body slouched for a moment before he pulled himself up by his strings. "Just, ah—did Dr. Zinn tell you about Dr. Antares?"

"Yes. Yes, he did."

"Then nothing out of the usual." Hodgins sighed, fiddling with something in his hand. Brian looked at it, and Hodgins followed his gaze. "You ever used one of these before, sir?" he asked, a bit of excitement rising up through his exhaustion.

"I've seen Geiger counters but never used them before. Care to show me?"

"Sure. So, it's called a Geiger counter. Which you know." Hodgins bit his lips and waved it over himself. It made an almost metronomic beeping. "It'll start beeping and kind of screeching if someone comes through with irradiated material on them." He paused. "It's the weirdest thing, with Dr. Antares. He spends all that time crawling in and around the reactor. He should be covered in uranium." Hodgins narrowed his eyes. "But I haven't had to take his pants once, and I've been here six months!"

Brian was proud in a profound way of how even his voice was when he said, "Why would you take his pants?"

"Oh!" Hodgins grinned at the chance to show off his knowledge of his job. "So, if someone comes through here"—he gestured to metal detector in front of the entrance door—"and I wand them"—he gestured vaguely at Brian's legs with the Geiger counter—"and it goes off, we have them take off whatever part of their clothes set it off. Alpha particles from uranium can't puncture unbroken skin, so they get caught in the clothes and can rub off on car seats or whatever. So we take their pants." At Brian's look, he hurried to add, "We have some backup overalls in the closet over there, but sometimes, we have to send guys home in their boxers."

"What do you do with the confiscated clothing?"

Hodgins tilted his head. "It goes in a big ditch over there." He waved in the opposite direction of the base housing. "We're mostly here to stop it from getting out of the building. It can't be transferred by skin contact, but if someone wore a pair of jeans out of here with uranium dust on them and then went to Arco for the Friday hoedown and sat on the bar stools, that would mean anyone else who sat on that bar stool might get irradiated too." Then he lowered his voice. "If the Russkies knew where to start looking and found a town where all the bar stools were slightly irradiated, they might begin to wonder what we're doing in here."

Brian kept his face receptive and nodded. "All right, so what were you saying about Dr. Antares?"

Hodgins sighed again, irritation flashing over his tanned face. "That *cowboy*, he does *everything* you're not supposed to do, but he never pops the counter. Never! I swear, one time, I was wanding everyone down just before dinnertime, and I saw him carrying a uranium pellet *in his T-shirt* over to the reactor. And I wanded him—*twice*—when he headed out around midnight and just—nothing. Last night, well, he was in and out of the reactor all night, left just before dawn, and he was clean as the undriven snow." He shook his head in disgust at the man's lackadaisical attitude towards being irradiated.

"You know," Brian said, "at Vandenberg, a lot of the guys who worked at Los Alamos came by to give talks. They said when they were all undergrads at Cal, they used to start a nuclear reaction in one building, then get it into the bed of a running pickup and drive across campus to where the labs were as fast as they could because the material was stored in a different place than the equipment."

Hodgins scrunched his nose. "Scientists, man."

"Yeah," Brian said with a smile.

"Captain Brian Flynn?" came a strong, bright voice.

He turned around as one of the nurses approached him, her black hair pinned up in victory curls, a pencil behind her ear, brown eyes smiling.

"Yes, ma'am?"

"Nurse Kiko Kelly," she replied, sticking her hand out for a firm shake. "Before you get started for the morning, mind if we do your physical? We'll want to set a baseline."

Brian felt a flutter of panic but squashed it down. "I thought all of my medical records had transferred."

She shook her head. "It could be weeks or even months before any of your files get here, Captain. And we need to know your normal starting as soon as possible."

"I was just giving a briefing to Hodgins—"

"Oh, no, it's fine, sir," Hodgins interrupted, and Brian narrowed his eyes; perhaps he'd been too successful putting him at ease. "I've got another hour on my shift."

Brian turned from one expectant face to the other and then closed his eyes, keeping his voice light and professional. "Thank you, Nurse Kelly. That's a good idea."

The nurse's station was in the right-hand corner of the building. It consisted of a front room with a big window facing the lab, two exam tables pressed against opposite walls, a filing cabinet supporting a telephone, and a door leading to an empty back office with a paper-strewn desk and a second telephone handset.

Nurse Kelly closed the blinds over the window to the rest of the lab, leaving them in the yellow lamplight. She hopped up on the far exam bed, skirt falling carefully over her stocking-clad knees, black pumps swinging as she gestured for Brian to take the other. He stayed standing, gritting his teeth. She crossed her ankles, picked up a blank chart, and looked at him over it.

"I'll start with the basic questions. Where did you grow up?"

"Nowhere you've heard of."

She raised her eyebrows and set the chart back down. "Are we going to have a problem, Captain?"

Brian tried to force his heartrate down. His hands were at his sides; much as he wanted to straighten up at her tone, he couldn't get them into parade rest without splitting the scrapes hidden by his uniform.

His breath was shaky, and he kept finding himself glancing at the locked door back out to the lab. *Not now, please, not now.*

"No, ma'am."

"Then take a seat."

He turned to look at the high bed, too high to just fall back on. *Probably easier for surgeries.* He put his hands on it and tried to jump up without twisting or bending his back. One of the bigger scabs on his back split, and he winced. He tried to smooth his face but wasn't nearly fast enough. Nurse Kelly lowered herself back down to the floor, heels clicking. She pressed her clipboard to her chest as she peered at him in the lamplight.

Her voice was soft, too, too soft. "Captain, are you injured?"

Brian turned his head to the side, struggling to keep his breathing steady. "Not in a way that compromises my ability to do my job."

She took a step closer, voice even. "That would be something I would decide, Captain." She took another step, and he flinched back from her, flushing at the reaction and unable to control it. She dropped her hands. "Captain Flynn, do you know what we're doing here?"

"What?"

"All of us—" She gestured out to the lab and up to the reactor platform hanging over the middle of it. "We are all here because the world has a scarcity of light. We need more light. We need light in rural places. We need light for sewing and doing dishes. We need light for reading and feeding babies. America is experiencing a scarcity of light. And that is why I like to think we've all come to this deserted, freezing place.

We're fixing the scarcity of light. Think of all the things we can learn and do if we have light. Think of all the places that will be safer; think of all the *people* who will be safer. How many things go on in the dark that could not go on if there were light to see?"

He could think of quite a few. He kept his face still.

She saw right through him. "Captain, I'm going to say something I usually wouldn't say to a man." She took a breath. "You're safe here. I won't—can't—tell anyone anything you tell me. Any paper records could be audited, but—" She glanced at the chart in her hands. "—I won't write anything down from this session unless you tell me I can."

Nurse Kelly set the chart on the bed behind her. "But everyone's job in this building is important. Mr. Jolley, the janitor—he's the reason we don't trip on crap and spill our blood tests everywhere. The scientists are trying to light up the whole world, the airmen keep the scientists from taking the uranium home to continue their experiments in their bathtubs, and my team is here to keep everyone alive as they play with the stuff responsible for killing a quarter million people in Hiroshima and try to make more of what killed half that again from what we dropped on Nagasaki. Everyone who works here has big roles, and while not everyone in this building trusts one another, I want my team to be able to rely on your team. So—" She took the pencil from behind her ear and chucked it toward the clipboard, where it careened over the bed to clatter behind the filing cabinet.

She held out her hand. "How about we start over. Hi, I'm Nurse Kiko Mabuni Kelly. My job is to help keep you alive. I'm not here to judge, and I'm not here to argue. I'm here to keep you well."

Brian's lips twisted as he frowned. He wished, briefly, painfully, that Bill was here, warm body tight against his side, soft hands on his, bright poet's eyes teasing him into a better mood. He crushed that thought harder than any he'd had that morning.

"All right. I have— Something happened. Before I left Roswell. Home. It's easier if you just see. It's okay if I take off my shirt?"

"Fine by me, Captain. I was a flight nurse over Düsseldorf in '43. Nothing I haven't seen before."

He nodded, eyes on the blank wall behind her as she stood, arms neutral at her sides. He unbuttoned his uniform jacket, face twisting as he worked it off his shoulders. He was grateful she didn't offer to help; he didn't think he could bear a kind touch.

He clenched his jaw until it creaked and crossed his arms at the waist to strip his undershirt, keeping his dog tags from getting tangled through long practice. He might have heard her gasp or might have imagined it. He wondered if these were the first boot marks she'd seen. His dark skin hid the majority of them, but the rounded heels of combat boots made a visible impression no matter the tone.

He made a motion toward the deep bruises on his chest. "These I can handle just fine; nothing broken or sprained, it just hurts." His voice caught on the last word. "But the back, that's what's giving me trouble. No infection I could tell, but, well…" He waited, and she looked at him levelly before walking around the exam table.

This time, he definitely heard a gasp, a soft "Brian, *what the—*" before she caught herself.

When she came back around, her face was professional. He felt a boot ease off his chest, just a little. Enough to breathe.

"You did a good job keeping them clean and disinfecting the—the scrapes. I'm going to clean what you couldn't reach and give you fresh bandages for the day. Come back to me at the end of my shift, and I'll change them out again. It looks—" Her voice strangled in her throat, but she kept talking. "It looks like you have experience with this, so I won't mother you, but the faster you heal, the better you'll feel."

She opened a drawer in the little stainless steel cabinet under the phone and pulled out alcohol swabs and clean towels. "We can go through your intake while I clean them up."

"You don't have to—" Brian started, but she shook her head, once, eyes fierce before she banked her fire.

"It's my job, Captain. Just let me do it."

He nodded.

She paused, looking at him. "The man who did this, he isn't stationed here, right?"

"No," Brian said. "He's back home in Roswell."

"With the aliens?"

He muttered, "That's what he would say." At her look, he explained, "He was in charge of the public affairs unit when that damn press release went out, blaming a fallen weather balloon on little green men. Never lived it down. Spends all his free time trying to catch one to prove he didn't make a mistake in '47."

Her eyes twinkled. "So you don't think aliens are among us? Indistinguishable from humans, here to steal our secrets and our resources?"

"The initial press release was an error of judgment. Everyone still keeping it going are just building on a hoax to get people to go through our tiny town on their way to LA or El Paso."

She nodded, heading around behind him, pattering to distract him. "Makes sense since they're building that new highway all through Utah and then down that way. But wouldn't it be something if they really were here? We're living science fiction here every day. Who's to say there aren't aliens in Roswell or anyplace else?"

Brian closed his eyes, counting his breaths as the alcohol stung.

"With the whole universe to choose from, what could aliens possibly see in us?"

Chapter Three: T-94 Days

Mr. KETCHUM. Then, too, Mr. Allen, I wonder how many of those blue discharges were issued. Maybe we are making a mountain out of a molehill.

Mr. KEARNEY. Will you yield?

Mr. ALLEN. Yes.

Mr. KEARNEY. You mean the blue discharges or the bad-conduct discharges, the total? I had the figures that were given on the floor. There were something like 117,000.

> *—Testimony by Mr. Omar B. Ketchum (Director of the Legislative Service, Veterans of Foreign Wars) to the US House of Representatives Committee on Veterans Affairs, April 7, 1949. Bernard William "Pat" Kearney (R-NY) and Mr. Allen speaking.*

Note: There were three white Congressmen (R-CA, D-LA, and R-IL) in 1949 with the last name "Allen," and at printing, it could not be determined which of them had served on this committee.

September 17, 1951

It was 03:30, and Brian and Antares were the only ones left in the building and had been for hours. Brian's new shift schedule had been a big hit, and this was his fifth night shift in a row; Dr. Antares had mostly been leaving him alone. Brian suspected Dr. Zinn had had strong words with him.

Dr. Antares had been doing something energetic with the material in the leaded-glass testing chamber on the ground floor since he'd gotten in at 22:00. Brian had tried to read one of his astronomy textbooks but finally found only his back issues of *Astounding Science Fiction* could hold his attention away from the constantly moving scientist. The man was currently leaning over, adjusting the experiments with a long-handled poker and even longer forge tongs, all while balanced on a piece of lead the size of a Thanksgiving turkey platter, protecting him from the in-floor secondary storage area for uranium fuel rods. The scientist was wobbling a bit. And then he was waving his arm a little wildly at Brian.

"Airman?" His voice came floating across the lab.

Brian called back, "What, Doctor?"

"Airman, come here. I need your help."

Brian dropped his magazine and hurried toward the scientist. Dr. Antares was crouched on his dinner plate, arms outstretched, trying to get the tongs into the back of the containment area. There were a number of flasks there, but his tongs were just shy of them.

Brian held his hands at his sides. "What am I doing?"

"I need you to hold the back of my pants so I can move the nuclear material to the next processing stage."

"Why do you need my help to do that?"

"Well, if Eisenberg didn't have such absurd monkey arms, then I would be able to reach it myself with these here tweezers. But he does. And I do not. And if I don't move it, we can't do the test on EBT-I tomorrow, so get in here, Airman."

Brian stepped forward, toes brushing the safe black edge of the yellow containment area, shoulders square. "No. That's not safe."

There was a sound of derision, and Dr. Antares stood, seeming to try to use his half-inch of height on Brian since orders weren't working.

Well, Brian had had a lifetime of men standing over him, staring down; he wasn't about to be intimidated by this cherub-haired scientist. "I don't know how you do things in Wyoming, but we need to—"

"We need to complete our mission," Antares said, jaw tight. "Millions of people need safe, clean electricity made from stuff mined out of American soil."

Brian realized there was something almost like golden flecks in the brown of his eyes. He tried to snap back to attention.

"Look—" Antares voice softened. "I don't need you to go near it. I know some of the airmen, they get nervous around the material—"

"Not me. I'm not afraid of anything," Brian said.

Dr. Antares's eyebrows quirked, eyes flaring as if he'd scented a challenge. Then his professionalism came back online, clearing his face and sharpening his bright eyes. "Look, I know it's unorthodox. But it's not dangerous. I just need a counterweight, okay? Something to balance me while I reach for that flask over there." He tilted his head. "We've spent more time arguing about it than it would have taken to just do it, Airman."

Brian's heart slammed in his chest even as his shoulders slumped. He looked up at the clock: 03:35. No one would really know. "Okay. What do you need?"

Antares looked like he'd have clapped his hands if he hadn't been holding highly irradiated tongs. "I'll just get as close as I can right here, and then you come over and stand on the second lead plate and hold on to my belt. Then, I'll lean in, make the adjustment—"

"What do you want me to do if you start falling?" Brian slid his lead plate up against Antares's, then clanked another down in its path. He stepped across the islands of safety to stand behind him, trying not to breathe.

Antares's smile was nearly wicked, and Brian reminded himself of ice and belts and blue ticket discharges. "You catch me, Airman. I trust you to catch me."

Then he was squatting, leaning forward, and Brian had to grab his belt before he could face-plant into the experiment.

Dr. Antares's skin was hot, sweating beneath his thin white dress shirt. His body was hot, too hot, hot enough that if he was under Brian's hands, under his tongue, he might be burning. He watched the clean arch of Antares's back, the way his muscles moved. A man who could dance. A man who could make him want to dance. Brian took a breath, and there it was, the sharp smell of another man working, the feeling of him under his hands, and Brian's own body flexed, filling itself in, the shell of him becoming a man again, and then—

"There!" Dr. Antares eased back on his heels as he turned in Brian's arms. Their faces were perilously close, Brian's hand still tangled in his belt. "Thanks," Antares breathed, voice low, and Brian jerked up, hand held out stiff like he'd hurt it, like it was dirty. And then he was jumping off the plate and onto the floor, risking his legs for those seconds but needing to get away.

"Airman—" Dr. Antares started, but Brian was barreling toward the bathroom.

It had multiple stalls, but it also had a bolt; he bolted it. He stared at himself in the mirror, and his eyes were—bright, wide, excited. They weren't the only parts of him, his body singing, tingling with the reaction, with the first man's touch, the first nonviolent touch since—

And then, like the chorus of a song, it was there, his father's voice centering him, telling him what he was. What he needed to not be. *Faggot. Fucking fag. Fucking waste of skin.*

Brian slipped into his father's mantra again. Reminding himself what the whole point of this assignment was. Trying to escape the inevitable blue slip from being in a city with clubs and boys and cigars and poetry readings, with quiet little motels where you could get a few hours of sleep against a warm chest, with bodies of men who'd come back from war knowing how good a man could make other men feel, not just in extremis, but in *life*.

But Idaho wasn't a place for lovers. It was supposed to be a place cold enough to freeze off this part of him, this cancer.

He was splashing cold water on his face when he heard feet approaching the door. His back was cold blue steel as he awaited the knock, the uncomfortable letdown, the hate-filled spewing, the— But the boots moved away. They sounded like work boots, not city shoes. Practical prairie boots for a man who was more used to horses and cattle than nuclear reactors. A practical man, good with his hands, and—

Brian nearly waterboarded himself splashing so much water in his face, trying to push the thoughts away. Then he dried off with paper towels because being caught crying, being weak, was about twenty times worse than being a fruit. He *needed* this posting. He needed to be away from his father, just for a few months. Just to get some of his self back after what had happened after Vandenberg.

He only had three and a half hours left in his shift, and he spent it writing up his weekly report in the nurses' locked office. He didn't include helping Dr. Antares since it wasn't in his duties, and it would only cause confusion and worry up his command chain. No one included everything they did in their shifts.

That was what the space between the lines was there for.

*

Dr. Eisenberg's arms really are weirdly long, Brian thought as the red-haired scientist held out the offending appendages for his morning wanding, a bit of snow falling off his collar to melt on the warm concrete floor. It was the end of Brian's shift. Dr. Antares had left while he was typing and retyping his report.

"You're new here?" Eisenberg asked, twitching his lab coat out of the way to help Brian get around his knees. "I was at a conference in Chicago, just got back yesterday morning. Wanted to get in before sunup to see how my experiments did overnight."

Brian hid a smile at the chatter and answered the question. "I'm new, yes."

"Where do you call home?"

"Roswell, New Mexico," Brian said, cringing for what would inevitably follow.

But instead, Eisenberg nodded and smiled. "Nuclear sunrises, right?"

"What?"

"The sunrises. We used to call them that at Los Alamos. The colors after the first bomb went off. They were purples and greens and reds. Splashes on the underside of the sky. The brightest light you've ever seen. Richard Feynman said he's one of the few humans to see it with his actual eyeballs since he didn't wear the eye protection. He was not, in fact, invited to that particular test. He just drove his truck to the edge of a mesa where he could see it. But, you know, Feynman invites himself to things." He paused, then leaned forward a bit, voice lowering. "You lived in New Mexico before 1945?"

"Yeah, my father was stationed at each of the army bases there in rotation when I was growing up; it was weird not to be moved around more but nice for our family."

Eisenberg took a breath. "Were they like that before?"

"What?"

"This'll sound superstitious, but the sunrises in New Mexico, were they like that before they set off the bomb?"

"Like what?"

"It's just, you wonder what we're changing, right? Bringing back elements like plutonium that haven't been on Earth naturally for billions of years, letting them loose in the atmosphere, and it just kind of makes you wonder."

Brian nodded, frowning a bit as he finished wanding his chest. "The sunrises didn't change after the tests. And it's not as if you were raining uranium down on people. The uranium is contained within the blast radius."

Eisenberg flashed him a smile. "Sure. I know the physics of it. It's just—anyways. It's good to know we haven't messed up the sunrises."

Brian watched as he headed over to the leaded-glass chamber with a spring in his step. This was the first posting he'd ever heard of where the scientists nearly danced to their labs. It was nice in a distant way to be a small part of it.

*

Dr. Antares was suspiciously quiet all the next night. When Brian finally couldn't stand it anymore, he went on a "patrol." Really, he was just looking for where Dr. Antares had squirreled himself away. Brian found himself searching the entire facility: basement labs, containment area, back lab; nothing. Nurse's station, decontamination shower, upstairs labs; nothing. His turquoise pickup truck was still parked in the gravel lot, getting lightly dusted with an early autumn snow. Brian had just come back inside when he heard the sound of a dropped wrench and a cuss, echoing as if it was coming from *inside* the reactor.

Brian took off at a dead sprint, shouting, "Dr. Antares, get out of there!" as he hurtled up the spiral staircase.

The reply echoed from the metal chamber calmly. "Call me Aaron, please."

Brian braced his fists on his hip and glared down at the top of Antares's head a few inches below the platform edge. "If you were my friend, I could call you 'Aaron.' But you're not my friend. You're my job. I'm paid to keep you safe. Or, barring keeping you safe, keep you from"—his breath rattled in his throat—"dying in such a way as you could kill anyone else. Get out of there or—"

"'Or' what?" Dr. Antares echoed without looking up.

Brian peered down. It looked like he was duct-taping pellets of uranium to the inside of the reactor walls with his bare hands. That was so *stupid*. Alpha particles couldn't go through skin, but they'd play merry hell if they got through a torn cuticle or a broken blister. "What?" he said, looking down into the hole.

"'Get out of there' or what?" Antares glanced up at him, but his hands were still smoothing the duct tape over the hip-high rows of pellets he'd already attached.

"Or I'll *get* you out."

"Okay. And then what?"

"What do you mean, 'and then what'?"

"Are you going to arrest me? I didn't see an MP designation in your file."

"I'm not an MP; I'm the security director. And why were you looking in my file?"

"Okay, so what are you going to *do*?"

What Brian wanted to do was *spank* him for being such a fucking *brat*, but that was exactly the wrong kind of thought. "Probably, I'd lock you in a broom closet until Dr. Zinn gets in. Then tell him you were violating his security procedures left, right, and center, and see what *he* said."

"Yeah, but Dr. Zinn knows I do this." Antares had turned his attention back to his hands, but Brian was nearly *certain* the man was smirking.

"He knows you climb inside the reactor without any kind of protective gear at all?"

"Uh-huh." He grinned up at him, then glanced to the side. "Well, not exactly. But he knows I do unorthodox things and get results. That's why he hired me."

"Unortho— What are you *talking* about? You could *die*. I don't understand why you're not dead *already*."

Antares smiled even wider, teeth white and even. "Captain Flynn, I eat uranium for breakfast."

Brian frowned, not particularly wanting to dive into that rabbit hole. "Whatever. Get out of there."

Antares shook his head, huffing. "We're back to this again? I *need* to be in here."

"*Why* do you need to be in there?"

"Do you *actually* want to know, or are you just trying to come up with a reason to make me leave again?"

Brian sighed and lowered himself to sit on the steel grate of the platform, peering into the reactor chamber. His back was healing faster with Nurse Kelly's help, but sudden movements were still not his friend. Dr. Antares stayed firmly inside the reactor. "What if I wanted to know?"

"Why?"

"Why do you think I requested this posting?" Brian leaned over to look more carefully at what Antares was doing.

"You *requested* to be put in the middle of the Idaho desert to do something you'll never be able to tell anyone that you worked on?"

"I did."

"What was the other choice?"

"Los Alamos, Travis, or Oak Ridge."

"Oak Ridge? Better weather in Tennessee than out here, but at Travis, you could get to San Francisco." Antares ripped off another strip of duct tape and began applying uranium pellets to it in careful little rows.

That's what my father thought too. "Yeah, but they're not working on what we're working on here."

"And that is?"

"Nonmilitary applications for atomic energy."

"Last I checked, 'Captain' was a military rank." Antares's tone was curious even as he kept working.

"Last *I* checked, the military served the civilian population in this country. Nuclear science is too powerful to be put only in the hands of soldiers."

"Soldiers like you?"

"I won't be a soldier for my whole life. I just won't. I've seen what that does, to my friends, my brothers." *My father.* "I want to make things, not just break them. Maybe make some things better." Brian grimaced; that sounded too close to a confession. "You know where Dr. Zinn was based before here?"

"Cal. Berkeley."

"I was up there with a—a friend on a weekend," Brian said.

Dr. Antares paused, looking up at Brian, eyes bright in the lab light, hands taping down the end of that row of pellets.

Brian kept going. "I heard one of Dr. Zinn's lectures. He talked about how plutonium has only existed on earth for nine years. Ten years now. It exists other places in the universe, probably whole entire planets covered in the stuff. But what we have today, all of it, we just made it ourselves. To be close to powering entire buildings, entire cities, entire *countries* with it? It's *incredible.* So I'm here to make sure that happens and keep everyone safe while it does; it's just an extra bonus if I get to learn something on the way."

Something passed across Antares's face, something like a spasm of pain or maybe recognition. "Fine," he said begrudgingly, pulling himself up out of the reactor to sit, legs still dangling into the tube below. He laid a hand on the casing in front of him. "I think the problem we're running into is that the interior containment section is insufficiently shielded. It's letting out too many of the irradiated particles, so we're not able to reach critical by reflecting them inward. I'm supplementing the existing resistance with a secondary layer."

"Of uranium?"

"See, if the thermal neutrons off of U-234 hit U-235 instead, there's nearly nowhere for them to go. It'll enrich a very few of them to U-236, but not enough to really matter for any of our purposes, and it degrades back down pretty quickly anyway. We need the thermal neutrons focused *in* to breed plutonium."

"Okay," Brian said, spreading his open palms on his knees. "Why didn't you just tell me that?"

Antares shrugged his broad shoulders, scrubbing his palms along his thighs. "I don't know; it's super top-secret information? I don't just go around telling the bartenders at the bar in Arco the recipe for plutonium."

"I have the security clearances."

"Security clearances are political to a fault. I don't know if you're here because you fucked up and Daddy had to find a new space for you—" Antares shut up; something must have moved across Brian's face. "Anyway," Antares said, backtracking. "Like you said. I don't know you."

Brian took a breath. "Can I help?"

Dr. Antares's eyebrows shot up. "What do you mean 'can I help'? You were just trying to lock me in a broom closet."

Brian shrugged and began unbuttoning his jacket. He stripped down to his undershirt, not looking at Dr. Antares as he did so. "I'm smaller than you; I can reach more of the inside of the reactor than you can."

"Brian, you can't—" There was a note of something near panic in Antares's voice, but Brian was already sliding into the tube.

"Get out!" Antares yelled, hand scrabbling at his shoulder, voice rising.

"You were *just* in here—"

"You're going to get— Get out! Get out!"

And then he got a grip on Brian's shoulder, trying to drag him up one-handed. Then *something* yanked him out of the chamber and sent him sprawling onto the platform. Dr. Antares scrambled back until his hips were against the waist-high railing, knuckles clenched white on the rails as if *Brian* was radioactive. Brian's heart was pounding, and his arms where he'd brushed the reactor walls were feeling hot, tingly like a sunburn.

"What—"

"Fuck. Fuck fuckfuckfuck *fuck*," Antares said, stalking forward and fisting his hand in the back of Brian's undershirt and dragging him to his feet. "Decontamination shower. Now."

"You were in there a lot longer than I was—"

"*I eat uranium for breakfast!*"

"That doesn't make *any sense!*" Brian said as Antares herded him down the spiral stairs and across the lab. "You are a higher priority than me. Get in the shower first if it's a problem."

"I don't need it, Brian!" Dr. Antares was shoving him closer to the closed glass door of the decontamination shower.

"What do you mean you don't need it? I thought you were fucking around! You can't be immune to uranium!"

"Of course I can. I'm different than you!" Dr. Antares was now fumbling with the door, one hand still tight in Brian's shirt, fingers pressed hot against his skin.

"There's no way to be so different—"

Dr. Antares whipped around, and Brian saw a terrible war in his eyes. "Please." Antares said, hands going to Brian's face, fingers light on his skin. "Please."

"I can't," Brian breathed, leaning into his palms just a tiny bit. "It's my duty to protect you."

Antares pressed his forehead to Brian's, hissing breath between his teeth. "It's a big deal for me to tell you why. And it will take a little while to explain it. Can I please tell you after you've taken the decontamination shower? I promise." He closed his eyes, and it looked like it hurt. "I swear on my home planet, Captain Flynn. I promise on my home planet I will tell you."

"Your what?" Brian planted his feet on the concrete floor, not letting him tug him any further, his eyebrows climbing toward his hairline, wondering if Dr. Antares had finally gone round the bend.

Antares glanced at the open door to the shower. "Fuck it," he said harshly and started unbuttoning his flannel shirt.

"I'm glad to see you're finally seeing the— Hey, *hey*, what are you doing?"

But Antares had already yanked the door open and shoved Brian inside the dark shower. He followed him in and latched the door behind them. There was barely enough room to stand apart, but Antares backed Brian up under the one shower head and jerked the emergency cord so icy water began to pour over both of them. Then he fisted the hem of Brian's shirt to pull it up over his head; Brian could either get with the program or get smothered by a sopping undershirt. As he was freeing his hands, he felt Dr. Antares's hands on his belt and flinched back so hard he slammed his battered back into the chilly steel wall. Antares backed all the way to the other side of the shower, hands in front of him, eyes flashing in the dim light.

"You need to get out of those clothes, quickly," he said. "I'm not trying to—"

Brian gritted his teeth. "Of course not." He unbuckled his own belt, and he was so *fucking* proud of how gruff, how controlled his voice was. "And we trained in decontamination procedures at Vandenberg. It's nothing I haven't seen before."

There was no such thing as modesty in the air force, but still, Brian thanked God the shower was night-dark and all the bruises on his chest had faded. If he kept his back to the wall, Antares wouldn't see anything worth questioning. Even still, he was glad the water was freezing and forced himself to think quelling thoughts as he shucked pants, underwear, and shirt. He shoved everything he had in the go box in the corner, hoping somebody had refilled the extra clothes bin or he'd be walking home in his birthday suit.

Brian grabbed the industrial bar of soap and lathered up. He said, voice rough, "You need to get washed off too, Doctor."

Antares tossed his shirt into the go bin and worked-on his own cowboy buckle. "I liked this belt," he said mournfully to the steel floor. "I won it at my first rodeo."

Brian was desperate for anything to distract himself as he rinsed off, to keep this professional. "You competed?"

Antares nodded, keeping his gaze on the floor, dutifully accepting the gritty soap Brian handed him. During his turn in the water, his glorious curls flattened against his head as he scrubbed himself. "Steer rastling. It's the highest-paying event that doesn't require you to bring any equipment. The trick is that the steer don't want to be on the ring any more than you do. So if you just tip them real fast, they can get up and go about their business."

Brian accepted the soap back and tossed it into the go bin as well, trying not to catalog what he could see in the low light filtering through the glass door: hair that made Brian's fingers ache to uncurl and re-curl it around his fingers; eyes firmly down now that Brian had pushed him back, had shown disinterest; hands careful, quick and thorough; chest and legs strong with riding muscles. Brian forced his eyes back up before he took in the rest of him.

"I never got to go to the rodeos," he said quietly in the dark shower, "even though they were big on the rez." He shivered in the cold, and his skin was starting to feel less tingly, which he hoped was a sign he'd shucked whatever alpha particles his skin had blocked off before they had a chance to find their way into his system.

"Next time one's in town, I'll let you know."

"You're still competing?"

Antares glanced up quickly, then locked his gaze back down. Brian caught a slight smile on his face. "I don't do well when I'm inside all the time. Sometimes, I just need to get thrown in the dirt and stepped on by a 700-pound steer, you know?"

"I don't think I *do* know," Brian said, a tiny teasing edge to his voice.

Antares turned off the water, and Brian opened the door and reached for the stack of thin, scratchy towels folded on a chair outside the door. He slipped one around his waist and one over his shoulders and back. Then he moved out into the lab and snagged a third towel to try to get his regulation haircut dry. Antares accepted a towel through the door and wrapped himself up in the same style.

As Antares was gingerly drying his curls, Brian ventured, "So, your 'home planet,' huh?"

Dr. Antares froze.

Brian continued, "You decided, since Dr. Zinn wasn't here to make you knock it off, you could go back to giving me shit about being from Roswell? The jokes got old about four years ago, for your information."

Antares very, very slowly lowered the towel he'd been dabbing his hair with, giving Brian big, wide eyes. "Yes, that's—that's exactly what I was trying to do. And I am sorry. In the future, I will not do that."

Brian toweled off his neck, looking at his bare footprints on the concrete. "Do you really have a genetic resistance to radiation? I heard from the guys you've never popped hot on the Geiger counter, not once in two years."

Dr. Antares nodded. "It's more epigenetics," he said, his voice catching. "It comes from, uh, growing up near the uranium mines. In Wyoming." He paused. "I guess I got all the radiation I was going to have."

Brian shook his head in disbelief but didn't push. He dragged out the spare clothes box from beside the shower and took stock.

It was empty.

Or as good as. Inside, he found one undershirt, a pair of boots, and a single pair of boxers. Antares took one look, resecured the wet towel around his waist, and said he had a change of clothes in his truck. He waited until Brian had put on the boxers, shirt and shoes so Brian could wand him with the Geiger counter. As usual, he came away 100 percent clean. He didn't meet Brian's eyes before fleeing the premises.

Brian listened to his truck driving along the gravel road as he wanded himself, going over his whole body. No spikes of radiation. Brian's shoulders unknotted, just a little. He took a breath and then headed back to the reactor platform to retrieve his uniform jacket, buttoning it up the best he could. He went to the nurses' office to borrow a blanket so, at the least, the airman who came in for the 07:00 shift wouldn't be greeted by his bare thighs.

Brian's shift was half an hour from over when Hodgins came in early to relieve him. Taking the longest and objectively shittiest shift had earned Brian the quiet kind of respect that could get grown men out of bed before the crack of dawn. Hodgins had taken one look at his still-drying hair and the rough blanket around his legs and begun stuttering apologies.

"I'm really sorry about this, Captain. The spares box was empty because a couple of scientists had to take the overalls yesterday afternoon, and we haven't had a chance to put anything through the wash—"

"Fine, it's fine."

"I can give you a ride to the barracks?"

"No, you've got your shift starting, and the scientists and staff will start arriving any minute now; you know Nurse Kelly likes to be here early."

The young man nodded miserably.

Brian fixed a smile on his face, carefully folding the blanket. "It'll be no problem." Brian opened the door, and a flurry of early snow hit his shins. "It'll be fine. I've been through worse."

He stepped outside, and there was Dr. Antares, leaning his shoulders back against the white cinder blocks of the building, one foot flat against the wall, arms folded, a black Stetson down low over his eyes.

He looked up, morning light glinting in his eyes. "Need a ride?"

"I'm fine."

Dr. Antares pushed away from the wall. "It's my fault you lost your pants to radiation; it seems the least I can do."

Brian worked his jaw, feeling the strap of a belt across his shoulders. But Colonel Flynn was three states away, and Brian was tired. The snow would probably delay most of the scientists who were getting used to seeing him walk home. No one would know if Brian didn't risk frostbite.

"Fine," he gritted out, and Antares looked surprised. As if he hadn't expected Brian to give in. But then his face lit up, a bright smile moving across it as he damn near skipped to his turquoise Ford pickup.

He opened the passenger door for Brian, muttering, "It sticks if you don't work the handle just right," which kept it from feeling too much like a date.

Not that it could ever be a date, Brian growled inside his head as he settled against the soft seat, leather cool against his bare legs. He just needed to get through this posting, and he would be—

Something flopped across his lap, and Brian startled, shoulder pressing to the door. He stared at Antares as he settled into the driver's seat.

"I thought you might be cold. It's a long drive to the barracks since we'll have to go slow to avoid the ice."

Brian looked down at a thick, southwestern blanket across his lap. There was something off about it. The materials said it was Diné, but the designs were something else. This had none of the characteristic geometric clouds or the stepwise formation of the mesas. He tucked his fingers around the edge, trying to work his nail between the fibers; nothing. He pulled up a corner to smell, and his stomach dropped, and he had to squeeze his eyes shut. A profound sense of longing for his mother overtook him, crashing around him like water from an icy mountain river in the brief seasons when the arroyos ran red with flooding rain.

His voice was harsh, caught in his throat when he said, "Where did you get a Diné, a Navajo blanket with Apache designs on it?" *With my tribe's designs on it*, he wanted to say.

"From a friend." Antares started the truck, and the scent of sage and fresh snow filtered through the vents.

Brian worked his hand over the blanket, the red and yellow squares building into diamonds in the corner, just like— "Some friend. This is worth more than a rent check."

The truck rumbled as Antares backed out over gravel. Brian looked at his wild, half-dried hair haloed in the storm-filtered dawn light.

The scientist said, "I wouldn't sell it for anything."

"When were you on a reservation?"

Antares's eyes widened as he reached his hand out as if he was going to snatch the blanket back. Brian's grip tightened on it irrationally, the first scent of his mother's people he'd had in two years. After his mother had died, his father had thrown everything that reminded him of her out with the garbage, no matter how Brian had begged. He forced his fingers to relax, forced himself to sit back, look harmless. It hadn't been that strange of a question, but Antares's eyes still held fear.

Antares sounded carefully controlled when he said, "I got it visiting my friend from undergrad. After defending my dissertation at UW, before coming here. I went down to the Four Corners—"

"That reservation is a six-hour drive south over not-much roads from the Four Corners; it's just outside of Roswell."

"—and my friend made sure I saw the reservation, got to know some of the people he's been working with there," Antares said patiently. He turned the wheel, driving them through the sweet wild grass on the roadside to avoid a slick of ice that had been a pothole the day before.

"Your friend. He's a missionary?" Brian couldn't help his mouth from twisting. Missionaries stole kids, forced or convinced them to leave their families, the rez, always willing with a bus ticket out, never particularly specific on where or how to get back home again.

"No, he's an artist."

Brian's eyes widened, speaking before he thought. "An *artist*? Who has money besides rich New Yorkers playing cowboy to move out nearly to the border to do *art*?"

Antares glanced at him. "James does well for himself, sells his stuff in New York to people who've never seen an open sky in their born lives, spends all the cash on the reservation, and then begs me for money at Christmas."

He huffed and worked the clutch, getting them up to speed now they were between potholes.

Brian said slowly, "I went to some galleries in Los Angeles. There was a lot of faux-Indian art. People profiting off cultures that isn't theirs. Off *my* culture."

He glanced up at Dr. Antares to see how he'd take this, and the man was shaking his head.

"That kind of thing is fucked up," he said. "No. James's thing is a lot more about painting sunsets and sunrises and sometimes putting little alien spaceships in them and then telling rich people he saw the aliens for real."

Brian cracked up. "That's all right, then. Fooling New Yorkers about the magic of the Southwest is a tradition as old as America; adding aliens just makes it avant-garde."

"Practically modern art," Antares said with a smile. He paused, looking at the slowly approaching barracks. "Are you going to be okay in there? I can bring you a spare pair of pants from the cabin when I come back tonight. It seems like you've been taking the night shift?"

"I'll be fine. I have a few pairs. And it'll just give me another reason to bum a ride into Arco on Friday."

"'Another'?"

"Hodgins told me yesterday there's a hoedown at the bar? We'll have two twelve-hour shifts this weekend, so I have the night off. Well," Brian said with a wry smile, "officers aren't ever really 'off' because if anything goes wrong, I need to fix it. But less on than usual. And I wanted to try out my dancing shoes." He glanced at his borrowed boots. "Or maybe buy a pair of boots that fit."

"I'll see you there, then, if not before." Antares pulled in to park, the snow fogging the windshield. Brian was startled. The drive had seemed much too short for the distance covered.

"All right," he said, working the handle. "And thanks. For the ride."

"You're welcome," Antares said. Brian was half out of the cab when he called, "Airman?"

Brian turned, snow tingling on his bare face. "Yes, Dr. Antares?"

"I can give you a ride in this evening. Since you don't have a car. Before your shift tonight. You start at 9:00 p.m., right?"

Brian shook his head. "Thank you, Dr. Antares, but I'll be just fine. Thank you for the offer."

And before he could say anything more, he shut the door, body shaking with more than cold by the time he got into his dark apartment.

Chapter Four: T-90 Days

"The primary objective of the subcommittee in this inquiry was to determine the extent of the employment of homosexuals and other sex perverts in Government; to consider reasons why their employment by the Government is undesirable; and to examine into the efficacy of the methods used in dealing with the problem."

> —*"Employment of Homosexuals and Other Sex Perverts in Government," Interim Report submitted to the US Senate Committee on Expenditures in the Executive Departments by its Subcommittee on Investigation, Pursuant to S. Res. 280 (81st Congress). December 15, 1950.*

September 21, 1951

The Mello Dee Club and Bar of Acro, ID was hot, crowded, and fetid on Friday night. It had nothing on the beach-smooth bodies of West Hollywood or even the rowdy cowboy bars of Roswell. It was something in between, all isolated men and the few women who made their lives in Arco, vying for attention that no one was actually going to get.

No one, except Dr. Antares.

He'd been dancing since he walked in the door, drinking a few beers but always finding a fresh partner when the fiddle players picked up a new tune.

Brian got it; he did. The simple pleasure of a warm hand on his arm during a hot dance, another hanging on the back of his neck, carefully painted lips hovering over his ear. He got it.

Hodgins had given him a ride into town. He'd picked up new pairs of pants and boots at the general store while the others got settled at the bar. He'd thought about finding a new coat but decided to wait until his paycheck came in. If he saved every penny, it would only be seven more months until he could make the down payment on a new truck.

Now, Brian was sitting in a back booth, shopping bag behind his knees, sipping a single beer and waiting. He hadn't made a space for himself on the packed dance floor, hadn't particularly intended to dance. He'd been sitting there for two hours, honoring the same beer, mechanically raising it to his lips when he felt someone's eyes on him. A few of the others had tried to call him up, but with women so light on the ground, the more men who stayed off the dance floor the better time the rest of the fellas could have. Hodgins had already disappeared with an older blond woman, seeming to forget he was Brian's only way home. Aside from watching Dr. Antares dance, Brian had mostly been occupying himself with trying to decide who he'd ask for a ride back to the barracks.

Antares was heel-toe dancing in his real, broken-in cowboy boots. Brian had seen him wearing them every night they'd been keeping each other company in the lab, but this was the first time he was seeing them used the way they were supposed to be. They were good boots, work boots. Nothing like the faux-cowboy chic some of the men affected the instant they crossed the Rockies. Brian remembered hearing Dr. Zinn tell one of the nurses that Dr. Antares had been a ranch hand before he got into physics. That he'd worked his way through school, over and over again, just fighting his way through, working summers at the ranch and winters in the lab.

A few times, Antares had caught his eye from the dance floor. And Brian thought—no, he *hoped*—no. He *wondered*. Was Dr. Antares wishing it was him in his arms? Was Dr. Antares wishing he could dance with Brian, could twirl him around or be twirled around by him?

He watched Antares dip a giggling woman who could have been old enough to be his mother.

And then it clicked.

The whole night, Dr. Antares had been picking the safe ones. The ones who'd come in with a girl they were tight with, the ones who weren't getting picked by the cowboys or scientists: the bar owner's wife, the cowgirl in ill-fitting Sunday clothes. He was picking them and dancing with them, but there was none of the tension the other men brought to it.

Brian let that realization give him courage, help him to stand, set down the beer that had probably been empty for half an hour. He stepped into the flow. He let his hips move a little, his hand close to his chest, and when Dr. Antares caught his eye again, he paused. Antares twirled his partner once more and let her go as the song ended. And he stepped into Brian, eyes only for him. He ducked his head.

"Need a ride?"

Brian nodded. "I think Hodgins is staying in town. If you've got the space, I'd appreciate it."

"Lead the way."

Brian used the chaos of the room to slip his hand, once, just barely there, across Antares's belly. He felt his stomach jerk against his fingers as the raucous, throbbing crowd around them moved, and then Antares was brushing past him to snag his black cowboy hat off the rack by the wall, long legs carrying him to the door.

Brian caught Dr. Eisenberg's eye, and there was a flick to Antares, *something*—like a two-by-four to the chest.

And he'd know.

By the time they'd made it out to the parking lot and Brian had caught a face full of snow, he felt chilled all over, hugging his arms around himself, shopping bag swinging from his elbow. He wondered what the fuck he thought he was doing. He sucked in the cold air, felt the stretch of scars on his back.

And *remembered*.

Antares looked at his hunched posture, took a step farther away, then carefully handed Brian his keys.

"I'm too drunk to drive."

"Then why did you—"

He cocked his head at Brian, considering. "Hodgins gave you a lift in, right? And then left with the widow Kleimeicher?" Brian nodded, and Antares rolled his shoulders.

"I don't particularly enjoy being trapped someplace without a way home, and I figured neither would you. The hoedown will still be here next Friday.”

Brian grimaced. “I wish I could offer you a couch, but all I’ve got is a twin bed across from a kitchen the size of a closet.”

“I’ll sleep it off in the lab. The drive to your place is long enough for me to sober up enough to be able to make my way to the lab without running myself into a ditch.”

“I can catch a ride with someone else or drop you at your place—”

But Antares was already opening his passenger door. “I live in a cabin way up in the mountains, Airman. Just let me take you home.”

Brian wanted to argue, but by the time he got around to the driver’s side door, Dr. Antares was already asleep against the passenger window, cowboy hat cocked over his knee. Brian let himself look for a bare, moon-slivered moment in the quiet of the parking lot. His mouth was a little open, his hair ruffled by the dozen hands of all of the women he’d danced with. A curl arced over his closed eyelid. Brian’s fingers itched to tuck it back behind his ear.

He gripped the wheel, got the truck into gear, and headed east on Highway 26, keeping his mind as blank as the dark-water emptiness of the high desert. They could be driving straight through to the Pacific or right out into space for all the land on either side of them gave up its secrets.

Brian glanced over at him once they pulled up to the airmen’s barracks, the blank windows of his team’s bedrooms staring down at them. He reached out a careful hand, fingers stiff with driving, and nudged the doctor’s shoulder. Antares woke with a start, jerking forward until his hands smacked the dash, fingers flexing as he caught his breath.

He muttered, “Waking up always feels like a crash landing.”

Brian wondered what planes Dr. Antares had been landing in out in Wyoming.

"You sure you're okay to drive?" Brian asked. Not that he relished the idea of everyone seeing Dr. Antares's truck in front of his barracks in the morning. But he wanted the man safe.

"I'm good," he said crisply.

"What's the chemical formula for table salt?"

"NaCl."

"How many electrons in U-238?"

"Ninety-two on the dot."

"Who's the US President?"

"Abraham Lincoln—no, don't give me that look and *don't* take my keys. It's Harry S. Truman. Good night, officer."

Brian slid out of the cab, meeting Antares in front of the truck. He pressed the keys into the doctor's hand as the other man caught him around the wrist, fingertips light over his pulse point.

"Thanks for the ride, Airman." Antares drew him in slowly, as slow as breathing. His face went to Brian's shoulder and pressed a kiss to the soft skin right behind his ear.

Brian froze, eyes shifting up to the watching windows, heart choking him for a long moment until he felt Antares drop his hands, heard him get in the truck, start the engine, and leave, taillights red in the distance.

Shit.

*

Brian didn't sleep.

He worked out until he couldn't breathe, playing his father's mantra with each rep. Once his muscles were shaking too hard for him to keep going, he took a brutally cold shower. Then he forced himself to do a dawn inventory of the entire barracks, making sure he knew where all the space heaters, flashlights, first aid kids, extra blankets, MREs, and utensils were, so he would know his men would be okay no matter what the Idaho winter threw at them and their hastily constructed quarters. He spent the rest of the day rebuilding every single wall he'd ever had, from the ground up if necessary: how to walk, how to talk, how to touch, how to feel. That evening, he walked through the melting snow to work, waving to the scientists heading home after finishing their Saturday experiments. He knew his face and demeanor were perfectly professional, even though, with every single movement, it felt like he was carrying razors inside his skin.

It was about 21:30 when he saw John O'Flanagan shrugging off his lab coat as he approached. Brian was almost grateful. The scientist had been giving him the stink eye since he arrived, and it looked as if tonight was going to be when he let loose.

His opening salvo came as Brian knelt to wand his shoes. "So, you're, like, colored?"

O'Flanagan was about three years younger than Brian's twenty-six. He was either a genius, a junior assistant, or someone's nephew.

Brian knew which one he was betting on.

"Excuse me?" Brian kept his tone neutral, continuing to wand up the man's thighs.

"Well, you're sure as shit not white."

Brian bit his tongue, hoping he would just let it drop.

"So, were you, like, in one of those integrated units?"

Brian shook his head. "I'm not Black. There's never been segregation for Indians."

"Ah, so all that McCarthy stuff must be awkward for you," O'Flanagan said, stepping forward and hitching his pants so Brian had to start over.

"I don't know what you're talking about." Of course Brian had been following the House Un-American Activities Committee hearings, but he had no interest in talking politics at his job. It could get him fired, talking politics at his job.

"'Better dead than red,' right?"

A voice came from behind O'Flanagan. "You're an ignorant asshole, John O'Flanagan."

Brian's back stiffened under his uniform, his face flashing hot and cold as Dr. Antares continued.

"You should be so lucky as to be Apache. Men from the reservations are fighting on the front lines at Bloody Ridge and Heartbreak Hill on the peninsula while you Harvard boys are thinking of new wars to start."

Brian pulled himself to his feet, giving Antares a quelling look.

O'Flanagan spluttered. "What the fuck are you talking about, Aaron?"

Antares stepped closer. "That's 'Dr. Antares' to you, John. Some of us actually finished our PhD programs, rather than having to get bailed out by our mommies."

John growled and surged toward him with a fist upraised, and Brian slipped his foot between his ankles and yanked. The man landed squarely at Dr. Antares's feet on the polished cement floor.

"Oh, I'm so sorry. Do you need help up?" Brian asked, hands clasped in parade rest and weight back on his heels, face carefully schooled.

O'Flanagan was still hoisting himself up as Brian said, "You're free of radiation, and you're free to go home." He hadn't finished the check, but this was one man's fertility and health Brian was not feeling intensely motivated to safeguard.

O'Flanagan looked between Brian and Antares and muttered, "Better dead than red," and then limped out.

Antares stepped forward, spreading his arms out wide for his own wanding. A small—very small—*very* carefully caged part of Brian flipped over in disappointment that Antares was heading home this early in the night. If he was leaving now, it meant Brian would be alone in the building for the night.

It's for the best.

Antares looked carefully at Brian and murmured, "I didn't think you needed saving."

Brian warmed, softening. There were a hundred other things Antares could have said, but that was just about the right one.

"No. It's certainly not the first fucking time I've heard it." He straightened his uniform. "And what would be the fucking problem if I was Black? We're an integrated force. I've served with Black men, and they were good men. Black men protect this installation, and if he's giving me shit, I'm fucking certain he's been giving Freeman shit. They have to put up with a whole lot more shit than I do most fucking days." He made a mental note to himself to check in with Freeman, see if he needed to have a conversation with Dr. Zinn about O'Flanagan's behavior.

"It's not like it's easy on the rez," Antares offered.

"I didn't grow up on a rez. I grew up in base housing." Brian finished wanding him; clean as always. "You're clear."

Antares looked as though he wanted to ask a question, hover around, get more information. But he took Brian's dismissal for what it was and left.

Brian spent a quiet shift alternating between a physics textbook he'd borrowed from Dr. Zinn and an old copy of *Astounding Science*

Fiction. He'd have to see the next time he was in Arco if there was any way to get copies of new magazines because at the rate things were going with the night shift, he'd run through the ones he'd shoved into his bag from his boyhood bedroom. He studiously didn't think about Dr. Aaron Antares, not even at midnight or 03:00 or 06:00. He didn't think about his smile or his hands or the soft feeling of lips against his throat. He thought of a long, cold night, the shape of the cherry tree on the hill, and nothing but the desert winds to keep him company.

*

The next night, Dr. Antares came into the lab after everyone else had left, hands loose at his sides, an easy smile on his face. Brian stood up and went to go stand in the brewing blizzard outside until he was sure Antares had gone back to his own work.

It only took Brian doing that six times that night for Dr. Antares to get the picture. The bags under Antares's eyes were pronounced the next evening, and Brian told himself he didn't care.

He knew he didn't look much better.

The next day, they didn't speak. Brian wanded him briefly and professionally.

Brian tried to read the astronomy and physics textbooks he'd brought with him from Vandenberg. Sometimes, he could lose himself in the math.

This time, he could barely remember the beginning of a sentence by the time he'd reached the end of it.

When he got back to the barracks, Brian's body dragged him down into sleep so still and dreamless that he woke barely able to move for stiffness. But his mind felt clearer.

The next morning was a Tuesday, and Brian's shift replacement arrived early, so when Brian stepped outside of EBT-I, he could see the far-off barracks in the predawn light, a few stars still in the sky. He heard a sound—

Dr. Antares leaned against the cinder block wall, boot braced against the white paint, thumb hooked in his too-tight pocket. With the cowboy hat, he looked like something out of some kind of dream. The kind of dream Brian used to dread, for the laundry it would cause, for the pain that any discussion of what, exactly, he dreamed about would bring. For the punishment for lying, or dreaming about lying with men, for all of it really.

But his father couldn't hit him with belts here. He couldn't hit him with his hand or a hanger or kick him with a steel-toed boot.

Not from three states away.

Brian ducked his head away from Dr. Antares's watchful eyes, hunched his shoulders, and headed out into the snow.

No reason to think Dr. Antares was waiting for *him.*

Maybe he was taking a smoke break, enjoying the predawn sage-perfumed high desert air. But unlike any of the other scientists, Dr. Antares didn't smoke.

Brian didn't either. He didn't care what the doctors said when they were wrong about so much else. He didn't think cigarettes helped keep his lungs strong. He always felt out of breath when he smoked, so he'd kicked the habit as soon as he left West Point.

Brian heard the crunch of cowboy boots in freshly crusted snow. But Dr. Antares didn't say anything, just hustled to walk beside him. Brian glanced over at him; again; again. He drank in every detail even as his chest tightened so much he could hardly breathe. The man kept his gaze on his boots, seeming content to leave his truck at the lab and walk for no reason into the windy Idaho autumn.

After another dozen yards, Brian couldn't take it. He'd harnessed the fury that had been grinding into his cold surface since the bar, and he let it slip, just a little. He pivoted, stopping, hand on Antares's shoulder as the dawn-dimmed stars looked on. "What are you doing?"

Antares didn't look up, focus still on the churned-up dirt beside the road.

Brian took a breath and tightened his grip, shaking his shoulder a little. "What are you *doing*, Dr. Antares?"

And he looked up, and Brian's mouth went dry.

He was stunning enough in full color, in the heat and noise and chaos of the lab. A chaos he seemed to breathe and feed off of and revel in.

A productive chaos, like the heat of an oven, changing the state of everything inside of it.

But in the last of the night's starlight, he was carved from ivory and ebony. Nothing, nothing like this had ever happened to Brian. Nothing like staring a statue in the face, nothing like trying to survive the heat of this man's breath on his lips.

Antares murmured, "I couldn't let you go mad again," his voice easy. "You're pissed," he said, gaze intent on his before skittering away. "You're pissed, and you're right to be pissed, and I—" He gave this utterly helpless little shrug, and Brian frowned, but Antares kept going, words tumbling out in a rush. "I don't want you to be. I want you to not be mad at me. I don't know how else to get there but by being *here*, being where you can *see* me." He gestured to the road in front of them.

Brian closed his eyes. "I'm not pissed at you."

And Antares scowled, holding out his fingers and counting down. "Three nights of no questions about my experiments; no hassling me on safety protocol; no waiting for me to get finished; no willingness to take a ride when it's no skin off my tight ass, and you don't need to be walking two miles back to your shitty barracks."

"I'm not mad," Brian repeated, turning away, staring at the road back to his admittedly very, very shitty barracks. But then Antares caught his shoulder, spinning him around, gripping tight, Brian's heart slamming in his chest.

Antares's face was feral, possessive, fierce, and Brian didn't know if he wanted to be scared or horny or some horrifying mix of the two. Antares spoke in a furious whisper. "I don't need to be something to you. You don't want it, then, I don't want it. But I don't want to hear the lie in your voice, Captain. I can't. I thought we were keeping each other company. So tell me why you're pissed."

Brian scoffed, letting his mask slip, just for a moment, bitingly sarcastic. "As if you don't know."

"I *know* what I did—" Antares started, but Brian held up a hand, watching Dr. Zinn's truck swish past them.

"No," Brian said. "No, Dr. Antares. I can't do this. Not here, not where—"

He shut his eyes, head pounding.

Two years. Two years, and I'm free.

"If you want to be my friend, please, don't put me in this situation. I can't, Dr. Antares. I can't do this again."

"'Again'? But—"

"Dr. Antares," Brian ground out with what he hoped sounded like finality and not him begging for his life.

Antares held his hands up, backing away, back toward the installation and his truck and all kinds of propriety he shouldn't have forgotten in the first place.

"Okay, Captain. I'll leave it alone. But if I promise to keep my hands—" At Brian's glare, he lowered his tone. "—my hands and my *everything else* to myself, can we go back to how it was before? Joking around? It was—" His voice got small, almost called away by the autumn wind. "—it was nice not being alone at night."

Brian nodded once, jerkily. "We can try. Good day, Dr. Antares."

"Good day, Captain Flynn."

Chapter Five: T-86 Days

"Upon approval by the appropriate authority of the recommendation of a board of officers, convened for the purpose, that the enlisted man be given a blue discharge because of undesirable habits or traits of character (AR 615—368). Under these circumstances, a blue discharge is mandatory. "Undesirable habits or traits of character" are those which render the individual's retention in the service undesirable and because of which his rehabilitation is considered impossible, after repeated attempts to accomplish the same have failed; or those which evidence a psychopathic personality, manifested by antisocial or amoral trends, criminalism, chronic alcoholism, drug addiction, pathological lying, or homosexuality during service, and because of which the individual cannot be rehabilitated to render useful service."

—History of the Phrase "Discharged Under Conditions Other Than Dishonorable" and Present Discharge Criteria for Three Services. Investigations of the National War Effort: Blue Discharges. United States Committee on Veterans' Affairs, House of Representatives, 1949.

September 25, 1951

Brian's studio was freezing when he finally finished the walk back, and no amount of fiddling with the thermostat could get the heater to do anything but blow frigid air. Brian leaned his forehead against the apartment door for three long breaths before going to the storage closet where he'd organized the space heaters the week before. He knocked on all of his team members' doors, handing the drowsy airmen heaters before asking Hodgins to make a maintenance request once he left for the lab for his afternoon shift. Brian snagged the last space heater and took it to his studio. He brewed a cup of hot water and laced his freezing fingers around it. Once he'd drunk enough to feel his body begin to thaw, he wound himself in his thin blanket and tried to force himself to sleep.

It took a long time.

That evening found Brian standing in his tiny bathroom, gripping the towel bar so hard the cheap metal began to crackle. The shower had been lukewarm at best, not enough to pound the chill that had sunken into his bones during the day in spite of the space heater.

He was just *so tired.*

He kept thinking about his conversation with Antares. He didn't understand how Antares was so incapable of toeing a line that seemed so clear to Brian.

He didn't know what to do.

Should he tell him? God, he *had* to know at this point. Getting his PhD in nuclear physics probably had nothing of the macho BS factor Brian had faced getting his degree at West Point, but how had the man survived to his late twenties, acting how he acted? Looking at him that way. Defending him to O'Flanagan. Following him out into the snowstorm. Giving him rides.

It wasn't a subtle pattern.

He'd seen blue discharges filled out for less. Far less.

Brian forced himself to release the towel bar and then tried to adjust it back into shape. It had a kind of bend in the middle now. He wondered if that would come out of his meager pay. Brian thought, just for a second, just for a moment, about what Antares had looked like in the decontamination shower, his hands on his belt, his shirt coming up over his head. He shut that down with the sound of a snapping belt.

Brian refocused. He knew what he had in front of him and drank as much hot tea as he could, hoping it would warm him up from the inside. Brian ate his dinner with his blanket tight around him, trying to warm his core from the outside in. He tried to plan who he would ask for a ride into Arco to get a better blanket because this was not going to fly even if the heat came back soon.

Brian looked at his small collections of books and magazines, carefully arranged on the top of his pinewood dresser. There were a few books he hadn't brought to the lab yet. *Leaves of Grass*, another poetry book, a slim thing, hand-printed, and carefully hidden in the back of a physics textbook during the bus ride here. He let himself grab the Whitman and tucked it under his arm. Brian looked out his narrow window. A double blanketing of ankle-deep snow had fallen on the volcanic desert while he'd slept through the day, crusty ice underneath and perfect powder sprinkled on top. Brian bundled up, his only jacket from Vandenberg over his uniform jacket, his nose tucked snug into the neck of it. He still felt like an icicle.

Brian shoved the barracks door open to start the walk in for his shift and found Dr. Antares idling in his truck outside. Brian took a breath and immediately coughed, his lungs seizing with the cold. He looked at the flurrying snow, looked at the fogged windows of the truck, and listened to the comforting rumble of the engine. Then he swung the passenger door open and clambered up. As he settled back against the seat, Antares pulled a thermos of coffee from between his legs and handed it to Brian.

"You okay there, Airman?" Antares asked, watching as Brian huddled against the heating vents in the car.

"It's fucking cold," Brian chattered through his teeth.

Antares began to laugh, then cocked his head, realizing Brian wasn't laughing with him. He slid the blanket off the back of the bench seat and settled it over Brian's knees without so much as an extra brush of his pinky. Brian relaxed a stitch as he started to warm up.

"They have to have heat in those things, right?" Antares asked.

Brian nodded, the motion jerky with the stiffness of his muscles. "It went out this morning, so we used space heaters. I just couldn't seem to get warm."

Antares frowned, chewing his lips as he considered the problem. He settled his shoulders and put the truck into gear.

"I know—I know we're not— There's— Look," he said, running his hand across the top of the wheel, fingers nervous on the thick indentations of the plastic. "Is it sufficiently heterosexual to invite you to stay with me, at least until this cold snap is over or they fix the heat? I've got a guest room, a fireplace, a soaking tub, for god's sake. I'm never going to use it—"

"Where the fuck are they putting you scientists up that you have a *soaking tub*?"

Antares gave him a slippery smile, something in his eyes making Brian's lie-spotting hackles pop right up.

"Like I told you, I have a place up in the mountains. It takes an hour on uncertain roads to get there and back, but it's mine, and it's private."

Brian rolled his eyes, his face feeling stiff. "That's ridiculous. How do you afford that?"

"Aside from my rodeo winnings? I was lucky at slots out at one of the casinos in New Mexico. Left me with enough to skip out of Argonne Labs housing. I've still got a key, so I can use their gym, but I sleep in my own bed every night."

"You gambled your way into a house?"

"Yep," Antares said, popping the *P* obnoxiously. "Last time, I was down there visiting my friend James. You should come with me next time I go back at New Year's."

"I won't go back to New Mexico unless I'm dragged by my hair," Brian said without thinking, leaving out *like last time.*

Antares frowned but let it go. "The guest room has a lock on the door and everything—"

"I don't think you're going to assault my virtue, Dr. Antares," Brian snarled. "I'm not some flinching virgin for not wanting to start—" He put his hand on the door handle, but the blanket weighed him down. He bit his lips, forcing his temper back.

"Sorry," Antares said, raising a hand between them, speeding up just a touch, probably figuring the farther they got down the road, the less likely Brian was to jump out of a moving truck. "I'm sorry, Captain Flynn. You stated your position, and I keep teasing, pressing up against it, and that's unfair of me."

And, oh, wasn't that an image, him pressed against a barrier. Some kind of glass, all of him out and on display, legs wide, Brian's hand between—fuck. Brian always lost control over his imagination when he was this exhausted. This was going to be the longest fucking night in the history of humanity, and Dr. Antares was still talking.

"What I mean is—I'll do better. I'm sorry. But I was trying to say, the offer of a warm place to crash is there. Friendly-like."

"I'll be fine. What're you working on today, Dr. Antares?"

The doctor's face fell before he could cover it, but he just bit his lip and then dutifully got on with rambling about his plans.

*

That night, Dr. Antares was a whirlwind, a madman, utterly ridiculous. The third time Brian caught him trying to juggle the four testing light bulbs just within his line of sight, he let his shoulders droop again and began to laugh. He locked the front door and followed Antares back into the upstairs lab.

"How are you keeping those in the air?" he asked, leaning against the door to the lab as the scientist approached him, weaving his way around a workbench, then switching to juggling them with one hand.

Antares smirked. "I'm telekinetic. Didn't you see that in my file?"

Brian flushed. He *had* looked at the good doctor's file, one dark night when they weren't speaking. "I saw three letters of reference and five letters of report. Was it in one of those?" he asked sweetly, and Dr. Antares *stuck his tongue out at him.*

And Brian wanted to snatch those light bulbs out of the air, crowd the scientist up against the steel workbench, and show him *exactly* how he could put that tongue to use. Instead, he gripped the edges of the doorframe and glanced up at the clock—*04:00 and all's well.*

When he looked up, Antares was laying the bulbs on the lab table, *clink* after careful *clink.* Once they were safe from rolling away, he untucked a pencil from behind his ear and made a note on his new design for the reactor's control panel. Antares caught his eye just for a moment and then looked back down.

But he didn't press.

Instead, Antares said, still not looking up, "Three more hours until the end of your shift." Something hovered in his voice. "So, Airman, tell me. Why West Point?"

Brian snapped his head around from where he'd been admiring the asbestos insulation around the pipes that could carry liquid metal to the reactor. "What?"

"Why West Point? You get tired of warm winters in New Mexico?"

"My father is a colonel," Brian answered, looking at the polished concrete floor.

Antares frowned. "Army, right? Since the air force just became its own branch in '47."

"Yeah, that was the year before I graduated. They came on the campus, lined us all up, and told us who of us were going to be air force officers and who were going to be army officers when we graduated. I think I made the cut because of the science major. I didn't know they'd do that when I applied to the service academies though. I thought— It doesn't matter what I thought. I had the grades; I wanted out of New Mexico. Out of that house. See a different kind of sky, be around a different kind of people. Free college and access to real laboratories were just the right amount of sweetener."

"Not so free when you're stuck in Idaho for two winters."

Brian quirked his lips. "Easier service than being in Korea; that's where most of my class is. Or was." He shifted his shoulders against the doorframe. "A lot have died."

"You wish you were there?"

Brian stared at him. His voice was harsh when he said, "I didn't see anything in your record about serving. That's something another officer would ask."

Antares looked down at his hands, clenching and unclenching them in the low lab light. "There's lots of different kinds of wars. But I know it can be easier. In a way. To be in the midst of the fighting. To see people lost and found, rather than waiting to hear about it months or years after. To be beside your friends when they die."

Brian expected to see Antares's usual mocking smile. Instead, he found something familiar in his expression.

Something like understanding.

Brian gritted his teeth and nodded, eyes feeling pressure. "Yeah. I—yes." His hands tingled. "Sometimes—sometimes I wish I were there. All my brothers are there." Then he looked up, out across the lab. From the doorway, he could see the base of the reactor tower, the steel spiral staircase. "But what we're doing here is good too, important too."

Antares turned to lean against the lab table behind him, and said, his voice wry, "You think the war in Korea is important?"

Brian frowned, taking a step toward him, trying to see his expression, but it was hidden in the shadows on his face. "The words of West Point are Duty, Honor, Country. In that order."

Antares waited for him to elaborate for a moment before saying, "I'm not sure I—"

"Country comes *last*. The work I could be doing there, with my background, with my degree, would be helping detect if China or North Korea was developing a nuclear weapon. Whether you think the US should be there or not, I think we can, between the two of us, agree neither of those countries should have control over a nuclear bomb. Hell," Brian said, rubbing his hand over his regulation haircut, "I don't think *we* should have the bomb either, for all the evil we've done with it. I'm still pissed the Nuclear Regulatory Commission idea—civilian control of all nuclear research—got shut down in Congress last year."

He paused, trying to say this right. Unused to being heard. "But I certainly don't think Chairman Mao should have the bomb. That would be duty, duty to use my skills to help as many people as I can. Honor, that would be protecting the people under my command while achieving that goal. A good leader, a good commander, can protect people, save their lives but also save their honor. Keep them out of fights that will hurt something impossible to fix inside of them. Keep them from breaking themselves in war. Keep war from breaking them."

He took a breath, and it made the tightness in his chest ache. "We have a duty to protect. To fight for those who can't fight for themselves. Keeping bombs out of the hands of madmen and killers is as good a start as any, better than most. All people, no matter where they're born, deserve freedom. Freedom from want, freedom from fear, freedom of worship, freedom of speech."

When he looked over to see Antares's reaction, he expected—well, what he got was something soft. Something like awe.

Brian tried to finish his thought. "There are a lot of guys who are into what Senator McCarthy is peddling, the 'my country right or wrong' crowd." He swallowed. "There's a longer version of that quote I heard from one of my instructors. 'Our country, right or wrong; when right, to be kept right; when wrong, to be put right.' We have a lot to set right after what we did in Hiroshima and Nagasaki. Nuclear scientists in particular. We have a duty *and* it's a matter of honor. We need to set our country right with peaceful atomic energy. To show people this awesome power can't just be used to hurt, but to help."

That was more words in a minute than he'd spoken to anyone in a long time.

Dr. Antares's voice was full when he said, "You're an *idealist*, Captain Flynn."

Brian bit his lip but nodded. "I have to be. Or else, what do we do? Let the cynics win? Let the war profiteers and segregationists and the anti-Indian bigots and—and—" He forced the words out. "—the anti-homosexuals, do we let them win? Let them have this country?" He shook his head, squaring his shoulders. "No. *Fuck* no. They can have it when they pry it from my cold dead hands. It's not *theirs*. It's *mine*."

"Are you going to save the whole world, Captain Flynn?

He flushed, but he was sure on this. "Somebody's got to. Don't you think it needs saving?"

Antares was closer now, his hands loose at his sides. "I do. And it'll only get better the more we fight."

Brian looked at him, alone in the dark light of the lab, and unlocked a tiny truth from under his heart. "It's—it's hard. Fighting alone. Not knowing what better looks like, what equal looks like. Not having, just—" He shoved his hands in his pockets. "It's an honor and a duty to work here, but it's also been—better. Than I thought it would be. Here. These past weeks."

Antares nodded, eyes wide, breath quickening in the close air between them.

Brian eased himself off of the doorframe, rocking on his heels. "I'm going to go and check the perimeter."

The scientist's face fell, and Brian chanced a hand, a spread of fingertips just on the hard edge of Antares's elbow.

"I'll come back after?" he said. "You can tell me more of your civilian-shaded opinions of the Korean War?"

Antares took the teasing for what it was and returned his smile. "It's a deal."

*

That morning, after Dr. Antares gave him a ride to the barracks, still gleefully chattering about international politics, Brian lay in his narrow bed. The barracks were warm again; turned out it had been an issue with a breaker, and Mr. Jolley had fixed it on his way home. The sunlight was bright in the azure sky, and Brian let himself run full wild with a daydream about Dr. Antares.

He'd pull Antares out of the ridiculous reactor, crowd him back against the hip-high railing, thigh between his, and just fucking *climb* him. Make him *know* in his *bones* that he was wanted. That his touch was *needed*. And Aaron—he'd finally get to call him *Aaron*—his hands would be under Brian's shirt, working the clips and clasps off as Brian crowded in closer and closer and closer, body hot and tight in the sage-scented Idaho air, body as much his as it was Brian's own.

Or: Aaron would wander over to Brian's little folding chair by the door. Aaron would be distracted with his calculations, and he'd slide down at Brian's feet with his back against the thick cinder block wall. Brian would lower himself beside him, folded up with a respectable distance between their shoulders as Aaron read aloud a passage in the research he was working on, and then another. He'd move closer and closer and closer as Brian's skin shrank by a full size for every inch he closed in. Then his hand would brush Brian's, and his entire body would light up, his shoulder suddenly warm as he leaned just a little bit closer.

It would be past midnight, and they would be the only ones in the building, the only bodies warming the air. Fingers intertwining on the pages, knee knocking against his, overlapping until they were halfway in each other's laps. They'd be laughing and smiling and arguing about casing design, and then Brian would turn, and it'd be all curls and smirks and lips, and he'd smell his inside smells, feeling skin brush against his. Brian would press a kiss to the corner of Aaron's mouth, missing an attempt to reach the intended target, and Aaron's eyes would flare. He'd gasp and say something like "fucking *finally*," and swoop in, hands bracketing Brian's face, knees crowding around his knees. Books lost on the concrete, bodies a single moving, trusting thing, and they'd laugh and knock heads and learn the taste of each other's mouths. Learn the shape of each other over their bulky clothing, then under one layer, then another. It would take the whole night, first his lab coat, then Brian's uniform jacket. They'd end up in the nurses' area, down to their undershirts and briefs, bodies hot in the twilight of the security half lights, hot and knowing, bodies slick with work, hands running freely and evenly across each other, always welcome and always full.

And Aaron would lean Brian against one of the examination tables and rut, bodies urgent and hot and tight. They'd shove hands between each other, laughing and bumping knuckles, bodies in need but also so, so trusting, and Brian would rest his cheek on Aaron's shoulder. Feeling it rising, feeling it riding out across him, feeling his heart begin to beat in time with his strokes, body shaking and unashamed, touched and unashamed, loved and unashamed. He would spend and feel Aaron's spend on him, and they would laugh and wash off in the shower, giggling and freezing and touching, and they'd get some snacks, and they'd just *be.* Still and quiet. And they'd go home to Aaron's magical, mythical cabin up in the mountains and go to sleep, safe in Diné blankets and a single shared quilt.

That was the fantasy Brian put himself to bed with, the kind of next-life promise he gave himself to make it through the hours and weeks here on the installation.

Chapter Six: T-83 Days

the dead are also remembered:

    there may be
here at the center of a chamber cut out
    of context
cenotaph for Jeff Rall who
    in youth fell
at Dunkirk, because war was more real
    than Blenheim's
in the Village; but the old teaching is
    he each year
closes the year from us and is to be mourned
    by women
openly, and the verse refers to him
    as to a
secret, a hidden liaison with springtime,
an allegiance to the unmentiond, a
    constancy
in avoiding the well-spring in searching for water
    where there was

a star regularly departed from an old alignment,
    not sorrow
nor happiness involved in the kept dimensions
    that allow
no continuous coordination of all parts to betray
    the still light
cast in the pool to the eye that has not
    demanded it.

    —Robert Duncan, excerpt from "Under Ground"

September 28, 1951

"Captain Flynn, can I see you in my office for a moment?"

Sitting on his folding chair beside the entrance, the warmth of the evening sun still strong through the cinder block wall, Brian felt more than chills, more like entire Arctic bites of glass sliding down his spine. But he stood up straight, put his shoulders back, and marched behind Dr. Zinn's cheerfully galumphing form.

Zinn ushered him inside his office and must have seen his stricken expression because he shook his head at himself. "It's nothing bad, Captain. I'm sorry, the social graces slipped away from me sometime between my first and second PhD. I actually have a bit of good news I'm not, technically, supposed to share. But—" He shrugged. "—if you don't tell, I won't either."

Brian cocked his head, but he sat and leaned into the flatbacked chair when Dr. Zinn gestured him into it.

"One of my administrative duties in our little shared civilian-military enterprise is to collect quarterly feedback from enlisted men about the officer commanding them and then provide that up the chain of command since, for operational security, there's minimal contact between you and Vandenberg. Nurse Kelly does the same for the nurses, Mr. Jolley for the maintenance staff, and Dr. Eisenberg for the scientists." Brian was back to feeling frozen, iced out, and on the ice flow.

Dr. Zinn riffled through the papers on his desk before retrieving a key. He swiveled on his chair to one of the unlabeled cabinets and drew out an Air Force blue folder.

He laid it gently on a drift of paper near Brian and then gave him a small smile. "If there were complaints, I wouldn't show them to you. But I figured—" He looked to the ceiling as if steeling himself to say something outside his comfort zone. "It can be hard being a leader. No one ever tells you when you've done a good job, when you're doing right by the people you manage or command." He flashed a grin at Brian that made him look like the young man pictured on the dust jackets of his books. "Well, that's stupid. You should know. You're doing a good job."

He stood, brushing his hands over his lab coat. "I'll go for a walk around the lab, see what monstrosities Dr. Antares is committing against my control panel tonight. Will"—he glanced down at the file, fingers nudging it a little closer to Brian—"half an hour do it?"

Brian nodded, neck stiff. The older scientist left, carefully closing the glass-fronted door behind him. Dr. Zinn might mean well, but there were all sorts of ways men could give coded messages to their superiors Zinn might not catch. Brian couldn't do anything about it if they did, but it was a profound kindness for him to try to give Brian a heads-up. A violation of the men's privacy, absolutely. But also a kindness.

Brian flipped it open. There were three pages, typed on the same typewriter without removing the paper. It looked as if each man had come in to write their evaluation on Dr. Zinn's typewriter. That eased some of Brian's worry about privacy since the men would have seen the others' words as they wrote their own or could read them anytime they wanted to come in and see.

Junior Airman J. Hodgins

Captain Flynn is a good man. He rearranged the shift schedule, so he's taking the ~~shit~~ night shifts. He makes sure our housing is as good as may be and never imposes on us, even though he doesn't have a truck, and though he could order us to drive him in, he just walks instead. Also, once he realized we'd never gotten the radios we needed to communicate between the perimeter guard and the base guard, he got those expedited, so we don't have to leave visitors waiting behind the locked gate while we drive in to make sure the installation guard knows what's going on. We'd been telling the last commander for months that we needed them, that it was a ~~crappy~~ unprofessional system we had, but nothing ever changed. But Captain Flynn got it handled.

Junior Airman R. Durbin

I woke up shivering before my shift because the heat had gone out, and before I could even pry myself out of bed to get some coffee onto my aching bones, there was Cap, heater in hand and promises to get it fixed on his lips. And you know what? He got it fixed.

Junior Airman L. Gamgee

Captain Flynn's been on our installation for about three weeks, and it's been night and day. We get days off now he's fixed it with the schedule, and he takes the shit shifts, never tries to fob it off on enlisted men. I wish we had more officers like that; he's the best I've worked with.

Junior Airman S. Ramirez

This is my first posting, and I just got here a month ago. The schedule when I got here was rough, the housing rough, and the scientists were a ~~nightmare~~ a challenge. But the one who made our lives the worst has cooled it since Captain Flynn arrived. God bless his patience with that man.

Junior Airman G. Freeman

I've been here for two years and have gone through four security directors; the snow, the secrecy, and the science isn't for everybody. The last security director, he tried, but he could never get on the same page with the scientists or the nurses, always late for his briefings or playing games around getting his blood tests in or bossing Mr. Jolley around. Captain Flynn treats every single person he works with like they are a professional who deserves respect, even when he hasn't gotten any kind of good sleep. He's the kind of person they mean when they talk about "an officer and a gentleman."

Junior Airman K. Kingman

The most difficult thing about this posting was one of the scientists who used to come in at completely random times, always messing around, testy and pissy with us, or chatting our ears off when we had other duties. Just, really hard to pin down to the protocol we need to follow. Since Captain Flynn came on, that scientist has kept a regular schedule, and on the rare days he overlaps with one of my shifts, he's a ray of sunshine. I didn't even need to ask him to put the test tubes back when he was wandering outside with them still in his pocket at the end of the long day—Captain Flynn just gave him a look, and he went to do it, meek as a mouse. I don't know how he did it, but Captain Flynn is great at civilian-military cooperation.

Brian sat with the pages for long minutes, reading and rereading them. He was sure he couldn't be the best officer Gamgee had worked with. He *couldn't* be.

But even he couldn't dismiss every single thing the men had said. He *had* made a schedule that made their lives easier. He *had* figured out how to quickly and effectively work with all of the different personalities on the installation.

He took a breath, trying to let those words take root in the rocky and mismanaged soil of his heart.

Then he got back to work.

*

The next night, Brian gave Dr. Antares a real smile when he came in. After everyone else cleared out, Antares came over to sit beside him, settling on the polished concrete floor, back against the cinder block. His pencil flew fast across his notebook, sketching a new housing for the reactor, glancing up at Brian occasionally. Brian stayed on his folding chair reading, but he liked to think he could feel the warmth of Antares beside him. He'd just reached the Calamus poems when Antares said without looking up:

"What you said about Mao Zedong? It's bullshit."

"What?"

"It's ahistorical bullshit. China only thinks they have to have a bomb because we have a bomb. If we gave up our bombs and turned all our uranium warheads into power plant fuel, they would give up their program. If we gave up bombs, they'd give up bombs."

"That's naïve."

"I don't think so. It takes a huge amount of their resources when they're struggling to feed their people. I wouldn't be surprised if they start some eugenics shit soon, limiting family size. It's not good in China right now."

"What do you know about China?"

Antares looked up, meeting Brian's eyes. "I read."

"Yeah? Any little red books I should know about?"

Antares snapped, "I didn't take you for a McCarthyite."

"Fuck him. But if you're going to People's Party meetings, don't tell me. God only knows when they'll ask me to start reporting on people's political preferences."

"I think the House Un-American Activities Committee wants nearly free energy more than little ole me."

Brian frowned. "Now, I was teasing before, but *that* is naïve. HUAC would rather we all live in the dark."

Antares just frowned as he crossed out a design. He flipped to a fresh page. Then he spun on his seat, lay back on the concrete, and propped his heels against the cinder block wall with his notebook braced on his thighs, hair spreading out behind him. Brian itched to touch it, keep the flotsam of the floor from getting mixed up in his curls.

But that was not his problem, not now.

Instead, he asked, "What do you mean 'it's bullshit'? Okay, I get what you're saying about ahistorical, but we don't have a time machine. We already dropped the bomb, killed two hundred ten thousand people. We don't have a time machine—"

"*You* don't have a time machine," Antares muttered.

Brian rolled his eyes.

Antares sighed. "No, you're right. We don't have a time machine. But, the thing is—" He flopped his head back on the floor, curls golden in the lab light. "It's just—" He paused. "You have to—"

He closed his eyes, letting his notebook fall to his stomach as he waved his hands above him, painting a picture. "Where I grew up on—" There was a long pause. "In Wyoming, you had to do double-entry bookkeeping on reality." He held up his hands like a big ledger. "On one page is what is true. What is reality. Like, take cows. When I was working as a ranch hand, saving up money for school, I was taught the basics by the old cowboy who owned the herd. Cows have to be protected from wolves. Cowboys fight wolves. On the other hand"—he shook a hand—"there's reality as you see it. I never saw a wolf take a cow. I saw mud, fences, ditches, other cows, hunters, even lightning take one idiot cow that just *had* to stand on top of a bare-assed hill in the middle of a summer thunderstorm. Never saw a wolf take a cow. If you practice good range riding, if you're regularly present with your herd, you get to know where the local packs are, and they aren't going to take most cows. Honestly, a herd of seven thousand head of cattle, it doesn't even actually matter if you lose one to foot rot and one to a random wolf. But you'll notice the ranchers spend quite a deal of time talking about 'dem wolves.' Because the wolves symbolize an *other*, a *thing* that comes for them. That they have to fight back, prove they are *strong* enough to fight back. So"—he wiggled one hand—"reality as we're told"—and then he clenched and unclenched the other—"reality as we see it."

Brian thought about it for a moment.

"Yeah, I guess I had to do that too. About—" He took a breath. "On my good days, when I'm okay with—" He looked at the bare white cinder block wall, jaw tense. "There was a while, when I was— I went to the parties, you know? The bars?"

Antares hitched himself up, palms flat on the concrete, looking up at him. "Yeah?"

"The ones for—" Brian waved between them.

Antares's eyes widened. "With how you reacted, I assumed you'd never—"

"No." Brian gave a harsh laugh. "Definitely, definitely have. Definitely. That's not the problem."

He could see the doctor almost jumping out of his skin to ask what the problem *was* and if they could maybe fix it and get on with things.

But Brian held himself back and continued, "Some of the guys, they talked like that too. About how are we going to build a better world if we can't see ourselves as righteous parts of it?"

"That's a good question. You said— There are good days. You know, even on bad days, there's nothing—nothing wrong with you. Us." Antares's face was so earnest it made Brian's eyes prickle.

He jerked his head to the side. "That's not what the Joint Chiefs of Staff would say. Have said. 'Undesirable habits or traits of character are those that render the individual's retention in the service undesirable, and because of which his rehabilitation is considered impossible.'" Brian's jaw ached. "'Because of which the individual cannot be rehabilitated to render useful service.' They would say I 'cannot render useful service.'" The weight of those words was like a boot on his chest.

"Then the Joint Chiefs and HUAC and the Senate and the fucking President and *certainly* Senator McCarthy should take a long walk off a short pier," Antares growled, and Brian cracked a smile. "I'm serious, Captain. Double bookkeeping. What we are, in this moment and in this place—it's illegal, and it's not wrong. There are—will be—places where we could be free. Be equal. Just try to remember that."

Brian said softly, "You sound like you've been there."

Something moved behind Antares's eyes before he said, "There's this quote I heard in one of my mandated philosophy classes at UW. It's by this abolitionist minister Theodore Parker. He said: 'I do not pretend to understand the moral universe. The arc is a long one. My eye reaches but little ways. I cannot calculate the curve and complete the figure by experience of sight. I can divine it by conscience. And from what I see, I am sure it bends toward justice.' Just remember that, Brian. Always bending, always toward justice." He met Brian's gaze and held it. "Because we bend it. That kind of thing only happens when people fight back."

This was solid ground for Brian. Fighting, he understood. "Yeah? You gonna be on the front lines of a queer revolution, Dr. Antares?"

Antares rolled his eyes, sitting all the way up. Brian carefully watched his face, not his stomach muscles. "Like you said—somebody's got to." Then he cracked a smirk.

Brian laughed. He stood and stretched his arms above his head, not missing how Antares tracked where his uniform shirt rode up.

"Well, does the Mr. Wilde of Wyoming want some coffee to fuel his subversive tendencies, or you gonna rely on the uranium you ate for breakfast?"

"Coffee would be great if you're making a cup."

"Sure. Anything in it?"

"As much sugar as you can stomach."

Brian made a face but headed to the hot water heater with a bit more spring in his step. He didn't believe in a queer revolution, but it was like he'd told Antares the night before. Sometimes it was just nice to know, for a few minutes, he wasn't alone.

*

"Captain Flynn, I have a call for you."

It was an hour into his shift the next night, and Nurse Kelly's dark brown eyes were concerned. Brian glanced at Hodgins. He'd been help-ing him study for the upcoming SAT test. He'd be taking a few days to go to Seattle to take it, then finish up his enlistment period, use his GI Bill to get an ag degree, and help out on the family farm.

"Who would even know to call for me here?"

She shook her head, taking a step toward him, and said, voice quiet, "Your father. Unless you have a much older brother who likes to get drunk and flirt with women trying to do their jobs."

Brian hoped his quick shudder was taken as disgust at his father's behavior. Which it was, but it was also for himself, for what he was about to have to do.

"Want me to tell him you're off shift?" she offered, already step-ping toward the nurse's station.

Brian's entire back was tense, all the way up to his neck. He could barely turn his head. "He'll just keep calling."

He turned to Hodgins. "Come and get me if I'm not back in fifteen minutes. Then head home; we can go over more of the algebra problems tomorrow afternoon before my shift, okay?"

"Yes, sir."

Brian forced himself to move, legs aching with it, Nurse Kelly be-side him.

"What's keeping you here so late tonight?" he asked to fill the air. He looked up toward the central platform as he passed it, trying to catch a restorative glance at Dr. Antares, but he must be inside the reactor again.

"Oh, just finishing running the weekly blood tests; I had to rerun a few because of a contamination error."

"Everything looking all right with them?"

"Right as rain."

They reached the nurses' office. There were two phones: one in the front exam area and one in the chief nurse's back room. Nurse Kelly took one look at him and picked up the receiver in the front room, palm tight over the microphone, and gestured him to the chief nurse's office. He shook his head at her, and she shook hers even harder back. She glared at him until Brian ducked his head, heart swelling with thanks. He'd be alone in the room but not alone on the line.

She uncovered the receiver and, using her brightest tone, said, "Colonel Flynn, for security purposes, all external calls must be monitored, so I'm going to stay on the line."

His father's tinny bark punched through the receiver. Kelly's smile stiffened, and Brian was reminded of a time at a fair when he'd chucked a ball of hardened sugar at one of his brothers in response to some taunt and split Ian's cheek open right over the bone. Sweet things in their natural form tended toward toughness.

"Sorry, that's policy," she said. "You can call him on the public pay phone in Arco, but I don't know the next time he's going to get out there without a truck." A pause. "Great, thank you for your help."

She covered the receiver again, palm flat and stifling. "I'm hanging up both lines in five minutes; if he starts to yell, I'm hanging up sooner."

"You don't have—"

"Brian."

He nodded and stepped through the doorway, then made eye contact with her through the glass window between the two rooms. He forced his lungs to expand, to get a little sip of air, and then he picked up the phone.

"This is Captain Flynn."

"What the fuck is this protocol?"

The man was *drunk*. Brian could smell the bite of it at the back of his throat. Bourbon always loosened up his father's muscles to make his hits land just that much more effectively.

"Sir, Nurse Kelly would know better than I do; I'm not a telephone operator."

He glanced over at her through the connecting window, wincing. She rolled her eyes and nodded. He tried to convey with his expression: *what people say to get bigots off their back has very little to do with what they actually believe.*

Brian hoped they both knew that.

"It's bullshit."

Brian stayed quiet.

"Well," the man said. "Calling to check in on you. I haven't heard from you. Hope you haven't been up to any of your old tricks."

Brian's blood drained out of his face, heart struggling to keep up. His vision was fogging up, but he forced his breath inward and out, hand on his chest.

"Answer me when I speak to you!"

"No, sir," Brian gasped out.

"Well," he slurred. "At least you haven't made a fuckup of it already. I was—" Something *tink*ed against the receiver on his end. *Probably the bottle.* "I was thinking of how we left things. You seemed to misunderstand what we did."

Brian thought of a belt, his truck's window smashing in, a crumbled Greyhound ticket.

He heard himself say, "In what way?"

"Everything," he said, overenunciating, "*Everything* I do for you is to make you the man you're supposed to be, not this—" He stopped himself. "I'm just sorry for you that you don't see everything I do for you. When you're a husband and a father, someday when you're a real man, you'll understand this was all for your own good."

Brian stayed silent.

"Answer me when I speak to you!"

He didn't want to agree with that. He didn't want to fight. He didn't want to be on the phone at all. He wanted to go back, read his textbook, and wait until he could breathe, wait until the shaking in his hands subsided again, wait until he was a person again. *Maybe see Dr. Antares smile.*

Nurse Kelly broke in, "I'm so sorry, Colonel. There's a call on the line—"

"Hold on a goddamn minute, you scarlet hussy. I'm talking to my youngest. It's his birthday soon and"—the colonel's voice dropped, becoming almost warm—"his red bitch of a mother isn't here to nag me about him—"

Brian clutched his stomach, body rebelling, the bizarre softness in the man's tone gutting him in a way shouting just didn't this time. He remembered this was what his father was and—

And there was a click. Blessed silence. Brian shook as he too, too carefully put his receiver down. His body was held apart at the atoms by the pain and rage and self-feeding hurt in his father's voice. A humiliating part of him wanted to call him back, to call back the first phone number he'd ever memorized. To apologize for not being good enough. For not being smart enough, strong enough.

Man enough.

A tiny voice in his head reminded him he'd gotten into West Point on his own because his father had wanted him to enlist and not become an officer; he'd graduated with a degree in physics on his own; the Air Corps had picked *him.* That voice was too petite, too crushed and choked out and belt-whipped down and cracked to hear right now. And Brian knew, from the long cold experience of nights spent sleeping outside when he was too unwelcome to sleep inside his childhood home, that he'd hear it again.

Just not now.

The quiet voice had been born under the stars on one of those long, cold nights in the New Mexico desert, walking to keep himself warm. It had been born, and he'd fed it after every beating, every beratement. Every fucking time he'd had the chance, he'd fed it. So he knew it would come back, would remind him he was better than this, worth more than this. But for now, for these few minutes, it could have been dead and buried for all he knew it was still there.

Nurse Kelly stood in the door. He couldn't tell if she'd been talking, but from the look on her face, she didn't expect him to be able to hear her just yet. He adjusted his hand on the desk and shifted toward the door, back to his post. But she held up a hand, brown palm sitting him down with the force of a drill sergeant's shouts.

"You've got ten minutes until Hodgins comes around for more tutoring. You're going to take the full ten—"

"But—"

"No, Brian," she said, tone quiet, firm. "You're going to take them."

She slipped fully into the room, leaving the door between cracked as if she knew he needed a way out of the room. "Did that frog spec who calls himself your father actually say he was sorry for *you* misunderstanding? After what he *did*? That fucking *toad*, Brian. Captain Flynn. That fucking—"

And she pressed her fingers against her closed eyelids before pivoting and squatting. She pulled a box from the bottom shelf of the chief nurse's high bookcase, under the blackboard's chalk chart of all of the most recent readings and results for all of the people in the lab. The desk lamp showed it was a box of black vinyl records. She shuffled through them.

Nurse Kelly pulled one out with a huff and laid it squarely on the chief nurse's desk in front of Brian's hunched body. "That's all I have to say about *that*."

And he started laughing. Broken and cracked sounding, but a real, actual laugh. The album sitting squarely in the center of the perfectly clean desk showed a laughing African American woman, with the words "Cry Me A River" beside her in a stark black font.

And with each choking laugh, he got a tiny bit more air in, sobbing laugh by sobbing laugh, Nurse Kelly grinning along with him. He wrapped his arms around his stomach, his hands tight in fists.

"You've heard this record?" she asked.

Brian shook his head.

"Well, I'll play it for you sometime. You're welcome to the player, nights when it's just you and the mad scientist up there."

He tensed, waiting for her to say something, something about what his father had implied.

She was looking toward the phone, but then she met his gaze as though trying to force her words into his brain. "Sometimes, the people who are supposed to love you are trash, Brian. Just *utter* trash. No fuck-ing point in trying with them. They might as well go cry a river for all the good they'll ever do you. Just—don't pick up the next time he calls. Just don't. If there's consequences, try to get out of them. But give yourself as much space between talking to him as you can, time to get him out of your head. You don't have to live like this." She waved where he stood, still hunched, even as his eyes dried from his laughter. "Take one step away. Then another. Then another. Eventually, you'll be free."

Brian's eyes felt hot, with a heavy pressure behind them. "I'll consider it, Nurse Kelly."

She quirked a smile at him. "See that you do. Why do you think I moved all the way out here to Idaho from sunny Boca Raton? After all the trouble my mother took, moving what was left of our things from California after she got out of the camps? Sometimes distance is all that protects us." She paused. "Distance and time. But time, we've got, Captain. And distance, we can make. No one can fight your demons for you, but I can be damned sure that while you work here, you don't face them alone. *Damned* sure."

He nodded, and as he stood this time, she let him, a gentle hand on his elbow as he maneuvered around her.

"Take care of yourself, Captain. Nobody else is going to do it for you."

*

The next night, Brian placed a call on the nurse's line to a number he'd found scribbled in the back of *Leaves of Grass*. He left a message and returned upstairs to keep an eye on Dr. Antares.

Chapter Seven: T-77 Days

"Case No. 3: Subject is white, 32 yrs., resident of the District, Sgt. US Marine Corps. Observed performance act of perversion upon below listed subject on October 20, 1947, by Pvt. Pyons and Cpl. Mast. Subject turned over to Shore Patrol. Civil Service notified.

Case No. 4: Subject is white, 18 yrs., S/2 USN, stationed at Naval Air Station, Anacostia, D.C. Observed engaged in an act of perversion with above subject on October 20, 1947, by Pvt. Lyons and Cpl. Mast. Subject turned over to Shore patrol. Civil Service notified.

[...]

Case No. 8: Subject is white, 24 yrs., resident of the District, CAF-2 Clerk. Made proposition to Sgt. Place. Admits to being bi-sexual, wanting men only when drinking. Subject fingerprinted and photographed at Metropolitan Police and charged with disorderly. Elected to forfeit $25.00. Civil Service notified. (Pvt Traband, November 5, 1947)"

—Excerpts from Pervert Records (Government Employees), submitted by the U.S. Park Police to the Hoey Committee. (Records of the U.S. Senate, RG 46). 1947.

October 4, 1951

Brian had come in early, catching a ride from Freeman, to help him figure out some transfer paperwork. He'd only just started his shift when the perimeter gate duty radioed that he had a visitor at the entrance. Brian headed out, so he was leaning against the front wall of the installation when the traveling shampoo salesman drove up in his battered Ford.

The salesman stepped out: tall and slim, underdressed for the weather, carrying a sample case. He gave Brian a crooked smile. "I've never delivered this far out before," he said. "I had to get an entirely new map."

"Thank you for bringing it so quickly." Brian stepped forward, pulling off his gloves to rummage in his pocket for his checkbook, snow stinging his hands. "I only called two nights ago. This is the only thing that keeps my hair from frizzing like I stuck my finger in a light socket."

The salesman raised his hand, long slender fingers just gracing the short hair behind Brian's ear and feeling the texture. Brian froze.

"Something not WASP, not white-bread in your family history?"

"My mother is Apache," Brian said. He could smell the man's cologne on the thin skin of his wrist.

The salesman smoothed his hair back down, giving him a small smile. "You picked the right product. I can't recommend anything better."

A truck door slammed, and Brian glanced over; Dr. Antares stomped into the lab without giving Brian a second glance, lab coat on and jacket over his shoulder. The salesman opened the sales case, removed a thick brown plastic shampoo bottle, and handed it over. Brian tucked it in the pocket inside his jacket and rocked back on his heels, boots crunching in the snow-covered gravel. He steeled himself for the question.

"Thanks. Does your sales area include San Francisco?"

"It does," the salesman said, and something shifted in his posture, a certain professionalism slipping off, a certain knowingness coming on.

Brian drew an envelope from the breast pocket of his uniform. He opened it up to show the man one hundred dollars in ten-dollar bills, representing a good portion of his first paycheck, and a slip of paper with an address and some book titles. "Can you go to this address and buy the books listed there? I'll have another envelope with the same when you bring them to me."

The salesman took the envelope. "That's going to be in two weeks. I could be here at 21:30 hours."

Brian closed his eyes, thinking. "That'll be the day after my birthday. That's fine. Thank you."

The salesman looked him up and down consideringly. "I can deliver them to you somewhere else, at home maybe—" and Brian smiled, shaking his head no.

"The guys here, all they care about is their work. They don't go through bags. They don't go looking for evidence."

The salesman tilted his head. "Lucky you."

He tucked the envelope in his pocket and dusted the snow off his jacket. "I'm in town tonight, staying at the motel in Arco." He paused, adjusting his coat against the gusts of snow lashing down the plain. "Room 216." He gave him a quick smile that dropped a decade off his face. "And the name's David."

Brian smiled, letting a bit of heat into it but not swaying into David's space the way he was swaying into his. "Nice to meet you, David. I've got company, but thanks for asking."

David shrugged, picked up his bag again, and sauntered back to his car.

Brian ran his fingers through his hair, named ten major constellations, and then went inside to continue his night shift.

*

Dr. Antares refused to acknowledge Brian the entire shift. He stomped out when he was finished without offering to give Brian a lift home. So Brian armored himself in his only coat, took a few stabilizing breaths of the warm lab air, and headed out into the predawn snowstorm, gusts whipping against the door.

It was nearly a white-out blizzard. *Only two miles to walk*, Brian reminded himself.

But still, he glanced down the curving road to the highway.

Antares's turquoise truck was bumping along at speed. It made something in Brian's chest hurt to see those cherry-red taillights. But he couldn't catch him now in this snow, and maybe Antares would sleep off whatever bug was up his butt by tonight. Maybe they could talk then. Brian started walking, tucking his gloveless hands in his deep, down-lined pockets.

The truck stopped. Brian kept walking. When he was close enough, he could see Antares's face in the rearview mirror. The truck rumbled forward another dozen feet before stopping with a jerk, like he'd thrown it in park in a huff.

Brian drew abreast of the truck, and the passenger door swung open. He looked up into the cab, feeling the hot air begin to melt the icicles in his eyelashes.

"What's going on with you?" Brian asked, hitching himself into the passenger seat.

Antares gripped the wheel, knuckles white. "I saw you," he gritted out.

Brian frowned, holding his hands to the radiator, flexing his fingers as the joints loosened. "I hope so; I'm the only one out here in this godforsaken blizzard."

"Last night. With that *man.* Touching your—" And he hissed out his breath, biting his lip to stop from finishing the sentence.

Brian frowned. "Touching my—"

Then he shook his head, rummaging in his pocket.

"What are you doing?" Antares said through clenched teeth.

Brian held up the brown shampoo bottle, shaking it so it sloshed. "I ran out of the bottle I bought when I was at Vandenburg. He's the circuit-riding Avon Lady for the western region. I called two nights ago, and he came on his eastward swing."

Antares snatched the bottle from his hands and flicked on the dome light to read the label as Brian watched, bemused. He shoved the bottle back at him. "Seems like a lot of trouble for shampoo."

"Says the man who can buy generic and still look like David in living marble," Brian muttered, stuffing the bottle back in his pocket.

"You think I— No, wait, don't distract me. Why can the Avon Lady man touch your hair, and I can't?"

Brian turned to him with such an expression of disbelief Antares reared back a little. His tone was flat with restrained frustration. "Do you not know about blue slips? Or are you just that excited to find out how hard it is to get a job after an otherwise-than-honorable discharge?"

"I'm not in the military—" Antares started, but Brian snorted.

"You're a nuclear physicist. You think you'll keep your security clearance if you're suspected of sodomy?"

Antares frowned. "No one at EBT-I would think to file

paperwork."

"*Maybe*," Brian allowed but nearly rolled his eyes. "*Maybe.* But I don't want to risk it. I don't know who's safe and who isn't. And even if you're right—"

"I *am* right, Brian—"

Brian talked over him. "Even *if* you're right, we wouldn't just— I can't just— There would be things to decide before anything. Things to figure out."

Antares switched tactics. "You could have gotten that hair stuff in the mail. Why'd you make him come out to the installation, if it wasn't to flirt?"

Brian actually did roll his eyes then. "I needed to see if his region included San Francisco. There are some books I need. Books a—friend— of mine had. That I never got to read. That I think will help. Help us."

Antares flipped off the dome light, letting Brian adjust to the soft-edged starlight again. Darkness swathed him while Brian's eyes relaxed, only the edges of his curls and the strong line of his nose visible.

"Books that you can't order through the mail?"

Brian nodded, feeling a flush rise. "Books that are *illegal* to order through the mail. I need to know some things. Some things I don't know, didn't have the chance to learn last time, when it was brief. Transactional. Chaotic. Things I need to know before I'm sure. About what to do." He waved his hand between their chests. "About this."

He felt the air move as Antares slipped his hand off the wheel, reaching across the darkness tentatively, fingertips just touching the crown of his knee.

"I can teach you—"

But Brian shook his head, and Antares's hand froze. "I don't—I don't want to be your *student*, Dr. Antares. I want—" And he scrubbed his face with his now-warm hands, words coming up scrambled and stupid and too, too naïve for words. "You know what? Never mind. I think I'll walk."

"Brian—" Antares said as Brian forced the door open and dropped to the uneven snow. He stomped his foot to force it flat and began back down the road. The wind howled, plastering his face in fat snowflakes like mosquito hawks dissolving against the flaming heat of his cheeks.

How could I be so stupid as to think, as to hope—

"Brian!" Antares's voice came from behind him through the still-open door.

Only 1.5 miles left. He could do this.

The truck rumbled into gear and rolled forward, the passenger door slamming shut with the motion. Brian kept his head down, ignoring Antares's muffled shouting, his hood carefully up to protect himself against the white wall of snow.

Antares pulled up alongside him, gesturing emphatically for him to open the door. Brian put his gloveless hands over his ears, mouthing, *I can't hear you*, and kept walking.

He did hear the truck stop and the passenger window creakily roll down inch by inch. Then the wheels crunched forward, rolling in neutral as Antares kept one hand on the wheel, both eyes on him.

"Brian, please. Get in the truck. You'll freeze those beautiful feet off."

Brian scowled, continuing to march on. One step away. Then another. The linings in his pockets felt so much colder after those few minutes in the warm cab. *Only 1.25 miles to go.* To his cold room in his cold barracks. He hadn't left the heating on, but he could turn it on when he got in, keep his jacket on, and make a cup of cocoa. *No, bourbon. Bourbon after the long night of silence.*

He could hear Dr. Antares muttering through the open window, choice words about his stubbornness, pigheadedness, idiocy, what sounded like exaggerated facts about frostbite—

Then, quiet. The truck still rolled along beside him, keeping pace, but Antares no longer chewed him out. When Brian glanced up into the cab, he saw Antares looking at him, expression thoughtful.

He held up one finger. "You had a queer Avon Lady come to the installation to sell you fancy shampoo"—he held up a second—"so you could ask him to buy you books on—let's call it—"

"'Alternative relationships,'" Brian supplied, still walking. Antares's shoulders relaxed now Brian was speaking again.

He held up a third finger. "Books you can't buy through the mail because of indecency laws."

Brian nodded.

Antares held up a fourth finger. "Because you want to be sure before we, before you and I—"

Brian stopped in the snow, squared his shoulders, and glared up at the other man. "I don't want to be a *wife*, Dr. Antares. Not even *your* wife. I watched my mother—my brave, strong, powerful mother—lose *everything* to that word, that title, that role. She died, and he wouldn't even let her body be buried on her own reservation; she's in some Christian grave at some church she hated. I don't want that for my life. I want to be an equal. Even in hiding. Even if it's a secret forever. I want to be an equal. But I don't know if that's possible for—" He gestured jerkily between them.

He took a breath, the freezing snow burning in his lungs, forcing him to remember he was *here*, not watching his mother sob as she picked up the pieces of the Pueblo wedding vase his father had just smashed, the one with the same pattern as was on Antares's blanket.

"Even if we could, without me being court-martialed or you being blackballed, if we couldn't be equals, I wouldn't want it. I won't live that way. I won't even risk it unless I know there's another way. A way between us, that's *different*."

Antares's face looked stricken, but there was something close to wonder, close to awe in it. He whispered, words floating through the flurrying snow, "Brian, please get in the truck. It's cold out."

Something in his softer tone, in the easier shape of his mouth, let Brian reach out, grip the cold handle through his jacket sleeve, and pull open the door.

His lungs felt as if they were expanding with every searing hot breath as he cranked the window up. A warm, thick weight settled across his lap, and Brian glanced over as Antares leaned back, having settled his Diné blanket across Brian's shivering legs.

Antares started to drive, setting an easy pace down the road. "I don't know if I've ever had someone take me so seriously they were willing to do book research on how to be with me," he said hoarsely.

Brian rolled his eyes, then tilted his head against the frozen window, his body suddenly exhausted what with the wild temperature shifts, the long day, and talking about his emotions. "Anyone who doesn't take you seriously is a fool, Dr. Antares," Brian said. "A goddamned fool who doesn't deserve your light in their life."

Antares made a sound, a soft, choking sound, but Brian kept his gaze on the horizon, speaking to the white blazing flats of the Idaho desert, words weaving and almost hypnotic.

"If I'm sure—when I'm sure—of you, of us, it'll be like Polaris," Brian said. "Twin binary giants, orbiting and swaying, giving off so much more light together than they ever could alone. It'll be the brightest star in the sky. It'll outshine the *sun*." He turned to Antares, whose eyes were shining. "But Polaris only orbits itself because the stars in question have equal mass. Even when no one can see them, they're in a balanced system. If they weren't, the larger one would consume the smaller one. Eating up its light, diminishing both. We have to be equals, Dr. Antares." He glanced back out at the road. They were nearly to his barracks. "Or we can be nothing at all."

"Aaron," Antares gasped hoarsely. "Please call me Aaron."

Brian nodded, waiting for the truck to stop in their usual place. He reached across the cab, wrapped his still chilly fingers around Aaron's, and squeezed once, tightly. "Goodnight, Aaron."

"Goodnight, Brian," Aaron returned, slipping his thumb across the bridge of Brian's knuckles.

Brian's body hummed, zinging for him to ask Aaron inside, to do what he'd been wanting to do since he'd grabbed the man's belt and held him steady over a radiation pit full of uranium rods. But he had a lifetime's experience with waiting himself out. So he let go of Aaron's hand and gently shut the truck door, then walked through the snowy quiet to his cold room, leaving only one set of tracks in the snow.

*

The next morning, the entire lab geared up for another attempt at the breeder reactor—the uranium in place, the other experiments bubbling along to themselves in the containment area, the light bulbs strung right in the middle of the building.

Dr. Zinn had sent everyone home at 22:00 except Aaron and Brian. He hadn't even tried to get Aaron to go home. He just told him, "The experiment had better be in the same state as we left it—or, ideally, a better one—when we get back."

Aaron was upside down, his curly hair all in a fritz. He was practically grinning about the possibility of the reactor finally producing plutonium the following morning. Brian watched as he double, triple, quintuple-checked his calculations.

Brian was glad he'd packed a book.

Well, books. It appeared to be a single book from the outside: a massive physics book. It was one he'd saved from Vandenberg. He'd read it before. He loved it, loved the way it made his head feel as if it were being unzipped from the back for the universe to pour right in. There was something so easing to the mind about thinking through the ways in which particles and neutrons and electrons reacted, interacted, and organized themselves.

The textbook easily concealed a slim volume of poetry in its hundreds of pages, hidden there since he left Los Angeles. Brian hefted the book out of his bag, flopping it on his lap, cover still closed. He slipped a finger between its well-worn pages, knowing just where to go to feel the spine of the handbound chapbook. He didn't need to look to find it, some part of him always knew where it was.

Whose name he would find in the dedication.

Footsteps approached, and he snapped the book shut, finger heating with how hard he was squeezing the paper around it.

But it was only Aaron, striding toward him at full speed with his nose buried in a thick sheaf of freshly typed calculations. Brian took a moment to watch him, something he rarely had a chance to do without the other man noticing.

Aaron turned sharply before he reached Brian, continuing what Brian had come to consider his "thinking circuit." Aaron walked the lab clockwise when he checked numbers and counterclockwise when he brainstormed about new experiments. He always seemed surprised to find Brian at the exact same place—the apex or the nadir of the loop.

Brian had no way of knowing what his opinion was on any given day, Aaron's eyes going to his with such raw questions before he shuttered them again, burying his face in the papers.

Brian watched him without fear of being seen because there was nothing and nobody in the world, maybe even in the entire universe, for Aaron right now that wasn't in the papers in his hands. And thus distracted, how did the man still manage to move as though he had muscles in places where people didn't? How did he constantly have Brian on guard, on the feeling of falling apart, on the precipice of jumping in?

Brian glanced at the book in front of him. If he was being *good*, faithful and true, he would have left that book in the dirty duffel bag he'd shoved it in on his way out of LA. He would have certainly left it in some abandoned gas station before he got back home to Roswell or, hell, just at his studio, where there was no possibility of him being blue discharged for reading it on duty.

And the thing was that evidence could be so thin for these fucking things. A look, a glance, a feeling; a slope of the shoulder, naturally red lips, a lisp. Anything a commanding officer decided was enough evidence.

But tonight in an empty lab, a book of queer poems wasn't going to cost him much. So far, Aaron had been right. Everyone in the lab was too focused on electrons and protons and neutrons to worry about the needs of anything larger than an atom. Even Brian's team had gotten swept up in the excitement of the next day's test, offering to come in early, to stay late, just so they could say they were in the building if it worked this time.

He slipped the book of poetry open, not looking at the dedication page since he knew what it would say. He flipped to the most dog-eared page, the one with a crease down the middle, carefully smoothed over and over again until it almost lay flat again.

> *I see your excommunicated garments there,*
> *I see your shoes upon the chair,*
> *I see your uncontrollable black hair*
> *lying like a serpent upon the floor*
> *of our desire, like darkness at the window Everywhere.*

Bill, his Bill, had drafted that first in the back of one of Brian's physics textbooks. He'd nearly knocked Brian on the floor, lunging over him for paper, saying the poem would escape if he didn't tether it quick enough. Brian had laughed, hugging his bare arms around Bill's chest, grinning and tickling until Bill had finished. He'd titled it "A Pair of Uranian Garters for Aurora Bligh." Aurora Bligh was Mary Fabilli's pen name. Brian had met her—swearing, drunk, savage, and incredible—at one of Bill's LA readings. She'd had a thick Central Valley accent untouched by a decade in San Francisco.

He flipped forward, blushing at "This Place Rumord to Have Been Sodom" and wincing at "Under Ground":

> *the dead are also remembered:*
>
> > *there may be*
> *here at the center of a chamber cut out*
> > *of context*
> *cenotaph for Jeff Rall who*
> > *in youth fell*
> *at Dunkirk, because war was more real*
> > *than Blenheim's*
> *in the Village...*

Bill had flown into a day of manic research, making sure he spelled everything right, using up all of Brian's bus money making long distance phone calls to New York to ensure they were still doing the annual Jeff Rall dinner, desperate to know that ten years had not been long enough for all of Jeff's friends to forget him.

It hadn't been.

Brian's heart pounded, but his fingers knew what he was looking for.

We have gone out in boats upon the sea at night,
lost, and the vast waters close traps of fear about us.
The boats are driven apart, and we are alone at last
under the incalculable sky, listless, diseased with stars.

Let the oars be idle, my love, and forget at this time
our love like a knife between us
defining the boundaries that we can never cross
nor destroy as we drift into the heart of our dream,
cutting the silence, slyly, the bitter rain in our mouths
and the dark wound closed in behind us.

Forget depth-bombs, death and promises we made,
gardens laid waste, and, over the wastelands westward,
the rooms where we had come together bombd.

But even as we leave, your love turns back. I feel
your absence like the ringing of bells silenced. And salt
over your eyes and the scales of salt between us. Now,
you pass with ease into the destructive world.

There is a dry crash of cement. The light fails,
falls into the ruins of cities upon the distant shore
and within the indestructible night I am alone.

He'd written that one for Brian, one long weekend paddling around the Salton Sea, camping amongst the sailboats, eating increasingly dubious sandwiches, the sun bright on their skin, and hands as free as they could get. Brian hadn't understood it then, but he saw it now, the silenced bells Bill had heard, the knives etched into Brian's skin, the ones he knew would cut between them eventually.

Brian read it again and again. Trying to think about gardens laid to waste and what it took to close dark wounds as Aaron made another circuit of the lab.

*

The next day's experiment failed to breed plutonium but succeeded in heating the liquid metal they were using higher and longer than they had before.

Brian consoled Aaron as he slouched against him the next night, backs to the hip-high railing around the recalcitrant reactor, murmuring, "Science is a progression of failures, each a little closer than the last."

Aaron had rolled his eyes so hard his head had ended up on Brian's shoulder. Since there was no one else to see, Brian let it rest there, feeling the warm weight of him and providing what soft comfort he had to give.

Chapter Eight: T-64 Days

You will perhaps make love to me this evening,

Dancing among the circular green tables

Or where the clockwork tinkle of the fountain

Sounds in the garden's primly pebbled arbors.

Reality is no stronger than a waltz,

A painted lake stippled with boats and swans

A glass of gold-brown beer, a phrase in German

Or French, or any language but our own.

Reality would call us less than friends,

And therefore more adept at making love.

—Adrienne Rich, "The Kursaal at Interlaken", 1951

October 17, 1951

Brian felt like he was snooping, but Nurse Kelly had said he could use the record player. So here he was, kneeling, going through the chief nurse's box of records.

The front door was locked against that night's flurries. The scientists could ring the bell if they needed in before dawn. Aaron had left before 22:00 for the first time in weeks, muttering something about needing his beauty sleep. Brian had viciously suppressed his disappointment. He'd thought—

Well, he'd thought wrong.

A birthday letter from a brother or his father would be the least welcome thing and was probably sitting in his unchecked PO box in Idaho Falls. But when he'd thought about what he *wanted,* he'd thought he and Aaron might sit together, arms pressed close, going over the results of a test. With only two days before his books were to arrive, he was going to—he had *planned* and *planned*—to maybe put his hand in the middle of Aaron's back as they went up the stairs, maybe let himself tuck a little closer to his side, maybe get close enough to feel the tickle of his curls against his cheek. Brian had imagined, had hoarded the imagining of what touches he might permit himself as a silent, unacknowledged, but certain-to-be-enjoyed birthday present.

But Aaron had left early.

So here Brian was, just after midnight, alone on his twenty-seventh birthday.

In the aftermath of the call, the conversation with Aaron, and the quiet, safe time they'd spent together, Brian had decided for the first time in his life to think more about what he wanted. Not whether it was possible or likely or even good—just knowing what he wanted. The easiest he'd come up with was to actually celebrate his birthday. To do it on his own terms.

And this year, he wanted to dance.

Who he wanted to dance with or how he wanted to dance, he didn't have a choice in that. But Nurse Kelly had shown him the record player. And he'd found what he was looking for: Lena Horne's "Stormy Weather."

The clock read half past midnight, and he was alone at EBT-I, and no one would ever know. He slipped the record free of its sleeve with a dry sigh and moved the needle to about where the opening would be. The sound of it lit up the small nurses' office, then flowed, filling every corner of the lab, from the basement to the steel-beam rafters.

He shifted his weight onto his toes, then his heels, and then up on his toes again. He swayed, hips stretching and growing loose with it, raising his hands around an invisible partner, middle and ring finger pressed together where he would tuck them into the belt loop of a warm, willing body. If the body in his mind had amber eyes that winked gold and curly hair, that was nobody's business but his. From this close, he'd be able to feel the small motions of Aaron's body, feel the sway and cuss of him. Cheek to cheek would be the most proper way if there was such a thing for people like them, but he—it was his fantasy. They would dance looking into each other's eyes, foreheads close and pressing to-gether, breathing the same air, moving as one flowing thing.

He spun as soon as Lena's voice started, singing the rain down.

He was waltzing, spinning, changing whether he was lead or fol-low, the music rising with him out into the lab.

He did his best Fred Astaire up the steps to the reactor and his best Ginger Rogers on his way back down, light-footed and swirling, working his way to the nurses' station before moving the needle to the beginning of the song again, humming the words, getting louder as they got into the second and third verse, voice tapping across the cinder block walls as he passed them. It was—*free*. He could breathe, and the orchestra breathed with him.

His feet followed his every whim, as he skipped, twirled, and pretended to spin an invisible partner, hips and heels always on the right beat, body weaving around Aaron's lab bench, and down over to the containment area.

He circled around, lifting the needle to play it again, then took himself to the basement where he nearly couldn't catch the tune, but he sang to fill the air, loneliness and cold water flooding down from a gray sky and missing an unnamed man.

The front door slammed open, and he jolted to a stop, hands dropping before hustling up the basement stairs, coming through the rear lab, hand on his service weapon. But the front door was still locked and the music was swelling so perfectly. So he let himself sink into it again and came back in on the second chorus, arms raised again, swaying, spinning around the corner, up the stairs to the catwalk where he twirled through the open door to one of the labs—

Aaron was hunched over his lab bench, a palm-sized brown box in his hands, tape on his thumb, wrapping paper half-clenched in his other hand, eyes wide as he looked up at Brian. Brian's arms were still up. He breathed hard as the music rose up the stairs and around them.

Aaron straightened, voice a little rough when he sang along, taking a step closer, and he was in Brian's space, package in his hands.

Brian whispered, "I didn't know you liked Lena Horne."

"There's a lot of stuff to learn about me," Aaron returned. He paused, looking at the scant space between them. "I know it's an invasion of privacy to have looked through your records to find the date. I promise I wasn't snooping just for snooping's sake. I was just—" He fiddled with the tape on his thumb. "I was curious, and I'm not great with controlling my curiosity. But once I saw, then I knew. And you didn't say anything, so I didn't spread it around. But—" He looked at the package in his hands.

"A sense of privacy is the first thing they take from you during hell week at West Point," Brian murmured, shifting his hands into his pockets. "I wouldn't stress about it."

Aaron nodded, long fingers slipping the last edge of the wrapping paper over, then slicking it down with the tape. He slid a calloused thumb over and over it until it was clear and flush. He held the package up between them. "Happy birthday, Brian."

"You got me a birthday present?"

"Yeah," he said, ducking his head. "Nothing fancy,"

"That's really kind of you, Aaron."

He shoved it at him a little, fingers brushing his uniformed chest.

"You want me to open it now?" Brian said.

"Yeah."

"Okay," he breathed, heart pounding bright and quick. He couldn't remember the last time someone had wrapped a birthday present for him. Certainly before his mother had left. The last few birthdays in that house had been a little rough.

Brian rolled the box carefully in his hands, feeling something small and hard move in it. He glanced up, figuring Aaron would tell him if it was fragile, but even this close, all he saw on the other man's face was bounce-heeled anticipation.

He slipped a finger between the newly applied tape and the colorful paper, uncovering a stiff-sided cardboard box. He tipped it, and something *thunked* against his palm.

He quirked his eyebrows, tilting his head as he slipped the lid off with a small sigh. Gleaming, in a white bed of what looked like tissue paper, was a key. He frowned, taking it out. It was—

"Is this a key to your truck?" he asked, words distant even to his own ears.

Aaron's face was still concerned, watching his expression. Brian had no earthly idea what his own expression was; his heart was too busy trying to jam its way out of his chest.

"It's for if I'm working some crazy hours and your shift ends or you need to get home quickly for something or—"

And Brian crashed into him, arms flung around him, face tucked into his neck, all propriety, all boundaries smashed just for a second, just for this moment. His breath hitched in his chest, his vision blurry, his knees barely keeping him upright as he left the configuration of their feet to Aaron, box falling behind him and the cold metal of the key pressed into the soft center of his palm.

"That's the kindest thing I can remember anyone ever doing for me, Aaron. I don't know how to—"

And Aaron was shaking his head, drawing back just enough to brush a lock of his hair back off Brian's forehead.

"Don't worry about it, Airman. Just take care of yourself. It's getting cold out there, and I don't want you walking if you don't have to."

"But if I have your truck, how will you—"

And Aaron lifted his eyebrows, quirking a smile. "I don't expect you to leave me forever. Just promise to come back for me."

"I will," Brian said, heart beating a riot in his chest. "I will."

Then Aaron took a long, deep breath and eased himself back, hands still on Brian's shoulders. "You said the Avon Lady man would have those books for you, not this evening, but evening after next?"

Brian nodded, mouth dry, fingers holding onto Aaron's long sleeves, unable to let go, just for now.

Aaron swayed toward him. "You've got another seven hours on your shift, right?"

Another nod.

Aaron shuffled a little, foot to foot, the music full and crackling with the high desert dust on the player. Aaron's voice was quiet, cracking when he said, "All I want to do is ask you to dance, learn some of that fancy footwork. But—" He scanned Brian's face as he whispered hoarsely. "I don't think I could keep my hands to myself if we did that."

And Brian just wanted to say *fuck it*. But here Aaron was, holding himself back by the skin of his teeth, and though Brian's breath was high in his chest and his heart simmering to a boil, he forced his fingers to let Aaron's shirt go, to let his hands drop.

"You have anything you need to do back here?" Brian rasped.

Aaron shook his head, eyes bright.

"Want to listen to some music with me?"

"Sure, Brian," he said in a soft voice. "Whatever you want. It's your birthday."

Brian nodded, reaching over to tug his hand, steeling his heart about how warm it was despite the chill outside, how tightly Aaron gripped him back. "Then let's go."

They sat together on the floor of the nurse's station, legs crossed and knees brushing, surrounded by records. They took turns operating the turntable, tried out the B sides, flopped on their backs to listen to the longer tracks. Aaron liked every Lena Horne record, listening as Brian talked about how much his mother had loved her, loved her voice and her Native American heritage and her pride and her beauty. Brian was surprised that Aaron kept digging through to find the race records, playing him "Go Down Moses" and "Swing Low, Sweet Chariot."

As the strains of "Didn't My Lord Deliver Daniel" faded, Brian tried to unpick the question that had been growing under his skin with each new record Aaron picked.

"How'd you get into race records? You're—" He gestured to where Aaron's top collar showed skin about as pale as a man could get without becoming transparent.

Aaron cocked his head. "They have some record stores in Denver. I'd pick them up on the way to visiting my friends in New Mexico."

Brian was about to take the brush-off for what it was when Aaron looked down, fingers light on the worn paper sleeve of the record.

"I like what they have to say," Aaron said. "About freedom." He turned to Brian, so deep in his space Brian had no idea how they'd resurrect their boundaries come sunrise. "You know, it's not normal, what America did. Ending slavery. Most places, they have slavery forever, or they never have it. Ending it once you have it, that's—" He looked as though he was trying to say something deeper than the words, but Brian didn't know how he was supposed to get it. Aaron ended up saying, "That's unique."

Brian spoke slowly, trying to follow him. "There are still people— lots of people—working without pay. In the fields of California and in prisons and, hell, in the houses of people from Santa Fe to San Francisco, Maine to Mississippi."

Aaron frowned, nodding. "I've seen that in the papers. But ending *legal* slavery, that's not nothing. That would be—" He tipped his head back against the chief nurse's metal desk, rolling it as he looked up at the low ceiling. "—that would be like if people like us could get married. Like, there would still be people fired and kicked out of their houses. But it would be so much better than it was before."

"'Married'?" Brian scoffed, voice cracking on the word, heart unable to take the idea. It was too vast a future to see. "I don't see that happening here, on this planet, at least." He gave Aaron a sad smile. Aaron just frowned, and Brian continued, "Maybe, someday, we'll have integration, like Eisenhower did with the army. But"—he shook his head—"—most of the men and women given blue discharges, they weren't queer; they just had racist commanders who didn't want integrated units. Same discharge if you were queer, Black, epileptic, whatever. You can't force people to be fair, to be just."

He felt Aaron's gaze hot on the side of his face.

"Do you really think things can't get better?" Aaron asked. "There won't be some place, some time, where people like us don't have to hide?"

His father's voice filled his mind, so strongly, so harsh: *Get used to this, son. It's all there's ever going to be for you. All you're ever going to deserve.* And something in him cracked.

Brian turned, expression feeling wild, voices pounding around them, and said in a broken whisper, "I *want* to, Aaron. I want to be able to see it here, to be able to imagine the country that I serve will ever love me back. I just— Most days, I can't. Maybe, someday, I'll be able to." He looked at him, all whiskey-colored eyes and untamed, impossible hope. "Maybe you can help me see it."

Aaron raised his hand, palm soft, just a ghost's touch on Brian's cheek, before pulling himself away as if he was reactor-hot. But he kept his eye contact firm as the music faded to clicks. "I will."

Then he leaned back, reached over to get another record, and let Lady Day carry them on until sunrise.

*

It was around 20:00 the next night, and the music had long since faded from Brian's mind. His bare back pressed against the sticky vinyl of the bench press in the gym—i.e., the barracks' spare unit—palms slick with sweat on the weight bar. Each gasp tasted of copper. He was on his second workout of the day, working his way up to his bodyweight to burn off as much energy as he could on his last night shift with Aaron before his books arrived. Aaron would be pulling up outside in half an hour. He started another set of sit-ups, the key to Aaron's truck jangling under his tank top, tucked between his dog tags.

The past two weeks had been a careful dance, both men waiting for Brian's illicit research materials to come in. Every day seemed to bring new challenges—the thinness of Aaron's T-shirts for one, the way he bounded up the stairs for another. Brian tried not to think about how well he filled out his jeans or the soft way his voice got when he muttered equations to himself.

Working out twice a day helped with the not thinking.

He'd been looking forward to this particular workout for days. Other than Freeman, who Brian would be relieving in half an hour, all of his men were at the Friday-night hoedown in Arco. That meant instead of a long workout, sweating through the long-sleeved shirt and sweatpants, Brian could wear his PT shorts, a thin undershirt, and nothing else without fear of anyone commenting on his scars.

Every person who had showered with him at West Point had seen them, and no small number of people had asked. One of the things he'd treasured at Vandenburg was the luxury of a shower all his own, the chance to avoid having to explain his body to anyone. Thankfully, he'd been able to complete his required PT in long pants and T-shirts that covered enough, so as long as he was careful at the gym and outside of medical exams, he didn't have to come up with excuses for the wide canopy of scars across his back and shoulders, down his thighs.

He liked working out, but not for how it made his body look. Generally, Brian tried not to look at himself. One of the first things he'd done in his new apartment at EBT-I had been to take the mirror off the wall and the back of the door. Getting dressed was usually a study in looking away. He didn't need to look at the uniform as he put it back on anymore; its first and, for him, only real wearer was the wielder of a belt. He didn't look at his too-dark skin, or his black eyes, or the way his slim shoulders fit into his uniform. At West Point, he'd rucked as much as the next cadet, but damned if he could put on a bit of muscle.

Brian switched to push-ups, the ache of them building up in his muscles as he thought about his form. There had been moments, bare and skimming, where he'd enjoyed what his body could do or what he could have done to it. When he'd enjoyed what it took to make it go, what it felt like to live inside it, to live outside it, and around it.

But mostly, he was grateful for the potato-sack uniform, for the colorless grays that hid his skin tone, for the jacket pockets where he could hide hands that shook whenever a superior officer screamed at him in a tone too close to home.

No, Brian liked working out for the way it made him feel, like his body was used and useful. It let him imagine fighting back and *winning*. Best of all, working out let him sleep without dreams of footsteps in the hallway or a hand on the doorknob.

He sat up, stretching out his lats and twisting his neck. He'd already done overhead press-ups, curls, and triceps dips, and his shoulders were cultivating a fine-tuned ache he knew he could enjoy and come back to whenever his body got too interested in Aaron's.

He glanced at the clock: 20:05. Time for another few sets on the bench press. He was pushing through the last of his first round at 150 pounds when he heard footsteps in the hallway to the gym.

He froze.

Only one door led into and out of the base gym; there was only one hallway in the building. He couldn't get back to his apartment without being seen.

But the room had a window, just big enough for him to fit through. It opened onto the ground outside the compound, and he could circle around to the back entrance unseen.

Brian racked the bar and sprang up, the footsteps getting closer. He was just forcing the window up with a *creak* when he heard:

"Brian?"

It was Aaron, frowning in the doorway.

Brian lowered the window frame with suddenly stiff arms, body curling in a little against the cold seeping through the single-paned glass. Brian closed his eyes, trying to decide what lie he would use. He'd fallen into a thresher when he was a boy? No, the newly pink scars from the last beating were still too visible. Birthmarks? No, Aaron was too close and stepping closer, only a few steps away. And he'd see them more clearly eventually if things went how Brian thought—hoped—they might. He forced himself to take a breath and his fingers to uncurl from the windowsill.

Better to know now if the scars are a dealbreaker.

Aaron sounded as if he was trying to speak around the hole in his heart when he asked, "Brian, what happened?"

Brian turned, bracing his hands back against the windowsill and forcing himself to meet Aaron's gaze. But his expression wasn't the look of pity Brian expected; it wasn't empathy. There weren't tears. Aaron's fists were clenched, eyes nearly amber with rage.

Aaron muttered, "I thought I'd seen my last whip marks," taking a single step closer. He cleared his throat. "I got in early since the snowstorm cleared faster than I thought it would. I realized I didn't know which apartment was yours, and this door was open and—"

Aaron took the final step forward, held out his hand spread wide, and, hovering, measured the width of a scar over one of Brian's shoulders. "Same width as the other marks; means probably the same implement. Some variation, but not much." He said softly, low in his chest, "Some of these scars have grown with you. So, your father or mother, uncle or brother? How you spoke about your mother before, I don't think she did this. Your brothers are all in Korea, and some of these are only a few weeks old. Did you have an uncle living with you, growing up?"

Brian gave a tiny shake of his head, barely a movement, but Aaron was close enough to see it.

He nodded, movement jerky as his voice came through harsh, furious. "So, your father. The full bird colonel takes his belt to you when you go home. Still does."

Aaron paused and took a step back, eyes closing, visibly trying to control his breath. He forced his hand away, balled his fingers into fists, and shoved them deep into the pockets of his thick winter jacket.

Brian had never had someone put it together so quickly, and he felt a strange wave of gratitude that all he had to do was nod, not put a single unsafe word of that in his own mouth.

Aaron didn't ask the question: *Why don't you fight back?*

Of course he did, of course he tried, but there was some part of him that was five and terrified and certain he was going to die, that the person who kept his first words, who'd held his hand through his first steps, would be the one to do it. Would always be the one to do it—

"Do you need a spotter?" Aaron interrupted his inner spiral.

"What?"

Aaron gestured to the bench press. "It looks like you're working your way up toward body weight. It's a good time to have a spot."

"You lift?"

Aaron nodded, gesturing to his own body with a smirk. "You think I keep this handsome physique doing nothing but crawling inside a reactor occasionally and harassing a single airman?" He wiggled his eyebrows and Brian gave a ghost of a smile. "The scientist housing has a gym, actually." He looked around. "It has this gym. Looks like they just bought two of everything and filled up an empty unit. I usually work out before heading home."

Brian cocked his head. "You work out before an hour-long drive home? Don't you need the sleep?"

Aaron's expression still looked as if he were chewing glass, but he was trying to keep things light. "Right back at you, bud. You going to let me help or not?"

Brian wished for a long-sleeved shirt, *but what would it even hide at this point*? He nodded, and Aaron circled to stand behind the bar as Brian ducked under it and lay back on the bench. Brian braced his feet flat on the floor and set his hips for stability.

He looked up, Aaron's curls swaying as he got a grip on the bar on either side of Brian's knuckles.

Aaron said, "Ready?"

Brian pressed his shoulders to the bench, adjusting to the sticky feel of it, letting the grating of the steel dig into his palms. "Yeah, I'm doing five sets of fifteen."

After the first set, when he was stretching his arms, Aaron said, "It's easier if you breathe."

Brian smirked, muttering despite himself, "Not the first time I've heard that."

"Really?"

Brian glanced at the door on instinct, but he knew they were alone here.

Still, it took effort to get the words out. "You don't always know things when you get started with—with alternative relationships. When you don't know where to get the books or other people. You figure things out for yourself."

Aaron nodded. "So, you don't need the books to tell you breathing is important."

Brian felt himself smile. "Generally speaking, breathing is important."

"Another set?"

"Yeah."

Aaron swapped in the next round after hanging up his heavy jacket on the weight rack. Brian moved behind the bench, hands light on the bar as he guided it up and down. Aaron barely tapped it on his chest before pushing it up again. Brian found himself matching his breaths, timing the shape of them, eyes tracing Aaron's face as he worked his way up to his bodyweight.

Once they'd finished, Aaron wiped his hands on his jeans, faint streaks of rust following them. He glanced at the jacket. "I don't want to get that sweaty; it'll just turn to icicles. Can you hold on to it for me? I've got another in the lab."

Brian frowned. "I have my own jacket."

A twinkle lit Aaron's eye. "I know you do. But I have an extra, and I don't think you do. Think of it as an investment in your not freezing to death the next time the heating goes out."

"I was going to buy one in Arco when my next paycheck comes

through."

Aaron shrugged, tipping his head to the side to stretch out his neck. "Then give it back to me then."

Brian swallowed and looked away. "All right, I'll get it back to you."

Aaron glanced at the clock. "I'll see you outside in twenty?"

"Probably closer to ten; I shower quick."

Aaron flashed him a grin but didn't linger, didn't press, didn't even try to figure out which unit was Brian's. He just headed right back up the hallway and out into the growing night. Brian walked slowly to his apartment, savoring the good ache in his shoulders. He'd been able to go longer, lift a heavier weight, feel more secure knowing he had a spotter if it was too much.

When he came back out, he wore Aaron's jacket over his uniform.

*

Aaron was heads down with a new casing design. Brian had hung his jacket on the back of the folding chair and locked the door after the last scientist left. Then he'd gone to keep Aaron company in the upstairs lab. Brian sat on one of the lab benches, gently kicking his heels as he read his old copy of *Astounding*. The cover illustration featured a soldier taking an underdressed Martian princess in his arms, her eyes wide and vacant. Brian glanced up to idly watch Aaron as he muttered to himself, frantically erasing a line on his hand-drawn schematics.

Brian heard himself asking, "You ever think of going to space?"

Aaron's entire body froze, and then in what sounded like a forced-casual tone, he said, "Uh, why do you ask?"

Brian drew one leg up to his chest, sturdy boot heel on the table, and set the magazine next to his hip. "We've got the rockets to do it, and the weather balloon that crashed at Roswell was working in the upper atmosphere. I bet we could get ships to space within our lifetimes, nuclear-powered ones even."

Aaron turned, eyes bright with something Brian didn't understand. "Why would you want to go to space?"

Brian tilted his head back, looking at the pipe-lined ceiling and imagining the clear-cut starscape above them. "Why go to West Point? Why come here? Why read poetry? Why read fiction? Don't you want something bigger, to see what's out there, to see what you can do?"

Aaron settled his hips against the lab table holding his drawings. "What makes you think out there is any better than here? What if the Earth is the best thing going in the universe?"

Brian huffed, frowning. "That would be beyond depressing. The best evolution has to offer the universe is people who kill one another with nuclear bombs, who treat half their species like dirt, who have entire societies built on racism?" He shook his head. "No, there has to be something else, something better out there. Maybe not perfect. Maybe other societies have worse racism or classism or other social goods or ills dialed up and down in different ways. But we can't be the *only* thing going."

"Enrico over at Cal would ask—if there's alien life in the universe, where is everybody?" There was something strange about Aaron's tone, as though he was saying words he didn't actually believe.

"It took one hundred and fifty years for my mother's people to know that Juan Ponce de León had landed in Florida in any kind of provable way. And with how Einstein believes special relativity works, if some group somehow heard our radio waves and came to investigate, if they traveled here as quickly as they could, it might take them hundreds of years." Brian gave him a slight smile, tapping on his magazine. "Maybe the Martians are coming, and we just have to wait them out."

Aaron looked at his feet. "And how'd that work out for your mother's people? Maybe you don't want people from other worlds here."

Brian tapped the magazine against his knee. "Now, that's ahistorical bullshit."

Aaron's head snapped up, and then he cocked it to the side.

"Look, white historians may not write about it," Brian continued, "but it just doesn't make sense to me that Columbus was the first person who went between this continent and Europe, or Africa, or the subcontinent, or even Japan. There's currents that will carry you all the way from Tokyo to Mexico. There's languages spoken back home—like Zuni—that sound nothing like any other local language. They had to come from *somewhere*. And for tens of thousands of years, thousands of different tribes lived and fought and traded and merged and split apart here on this land, long before Europeans arrived."

Brian took a breath. "What I'm saying is, genocide and colonialism and empire building are the *outliers* for how sentient beings interact. The most common way sentient things have interacted, as far as I can tell, is peacefully." He held up three fingers, counting them down. "Through trade, mutual discovery, or intermarriage." He shrugged. "There's no reason to assume another culture is as bloodthirsty as the Spanish or English or French; everything else being equal, the first aliens we're most likely to meet are refugees, explorers, traders, or just madmen out to discover the universe."

"So, if you went to space, which would you be, Brian? Refugee, explorer, trader, or madman?" Aaron's voice held a strange tension.

Brian bit his lip, thinking. "I'd like to think explorer. Some days, refugee. Just, what if there is someplace, like what you said, where we're equal? I don't have much to trade." He quirked a smile. "I like to think

I'm not mad. But you left out one option."

"I did?"

Brian nodded, smirk growing. "Trade, mutual discovery, or *inter-marriage*." He blinked, his eyes big and doe-like as he tapped his finger on the swashbuckling cover of the magazine. "Maybe I'll be a Martian war bride; you ever think about that? Get swept off my feet, taken to a strange new world by a gallant stranger." He blinked one more time before cracking up and shaking his head. "Not that there's a lot of takers."

Aaron's voice was rough when he said, "I don't think you'd want that, leaving a place you know for a new world. Hard to be equal if you're a war bride. No friends, no context. Is that the kind of future you'd *actually* want?"

Brian slid his fingers across the creased cover. "Depends on the gallant stranger. Depends on the new world." He looked up at him, gaze meeting and holding his. "Some days, I can imagine all kinds of things, Aaron. All kinds of worlds. I know it doesn't seem like it because I have to survive this one, but some days, more and more, I can see them. I can *hope* for them. A place that's equal, where promises are kept, where people have full lives, live with dignity, out in the open."

Aaron looked as though Brian had stripped down to his skivvies and begun to do push-ups. "Oh," he whispered. He visibly tried to collect himself. "Oh, that's—that's good. That's good you can imagine them. You can't be what you can't see." He took a breath, words stumbling over themselves. "I'd love to keep chatting, but I need to get this done before morning."

Brian waved his hand and checked the clock on the wall behind Aaron: 04:40. His body was settling into stiffness from the workouts. Without thinking about it too much, he hopped off the lab bench and folded himself onto the floor before stretching his legs out. With Aaron distracted and after that odd exchange, Brian found his mind wandering even as he pulled his legs into a pike position, grasped the toes of his boots, and pulled himself forward until his lower back ached with it. He stretched his calves, his ankles, his arms and wrists and neck. Then he tucked himself up against the base of one of the lab cabinets, magazine on his knees, and got back to reading.

Aaron was quiet on the ride back to the barracks at the end of his shift, quiet enough that when they trundled to a stop, Brian turned to him.

"You sure you're okay to drive to your cabin?"

Aaron glanced over at him, but it wasn't exhaustion Brian saw on his face; it was something more like curiosity, like wonder. "I'm all good. Thanks for asking." He resettled his shoulders. "I'll see you tonight, all right?"

"Sure. Drive safe," Brian said, forcing himself out the passenger door before he could do something telling like grip Aaron's wrist, squeeze his hand, touch his cheek. Ask again.

*

Brian did his morning workout, body loosening with the exercise. He kept it light, tiring out his core and legs. Upstairs, after his shower, he lay on the bed with Aaron's coat under his head. It was so much softer than the flat nothing he'd been given for a pillow. All he could think of was the scientist. He imagined giving the coat back. He would go to Aaron in his cabin up in the mountains, press him against the rough-hewn wood of his door. He would get in hot and close, thighs to thighs, muscles thick from the kind of labor neither of them admitted to liking, but both knew they, in fact, loved.

Aaron would smell warm and slightly chemical, the way he had in the bare moments when Brian wanded him down or when they sat close together, the other doctors long gone, and there was protocol to follow but not much time for anything but time.

Brian imagined he would taste hot and slick, and Brian would just lick his way inside, push his body close and close enough, make sure nothing was lost between them. And Aaron—his hands would grip and grab Brian's ass, rub over his biceps, enjoy the clean line of his stomach, the hard bones of his hips. Making sure he knew he was wanted for his form, his body, not some imagined femininity.

And he would shove his freezing cold hands against Aaron's burning skin because he was *always* hot, radiating with it, and finally, *finally*, finally getting his hands where they needed to be. Finally getting the warmth he'd been missing all this time. He'd make a topographical map of every line and curve and kink of Aaron's body. Did he have scars too? Did he have a space between his shoulder blades always tense against a blade, no matter how good things felt or sounded? Did he feel as though he was full of bile and vileness just waiting to get free? Or was he as easygoing as he looked on the outside?

Brian wondered what he'd meant when he said he thought he'd seen the last of whip marks. The thought of Aaron carrying them on his own skin twisted something in Brian's stomach, thinking of that. He wondered if Aaron's clenched fist had felt like this, a surge of protective feeling—this junkyard dog, castle walls feeling. When Aaron's eyes had filled with fury as he realized how it had been in the colonel's house growing up, what weights Brian was still carrying, Brian had felt as if Aaron wanted to protect him. Maybe that was what the jacket was about. But it didn't feel as if Aaron wanted to *possess* him, to own him. It felt as if he was angry *for* Brian because Brian deserved better than he'd gotten, deserved better than what was on offer here, and wanted in some small way to be a part of fixing that for him. It was an unfamiliar look; Brian couldn't recall seeing it in anyone else's eyes before.

It meant a lot to him.

Aaron treated him as if he deserved care. As if he deserved to be safe. Brian thought of that, of hard hands made soft by intention, of a cowboy's half-smirk, and the sound of Aaron's laugh as sleep took him deep and low.

Chapter Nine: T-63 Days

"As has been previously discussed in this report, the pervert is easy prey to the blackmailer. It follows that if blackmailers can extort money from a homosexual under the threat of disclosure, espionage agents can use the same type of pressure to extort confidential information or other material they might be seeking. A classic case of this type involved one Captain Raedl who became chief of the Austrian counterintelligence service in 1912. He succeeded in building upon excellent intelligence in Russia and had done considerable damage to the espionage net which the Russians had set up in Austria. However, Russian agents soon discovered that Raedl was a homosexual and shortly thereafter they managed to catch him in an act of perversion as the result of a trap they had set for that purpose. Under the threat of exposure Raedl agreed to furnish and he did furnish the Russians with Austrian military secrets. He also doctored or destroyed intelligence reports which his own Austrian agents were sending from Russia with the result that the Austrian and German General Staffs, at the outbreak of World War I in 1914, were completely misinformed as to the Russian's mobilization intentions. On the other hand, the Russians had obtained from Raedl the war plans of the Austrians and that part of the German plans which had been made available to the Austrian Government. Shortly after the outbreak of the war Captain Raedl's traitorous acts were discovered by his own Government and he committed suicide."

> —*"Employment of Homosexuals and Other Sex Perverts in Government," Interim Report submitted to the US Senate Committee on Expenditures in the Executive Departments by its Subcommittee on Investigation, Pursuant to S. Res. 280 (81st Congress). December 15, 1950.*

October 18, 1951

H odgins called on the radio, buzzing and crackling on Brian's belt. "There's someone at the gates for you."

Brian stood up from his folding chair. This time of year, 21:30 was full dark. *Just when he said he'd come: military precision.*

He drove the same battered Ford, hair a bit shorter. And Brian saw something he hadn't quite realized before, hadn't been able to see.

As David swung himself down out of the driver's seat, Brian asked, "Did you serve on the continent?"

He paused, looking at Brian oddly. Then his body unslouched, shoulders tightening, pushing back and down. An old posture, well beaten into the grain.

He said, "I was at Normandy."

Brian looked over to the truck. "Not a career man?"

David leaned back into the cab and snagged an old army duffel, heavy with books. "Didn't even get the GI Bill before they sent me packing. Turns out 'semper fi' means something different for, well…" He looked Brian over before he glanced back at the duffel. "I'm pretty sure you know."

"Yeah." Brian replied. He ran a hand through his hair. "Things seem to have worked out for you?"

David shrugged. "I would have liked to go to college. But there are these sounds and smells that come back with you. After a day like we had in Normandy. And this job…" He looked over the high volcanic desert plain. "I can see everything that's coming at me for miles and miles around. You were in California?"

Brian nodded.

"I spent an afternoon in one of the coffee shops on your list, where they sold the books. You know they're thinking of opening a bookstore in San Francisco?"

"Yeah?"

David nodded. "They're going to call it 'City Lights.' You might want to take a look if you're ever back there." He looked to the side, voice a little far off. "But you probably noticed that Californians, they don't measure distance in distance; they measure it in time? Like, 'Oh, I'm an hour away from San Francisco,' or 'I live forty-five minutes from Oakland'?"

Brian smiled a little. "I hadn't really caught that, but yeah."

David kept going. "I went through a valley last summer over in Montana. Just on my own. Just going between places, covering my territory. I was on the way out of Idaho, heading east. I pulled over to the side at the top of the pass, checking the map. Seventy miles to the next mountain range. Over the edge of the lookout was this incredible, green heaven in a bowl of high valley. I was going seventy miles an hour. Looking across to the next pass, looking over all that impossible beauty, I could see time. I could see the next hour of my life. These mountains, these massive nameless mountains, just for me." He took a long breath. "So, yeah. No pension. No GI Bill. But they can't take the mountains away from me. Or the high desert. Those are mine just as much as they are any man's."

Brian nodded. "That's a good way of thinking about it."

"For me, it's the only way to think about it." He rolled his shoulders back. "Anyway." He paused and handed over the duffel. Brian handed him an envelope with the last hundred dollars, and he took it and tucked it into his inside jacket pocket. "I got you what you looked for and a couple of others besides that some of the folks there recommended. There's a few ones that came out recently that you probably didn't know the titles of."

He paused again. "I will admit, I read a couple of them. It was a long drive, and San Francisco is pretty early in my route. Good ideas in there. What it might look like if we didn't have to hide, how much healthier it would be. What it means to love someone, even. Wherever you got those titles, it was good."

"Well, if your route ever includes LA, go down to—"

"That's the southwest Avon circuit."

"Ah. Got it."

Another pause, and David glanced back at his truck before asking, "You doing okay on that hair product?"

"Yeah, I'm using it sparingly. Not a lot of hair to work with." He weighed the bag in his hands. "Do I owe you anything else? This feels like more than two hundred dollars of books."

David shook his head, a slight smile on his face. "Call it a late birthday present. I actually feel like I owe you. Last night, I stopped over in Boise. Saw a poster about an open Veterans of Foreign Wars Lodge function; can't be a VFW member, of course, with the blue discharge. Found an old friend there. Same unit, same charge. He went back home here. Had a brother who didn't much mind why he'd been discharged, just glad as sin he was still alive. And we— Well, just so you know, you've got a new friend over in Boise there who knows Dorothy. That's where I'm heading next. Taking some well-deserved vacation days, taking some time to catch up."

Something incredible swept over Brian, seeing something different in David's smile, the way he was itching to get back into his truck. Brian said, "I'm really fucking glad for you."

He smiled. "I'm really fucking glad for me too. He was something in France and has only gotten better with age. I'd better get going. He'll be waiting for me." The man pointed to one of the books. "I scribbled his address in there. If you and— Well, I assume there's somebody special if you got all this stuff. Come on by. We'll cook you some hot food. Give a place you can hold hands without looking over your shoulders."

David gave Brian another smile, with none of the coy carefulness of the first one he'd given him, and patted him on the shoulder. "Stay safe out here, Captain. I hope we see you around sometime."

Brian headed back inside and tucked the duffel firmly under his folding chair. Aaron came down out of his lab, took one look at the duffel, and a grin sparked across his face before he controlled it. He didn't pry or prod, just took the steps two at a time as he disappeared up to the control room.

*

Brian waited with a jiggling knee until the last scientist was out of the building, and then he locked the door.

"I'm heading to the basement to read," he hollered up the stairs. "Call me if the Russians invade."

"Will do!" Aaron echoed back down.

Brian hefted the bag over his shoulder and thundered down the stairs. He looked around and tucked himself between two massive equipment cases right under a hand-painted sign that said: "DO NOT ENTER Without Permission of REACTOR CHIEF OPERATOR." He sat with his back against the stainless steel for good measure and unzipped the duffel. The smell of paper, of bookshops and dry paper and ink, filtered around him.

All of the books' covers were hidden, carefully and tightly, in brown paper. On top was a long bookmark David must have slipped in:

This came out since you were last on the left coast; I believe it may have what you were looking for. —David DuFrois

Brian unwrapped each book, fingers careful of rough-printed covers and handbound spines.

Adrienne Rich, Christopher Isherwood, W.H. Auden, Gerald Bernard Francis, Marguerite Yourcenar. Poetry, love songs; hints, guesses. The contents of Bill and Mary and Jess's shelves. One he didn't recognize: *Quatrefoil*, by James Barr.

He started there, back aching until he lay on the rough-finished concrete floor, duffel bag full of queer books for a pillow.

This first book was an experience. The men were masculine and confident. Neither were "wives" in the relationship, neither were hidden. One of their sisters even encouraged them.

Brian knew before it happened that one would die because in these books, queer men never, ever lived.

But while they lived, they were happy.

Brian dove into the next one, let the world flow over him, taking notes in his mother's shorthand that used Apache phonetically with English letters. When his pencil wasn't in his hand, his fingers kept creeping up to trace the outline of the truck key, tucked safely between his dog tags.

He tracked how to do simple things: Who picked up the tab? Who would make decisions if one made more money than the other? Who would pay taxes? Who would go on the house lease? These decisions were made for better or worse—mostly worse—for women in society's drawing rooms and smoke-filled parlors. But with *them*, they didn't have to live that way.

Then to the practicals: cooking, sleeping, shaving, two bedrooms or one. Even the most gnostic of the poets touched on these basics from time to time. Renting two bedrooms would reduce confusion, but anyone who grew up in the midst of the last panic—the Great Depression—would understand two men and two beds in a room.

But Brian didn't want to think only of the practicals of concealment. Outside the cities, no one much went into homes to inspect the layout. He hadn't had visitors the two years he'd lived at Vandenberg, except for the unannounced, disastrous appearance of his father. He didn't see himself becoming vastly more social as he grew older.

By midnight, Brian didn't want a single period more of information on how to hide, how to be seen as less Native, less queer, less what he was.

He knew from hiding; he knew from sin.

What he needed to know was how to *live*. How to figure out who swept the sidewalk and who cleaned the porch, who wore the pants in the family. And then he read this line, this tuning, impossible stanza—

Let us return to imperfection's school.
No longer wandering after Plato's ghost,
Seeking the garden where all fruit is flawless,
We must at last renounce that ultimate blue
And take a walk in other kinds of weather.

It was called "Stepping Backward," and those lines just kept sticking with him, reminding him of the conversation about different worlds he'd had with Aaron. Maybe love was that simple: walking together in all kinds of weather.

Maybe—maybe that was all it was.

He kept reading and reading until his watch told him it was 06:45, and then he slipped the slim Rich book back into the bag, zipped it, and headed upstairs. Ramirez was upstairs, ready with the Geiger counter as Aaron skulked beside him. But Brian took the fifteen minutes to check in with him, to make sure he knew about the upcoming experiments, to make sure he'd been able to get everything he needed in Arco. Right at 07:00, Brian nodded, and he and Aaron headed out into the waiting dark.

Aaron was practically vibrating out of his bench seat when Brian got into the truck. As soon as Aaron had them on the road, he rushed out with, "Did you get a chance to look at the books?"

"I did," Brian said, keeping his tone solemn.

Another few seconds passed before Aaron broke. "And?" His voice rose to squeak on the word, he was holding himself so tightly.

Brian took a breath. "We can talk more tonight once the others have gone home. But—I have hope."

Aaron let out a low whine, hands tightening on the steering wheel. Then he loosened them and reached over, laying his hand palm-up on the bench seat between them.

Brian looked at it for a long moment, at his calloused fingers, loosely curled—a hand that had held reins and uranium and weights and beer bottles and, most recently, a key.

He slipped his hand into Aaron's and gripped tight for a long moment, palms hot and pressed to each other. Brian swore he could feel Aaron's heart beating under the rumble of the truck through the morning snow, banks of fog rising from it as the day dawned warmer than it had in weeks.

He held on until they reached the barracks.

*

Dr. Zinn elected to toddle around the lab until *damn* near 23:00 that night, futzing and fussing with the experiments.

On a normal night, Brian would have been soaking up the information he was sharing, the brilliant ways his brain worked, the ideas and relationships and contexts he normally hungered for.

On this night in particular, if Brian thought he could have done it without getting fired, he'd have hoisted the man into a fireman's carry and dumped his ass in the snowfield outside the perimeter fence.

But instead, he and Aaron followed Dr. Zinn around the lab, pressed urgent buttons, and held requested wrenches. They generally did anything they thought would help him finish whatever it was he thought he needed to do and get him *out of the lab* as quickly as possible.

When he finally bid them both goodbye, Brian shut the door, counted to thirty, and threw the bolt. He turned to see Aaron leaning against the door to the uranium storage vault, the low yellow light highlighting his soft curls. He had his Stetson in his hand; the only evidence of his nerves was him tapping it in a rough rhythm on his upper thigh.

"You want to do this in here?" Aaron asked.

Brian frowned; what were they going to do, go stand in the snow to talk? *That's one way to ensure we keep our hands to ourselves; Idaho frostbite as chaperone.*

Aaron seemed to have followed the thoughts on his face, and he jerked his head toward the door. "We could sit in the truck." He took a step closer. "You still have your key?"

Brian flushed. He did. He just didn't think he was going to have to show Aaron where he'd been keeping it. He'd thought the whole point was he'd only use it when Aaron wasn't around to give him a ride. He nodded, hand going to his collar, and he tugged the button open as Aaron's eyes yanked down to follow the motion of his fingers. He slid the chain back and over the top of his head, the metal body-hot, until his dog tags slipped out, with the key to Aaron's truck clinking among them.

Aaron's eyes were huge as he took quick steps to gather the offered metal, pooling it in his broad palm.

Brian asked, "Why do you want to talk outside?"

He thumbed over the tags and held the key up, the tags clinking down to the other end of the chain. "I guess I'm less interested in speaking with Captain Flynn, Security Director for EBT-I, and more interested in speaking with regular, brilliant Brian Flynn. Brian seems to have an easier time coming out from behind the captain's bars outside this building."

Brian looked into Aaron's eyes and felt seen, understood in a way he hadn't thought anyone would understand him.

Aaron's voice was quiet, his breath warm on Brian's cheek when he said, "We'll lock the front door to the lab. With the headlights in this fog, we'll be able to see anyone coming from miles away."

"Okay," Brian said, scooping the key out of Aaron's palm. "I'll get her warming up."

Brian sat in the driver's seat, hands on the wheel, foot on the brake as Aaron unfolded the Diné blanket so it could cover both of their legs. With the heater on, it was easily warmer than the lab. The night was so dark the high desert around them seemed a black sea, only broken by the occasional glint of moonlight on silver-edged sage and the high, impossibly white mountains to the north.

"So," Aaron said.

Brian said in a rush, "I haven't finished reading, so I don't want to make any major changes yet. But I want us to be equal." He took a breath. "I don't want one of us in charge and the other not. Decisions, big ones at least about careers and money and living places and leases and family, those need to be ones we talk about." He paused. "As equals." *Just to make that clear.*

Aaron seemed to be smothering a smile. "Got it. I gathered that. That's no problem for me."

"Really? Because you said you wanted to *teach* me—"

"I used the wrong words. I seem to do that a lot with you. What I was trying to say was—there are things you know that I don't and things I know that you don't. Friends teach one another things, and to me, anything further than what we're doing is an extension of being friends."

Brian frowned, turning to face him. "I don't just want to be friends, Aaron."

Aaron rubbed his hand through his curls. "I didn't mean it like that. I meant it like music. Friendship is the piano. Without it, any vocals sound weird and harsh and can get off-key fast. Friendship is what keeps everything in tune."

Brian nodded. "It's like the containment area for the reaction."

"Yeah," Aaron said, back on familiar ground. He leaned a little closer. "You said being taught isn't what you want. What do you want, Brian?"

Brian buried his face in the other man's shoulder, feeling him stiffen under the contact and then relax into it, hand going to his knee, its warm weight carrying messages from another world.

He spoke to the warm fabric, breath puffing through the other man's clothes. "At Vandenberg, I had—someone. A man. He wasn't bad; he wasn't cruel, but he was older. And I was young. So very young. I went to the clubs and the bars, and he was a poet, and—" Brian squeezed his eyes closed. "He taught me, and it was good, so good, but if he didn't feel like seeing me, we didn't see each other. If I wanted to talk about something he didn't, we didn't talk about it. I existed on sufferance. And the thing was, with how I grew up, I was used to it. Expected it." He sighed, frustrated with himself. "It was the best I thought it could be."

Aaron made a hurt sound, and Brian pressed his forehead in closer, some animal part of him craving warmth.

"After what happened there and after what happened in Roswell, with my father"—Brian forced the words out—"I made the connection. The one he wanted me to. That what I'd been, with Bill, had been the cause of—" His chest ached, but he kept going. "Coming here, I'd assumed there'd be no clubs, no men to see or be seen by, and I would just freeze that part of me off. Kill it."

Aaron shifted against him, hands clenching in his lap, but he seemed to be forcing himself to give Brian space to speak, to be what he needed to be for this moment.

"And I met you, and you seemed to have no earthly knowledge of fear," Brian continued with a dry chuckle. "I had nothing but fear. Fear keeps you sharp, keeps you safe, as safe as anything can, how I grew up. And some men, they feed off that fear."

"I don't."

Brian smiled a little, small and secret, pressing closer to the dusty, chemical smell of him, like sage in New Mexico, like the rain at West Point. "I figured that out. At the Mello Dee Bar in Arco, you weren't looking for prey. When you talked with me, you didn't go on and on about what I knew or didn't know. You just, sort of, took me as I was."

Aaron was silent, but his fingers were a solid grounding path on Brian's knee, tracing patterns in the thin fabric of his uniform.

Brian said, "So, equals. And with sane boundaries." Face still hidden in the other man's shirt, he felt Aaron cock his head as if he were questioning the word.

"I think I may need you to define that term," Aaron said, "since we both know I'm no expert there."

Brian chuckled a little. "I don't want to get a blue discharge. We can't have evidence that might be used against us. Nothing where other people can see, unless we know they're safe. If there were someplace where everyone expected us to be equals, where we didn't have to hide, we wouldn't need to do all this. But things get so warped when things are secret. When we can't be open about who we are. I don't want whatever we are together to get twisted up in the ways the world will try to break us."

"Can you think of anyone you think of as safe?" Aaron asked, tone neutral.

Brian smiled. "Well, David—the Avon Lady man—told me he and his new boyfriend want to have us over for dinner, so there's that."

Aaron chuckled. "You do move fast once you've got your feet under you, Brian Flynn."

Brian started to object. "I—"

Aaron kept going. "What I do know from—" He paused and looked at Brian's face before making a decision. "—growing up in Wyoming is that there's a lot to look forward to, even within those bounds." Brian got the distinct impression that wasn't how he'd planned on ending that sentence when he started it. But Aaron was still speaking.

"Kissing, for one. Handholding. Going out on dates. Not"—he spoke over Brian's rising objection—"where others can see and not the way men and women do out here. But two friends going hiking, camping out, exercising together, taking classes if there's that kind of thing around. Horseback riding, rodeos, festivals, shows. I hear what you're saying, that in this time and this place, we can't have our hands all over each other. It would be easier to be equal if there were people around us who expected it. But there are things we can do in public, particularly in places where female company is thin on the ground."

Aaron frowned a little. "And that's just if we want to do things in public. Two bachelors living together is the standard way of things in many places and won't be looked at one way or another." His smile quirked a little. "But moving in together is a bit of a way off, no matter how shitty your barracks are. I guess what I should be asking is, now we've got some parameters, what do you want to do?" And he turned, just a little, finger and thumb going to Brian's chin as he caught his breath.

"I mean," Aaron murmured, "we haven't even kissed yet." And Brian was scrambling to lunge forward to fix that problem *immediately* when Aaron leaned back, just a touch, hand pressing against his chest with a smile.

"As for what *I* want—I want you. Plain and simple. And I want you to know it. I want you to know it's *you* I want, and since it seems to take some time for these things to sink into your big, busy brain, I was going to take my time in showing you."

He trailed the backs of his fingers up the side of Brian's face to sink into his hair. "I want our first kiss—our first *everything* to be special, Brian. Special enough to make you want to see the stars."

And Brian closed his eyes and muttered, "You don't need to treat me special, don't need to convince me. I already want to see the stars. I want to be on the first ride to the moon. That's what all the textbooks are for, all the waiting, and studying, and hoping." He gave him a smile. "But I could argue this was pretty special. You did get me to talk about my feelings for a whole ten minutes."

Aaron threw his head back and laughed, body shaking with it, before slinging his arms around Brian and pressing his massive smile into the soft skin of his neck. "I believe you could argue that. But let's do something together, away from here. What are you planning for Thanksgiving?"

Brian made a face where Aaron couldn't see it. "I think I have to go home."

"Brian—" Aaron started, and Brian felt him decide not to push there. "All right, we'll find another time. Maybe right after? And for now, we continue as we were, but when we're safe, we can—" He put his palm on Brian's neck, curling his fingers against the collar of Brian's uniform, tingles racing after the motion.

"Yeah. All right." Brian took a slow, deep breath. "That will give me time to read the rest of my books, to figure out what I want. From this. From us. As equals."

He pressed his face into Aaron's hair, breathing in the soft, warm scent of him. The other man's hand came up to grip his elbow.

"You do that, Brian. I'll be right here."

Chapter Ten: T-49 Days

Q. Mr. President, I wonder if we could retrace that reference to the atom bomb? Did we understand you clearly that the use of the atomic bomb is under active consideration?

Truman: Always has been. It is one of our weapons.

Q. Does that mean, Mr. President, use against military objectives, or civilian—

Truman: It's a matter that the military people will have to decide. I'm not a military authority that passes on those things.

Q. Mr. President, perhaps it would be better if we are allowed to quote your remarks on that directly?

Truman: I don't think—I don't think that is necessary.

Q. Mr. President, you said this depends on United Nations saction. Does that mean that we wouldn't use the atomic bomb except on a United Nations authorization?

Truman: No, it doesn't mean that at all. The action against Communist China depends on the action of the United Nations. The military commander in the field will have charge of the use of the weapons, as he always has.

> *—At a press conference on 30 November 1950, President Truman was asked about the use of nuclear weapons.*

November 1, 1951

Brian had been watching the approaching turkeys with apprehension. First, they'd colonized the nurse's station. Well, he only had to go there once a week for his blood test, so he could pretend the fourth Thursday in November wasn't nearly upon them. Then they were seen covering the small window into Dr. Zinn's office. Well, fine. Probably a prank. But when he came in for his evening shift, the lab still full of scientists prepping for the morning's experiment, and a bunch of meat-fisted future sandwiches were draped on the cinder block wall right over his metal detector, he was a half breath short of yanking them down.

"Turkeys get you down?" drawled a wry voice, and Brian tipped his head all the way back, trying to count the beams between him and the full ceiling. He got to fifteen before Aaron got tired of waiting, sauntered toward him, and slid a finger across the inappropriately yellow fowl. "I never much got the appeal," he said. "They're the dumbest animals alive in captivity and only barely better than chickens in the wild. Ever try to drive through a flock on a county road? A fucking nightmare. Twenty-pound balloons of malice and idiocy, all crowded together like a shark's wedding."

"I've never seen them in the wild," Brian said, breathing shallowly. Aaron was a half-step away from him. On the other side of a stand of paper turkeys, sure. But that wouldn't stop him if Brian just pushed.

But they had their rules.

"They're dumb as fuck," Aaron said, turning to look at Brian under the gently swaying turkeys. "Better off cooked on a platter. Except they taste like angry napkins and disappointment, so there's no real fucking point in cooking them either."

"It's that I just don't like the story, the 'it's okay we killed all your people because it got us this great turkey' story," Brian muttered, too low for anyone around them to hear. "Every fucking year at Thanksgiving, the same goddamn story. And it was always wrong, always fucking ridiculous."

"That part fucking sucks too," Aaron said, and Brian saw there wasn't one ounce of pity in his words. One solid cent of disbelief or apology. Just a friend, seeing life had not been what it ought to and comparing the world unfavorably to his own vision of it because of its treatment of someone he cared for.

"There isn't enough cranberry sauce in the world to cover the stench of genocide," Brian said, forcing his voice to stay low as his face heated. He rarely—if ever—let himself talk this way out loud. It was a quick ticket to a rough day, making fun of a major American tradition. So he kept that shit to himself. There was no Scrooge for Thanksgiving. He could hate it all he wanted inside his own head.

But Brian figured Aaron was a safe person to vent to. Despite Aaron's obvious loyalty to his country—and what else could you call freezing your balls off in central Idaho as winter came roaring out of the sawtoothed mountains—Aaron never seemed to feel as if he had to defend it. Like America was big enough to stand up for what she needed to be, to accept the faults and flaws in evidence without him flying to her aid like a damsel in distress.

"Have you decided what you'll do for the days off?"

Brian froze. He and Aaron had gone to Idaho Falls the previous weekend to explore, and he'd checked his PO box only to find a single letter. Return address: Colonel B. Flynn, 509th Composite Group, Roswell, NM. It contained a letter informing him he was required to come back to Roswell for Thanksgiving, with a Greyhound ticket inside. He had no right to pretend he didn't have a family to go back to, no matter how much he wanted to.

"Hey, hey, sorry," Aaron said, rubbing his own face with his hand. "I know it's not the time and place. We hadn't talked about it yet, but I'm going to head back into Wyoming, staying at a cabin near some hot springs for a few days. Use the seven-hour drive to clear my head. Maybe come up with some new ideas for how we can heat the water for the turbines."

Brian could see it so clearly. Drive the seven hours across Idaho, across the Rockies, deep into Wyoming with Aaron. Singing along to what passed for patchy radio out there. Bedding down in their own quiet nowhere, soaking in the hot springs, cooking simple meals. And no one, *no one,* would bother them. They would have a cabin—a nice, snug cabin—to themselves. With curtains. And they could *finally—*

Aaron seemed to have been following Brian's thoughts when he stepped back, putting his hands behind his back. He rocked on his heels and said, his voice quiet, "I don't suppose you'd want to keep me company? It's a long drive, and I could use someone to spell me for it." He glanced up at the beams holding up the ceiling. "I'm heading out before dawn the Wednesday before the Almighty Turkey Day. It's a long haul across the Rockies and—" Bravado dropping, his eyes met Brian's, but only for a moment. "And I could use the company, Bri. I really could." His tone was soft in a way that was more about intent than volume, as if he was outlining a future, a vision for them, giving Brian a preview.

Brian knew the right answer, the *duty* answer, but instead, he muttered, "I can pay my half of rent on the cabin. I've saved some cash up."

Aaron's eyes widened, eyebrows going all the way up. He rocked forward as if he was going to touch Brian but then shook his head at himself.

"The rental was one hundred dollars for the week, so you cover gas and food when we get into town, and we're all good. Pack the heavy jacket; we're going to need to get the fire started in the cabin, and it can take a few hours to warm up."

"You've been there before?"

Aaron nodded. "I rent it from a buddy of mine from UW. It's his summer hunting cabin."

"And he'll be there?'" Brian asked, hope and warning warring in his heart. He didn't know what to think of Aaron having another buddy there.

But Aaron just scoffed. "Charles? Fuck no. He goes and hides in Florida as soon as the first snowflake falls. Got it all worked out with his thesis supervisor and everything. No way, no how he's out there with any kind of weather. But he left it all set up."

Brian's shoulders relaxed, and he tracked one of the scientists as he cantered down the spiral staircase. "That sounds like a good way to live. I'm in. We can talk about it later?"

"Yeah," Aaron murmured, eyes bright.

*

It was a bit past 02:00 when Brian asked the big question, back against the stainless steel of the only part of the control panel Aaron hadn't disassembled yet, a spray of tools arrayed around his folded legs. "There's going to be snow in Wyoming, isn't there?"

"Yeah? Just like there's snow here?"

"The thing about snow is—it's rude."

Brian could see Aaron's eyebrows spark up at this, but he remained bent over the console he'd ripped off the main control panel, tweaking something in its inner workings.

"How so?" Aaron asked.

Brian was 99 percent sure Aaron had disassembled this particular control panel during this overnight retrofit because he knew Brian could keep an eye on the front door while he got into things he wasn't technically supposed to touch. Brian would, in fact, sit on the floor next to him as he yanked the cover off and dove inside. Brian would stay to hand him tools, wrapped tightly in Aaron's jacket.

But that didn't mean he was going to admit it.

"Back home, snow doesn't come to us for more than a month or two. We *visit* the snow up on the mountains, on the reservation. We drive to Sierra Blanca, enjoy the snow, then come back. In *Idaho*," Brian said darkly as he looked toward where the thick concrete and cinder block walls restrained the snowy desert outside, "it comes to stay. Like an uninvited guest. It's *rude*."

Brian heard a strange, choking sound and looked over at Aaron.

He was hunched over inside the console, shoulders shaking, hands braced on either side of the central panel. He made the sound again, a kind of out-of-control gasping.

Brian shuffled closer, let a hand come to rest on the middle of Aaron's back, ready to pull him around if he had somehow managed to use his genius brain to start choking on something. But at the touch, Aaron turned into him, and Brian caught a glimpse of his broad grin before he buried his face in Brian's shoulder.

"What—"

"You're ridiculous," Aaron gasped, laughter finally spilling out, vibrating up Brian's neck and straight back down his spine. "You spend all day in this formal 'I'm The Best Soldier In The World' thing with the uniform and the rules and the too-tight pants, and the—" Aaron waved his hand behind Brian's back as his arms slowly rose to Aaron's elbows and held him tight. It was like his body knew how to react, even as his brain was still desperately behind.

"And then, it's dark and late, and there's so little sunlight left, and you sleep through most of it to give your men a better schedule. You have to be exhausted, and you're *still* here and not reporting me for fucking around with the console *again.* You're reading your books and thinking about *equals,* and you're just—you're so serious all the time sometimes! And *then* you're, like, *bitching* about the weather! You're *whining!* Because it's cold. And you've—" Aaron leaned back, wiping his eyes. "—you've gone through some shit that I don't think anyone can adequately understand. But instead of being angry or hurt, instead of having your heart break or fall to pieces, you just keep on. But then you get fussy about the fucking *snow.*"

Brian considered being offended, but instead, he raised his hands, slow as breathing, and carefully traced lines on either side of Aaron's face, watching as his eyes widened, a real question rising in them as Brian said as softly as he could:

"I fucking *hate* snow. You are so lucky I like you enough to spend my vacation wading through *even more of it.*"

Chapter Eleven: T-29 Days

Some corner of the mind retains
The medieval man, who still
Keeps watch upon those starry skeins
And drives us out of doors at night
To gaze at anagrams of light.

Whatever register or law
Is drawn in digits for these two,
Venus and Jupiter keep their awe,
Wardens of brilliance, as they do
Their dual circuit of the west—
The brightest planet and her guest.

—Adrienne Rich, "For the Conjunction of Two Planets," 1951

November 21, 1951

Aaron picked Brian up at just before 05:00 on the Wednesday before Thanksgiving, clutching a mug of coffee and holding out another for Brian. Brian had stomped out into the snow with a duffel holding all the good cold-weather clothes he had. He wore the jacket Aaron had lent him over a T-shirt and some uniform pants and felt freer than he had in months. Aaron glanced at the small duffel significantly but didn't say anything.

He patted the wheel. "You okay taking shifts? I usually do this on my own, but it would be a treat not to be battling my own eyelids four hours in."

Brian said, "Sure, I can take the first one," and moved to reach for his key.

"Nah, I've got the first leg. You can familiarize yourself with the route." Aaron paused, a smirk flickering across his face. "And you can try to find us a radio station."

"You know there's three total radio stations in this part of Idaho?"

"Well, you can try to find us some more."

Brian rolled his eyes. They were on the highway now, trundling along and picking up speed, EBT-I fading behind them over the curve of a volcanic ridge.

"Fine, then you can provide me other entertainment," Aaron said.

"What kind of entertainment?"

"Road trip games!" Aaron grinned.

"I've never played car games before."

"Four older brothers, growing up in a rural area, and you never played any car games?"

Brian frowned. "We didn't talk on car rides."

"What did you do? Read?"

Brian shrugged. He'd read; his brothers had tried to mess with his books; his father had screamed at them; they'd all sat in stony silence. He said, "I have heard of some of them. There are no signs for two hundred miles, so playing the alphabet game is out. And there will be nearly no other cars for about the same distance, so license plates is no good."

"And your objection to twenty questions?"

"I shudder to think what you would come up with. Maybe I could read to you?"

"Yeah?" Aaron said, eyes brightening.

"Yeah. I packed my books." Brian rifled through his duffel before stilling. "I don't know if they're really your thing."

"The books you got from the Avon Lady man—from David? How are those 'not my thing'?"

"Some of it's poetry. Modern stuff."

Aaron shrugged. "Given that I at least partially owe the current pleasure of your company to those books, I'm open to it. If I don't like it, I'll just tell you."

Brian began digging through the front of his bag for his copy of *Leaves of Grass* as Aaron cruised them down the snow-dusted highway.

"I've seen that one before—you read it in the lab sometimes."

Brian chewed his lip, looking at the God-scale mountains, dwarfed by the snowstorm clouds glowering over them. "It's one of the few I was able to keep when I was leaving Los Angeles. It's assigned in colleges, so I figured it wasn't—"

"—too obviously queer?"

"Yeah. The other one I saved I just tucked in the back pages of the textbooks I could grab before I was hauled out of the dorms. All the other poetry books, I had to leave behind."

Aaron frowned at the road. His fingers squeezed and released the wheel a couple of times. He ran his tongue across the front of his teeth and said in a soft voice, "Look, you don't have to tell me. And I'll only ask once so you don't get badgered on this road trip. But what happened?"

"I don't want to talk about it. It's in the rearview mirror."

Aaron glanced at the actual rearview mirror. "Sometimes," he said slowly, "things in the rearview mirror can overtake you, and it helps if everyone in the vehicle can see them coming."

Brian exhaled, looking out the window at the snow-strewn sagebrush and hand going to his key. "Fine," he said, pausing, voice flat and dry as the high blackstone desert around them. "Last August, my father flew in to visit Vandenberg unexpectedly. My dorm chief let him into my room. It was a Saturday, and I was out. I had poetry books, had gotten them in a coffee shop, a little place in West Hollywood. Someone I was with had written a book of poetry."

Brian dug in the bag, pulled the slip of a thing out, brown paper cover and hand-sewn spine. He traced a finger over the hand-drawn line art on the cover. "He thought he was being romantic and dedicated the book to me. By name. My father read the dedication and formed a logical conclusion. My father took the book, went to one of his friends. An officer. Initiated a blue ticket investigation. When I got back from a night out with that friend, there were two MPs at my door. I'd been out celebrating because I'd just gotten into UCLA's physics PhD program, and my commander had approved me finishing out my last two years there. They took me to the basement. I was interrogated all night."

Brian paused, gritting his teeth, swallowing. "By morning, I agreed to accept an immediate transfer rather than a blue ticket." He paused. "I had to agree to never see him again and destroy all of my copies of his books." He tucked the copy back into his bag, carefully inside a hardback that would keep it from getting crushed.

He couldn't look to see Aaron's reaction. His hands were hard as stones on the wheel, shoulders tight with it. His voice held, something.

"That was the last you saw him?"

Brian shook his head. "I—I found a pay phone at a gas station while my father was buying smokes. My friend, he offered to come and get me—said, 'fuck him,' and I should just go AWOL, just take the blue ticket and go." His shoulders ached with tension. "But I need the money. I need the GI Bill money to be able to go to grad school. He said he would take care of me, but I couldn't just be his thing." Brian's voice grew hard. "I'm not a pet, Aaron."

"No. You're not."

"And I don't think Bill would have treated me that way. But I wouldn't have a job, couldn't get a job. Do you know how hard it is to get a job with a blue ticket in your discharge papers?"

Brian glanced in the rearview mirror. "I would never work someplace like EBT-I as a scientist. Couldn't work there even as a glorified security guard. The whole rest of my life. No research, no science. So I thought, what's two years? Two years of pretending? I'd gone twenty-seven years before, and only one more year, and I can get what I want?"

"So you went from Vandenberg to here?"

Brian huffed a laugh that didn't have any humor in it at all. "No, it took a couple of weeks for the transfer to go through. But I wasn't welcome on base. So my father drove my truck back to Roswell. Said he didn't want to pay to put me up so near a city that was tempting me to sin, and he had to get back to his stupid alien hunting hobby." Aaron made a noise, but Brian kept going. "Then he engaged in his own methods to try and reinforce the lesson. The night before I was supposed to drive up here, he pulled me out of bed, dragged me outside by my hair, told me to watch while he burned my truck down to the chassis. Told me he'd heard from the MPs that faggots fucked in trucks, so he was helping me avoid temptation. Then he gave me five minutes to pack and handed me a Greyhound ticket. Fifty-one hours later, I was here."

The truck around them hummed for a second as if a fluorescent light had been screwed in slightly wrong. A warm, warning buzz. It got louder until Aaron took a quick breath in through his nose and slowly out through his mouth.

"Okay," Aaron said. "Okay." He swallowed. "He shouldn't have done that."

"What?"

Aaron spoke through his clenched teeth. "Your family shouldn't hurt you."

Brian sneered. "Well, lucky you, your family doesn't hate you. Congradu-fucking-lations."

"I mean it, Brian."

Brian felt that steam rising in him and forced it to cool. It felt good to be able to control when and where he was angry, felt like maybe he wasn't a bomb about to explode and hurt everyone around him. He pressed his hand to the cool glass of the window. "Maybe," he allowed. "Maybe that's why I'm here. I'm going to catch it real bad at Christmas, but I just didn't want to—"

"Spend a shitty holiday with people who hate you? Good fucking reason."

"Yeah," Brian said to the drifting snow outside his window.

"We'll make Christmas plans."

Brian could hear him swallow, his voice getting small.

"Don't go back, Brian."

Brian frowned. "I can't just leave my family like that, Aaron. I'm his only son left who *can* come home. All my brothers are in Korea."

"Blood does not have to mean loyalty. You don't have to be loyal to those who are not loyal to you."

"You don't get to tell me what to do."

"I'm not—" Aaron paused, thinking. "So when you said you didn't want a blue ticket, I guess I thought that was a distant fear. Not a practical one. That's why I—"

"Flirted like there was no tomorrow? Scared the shit out of me every time I thought someone might catch us—"

"I still don't think anyone would—"

"I had ten classmates from West Point class of 1948 given blue discharges. Two to three *thousand* navy personnel a year are getting them. And that's just the navy. Suspicion is *enough*, Aaron. It's more than enough. It's not like they threw away the file they started on me at Vandenberg. Filed right there under 'Brian Flynn—Blue Ticket Inquiry.' They're watching—"

"But," Aaron broke in, was trying to reason this, solve the problem, and Brian's irritation rose. "*How* are they watching, who *specifically*—"

"My father can see *everything*. How did he know to come on that day, how can—" Brian gripped the side handle as hard as he could, unable to breathe, fingers cramping with it, trying, trying, breath coming harder and harder and harder until his body shifted as the truck swerved into the shoulder and settled to a stop.

Aaron's hand came warm and firm between his shoulder blades. He didn't say anything fucking stupid like Brian's friends had in high school or the nurses or the rare fellow pleb. He didn't say *breathe* or *it will be all right* or any such shit. He just slid across the bench seat, arm over Brian's shoulder as he hunched over the dash and took loud, slow, steady breaths. Over and over, even as Brian jerked and writhed through it, couldn't see, couldn't breathe, *so sure he was going to be caught, going to be found in his tiny, tiny, safe hole he'd found, dragged out by his hair, beaten with a belt, raked across the back with the cherry switches he'd been ordered to pick out himself...*

But eventually, humiliatingly, as it always did, the horrible, clenching, wracking thing passed. And he was limp and sore and fizzing with it and cross in Aaron's arms. He wanted to shut down, to take back what he said, to get some quiet to get himself under control. But then, just barely, he heard Aaron's voice and realized he'd been muttering the whole time.

"You think if I dismembered him and put a different body part in every county in New Mexico, anyone would ever notice? Like, one body part per county. That's enough distribution..." Aaron went on. Brian faded out and when he came back in again, Aaron was saying, "Do you think he knows how to swim? I bet he doesn't. Desert man his whole entire life. I'll just float him over the Atlantic and let him take a fucking swim, see how *he* likes not breathing."

Brian laughed. It sounded *terrible*, raw and ugly and wracked, but it was a real black humor laugh.

Aaron shut up at the sound, but Brian waved him on.

"Go on, keep planning my father's murder. It's soothing,"

"All right," Aaron said, thinking. "What if I could turn him inside out with my mind? Let him die seeing his own shriveled heart?"

"Very *Tell-Tale Heart* of you. Edgar Allen Poe went to West Point, too, you know."

"Classy. I could, I don't know, make him eat plutonium until he burned up from the inside out? Run him through an industrial paper shredder? Walk him out to Sierra Blanca and leave him there in the pale snow, no liquid water or real food in sight?"

"We could just put some good old-fashioned rat poison in his Jack. That'll do the trick."

"Simple, clear thinking. That's what I like out of my airmen," Aaron said, voice dark and encouraging. And then, "Feeling a little better?" his eyes carefully on the horizon.

Brian nodded, but as Aaron got to moving away, he snagged his knee, fingers gripping in. "Maybe." Brian worked his jaw. "Maybe just a minute more? Just thirty seconds," he added, bargaining himself down.

Aaron leaned away, and Brian's heart felt—how could he feel so betrayed, they weren't *doing anything.* But all Aaron did was turn the key, getting the truck going. Heated air blasted through the front dash, warming them both up.

"I'd like a bit longer than that, if you're up for it," Aaron said.

Brian grumbled about wasting valuable moonlight, but when Aaron tucked his arm back over his shoulder, he let him. *Oh*, he let him.

Brian spoke quietly, wanting to make it clear he was making a rational argument, no matter how his stupid body responded to a perceived threat. "Any one of those scientists, any one of those airmen, could restart the blue ticket inquiry with a single phone call. The file at Vandenberg, it has a photograph of the dedication page. Not that the book isn't, in and of itself, incriminating since Bill isn't particularly subtle. But all my file at EBT-I says is there's 'further information at Vandenberg Air Force Base.' So someone would have to go to my file and look for it. And someone could call and ask someone to do it, and nobody is really going to go to the trouble to check that out. But if someone had a reason to—"

Brian pushed his back into Aaron's warm, broad hand.

Aaron said, "I don't think that will happen here. Here's why." His hand, still soft, gentled across Brian's shoulder as the parked truck cooled around them. "A month ago, Dr. Zinn—" He paused. "I didn't tell you before because when it happened, it was during the days when we weren't talking. But Dr. Zinn saw me looking at you. When you were on guard duty. I was trying to do a chemical reaction equation in my head, and sometimes I look at things I—" He looked to the side, muttering, "If you can tell me about Vandenberg, then I can say this."

He got it out in a rush. "Sometimes I look at things that I like the way they look, that I think are beautiful, and it helps me think about equations. Dr. Zinn asked me to his office, and he shut the door. And he said—" Aaron paused, and Brian looked up at him.

His eyes were closed, and he spoke slowly as if reading off the backs of his eyelids. "I'm trying to remember how he said it. I think it was, 'Brian is a good kid, and you're a good scientist. And I think you could be good for each other. And I think as long as you're able to keep doing your job, no one here is going to bother you about anything. But he's in the military, and they handle things different there, so make sure you're not endangering his career. And all the nonsense in DC, the probes, the Hoey Committee, and HUAC—they're not going to go hunting out here in Idaho. But tread carefully, is all I'm saying. And know I won't sign off on any report to Brian's chain of command, and I suspect none of his men would make one. They like him too much.'"

Brian didn't know if his eyes could get any wider. His heart was kicking up in his chest. "I need—out."

"What?"

"I need out!" Brian fumbled with his seatbelt.

"Hey, wait. Where are—"

But Brian was out of the truck. He ran into the snow-dusted sagebrush, dropped to his knees, and slammed his hands into the black volcanic earth.

"*Shit,*" he said, hearing Aaron's door click shut in the windy-worn desert quiet, but there was no sound of him coming for him through the sage, and Brian was glad.

"Shit!" His head was swirling. Had he just been avoiding this with Aaron for no reason?

No, he *had* a reason. The men on his team could have reported him. It didn't matter what they said in their commander reviews, what Aaron or even Dr. Zinn thought of their loyalty. They still *could*, on a whim, on a hidden grudge, on a bad *day*. Aaron was sweet to think they wouldn't, but there was no way they could care for Brian that much. To hide something like that, just to protect him. He could never assume there was someone on his side. No one, *no one* was ever on his side.

God, that sounded bad.

"Shit," he muttered, keeping his face down, pressing it to the backs of his hands where they gripped the sharp volcanic gravel, letting the pain work its way through his arms. He welcomed it. It reminded him he was here, not drowning in the—regret?

"Shit," he whispered.

Aaron's cowboy boots step-slid down the embankment, his long legs moving through the waist-high sage. Aaron squatted in front of him, peering down. Then he heard him sit back, thick black gravel shuffling as he folded his legs. He heard him lean back, adjust his arms, hands rustling the sage leaf mixed gravel.

"I can still see a couple stars," Aaron said.

Brian huffed a breath into the dirt beneath his lips. "I can't."

"Yeah, well, maybe you could look all the way through the earth. You'd have a good view of Scorpio."

Brian frowned, looking up at him. "Why would you know that?"

"Maybe I'm an alien."

A chuckle forced its way out of Brian's chest as Aaron kept going.

"In alien school, before they let you become a starship captain, they make you memorize all of the skymarks of your destination. Like, we've got our own navigation system to run our spaceships, but sometimes, you need to engage in a little casual astral navigation so you don't get sucked into a black hole after your satellite dish gets hit by an erratic comet."

Brian looked up and laughed, a real, if cracked, sound. "I don't even know half the words you just said. Black hole? Satellite dish? Erratic comets? You've been reading too much *Astounding*."

Aaron tilted his head all the way back, the long line of his neck catching the first sliver of dawn. It sliced through his hair, highlighting the edges where, moments before, he'd been fading into the black ink sky.

"I know," he said with a sigh.

And Brian—there was no one out here but coyotes and cows, the sage rising high over their heads, shielding them from the road. He rolled forward on his knees, ignoring the painful crunch of the gravel. He put his hands on Aaron's shins.

Aaron kept his head back, and Brian was reminded of how he'd gotten a feral cat to start accepting food at Vandenberg. It would come up, rub itself along his legs, but only if he wasn't looking at it. Only if he kept his body entirely neutral, pretending he couldn't see it.

He crawled another half foot forward, knees pushing against the soft-tooled leather of Aaron's cowboy boots.

"Aaron," he said.

At his name, Aaron tipped his head forward, looking at him, only a breath between them. "Yeah, darling?"

"I—" Brian said.

Aaron brought up his hand, pressed his fingers to Brian's lips. "If I'm going to be your first kiss in three months, it's not going to be in the middle of a fucking field in Idaho."

Brian frowned, the movement making his lips move across Aaron's calloused fingertip. The warmth building in the pit of his stomach had been missed and was profoundly welcome. "Then how's it going to be? We've been waiting a month, more than. I figured you had some kind of plan, and after you waited me out, the least I could do is give you time to think."

Aaron looked at him, considering. His eyes dipped down to Brian's lips, the lines of his shoulder as he knelt forward. "You are going to be soft and safe, warm and comfortable. Full, not hungry or thirsty. Not scared or defiant. You're not going to be proving anything to anyone. I'm going to kiss you because you want me to and because I want to. Because I want you, Brian Flynn. And because you want me. Not a statement, not for anyone else. Just us."

Brian paused. "And what if I wanted—what if I said that was true now?"

Aaron cocked his head. "You're a lot of things, but I've never known you to be a liar. For one thing, you can't possibly be warm. It's as cold as Satan's nutsac out here."

Brian laughed, leaning back a little on his knees.

Aaron's hand didn't leave his face. He rose, leaning forward with Brian, fingers going deep into his hair, and Brian couldn't help it, he closed his eyes, preening into the movement. It had been months since anyone had touched him with intent, where he was *certain* they couldn't be seen, months since he could even think of enjoying this kind of focus. He pressed back against Aaron's hand, holding tight to this spare, bare moment. He couldn't let it go. Not for a half second.

"There you are," Aaron said. "There you are."

*

They talked about easier things for the rest of the drive. Brian told him the plots of different science fiction novels he'd read. They both agreed they wanted to know more about Middle Earth, wondered what happened to the One Ring after Bilbo got home. Brian read him parts of the Whitman book and then the Rich book. Aaron listened, half smiling, smirking at the dirty bits. Aaron told Brian about different kinds of experiments he'd run in grad school, the same kind of light versus heavy water versus liquid metal debates they were still working on in the lab, but with more drinking.

As they crossed out of the Rockies, Aaron finally found a radio station. It was mostly playing the same ten songs, so after a half an hour, they started to memorize them. Aaron had a nice voice, low and sweet like warm honey and bourbon. They talked about the kind of food they liked to eat, the dances they enjoyed.

Aaron shared more about himself, some of the men and some of the women he'd loved. He said he was bisexual. And when Brian murmured he hadn't heard that term before, he just said, "Look, I'm a physicist. I don't really get involved in plumbing."

Brian had laughed for about thirty seconds as Aaron gave him an amused and questioning look.

Brian replied to the silent question. "It's just—something. To talk openly. With someone who understands." He took a breath. "So, bisexual means, men and women?"

Aaron tilted his head. "Not for me, not really. Do you really think the world has only two kinds of people, two genders?"

"What do you mean?"

Aaron turned a little, hand steady on the wheel, holding up two fingers with the other. "I mean, if people were left to their own devices, I figure there's always going to be a lot more ways of being than just two." He glanced at Brian. "Like, growing up, I knew people who didn't feel right being called cowboys or cowgirls, so we'd just call them range riders. The day you first met with David, you mentioned that Polaris is a binary star system, right?"

Brian nodded.

"Well, there's perfectly balanced groups of three and four stars too. Relationships can work like that—like molecules, polycules. And there's stars that give off a lot of heat and no light, or a lot of light and little heat—for a star, anyway." He smiled a little. "I figure gender, sexuality, affection, friendship, they're all like that. Some people like sex but not romance; some people don't like sex or romance but make lifelong platonic friendships; some people like romance but not sex. Some people like people who aren't in the weird gender binary most Americans are so obsessed with these days; some people like women, and some people like men." He grinned. "It's big and complicated and as wonderful as the sky."

Brian blinked as he began to rearrange his thoughts.

In a quieter tone, Aaron continued, "And for every single freedom we grant other people—to be bisexual or asexual or queer or heterosexual, to want romance but not sex, sex but not romance, friendships without either; for every time we accept that gender isn't so much a binary star cluster as a bimodal distribution and sometimes entirely outside a number line; for every time we stop worrying about who's in whose bed and how many people they share it with, as long as everyone involved is being safe, informed, and good to one another—that is *more* freedom we each have ourselves. To define for *ourselves* what equal means, what free means, what love means."

He forced his voice a little lighter. "If we don't sort everything into predetermined categories given to us by a society that could care less whether we live or die, we're left with making our own houses, our own definitions of home. So, what then?"

Aaron quirked a smile. "Then a relationship, particularly one built within a house, can be divided into tasks and strengths. Who takes out the spiders and who doesn't; who washes the dishes and who sweeps; who cooks and who scrubs and who shops for food and who plans the meals; who pays the taxes and who gets the mail and who writes the budget, and who speaks at the city council meeting; who picks up children from school and who teaches them to be and love themselves. Who cares for elders and who fixes the truck and who reminds the other or others to eat and to sleep."

He shrugged. "Just tasks and balance, communication and dreams. If you start as equals, like you've been saying, then you get to figure all of that out how it works for the people in the relationship, not some cardboard cut-out life."

"Part of me wants to say that sounds like a lot of work, but it also sounds a whole hell of a lot better than two people trapped in a hateful house, caged by roles they didn't choose and don't think to understand. It sounds like a way to fight back, every day, by choosing to treat other people as equally valuable in the world." He set his palm on the dash, thinking. "It sounds like a vision from another world."

Aaron ran his palm down Brian's shoulder to where his T-shirt ended and his skin began, warm and solid and there. "It could be a vision of the future, too, here. Not everywhere, but sometimes, and some places."

Brian raised his eyebrows, reaching over to press Aaron's palm closer to his arm, to hold his hand there. "Before I start to collect social security?"

Aaron blinked, squeezing him once, tightly. "Maybe."

Pressure built behind Brian's eyes. "That's a long time to wait."

Aaron patted his hand and placed his own back on the wheel again. "It is. It would be worth it to see it though."

"Yeah," Brian said, voice low and a little doubtful. After a moment, he turned to Aaron with a smile. "On a different topic, if we had a spaceship that could take us anywhere in the universe, which planet would you go to first?"

Aaron met his smile and the new tone brightly. They chattered and listened and talked and traded places driving as the plains of Wyoming opened up around them, wide and impossible and as far-reaching as a dream.

Chapter Twelve: T-29 Days

IN paths untrodden,

In the growth by margins of pond-waters,

Escaped from the life that exhibits itself,

From all the standards hitherto publish'd, from the pleasures,
    profits, conformities,

Which too long I was offering to feed my soul,

Clear to me now standards not yet publish'd, clear to me that my
    soul,

That the soul of the man I speak for rejoices most in comrades,

Here by myself away from the clank of the world,

Tallying and talk'd to here by tongues aromatic,

No longer abash'd (for in this secluded spot I can respond as I
would not dare elsewhere,)

Strong upon me the life that does not exhibit itself, yet contains
    all the rest,

*—Walt Whitman, excerpt from Leaves of Grass, Calamus po-
ems, "In Paths Untrodden," Deathbed Edition (1881).*

November 21, 1951

That afternoon, they stopped over in Winchester, WY, to get supplies for the week: pancake mix and corn oil and popcorn and frozen bacon they could chuck in the cold cellar, spices and dried pasta and rice and canned veggies for stews, and some kind of tiny cupcakes the trading post owner had made in her very own kitchen; they were nearly all frosting, and Aaron adored them. They'd eaten a massive lunch at the trading post: bison burgers and veggies nearly embalmed in butter and even what passed for milkshakes. Then they'd driven another forty-five minutes on dirt roads, their tire tracks the first since the snowfall. As soon as Brian lost sight of the highway in the side mirror, his shoulders relaxed, his entire body slouched down a little in the seat. He might have caught a slight smile on Aaron's face, but the other man kept his peace.

The cabin sat in the middle of a snowfield. The stark Rockies were a mere threat in the western sky; stands of towering pines nearer the cabin were heavy with snow.

As Aaron slowed the truck, he murmured, "You know I don't have any expectations, right?"

"Are there two beds?"

"I mean, there could be. There's a cot."

"Hmm."

"What I meant to say is—you've got the key. You want to drive off, I'll find my own way back. I just—I don't want you to feel trapped."

Brian turned, frowning a bit as he quietly laid the flat of his hand against Aaron's neck, fingers tracing the place where the stubble faded to smooth skin. "I don't think I've ever met someone who spends more time trying to make sure I'm not trapped, who makes me feel less trapped. Who makes me feel more free." He smiled, just a little. "Don't worry about it."

Aaron caught his hand, pressed it closer to his cheek, and Brian felt something kick in his stomach, a flood of blood switching directions, his breath coming faster. "Okay," Aaron said.

He pulled in to park in front of the cabin's porch, and they got to work in the bare bits of sunlight they had left. They worked in easy parallels, habits learned fast and well in long nights at the lab. Brian unstrapped the tarp from the back of the pickup as Aaron opened up the cabin and lit a fire. Aaron showed Brian where to find the quilts from the big chest that doubled as seating. He layered them carefully on the large bed in the middle of the room. Aaron propped the door open with a river stone, letting the cold wind sweep away all the stuffed-up smells. Then, together, they hauled their bags and gear in, box after box after box.

Brian found a banker's box right up against the cab, carefully ensconced in a second tarp, perfectly watertight. Everything else had gotten gently dusted in snow the entire drive, but it was as dry as tinder.

He opened it up and called out, "Umm, Aaron?"

"Yeah, darling?" came the drawl from just behind him.

He glanced over to see Aaron perched on the tailgate, black Stetson tipped over his face to keep the snow off. "Why do you have the chief nurse's record player?"

"I do not. That is *my* record player."

"Why do you have the chief nurse's records?"

"Those definitely are her records."

"Did you—"

"I did not *steal* her records. She, for one, wouldn't know if I had since she's off for the holiday. But I *asked*. And she said I could borrow them. Because she's not going to be playing them over the vacation, and

I wanted to. And she said, 'If you damage those, Antares, you will find your weekly blood draws become a point of trial. Do not fuck up my records.'"

"Is that why your luggage was in the bed covered in snow, but the records were protected?"

"That *is* why. That woman scares me. I am frightened of her."

"Well, at least you're man enough to admit it."

"Oh, I am all kinds of man to admit it." He slipped a smile. "You know, my mother was a doctor."

"That's rare. Where did she get her degree? I thought there were a couple of women fighting for them at Harvard but hadn't heard about anyplace out west."

"She's...Swedish."

"'Antares' is a Swedish last name now?"

"Yes?" he said hopefully.

"Okay. I'm just throwing it out there. Whatever bizarre background lie I end up finding out you've been spinning to amuse yourself these past months, it had better be entertaining. Because all this setup—"

"Oh, it's a good one." Aaron smirked. "It's out of this world."

Brian laughed, heart beating a touch faster. He hoisted the box of records over his shoulder and hopped off the bed of the truck, leaving the record player for Aaron to grab.

He stepped into the cabin, and his shoulders ratcheted down the last few inches.

The cabin was one big room, a cast-iron wood-fired stove pumping out heat in one corner with a massive fireplace taking up the back wall, crackling merrily. A queen bed was centered against the main wall and— as promised—a freshly set-up cot on the other side of the room with a little privacy screen in front of it. There were quilts newly laid and stacks of food in the corner farthest from the fire. The bole of a pine sapling, shorn of its bark, hung on thick knotted ropes from the bare wood rafters with some wire hangers ready for their clothes. A few paintings of Wyoming skies hung on the wooden walls, and a massive heap of Diné rugs covered the floor.

Brian knelt, hands tracing and retracing the patterns in the rugs. The smell that rose from them was— He wanted to roll in them, on them, fold himself up in them like his mother had wound him in her blankets when he was small and the base heating would go out.

Aaron came in behind him and set the record player against the stacked log wall. He was framed in the doorway, the sunset and snowscape behind him, face lit by the warmth of the roaring fire.

Brian stood. "It's pretty warm in here," he said, taking a step forward.

Aaron nodded, eyes never leaving his. "Yep, it heats up pretty quick with both the fireplace and the stove going."

Another step as he shrugged off Aaron's thick jacket and let it fall on the rugs. "And I'm pretty comfortable here."

Aaron's eyes were getting wider even as he kept his voice steady. "I'm glad to hear it."

Another step. "That was a good meal we had. I'm not hungry or thirsty. Are you?" He watched Aaron's throat bob, almost close enough to touch now.

"Not for food," Aaron muttered, gaze not raising from Brian's lips, "that's for *damn* sure."

He took the last step, bodies not touching, held apart by less than the space of a breath. "And I'm never going to be soft. But you make me feel as safe as I've ever been."

"*Brian*," Aaron managed, and Brian eased forward until his

forehead just touched Aaron's, breaths mingling hot and close.

"I'm going to kiss you now. That all right with you?"

"Yes. God, *please—*"

And Brian pressed his lips against Aaron's, feeling the soft, hot shape of them, smelling the close-in smells of him, and then Aaron groaned and slipped his tongue into his mouth, twisting and *perfect*. Aaron's hands went to his hips and jerked him tight against his body, Brian's thigh going between his as he grunted at the sudden contact.

Aaron pulled back. "You good?"

Brian grinned and leaned back in to spin them so Aaron had him backed up against the open doorframe, the furnace of a man in front of him keeping him warm against the snowy chill outside. He hitched his leg over Aaron's hip, and he ground forward with a gasp of relief, *finally* touching and being touched.

Aaron swayed forward, slipping his hand behind Brian's head so he could kiss him without him smacking in the rough-worked wood. Brian's hands were in his hair, carding and letting the careful curls play over his fingers.

"You can pull it, if—"

And Brian shook his head, taking a breath, body still tight against his. "I can't—"

Then Aaron touched their foreheads together again. "Then I'm fine with what we're doing." And Brian heard the soft glee in his voice.

"Just 'fine'?"

He drew back, amber eyes sparkling like gold dust mixed in them. "Captain Flynn, are you fishing for compliments?"

Brian narrowed his eyes, but Aaron just laughed and kissed first one cheekbone and then the other.

"I am good," he said before kissing the tip of his nose. "I am great."

And he nudged Brian's head down to lay a smacking, happy kiss to his forehead. "I am *fantastic*."

Brian caught his lips again, and he tugged up Aaron's button-up shirt to trace senseless patterns on his bare skin. "In that case, want to move this inside?"

Aaron glanced at the open snowfield, the sun setting behind the towering mountains.

"Sounds like a plan."

He traced his hands down Brian's arms only to tangle their fingers and tug him into the cabin. The door shut with a soft *snick*, and Brian pulled Aaron toward the bed, but Aaron hung back, frowning.

"Want to play a game of cards?"

Brian glanced at the bed, thick with lavender and gray quilts, and then back at the scientist. He cocked his head. "I thought—"

Aaron met his gaze, let him see the utterly unbanked fire in them. "Yes. *Yes*, Brian. Yes. But we have time. We have time, and we don't have to rush—"

Brian crossed his arms over his stomach and pulled off his shirt. Aaron shut his mouth, gaze sweeping across the exposed skin. He didn't linger on the scars or avoid them, just traced them with the same intensity as he admired the rest of him.

Brian said, "We can play cards after."

"'After' works too."

Brian gave him a smile and backed him into the shut door, looking him in the eye. "But, for now—"

He leaned in to kiss him, and Aaron met him halfway. Brian slid his hands under Aaron's shirt with a deep sound of approval. He was hot, his hair growing thicker the closer his fingertips inched toward the button of his jeans. Aaron groaned at Brian's searching touch. Aaron's stomach jerked against Brian's fingertips, and Brian found himself grinning. It was a good, deep-in-the-bone feeling, this joy, this *pride* in making another man moan, making his body react to him.

Brian sank to his knees. He looked up, mouth about level with Aaron's belt buckle. "Any objections?"

"God, no, Brian. The way you look down there—" And Aaron's fingers slid softly in his hair, tracing and retracing the shell of his ear, gentle and safe against his skin. Brian buried his face in Aaron's thigh, the rough, sweat smell of him, the scent of his truck, the snow, and the smoke off of the stove all mixing and grounding him like a live wire, here; just here.

He grinned up at Aaron and then fumbled the buckle open with his help, fingertips catching on the snow-cold metal. Unslipping the top button. He could feel him against the heel of his palm, hot and warm and straining against the denim. Aaron was shaking above him, his fingertips digging into the rough wood of the door behind, his breath kicking up.

Brian undid another button on the fly as Aaron gasped at the sensation, at Brian's quick fingers so close to the source of him. Brian leaned in, tracing the shape of him through the denim with closed lips, reveling in the smell, the curve of him. As Aaron tried to keep himself from jerking his hips, Brian followed each newly opened button with an open-mouthed kiss to his cock where it stood up proud in his white boxers. Aaron's hand clutched his shoulder, thumb working in wide open sweeps across the exposed expanse of his collarbone. Brian slid his hands around to the sides of Aaron's waist, hooking his fingers in the belt-loops and tugging. The Levi's slid over his hips, catching at his spread thighs.

"Bed," Aaron gasped, voice already wrecked; Brian looked up at him. Breaking through his glazed-eyed lust was a hint of practicality. "I can't get my boots off from up here, and I want to touch more of you."

Brian pressed one last long, lingering kiss to his cock before he worked a hand inside his boxers to get a good handful of him as Aaron groaned at the sight. Then he stood, crowded in close to kiss him breathless against the wall, and swallowed every sound, bodies one clean line.

"Think we can make it to the bed like this?" Brian asked.

Aaron steeled himself. "Only one way to find out."

Brian took a step back, hand moving slowly, Aaron following, his hands going tight and sure on Brian's hips. Another step. Another. The queen bed bumped against the backs of his knees, and he sat, pulling Aaron in so he could lick a swipe across the other man's head as he trembled.

Brian smirked up at him. "I'm not sure we can keep this up while you get your boots off."

Aaron swallowed, blinked hard at the thought, then nodded jerkily. "Probably not."

Brian released him, trailing his fingers up his stomach before tasting the warm skin just beside his navel. Then he made room on the bed, bending over to unlace his own boots enough to get his feet free of them without taking off his uniform pants. Aaron sat to kick off his cowboy boots and jeans and struggle out of his button-up.

Brian caught his fingers halfway down his chest and stilled them. "Let me."

He nudged him toward the head of the bed, and Aaron moved easily, crawling backward as Brian followed, always within kissing distance, until his head was on the thick, dark pillows, curly hair haloing around him. Brian kissed his exposed chest as Aaron's fingers traced immeasurable patterns across the scarred skin of his shoulders, ruffled the hair at the nape of his neck as he preened into it. Brian wanted to taste every part of him, wanted to be able to close his eyes and remember the shape of his pec under his tongue, his belly button against his smile, his hips in his hands.

He looked up to Aaron for permission just before he slid his fingers into his boxers again. At the man's enthusiastic nod, he slipped them over his hips and off. "*Oh*," Brian said. "Oh, but I missed you."

Aaron's tone was a little teasing. "You haven't really seen me before; that shower was too dark to see much of anything."

"True, but I missed the thought of you. Knowing you were there and I couldn't touch you and now I *can* and—"

"Hey, hey, yeah. I get it." Aaron's hand went to his cheek as he smiled at him. "I'm glad you're here too."

"Yeah," Brian said. Then he crawled into Aaron's lap, careful of his dick between them, thighs on either side of his strong hips, and kissed him, soft and sweet. "I'm real fucking glad."

He worked a hand between them, fingers brushing his own cock through his uniform pants on his way to sliding, dry and warm, down Aaron's dick.

Aaron closed his eyes, hissing a long breath between his teeth, and ran a calloused fingertip around the inside hem of Brian's waistband. He shivered at the sensation, hips bucking a little before he stilled them.

"We can get you out of these?" Aaron asked.

"I want to focus on you. But after, sure."

Aaron reached up to pull Brian deep into a kiss, tongue warm and full in his mouth, smile tucked tight against his lips. "Promises, promises."

Brian grinned, slipped out of Aaron's lap, and watched him lay back with a self-satisfied grin, arms folded behind his head. Brian kissed one hipbone, then the other, carefully avoiding the dick that bopped red under his chin. Aaron made a noise of protest, and Brian smirked up at him before swallowing him in one fell swoop.

This he remembered how to do perfectly. The musk of it, the way the skin got slick under his lips, the hard-soft of it, how to move around the muscle of him. His blood rushed in his ears, unsure where to go, his dick as hard as it had ever been, but he was content to wait. To focus for a few minutes on this, on remembering this.

He heard a soft sound, like a cloth being pulled, and looked up to see Aaron's hands clawing at the bedsheets, palms full of great, creaking fistfuls of quilt. But Aaron kept his hips still, struggling not to jerk up into Brian's mouth. Brian appreciated the courtesy, but he didn't want Aaron restrained.

He wanted to see what he was working with.

He slipped a hand under Aaron's hips, encouraging him into his mouth. Aaron gasped in relief, body moving in slow undulations as Brian fisted around the base of his dick, protecting his lips and giving that little bit of extra pressure. He knew this and loved it, the feeling of Aaron bucking between his palm and up into his mouth, the free feeling of his strong body dancing against the sheets. *We're going to dance this weekend*, he promised himself. *I know it.*

Brian urged him up, closer, harder, body humming with it, with Aaron's sounds and smells and joys and pleasures, wild from being in the middle of this, of causing this with him.

Then Aaron ground out, "I'm going to—"

Brian pulled off to gasp, voice sounding fucked-out and wanton, "In my mouth, I want to taste you, *please*—"

"Oh, *fuck*—" Aaron groaned, head flung back and hands near-tearing the quilt.

And gave one, two, three quick thrusts as Brian tried to keep from getting bucked off before he was coming in his mouth, salty and hot and sour and so perfect.

He eased him through the spasms, hand soft and guiding on his bare side, then released him with a slick sound once he felt Aaron pull back from the overintense sensation.

Brian tasted him one last time before crawling up his naked body. He slung a uniform-clad leg over his hip and laid his head on the low valley between his pec and his shoulder.

"I tend to—" Aaron yawned. "—fall asleep after. You all right with a nap?"

Brian nodded. Not tired but wanting a chance to breathe, to carefully file every one of the million, trillion sensations he'd just had.

Aaron's hand traced another of those impossible patterns up his back. "You're something special, darling."

Brian was pretty sure Aaron was already asleep when he whispered to the fire-warmed winter air, "You too."

*

Brian woke from a light doze, body soft and loose in a way he hadn't felt in months. Aaron had rolled on his side in his sleep, and Brian had followed him, unwilling to be away from that expanse of smooth skin for even a moment. He'd tried to keep a tiny bit of a distance, unsure how Aaron felt about being the little spoon. But Aaron had kept wiggling back, closer and closer to him, as if even unconscious, his body knew more about being held and holding another person's body than Brian could scrounge together from his best memories and most educated guesses.

He traced with his eyes and then his lips the expansive curve of

Aaron's back, the work-wrought muscles, the places he'd grown straight and strong, the places his body dimpled or arced in the normal, unique, human ways bodies did.

The cabin smelled of woodsmoke and warm wool and sweat. He closed his eyes. There were some feelings Brian could only have going seventy miles per hour. Thoughts too heavy to hit at anything other than top speed in his truck. When he'd been with Bill, around the others, he'd spent a lot of time in his truck, just driving. Thinking. Crying or screaming or laughing, sobbing or whimpering, thinking about it. He could save emotions up. He was good at it. At Vandenberg, he could save all of the emotions he'd cobbled together for the entire week, his feelings at having to listen to others mock queer folks or the threat of the blue discharge or the shame when someone got discharged and he did nothing about it, not even sharing a sympathetic look because he didn't want to draw attention to himself.

Southern California was good for driving. He would take himself straight down the coast and out to the eastern parts of San Diego County, see where the great white stone eggs of granite lay scattered over and under the scrub brush. He would go deep into the eastern Kern County mountains, the topography something he knew as well as the lines in his own face. Once, he'd found this little hotel hours after he was all cried out for the week. This sweet space with a hot spring beside the "killer" Kern River. Men and women used the hot spring, more naked than not. He'd sat beside the pool, watched, maybe, reading his book. No one got hurt, no one hurting. Just people in their full bodies. Free.

He'd faced doubts. He suspected every queer person had. Was he twisted, warped in some fundamental, impenetrable way? Was he not trying hard enough to like women in this way? But it wasn't soft arms or hips that slid right into his palms that he wanted; it was this. A hard body under his tongue, a bobbing throat as he worked his way down the other man's body and tried his best not to let his knees buckle. A man beside him, in the truck, in a cabin. In his bed.

He hadn't gone into the hot spring in Kern County. He knew the reaction his scars would bring, the pity and the stares. The questions. But he liked to think about it, going there some moonlit night with someone he liked, with someone who knew him. He dreamed about it for a while before what happened, happened and took his dreamscape away from him.

He wondered if Aaron would want to go to the hot spring here with him. He'd mentioned there was one on the property. He thought about it, slipping into the simmering, algae-slick depths, bodies strong and sweating. He could splash him or take off his shirt or just—be. For a few minutes. He looked over at Aaron, counted the soft rise and fall of his breaths. He laid a heavy arm over his waist, feeling the remains of sweat and liking the way his belly fit into his palm.

He'd see.

Later.

Chapter Thirteen: T-28 Days

Is any light so proudly thrust

From darkness on our lifted faces

A sign of something we can trust,

Or is it that in starry places

We see the things we long to see

In fiery iconography?

—Adrienne Rich, "For the Conjunction of Two Planets," 1951

November 22, 1951

When Brian awoke again, Aaron was stirring something golden and spicy as it simmered over the fire. A soft lavender quilt pooled around his hips as Brian sat up to survey the cabin. From the stack of cans beside the hearth, he guessed the concoction had begun life as some kind of canned juice, something with rich apples now mixed with nutmeg and allspice and cinnamon.

Aaron glanced over before grating a bit more of what looked like cinnamon into it. "Apple cider is a necessary remedy to the absolutely fucking freezing nature of the winter in Wyoming."

Brian nodded, stretching his arms up and up toward the arching log ceiling. "What time is it?"

"Late. Or early. Depending on how you count." Aaron gave a soft smile. "Mid-shift for us."

Brian nodded, yawning.

"You hungry?" Aaron asked, and Brian shook his head, swinging his legs to the thickly carpeted floor.

"Outhouse is outback?"

Aaron nodded, gesturing with his ladle.

Brian slid his shirt back on, then snagged both their coats and pairs of socks. The wintry blast of cold only made his heart beat faster, and with each crisp crunch of his boots through the light crust of the snow, something bubbly rose in him, a half-remembered melody, something like glee, something like joy. He looked out over the horizon, massive and impossibly huge on one side and broken up by the towering Rockies on the other. Not another living thing in sight.

He hummed the chorus of "Stormy Weather" to himself as he did a little spin, feet sure in the crunching snow.

When he was finished, he stepped back out. And looked up. And up. And up.

"Aaron?" he called, and he heard the *clank* of the ladle and the hurry of a man struggling into boots. "It's no hurry! It's just—"

But Aaron poked his head around the cabin, wearing his shirt-sleeves and half-buttoned jeans and boots, and Brian laughed and jogged toward him, slipping off one of the coats. He wrapped it around his shoulders and zipped it up over his chest.

"You'll catch your death. I just wanted to show you..." And he looked up again.

Aaron followed his gaze, shoulders sagging with wonder as he saw.

The Milky Way, on brilliant display, arced nearly technicolored across the sky. Brian blew his breath to the side to avoid it fogging up between them and stepped in a little closer to Aaron's warmth.

"What you said before in the lab—you really think there's other societies out there? Other worlds? Do you really think we could visit them?"

Aaron stiffened, then relaxed. "You want to be like Lazarus Long? Take a rocket ship to the stars?"

"I was more thinking Andre Norton's Captain Garin Featherstone, but yes."

"'Andre Norton?'"

"Andrew North? She goes by that in the magazines, but I met her at a book signing when I was in LA. Brilliant lady."

"People shouldn't hide who they were. It just makes it harder for the next person after them to find their place in the world."

Brian froze at the frown in Aaron's voice, feeling like he'd had a snowdrift dumped on his head. He barely heard his own voice when he gutted out, "Sometimes people need to hide to survive."

Aaron looked at him in confusion, hand going for his shoulder. Brian shrugged him off, taking a step back in the snow, trying to get room to think.

"That's not what I—" Aaron started.

"It's not like *you* have to worry about it. You've never hidden anything in your damn life."

Aaron dropped his hand. "You don't know what you're talking about."

"Yeah?" Brian shoved his hands in his pockets, shoulders hunched against the blow he knew was coming for talking back. "So explain to me, Dr. Antares. How could you possibly know what it's like to hide everything about who you are, when you have somehow managed to exist for all of your twenty-seven years on this earth without ever having to learn how to conceal the most basic, most fundamental parts of yourself?"

Aaron just stared at him, something painful and intense moving across his mobile face. He looked at the sky and then snapped his gaze to the ground, wincing like he was hurt. He shook his head and took a step back. "I can't. I can't. If I'm going to do this for real, not just to tease I need— It's not *just* my decision."

"What on earth are you talking about?" Brian snapped.

"Just because I want to, I can't just—" Aaron ground the heels of his hands into his eyes so hard it looked painful. "But you've told me all these things about *you* and—" Aaron took a breath, sounding hard in his throat. "I need to call James. If we're going to do this, I need to call James first."

"Your artist friend on the rez? What does he have to do with this?"

"What? Yeah. Him. Look, I need to have a personal conversation, and you can't listen."

"What do you mean a 'call'? There's no phone lines out here."

"I have a—let's call it a radio."

Brian glanced at the receiver-less roof of the cabin, remembered driving the miles and miles without clocking any kind of antennae or repeater or anything. "What kind of radio...? Aaron—"

But Aaron was walking away, headed toward the truck as he called out, "I'd get inside if I were you. The cider should be almost ready."

"Aaron," he said, the fear and confusion thick in his voice. "What's going on?"

Aaron paused at the porch, hand bracing on the wall. "We can talk about this after." He turned to look at him, and Brian had never seen that expression, something like raw fear and pain on his face. "I promise."

Brian watched as he walked around the side of the cabin, hauled himself up into the truck, and started it up to get the heater going. Through the truck window, Brian saw him pull something out of his pocket before he turned away and held it to his ear. He'd asked for privacy, and whatever else was going on right now, Brian could honor that.

Brian headed back into the cabin and shut the door. The cider did smell ready, but he couldn't drink. He paced around the cabin, his stomach in knots.

What was Aaron doing?

Even if Aaron somehow had a radio that worked without an antenna, Brian wondered if James would even pick up. It had to be past midnight and was an hour later in Roswell, thanks to the way the Central Time border cut the Southeast quarter of New Mexico off from the rest of the state's Mountain Time. He paced across the room again, hand drifting up to the key to Aaron's truck, hand tight on his bare chest under the loaned jacket.

A millennia or a few minutes later, Aaron yanked open the cabin door, hair haloing as if he'd been tugging at it, muttering to himself, "I don't care what he says. I'm the one here. I'm the one who knows you. He doesn't know what he's talking about." Brian kept the bed between them.

Aaron looked around the room, orienting himself, and then took a breath. He shut the door carefully. His voice was low, tense in a way Brian had never heard it when he said, "I'm going to tell you something serious that is going to sound like a joke. I need you to listen."

"Aaron, what the *fuck* is going on—"

"Brian, I'm an alien."

Brian cocked his head, looking at him. "Is your family from Czechoslovakia? Sneak through on a prewar tourist visa and never filed the immigration paperwork?"

A small smile flitted across Aaron's face before he grew serious again. "My family's from a lot farther out than that." He ducked his head low and there was something almost pleading in his voice when he said, "Think about it. Haven't you seen things, heard things? Doors closing untouched, juggling acts that don't make sense? How *I am* with—everything?"

"I just figured— You said you're from Wyoming. And that's why—"

"Why I act like I grew up in a place where I didn't have to hide who I was? Just how open-minded do you think cowboys *are*, Brian?"

Brian stepped around the bed, advancing on Aaron, keeping his hands by his sides but backing Aaron up. "This isn't funny. I told you things about me, things I've never told anyone. *Trusted* you with—" And he swallowed that back down, forcing his voice low as Aaron's eyes widened, echoing the hurt Brian felt boiling over in his chest. Brian heard his voice rising and didn't know what to do to stop it. "You know all these secrets about me, and now you're—what—you're making fun of me? Because of where I'm *from*? Does now really seem the *fucking* time for alien jokes?"

Brian yanked himself away from Aaron and spun toward the door, needing fresh air before he said something he couldn't unsay, did something he couldn't undo.

The door, which had been shut moments ago, flipped its own lock and swung wide open, letting the midnight chill in. Brian stopped for a long moment. Then he went over, checked the lock, and shoved the door shut. He took a step back, heart kicking up, as the deadbolt flipped over, and the door opened, just a crack, not enough to let the snow in, but enough to make the point.

He turned and caught Aaron's gaze for a long moment.

Aaron took a deep breath, and then every one of the head nurse's records rose up out of the record box to dance like electrons around him, like he was the nucleus at the center of an atom.

They glittered black, spinning idly where they hung in the air.

"Like I told you." Aaron said with a quaver in his voice. "I'm an alien." Then he raised his hand and floated all of the whirling records into their sleeves in little orderly lines. *Like the brooms in* Fantasia.

Brian stumbled back and sat on the bed, the quilt still mussed from their shared sleep.

"You're an alien." His voice seemed distant. "You're from outer space."

Aaron stayed still, his hands in the air, the last of the records slipping into the box. "I'm from the fourth moon off of the Antaran binary cluster." His tone was nearly even, only a little shake in it showing the strain he was under to keep it that way. "It's a world with twelve billion people and a horrifying culture of slavery; lovely double-moon sets if you come at the north-shimmers; no discrimination based off of who adults are romantically, sexually, or platonically connected to; and full equality across genders. Great dancing, not that I've seen it in a hundred years." His mouth took a sardonic twist. "Aaron of Antares IV, at your service."

Brian slowly collapsed on the bed. He folded his chest over his knees, head hanging.

"Shit, Brian—"

"I need—I need a minute."

Aaron would be able to catch me with that neat telekinesis trick he just pulled even if I wasn't sitting, he thought hysterically. He thought of that time in the reactor, when Aaron had hauled him up from an angle where he had no leverage, all the times Aaron's truck door had seemed to open without him touching it. He thought about him juggling the light bulbs. Brian's breathing got faster, and he laced his fingers behind his head.

Cowboy boots entered his field of view. "Breathe, just breathe, Brian. It's going to be okay. I'm really sorry, just breathe."

You try to breathe.

Jesus Christ. Fucking aliens. The colonel was right.

Oh, oh God.

"Would something to drink help? I don't know what to *do*, Brian." Aaron's voice was muffled by the pounding in Brian's ears. "I've never told anyone before."

Brian heard the rattle of the stockpot over the fire. He glanced up to watch the ladle float off the wall, slip into the mulled cider, dipping in and then pouring it shimmering in the firelight into a hovering ceramic mug. Then the mug floated into Aaron's outstretched hand, and he cradled it, smelling its spiced warmth for a moment before stepping toward

Brian, hand outstretched.

And all he could think of was all the times Aaron had handled uranium with his bare hands, and Brian hissed, "Don't touch me!"

Aaron's eyes were unshielded, and it was like Brian was watching a heart break in real time. Aaron took a half step back and blinked hard before searching for a place to put the mug down. He finally tucked it against the bed leg, fingers fumbling but careful.

Brian shoved his hand out, gripping Aaron's wrist too tight for him to back away any farther. He forced his mind to function, to stop from hurting Aaron any more than he already had. Aaron whose skin was warm under his fingertips, whose eyes were brimming over.

Brian made himself say, "I didn't mean it that way. It's just—you're always touching uranium. Is this how you always test clean? And how have I been clean all this time? Am I going to—"

"No, no, God no. I pass all of the tests the normal way. I process it, just like you do calcium or iodine or sodium. I never pop hot, remember?"

"Okay." Brian's breath shuddered, but the science of it grounded him. "You're going to have to explain in a little more detail how you don't set off my Geiger counter."

"You want to know why I can pass your fancy security device after touching uranium, but you're just going to let slide that I'm from a moon off Antares and can float things with my brain?"

"I am absolutely not letting those things slide, but as security director, I feel like I should focus on the uranium bit first."

Aaron huffed a wet-sounding chuckle and slowly lowered himself to the floor, legs crossed, in front of Brian. He looked up at him. Brian realized he still hadn't let go of his grip on Aaron's wrist and loosened it so he wasn't in danger of bruising the man—alien?

Aaron turned his wrist over and, careful as breathing, picked up Brian's hand and held it between the two of his. He traced his fingertips over the lines in Brian's palm, motions smooth and meditative, just this side of ticklish as he spoke. "You have to understand that the neighborhood I grew up in, planetwise, is really different from yours. We're in the pathway of a lot of supernovas. And we're mostly protected from the coronas, but they slice through us often enough that our whole planet has fresh supplies of uranium, neptunium, thorium, pretty much anything like that you might want to see. Lots of the stuff our boys at Berkeley have been working on."

"My boys, not yours," Brian heard himself say.

Aaron's hands stilled around his, frozen as a mountainside before he said, voice careful, "I've been working in the US nuclear program longer than you have. I would say they're as much mine as they are yours." He took a long, slow inhale. "But, for us, every species on our planet evolved not just able to stand uranium but to use it."

He glanced around. "That's why my telekinesis, my TK, is so strong. A lot of folks from my ship—once they realized this planet had nearly nothing of the stuff we'd always assumed was as abundant as salt or carbon is for you—they just became, well, more and more human. But being at the lab, every day, interacting with it—" He shrugged. "It helps."

"You didn't actually need my help reaching that beaker the first night. You could have just used your TK."

A grin cracked across Aaron's face. "So that's what you're choosing to remember."

"Still figuring out if you're a security threat."

"I am," Aaron said, voice soft. Brian's shoulders stiffened, even as Aaron's fingers traced gentle curves and whorls into his palm. "I'm here not just to help with what Nurse Kelly calls the 'scarcity of light.' I need to steal a few measures of the plutonium. To get my people back."

"'Your people'?"

Aaron swallowed and glanced behind him to where he'd set the mug of cider. "Yeah, my people. You want that cider? This is going to take a bit."

Brian nodded, then watched as it glided through the air toward him and gently set itself on the floor beside his foot.

The smell was warm and crisp and bright as Brian lifted it, took a long sip, and said, "All right. You should get some too. I'm guessing being Antaran doesn't make you immune to winter chills."

"It does a little bit actually. We run at about forty Celsius as our baseline temperature. Well, males do. Nonbinary people are usually at about forty-two Celsius, women at about thirty-nine. That's why I pushed, in the car earlier, about gender and sexuality and romance. There's so many different ways of being on my home planet, and I think you'd find that way of thinking really freeing."

Brian blinked hard, once, and then decided he could ask more about that later. But he had something more important he had to do first. He leaned close, making sure he had Aaron's attention.

Aaron looked at him, a question on his face.

Brian said, "I want to say—I'm sorry for yelling. I let my temper get away from me, and I shouldn't have." He paused, setting his jaw. "I don't want to be the kind of person whose lovers are scared around him, have to tiptoe around all his...issues. I won't do it again, or at least I'll try my damndest not to."

"Is that what we still are?" Aaron said, voice small. "Lovers?"

Brian frowned a little, reaching up to trace his fingertips over Aaron's cheek as the other man's eyes gently closed. "I can't think of any word I'd rather use," he said softly. "Maybe there's something you'll tell me that can change my mind, but Aaron, I *know* you."

Aaron gave him a quizzical look, and Brian was surprised to hear himself chuckle.

"Maybe not every piece of you, just like you can't know every piece of me in the time we've known each other, the ways we've come to know each other. But you're a man who cheers up his friend when he's down and listens when he says no, even if it's over the smallest things, and who keeps memories and other people's secrets. You care about what's right and work hard to fix this shitty world."

He met Aaron's eyes, voice getting stronger, warmer, more even. "And you've shown yourself willing to listen to me ramble on about everything from Heinlein to Auden to linear algebra's applications to uranium mining." His voice gently teased. "That's the highest quality I can think of for a lover." He swallowed. "And before we cross the state line again, I still have to think about it, the idea that you want to steal the plutonium we're all working so hard to create—that you've been pivotal in getting us closer to having at all. But I understand something about wanting to escape, to get to someplace more free." He nodded to himself. "I'll think about it. Tell you where I come down."

Aaron leaned forward, burying his face in Brian's knees. "You can't imagine how many times I've wanted to tell you, Bri. I *wanted* to. You *know* how I am about secrets—"

Brian eased his fingertips through Aaron's curls, settling them close to the scalp and moving through them. Trying to echo the helpless patterns the other man was tracing on the backs of his shins, trying to wring some comfort out of their shared touch. "You said it wasn't just your secret though. How about you start there?"

Aaron drew back, eyes damp and mouth set. "All right. But..." He glanced back over Brian's shoulder. "You mind if we sit up there? I kind of want us to be at the same level for this."

"Equal," Brian said.

Aaron's lips quirked, but he stayed serious. "Yes. Equal."

Chapter Fourteen: T-28 Days

The truth at last cried out to be confessed:

He must remain eternally a guest,

Never to wear the birthmark of their ways.

He could be studying native all his days

And die a kind of minor alien still.

He might deceive himself by force of will,

Feel all the sentiments and give the sign,

Yet never overstep that tenuous line.

—Adrienne Rich, excerpt from "By No Means Native," 1951

November 22, 1951

"The first thing you need to know about space travel—the real kind, not Dr. Lazarus Long's—is it isn't fast." Aaron had a big wooden bowl of popcorn on his lap and was floating the popped kernels in a little mobile of the Milky Way around them.

"From here"—he pointed to a kernel he'd previously designated as 'Earth'—"to the moon is about three days with the kind of rockets your people can build within your lifetime."

"'My people' as in 'Earthlings'?" Brian asked, snagging the kernel representing Earth to munch on.

Aaron grumbled and floated another out of the bowl. He shook his head. "I don't like to use diminutives for other species; I wouldn't like to be called an Antarette or Antarina or Antaran-chan. 'Gaians' probably works fine, from the Greek personification of Earth."

Brian clicked over to the reminder that the man currently lying between his bare legs, his back tight to Brian's chest, was a different species. Somehow, that part wasn't hard for him; it was the astromechanics he kept getting stuck on. "All right. So, three days from Earth to the moon."

"For *Gaians*. For my people, with centuries of spaceflight experience, point-to-point, that distance would take—" And he started to do the calculation in his head, but he captured Brian's hand and traced the numbers across his palm with his fingertips. "—about .2 seconds."

Brian took a deep breath, easing Aaron's body up and down with it. "Point-to-point?"

He could hear the smile in Aaron's voice. "Well, space is a vacuum, right? So most of what space travel is about is positive and negative acceleration. And the human—or Antaran—body can only take so much of that before we turn into one of those mosquitoes we hit going through the hot springs in Thermopolis.”

Brian made a face where Aaron couldn’t see it; they’d had to pull over and clear the windshield after *that* bug guts–fest.

“Okay, so from Earth”—Brian pointed to that spiraling kernel—“to the moon”—he pointed to another hovering above the hearth about ten feet away—”is three days for us, and .2 seconds for you. So how long did it take for you to get from Antares IV to Earth?”

“One hundred years, using Gaian time.”

Brian frowned. He leaned around to peer at the side of Aaron’s face, raising his fingers to trace the barely-there crow’s-feet. “So you’re—”

“About one hundred and twenty-seven years old.”

“Well,” Brian said faintly, “you look great for your age.”

Aaron’s back shook as he tried to suppress his laughter, but he finally burst out. He set the popcorn bowl to float gently down to the floor, then flopped over and buried his face in Brian’s stomach. Brian played with his raucous curls until Aaron simmered down to quiet chuckles, pressing his smile into Brian’s skin. Then Brian cupped his cheek and brought him up to look at him more carefully.

“Did you really live one hundred and twenty-seven years before you met me?”

Aaron shook his head. “No, with special relativity, it’s a little more complicated than that, and we don’t travel in a straight line.” He smirked to himself. “It’s a pretty queer route if I do say so myself.”

Brian rolled his eyes, and Aaron kept going.

“If we traveled at the speed of light, it would have taken us about six hundred and four Gaian years to get from Antares IV to here. But we can’t travel at the speed of light; no one we’ve ever met can. And we can’t go in a straight line, not just because most of my crew are people who might be called queer here, but because there's a few stars and planets and such in the way."

"So, did you take a shortcut between the stars?"

Aaron grinned. "That's exactly it. There's spaces where we can cover greater distances more quickly than you would expect— like how it's faster to run through air than through water—and we've had millennia to chart them and train computers to navigate them for us while we sleep. Like Einstein says, time works differently when you're traveling at anywhere close to the speed of light, and my people, we sleep the whole journey, or nearly the whole thing. In English, you'd probably call it 'stasis' or 'cryosleep.' But when we set out for Earth, it was 1847 here, so one hundred years is right enough. But I was sleeping for all of it, so by my reckoning, I've lived the same amount of life as you."

Brian nodded. Somehow, it felt better knowing the man whose dick he'd had in his mouth didn't have two full lifetime's worth of experience on him. He circled back to the science. "So, space travel is slow, given the distances you're covering."

Aaron nodded. He pointed to two kernels. "So, if that is the distance between the Earth and the moon, then the distance between Earth and Antares IV is as if we did the drive between here and Washington DC—"

"That's not so bad—"

"—two thousand five hundred and forty-nine times."

Brian closed his eyes as he tried to get his head around those distances.

Aaron paused, chewing his lip. "Space is really big, really empty, so space travel—even really good space travel, and Antarans have some of the best in the galaxy—is cosmically slow."

"All right," Brian said. "So, why did you come here? What happened in 1847? With the whole universe to choose from, what could you possibly see in us?"

Aaron tipped his head to the side, eyes searching. And, for a moment, Brian wasn't sure how he'd ever thought Aaron was human. Humans didn't usually have what looked like gold leaf strewn across their irises. No human had ever looked at him as though he was something precious, something to be protected at all costs.

"Do you really not know?"

Brian's heart dropped. He had an awful feeling it was something horrible.

He thought back to other travelers, those who sought trade, mutual discovery, and intermarriage, those who sought conquest, dominion, and empire. In a hushed voice, he said, "What is it? Is there something here? Something you can't get anywhere else?"

"In a way, yes. But it's not a resource; you have far less plutonium than Antares IV. Nearly none when we landed; a bit more now." Aaron gave a slight smile. "You know they use it as casual-wear jewelry on Antares II? And have the—the slaves do prize fights over wooden trinkets, since trees don't grow on that moon."

He covered his face with his hands and inhaled slowly. His shoulders bowed, and then he turned around to settle his back against Brian's front. "As for why we came here. It's fair to ask. It's good to ask." A slow tremor began working its way across Aaron's body. Brian rubbed his hands down his arms, trying to give what comfort he could. Aaron leaned into it, taking it wholeheartedly. He sounded rough, rushed when he said, "I'm sorry. I haven't had to tell anyone this in a long, long time. All my people, they *know*. They were there. And the people we've met since we crash-landed—"

Brian frowned, detail catching at the back of his mind. "When you crashed, did you land between Roswell and the reservation?" His voice rose with excitement and exasperation. "Is that why your friend—James—is on the reservation? Is that why you have so many rugs with our designs? Was it not a hoax? Was it *real*?"

Aaron coughed and drew one knee close to his chest, arms tight around it, long back arched with misery. The spiraling galaxy of popcorn had stopped where it hung, every star frozen in place. "Oh," Aaron said, and Brian had never heard him sound so bitter. "Oh, no. It's real. The US Army Air Forces caught us as we were on a shallow trajectory, heading down toward Appomattox, and forced us out of the sky." His body shook, but he was still warm.

Brian tried to hold on to him tightly.

"I lost fifteen people, Brian. Friends, shipmates. My...my sister. She was one of the ones who burned on the way down."

Brian reached a shaking hand to tuck a single finger under Aaron's grip, where he squeezed his own wrists white. He pried up one finger and then another when Aaron let him, then another, until Brian had his whole hand in his. Aaron was starting to really shake with the tension of holding himself so, so tightly.

His voice as soft as snowfall, he said, "Oh, *Aaron*," and the other man turned. Brian wrapped his arms around him, bringing his head down to his shoulder. Aaron was silent and motionless for the first time since Brian had met him, only the barest tremor with each carefully modulated breath, just the wetness trickling down his neck.

After a few moments, it passed, as it always did. Aaron sighed, body moving with it more than it had for long minutes. He spoke into the pillows propped up behind Brian's shoulders, settling his knees on either side of Brian's hips.

"That was four years ago. Most of my people escaped the air force; they only killed five of us once we reached the ground. I was—I was the captain. *Am* the captain, once we can get her back up in the air. It took me fifteen minutes to get out of the wreckage, to freeze the bullets right out of the air." He shuddered. "Fifteen minutes, and I lost five more of my people. From there, James—he's good with memories—he convinced them we'd been a weather balloon. Well—" He gave a snort that might have been a sob. "—most of them. He missed Lt. Walter Haut, who sent out the first press release. We got that cleaned up, but you know, rumors only grow."

Brian nodded, searching the stilled galaxy behind Aaron's head for the sense in that. It was believable, of course. *Of course*, the military would force down an unidentified aircraft cruising low over the Southwest. *Of course*, they would approach the craft with guns drawn. He wouldn't be surprised to find his father had been there; it was his base that had sent out the release, his base that had become the laughingstock for such a memorable fuckup.

Aaron uncurled a little, body losing some of its painful tension, meeting Brian's gaze again. "Most of my people, the two hundred and six who survived the crash, found refuge on the reservation. James convinced the tribal elders to let them stay while we healed."

"He used his powers?" Brian asked, voice tight, his mind beginning to spin.

Aaron shook his head, a hard no. "No, never, never for something like that. He offered to trade skills, technology, resources. The tribal council has been wanting to open a ski resort on Sierra Blanca, a hotel, the whole thing. Our people said they could help, save on the building costs, do some of the engineering. It was an offer of help to a sovereign government in exchange for shelter, made in good faith and honored in the same way."

"And you? What were you doing while James was being your diplomat?"

"Well, I was the captain. I had to get my people home. It wasn't supposed to be a one-way trip, and then we landed and—"

He laughed, covering his face a little, fingers trembling just a shade, enough to be visible in the soft firelight. "And we didn't have enough plutonium to get home. The longest half-life for the stuff, any isotope, any version, is eighty-two million years, right?"

Brian nodded.

"But most isotopes are either 14.4 or 87.7 years?"

Another nod.

"Where I grew up, this didn't matter. We were getting bombarded all the time with the stuff. It showed up everywhere. But here, until December 14, 1940, there was *none*. Traces, tiny, itty bitty traces spread through the crust, but functionally, it was an extinct element. Not that we *knew* that. Not that we *thought to test*." His voice was full of self-recrimination. "We weren't exactly a sanctioned mission, weren't exactly overflowing with resources. But in hindsight, it was so *stupid* not to bring enough fuel to go back home once we've finished our research. We just *assumed* it would be here. But when we landed, the amounts in existence were miniscule and tightly, incredibly tightly, controlled."

"We built the first draft of the bomb in 1940."

Aaron nodded, face sobering. "Yeah, that's when you started manufacturing plutonium, but just for weapons. And no matter how good James is, there was no hope of getting it out of those facilities. He can convince a few people a month, not the hundreds we'd need, and certainly not with his powers dimming by the day without plutonium or uranium nearby."

He sighed, running his hands over his face. "It's just—it would be like you all, traveling to another planet and expecting to find wood to burn. It's *everywhere* at home. Even in the high desert, you've got sage that grows old enough, thick enough to make a gnarled walking stick out of eventually. But some places, like Antares II, there's *nothing.* It's all grasses, even giant grasses, like your palm trees. But nothing with rings, nothing like you'd understand wood to be. And maybe you'd plan ahead for that. But what if you'd gone to one planet, a dozen, a *hundred* other planets, and every single one of them had enough wood for you to burn? Maybe you'd stop using up your precious spacecraft storage space on wood. Instead, pack extra medical supplies or testing equipment or, hey, refugees. Escaped slaves."

He covered his face again. "And it wouldn't be *stupid*, precisely. Just an educated risk. And everything in space travel is risky and everything in space travel is hard. So, four or five generations ago, we stopped carrying enough plutonium onboard our research vessels to make a round trip; that's what my ship was before we stole her. A research ship. We brought just enough fuel to get us here. We figured we could harvest as we went. It always worked." He huffed a humorless chuckle. "It always worked *until now.*"

"You didn't send, I don't know, a scouting ship?"

Aaron shook his head, his curls dancing across his forehead.

"So, on Earth, for millennia, the way you've interacted with stars is with your eyes, right? First watching them, then using little bits of glass, then better bits of glass, all the way up to the massive new one at Palomar Observatory—"

"The Hale Telescope? Five meters if it's an inch."

Aaron smiled, and it moved softly across his face. "Yeah. So, another species, a few galaxies over, they developed—well, I think of it like an early warning system. Like for a tsunami, to give people enough time to get to higher ground. But theirs is for things like novas and solar flares and planetary collisions. Each node in the network takes information in and distributes it outward, far faster than the speed of light using those thin spaces we talked about. Each node just receiving and repeating, repeating and receiving. We call them satellites."

Brian nodded. "Like a three-dimensional blanket, with warps and wefts and whatever you'd call the thing that goes between the intersections of the warps and wefts on the z-axis."

Aaron kissed his forehead. "Exactly, my brilliant man. Exactly."

He kept going. "Now, that early-warning system was only for galactically large things. But through centuries of negotiations and treaties, we got permission to build our own network into it, add capacity and piggyback on what was already there. Think of it like if someone decided to build a massive highway system in the United States. Some interstate highways would parallel state highways and county highways, others would cross over them, others would take them over entirely."

Brian nodded. He'd heard conversations about something like that being planned in DC.

Aaron continued. "Our entire astronomical navigation process relies on that massive network of receivers. Fifteen generations ago, we used plutonium-fired engines on small, superfast satellites. No living things on board meant we weren't bound by the physics of living things, and we could send them anywhere we wanted to, as fast as we could. They're stationed around thousands and thousands of planets, starting with those most likely to harbor life from our flyby guesses but including your oddballs like Mars or Venus."

"Wait, there's no life on Mars?"

Aaron smiled. "Not that we have heard."

Brian paused, trying to think this through. "All right. So, you started traveling to earth in 1847 and crash-landed here in 1947. Something you heard in that year must have brought you here?"

Aaron nodded, looking to the side. "We started planning a bit before then."

"But radio wasn't invented until you'd been flying for over thirty years? Wait—did you hear the *telegraph*?"

Aaron shook his head, pained. "I wish it had been something like that. But the thing was, we weren't a scientific mission. It was—" He looked down at his hands twisting the lavender quilt. "You're going to think this is *so stupid*."

Brian gently gripped Aaron's chin and lifted it to meet his gaze. "You're a lot of things, Aaron of Antares IV. But I would never in hundred years call anything you do 'stupid.' If you don't want to tell me, that is okay too."

Aaron closed his eyes, shoulders hunching. His voice was rough, a near-whisper. "We're abolitionists."

"'Abolitionist'? Like Frederick Douglass?"

Aaron's eyes flicked open and caught Brian's before dropping again. "Yeah. I'd mentioned earlier, Antares IV—actually, a lot of the planets we visited—have slavery. Legal, people-are-property slavery."

He shuddered as his arms went around his stomach, rocked into his own tight grip. "It's binary, in every system we've visited. Every culture we've ever heard of, are ever taught about. Societies, they have slavery—or they don't. The ones without it never had it. The ones with it never give it up. Like I told you when you asked me why I liked 'race records.' You can—"

He choked, body shaking, for a moment before he forced himself to say, "There aren't a lot of ways to keep a massive minority, or sometimes even the majority, of a population without rights. But that network of satellites, both the old network and the new one, they can take pictures, send them back. We can tell how many bodies are on a planet. And we could—well, my sister and I—" His face tightened again. "She was the engineer. She stole time on every single one of those satellites, used their imaging, and scanned for places, for worlds, where we could see people shipping other people massive distances, packed together in conditions no soul would choose. Slave auctions, plantations, chains. So many *chains*." He shuddered. "Slavery, it looks the same. Most places. There's shipping routes, places people are stolen from, places they're brought to. The conditions of transfer look much the same, can be picked up by a computer program."

"So she looked for slave planets and free planets?"

Aaron frowned. "She was looking for one specific thing. Just one. Worlds where some places were free and others were not. Where there were places with transit routes, like triangle the transatlantic slave trade made to only some parts of the planet. And places that were nearby but *not* part of that route. She could tell from the routes, from the *weight*, which ships were brutalizing humans and which were carrying cotton. She looked for worlds where those shipping routes *changed*. Places where enslaved people were forced to travel to at one time, and then *no longer were*." His breath rattled in his throat. "She was looking for hope, for evidence of change. We all were, all of us who wanted to end slavery on Antares IV."

Aaron looked up into Brian's eyes before tipping his head forward, forehead close and tight to Brian's. "And Earth was it. The only place we found, the only world in a thousand worlds where some nations enslaved people and some didn't, where slavery used to thrive in some places even within countries and then stopped." He was quiet for a moment. "So we came here. To figure out how you did it, to ask the questions those silent pictures could not answer. We could read the patterns, see the *shape* of your change. But we couldn't read your history or meet your leaders, couldn't speak your languages or sing your freedom songs. So we came here."

His expression brightened a little. "While we were sleeping, you all started sending out radio waves. The closer we got, our ship started to pick up more and more, feed them to us in our sleep, hum them to us in our dreams, teaching us your language, your music. The first radio broadcasts were played into our sleeping containers, the first TV too. We were slowing down for six months, everyone learning Diné and English and French and Spanish, learning to love the music. I had to ban people from singing 'Somewhere Over the Rainbow' in the galley." A fractured smile moved across his face.

Brian's vision swam. His head felt light, hands tingling. He said, his voice cracking, "That's really amazing. It's just such a cruel world, isn't it? We never seem to win."

Aaron pressed his forehead tighter to Brian's, as though he were trying to whisper this truth into him. "They're all cruel worlds. But there's bravery and kindness and justice everywhere too. There has to be, or else what's the point?" He kissed first one of Brian's cheeks and then the other. "And if we can't find justice, we create it. Sometimes we just need help figuring out how."

For a long moment, they looked into each other's faces, each searching and finding what they were looking for.

"So," Brian said at last over the lowly crackling fire, "how'd we do it? How'd we end legal slavery?"

Aaron's face grew still, fingers gentle on the back of Brian's neck. "Some of your people fought a war, Brian. And we've got to get off this planet to go home and start one."

Chapter Fifteen: T-28 Days

As often as I call; the flight of wings

Surprises empty air, while out of clay

The golden-gourded vine unwatered springs.

I have inhaled impossibility,

And walk at such an angle, all the stars

have hung their carnival chains of light for me:

There is a streetcar runs from here to Mars.

I shall be seeing you, my darling, there,

Or at the burning bush in Harvard Square.

—Adrienne Rich, excerpt from "Vertigo," 1951

November 22, 1951

They took a few minutes to catch their breaths. Aaron got something bubbling and warm on the fire while Brian restoked the amber coals. The idea of discussing a war just felt too big for the room; he had so many questions, but he wanted to ask them right, not break this fragile thing they'd been building between them, that they both so clearly wanted to keep going.

They'd both, pointedly, refused to buy anything even vaguely Thanksgiving-ish at the market aside from the cider spices, so what Aaron had over the stove was a thick vegetable stew, spices floating and curling out of their canisters without his hands touching them as Brian watched.

"This'll be ready by lunchtime," Aaron murmured.

Brian frowned. "What time is it now?"

Aaron cocked his head. "Feels like about 8:00 a.m.?"

Brian quirked a half smile, standing up as he dusted his hands off on his jeans. "About time for you to take me out."

Aaron raised his eyebrows. "Yeah? Where to, Airman?"

"Well," Brian said, stretching his arms high above his head, feeling the long lines of tension release into the quiet air. "Not back to my shitty barracks, that's for damn sure. We have four more days in this cabin, and I intend to make good use of every one of them."

"Yeah?" Aaron said, a flicker of flirt about him, and Brian smiled.

"Maybe that, too, later." Aaron stepped toward him, and Brian watched as his toes sunk into the thick rugs as he stood an arm's breadth from Brian.

Brian took it. Took the moment, took the time to study him over. No furtive glances, no half-remembered looks. Aaron's body was strong, lambent in the firelight, shoulders broad and muscled, biceps thick enough Brian wasn't sure he could reach around them with two hands. His muscles played under the skin of his forearms as he hitched his hands in his pockets. He had hair on his lower belly, up to his chest. Brian let his admiration fill his face, so by the time he met Aaron's eyes, they shone with heat.

"Later would be good," Brian confirmed, gazing into Aaron's golden-flecked eyes.

Aaron's hand reached toward his hip and then stilled, stopped in midair.

Brian caught it, drew him in, and laid Aaron's palm against his own bare side. "But maybe we get out of the cabin for a few hours first? You said something about a hot spring?"

"I did. It's back toward the hills. About a twenty-minute walk. It's—" He hedged. "—it's nothing massive, not like when we drove through a quarter mile of hot springs and rivers and streams in Thermopolis on the way here. Just some tubs sunk into the ground." He paused again. "I was about to say I carried them out on horseback, but I didn't. I used my..." He twiddled his fingers.

Brian reached for his hand and touched his lips to his knuckles. "That's something I'd like to see."

Aaron's said softly, almost a whisper, "You don't find my abilities disturbing?" He paused as Brian kissed his palm, tongue flicking out to taste the lifeline running strong across it, then added, stumbling, "They're not very human."

"What can I say? I like science fiction. I think they're incredible."

"Oh. Okay." Aaron seemed like he was trying to hide a smile.

They got dressed and buttoned each other into their thick winter jackets. Brian took Aaron's black cowboy hat off the hook on the wall, distracting him with soft touches every time he tried to mount a rescue operation for it. He still had it on his head when they stepped out into the silent morning, laughing as sparks of snow flicked down from the sky to crowd Aaron's golden curls.

"So, why Wyoming?" Brian asked, and Aaron glanced over at him, amber eyes blinking away the snow that circled around them.

Aaron turned back to the path that led through a thin smattering of trees between two low hills. "I wasn't lying when I said I'd worked as a ranch hand, worked the rodeo circuit," he said, waving his hands. "I don't like lying, and I'm not particularly good at it. As you can tell."

Brian traced a hand down his back, knowing the thick jacket would mask most of the contact but wanting him to know he was here.

"After we escaped the military, I split us up into groups. Those of us who knew enough of the science to be able to pass as nuclear physicists, and those who didn't. We went to the places the news reports told us had the best chance of having plutonium or being able to develop it." He ruffled the snow out of his hair. "We've got folks at Oak Ridge and Cal, and UW had a good program, small enough a transfer with the kinds of transcripts James could build for me would get right in." Aaron shrugged. "We don't have doctorates on Antares IV; it's more of an apprenticeship system. But I was about at the right level. And, I mean, there are a lot of places you all are a bit behind. Can you believe people here still think the universe is only 4.55 billion years old?"

"That's what I heard from Clair Patterson at Caltech—"

Aaron shook his head, quirking a smile in the wan sunlight. "Try thirteen to fourteen billion years. Anyway, I could fit into that environment pretty well. There's no expectation physics PhD candidates will know anything about history or culture. How to act in public. Pretty much anything. And it's not like I had a lot of money for socializing."

"No alchemists on Antares IV? You actually have to work for money like everyone else?"

"Hah, no. I was telling the truth about paying for my cabin with casino winnings; they're a little bit easier with TK. With telekinesis." He screwed up his face. "But cheating casinos usually means cheating tribes, so I try not to do it if I have any other choice. Thus, working as a cowboy. We have to work shit jobs for drinking money like everyone else."

Brian's step faltered, and he recovered, but Aaron noticed.

"What?"

"Why do you still have slavery? I can't imagine a world where everyone has TK letting themselves be enslaved—" He shut his mouth, his own words echoing back to him, warping, twisting inside him. "I can't believe I said that. I've heard that, exactly that, so many times. *'Why don't you fight back. You're a man now, why would you let— If you were a real man—'*" His vision was blacking out, body shaking, the cold air hard, tight in his lungs, his hands icy with it. But Aaron's hot hands were on his face, his eyes close to his.

"Breathe. Name me five noble gases."

"Helium, neon, argon, krypton, xenon."

"Good, now four constellations."

"Sagittarius, Capricorn, Libra, Scorpio."

"Three Southwestern tribal nations?"

"Diné, Hopituh Shi-nu-mu, Abachi."

"Two science fiction authors."

"Andre Norton and Heinlein."

Aaron closed the gap between them, resting his forehead against Brian's as the panic receded. "And one incredibly brave airman who I'm falling for."

Brian blinked; he hadn't realized he'd closed his eyes. He took a step closer, the snow crunching under his feet. He laid a soft, chilly kiss on Aaron's mouth, humming into the sweet smell of him. "Me too."

Their breath clouded around them, and for a moment, the wind seemed to still, the snow seemed to pause, and it was the two of them in a bubble of their own making. It felt magical until Brian looked up and realized the snow was catching on the air just outside his reach.

He huffed a wondering chuckle. "You made us a snow umbrella."

"You seemed to be going through enough without getting snowflakes down your collar; I know how much you hate snow."

Brian nodded, getting his bearings back, and said quietly, "I might be able to tolerate some snow if you're here."

After another long minute, he wrapped his hand around Aaron's wrist, getting him walking down the trail again. The snow continued to cascade around them, Aaron's invisible barrier keeping them dry even as they stepped under the drip-needled pines.

A wall of logs cleverly jointed together enclosed the hot spring, protecting the three tubs sunk into the ground. A network of ceramic half-pipes came out of the hillside, snowflakes melting nearly as fast as they fell, steam curling up into overhanging pines.

Brian ran his fingers up the log fence, getting a smear of sap on his fingertips for his trouble. Hot water began to gush into one of the tubs. The design, a series of overflows, allowed tubs with three different temperatures from the same source, each cooling the water for the next one.

"You made this?"

Aaron glanced up where he'd been messing with the rocks at the source of the spring. He ducked his head and nodded. "It's just so fucking cold here. The first time I came up, I thought I was going to die. It was only May, but it was not pleasant." He patted the log wall. "But I found this place when I was out exploring and realized I could make it better. Make it good."

"You did," Brian said with a smile. "Now, where should I put my boots?"

They undressed as the tubs filled. Aaron took the hottest tub while Brian took the cooler one, still a pulse-quickening heat but not as much of a shock as the other man seemed to seek.

Brian settled into the warming curve of the tub, letting the water tickle its way up the short hairs on the nape of his neck. He rested his head on the edge of the tub, curled white enamel hard against his bones. He looked up, the steel-gray sky above seeming so close.

"So, you said you wanted to steal all the plutonium."

Aaron sputtered as if he'd inhaled a lungful of sulfur-tinged water. Brian wondered if Antarans could breathe underwater; he hoped Aaron wasn't trying to find out how to avoid the question.

"I mean, not all?" Aaron said, finally. "And we've been helping the nuclear program a lot. We wouldn't have as much as we have now without—"

"Breathe, Aaron." Brian was glad to be the calm one this time, deciding the course of the next few months as he heard himself say, "I'm not going to turn you in. I just need to know your plan."

"My—" There was a pause and then the sound of approaching feet. "Scoot up," Aaron said.

Brian tipped his head back and cocked it at him, wrinkling his nose when Aaron dripped on him. "This is a one-man tub."

"There's more than enough room. It's seven feet long if it's an inch. You need to—"

And Aaron started poking his chilly foot behind Brian's back, so Brian had the choice of either getting stepped on or leaning forward; he grumblingly chose the latter. Aaron slid in behind him, all slick skin and heat.

Brian completely forgot the question.

Aaron's knees tucked in close to his sides, Brian's hands settling on his shins. He flexed his toes in the water, watching little bubbles form and drift upward in the cloudy sunlight.

"So," Aaron rumbled behind him, and oh, but Brian could feel his words before he heard them. "My plan."

Brian twisted around as much as he could manage, squinting at the other man. "Are you trying to distract me?"

"No, but if I'm going to be interrogated, I want to be cuddled while it happens."

"I wasn't—"

"I know Captain Flynn when I hear his voice. I can practically see your captain's stripes shining out of your skin right now."

Brian would have flushed anew if he could, but between Aaron's naked body and the hot tub, his blood was all already under assignment. Still, he tried to keep his voice reasonable, balanced. "If you get what you need, I get fired. You could take the first batch of plutonium we produce at the scale you need and disappear down to the rez; no big mystery who took it. Given everyone and their cousin Jan knows we spend time together, that will sure as shit look like a conspiracy after the deed is done. Not blue ticketed, but a dishonorable discharge seems pretty likely. Maybe sent to Leavenworth. A yellow ticket might be easier to explain than a blue one, but it's not my goal. So. What's your plan to keep that from happening?"

Aaron paused, long fingers tracing patterns on the enamel tub. He said, so softly the gurgle of the hot spring nearly hid it, "I thought you might come with me. Join my crew as military advisor, as an equal.

There's no one that would look twice at us, or even if we weren't together. You're brilliant and would find a role you'd enjoy on the ship with ease. Astronavigation, security, defense, weapons, diplomacy, nuclear physics. You have so many options, and we need the help. Some of my people intend to stay, some were lost in the crossing. My friend Mara, she's a biologist, has been working on a serum that will make any human immune to radiation, so nothing in our ship or home environment will poison you."

"Why's she doing that?"

"She has a lover on the reservation," Aaron said, and Brian could hear his smile. "Wanted to make sure she was safe if she chose to come along. My people would treat you as one of our own." He'd sped up as though trying to finish his case before Brian interrupted again. "As an equal. I thought you could come see Antares, help us free our world. It's a fucked up place in many ways. But with your brain and your bravery, you could help us fix it. It's the work of a lifetime, something I couldn't expect you to know an answer to just like this, but—" He met Brian's eyes. "That was my plan."

"How long have you been planning this?"

"Since the moment you kept me from flailing into the testing chamber. You don't take my shit, Brian, but you also know how to bend without breaking. You set your rules, and you hold to them, but you also let yourself change your mind based on convincing input. That's pretty much my ideal for a friend or a lover. And the chance to get to introduce you to my crew, to people who would let you be who you are without fear of recrimination or violence? With active welcome and support? Making sure you got to have that within your lifetime, that would be incredible to experience alongside you."

Brian breathed, filling his lungs until they ached with the cold, crisp air; he imagined breathing air made by something other than trees and tasting food grown on another world. He considered Aaron and blue tickets and all the things he could learn flying in a spaceship powered by plutonium and what it would mean to free an entire people from slavery.

"Yes."

Aaron's stomach tensed against Brian's back, his hands slipping into the tub to wrap around Brian's waist. "Just like that?"

"Would I get to study physics? Go to the stars? Know things no one else on this planet will know within my lifetime? See worlds and ways of being no one on earth could conceive of, use my mind and my heart and my body to help fix real problems in the world?" The pain in Brian's voice surprised him, but what he said felt true.

"Yes."

"And I would be free to love who I want? Be treated as an equal by the people I work with, no one making cracks about my skin or hometown or who I am?"

"Yes, except for the hometown bit. The crew's saved up a fair number of alien jokes, and they love to try them out on people. But they'll run out of steam eventually, particularly if you don't rise to the bait." There was something warm, spreading in that tone.

Brian shrugged. "Then if we can get the plutonium production online, I'm in."

"That's a big 'if.'" He sighed, puffing against Brian's nape. "It's not going fast, the research. It's hard work making a new element. But Brian, me taking what I need to get my people home? Like you said, that would be violating every rule you're there to enforce. I wouldn't just be bringing radiation out with me by accident. I would be bringing it on purpose."

Brian frowned, rubbing his fingertips against the calluses on his heel. "We bury enough of the spent fuel out in the pit outside, as long as you're not smashing the lab on your way out, they can replace anything you take. And honestly, it seems like paying you for your expertise."

He leaned his head back against Aaron's shoulder. "I've known what it is to be without a home. And to need to get back. I've been trapped, Aaron." He paused, gritting his teeth trying to think how to say it. "I've been trapped before, and I wouldn't wish that on someone else. If this is about getting you home, helping your planet, isn't that bigger than us and the Russians? Isn't that something that might be worth bending a few rules for?"

"You might go to prison."

"If I didn't come with you, yeah, I might." Brian let it hang in the air, the possibility, the hope. "I trust you, Aaron. I don't have some empirical reason to, and there's a lot of history to suggest I shouldn't; but I have hope. So I trust you're not going to hurt me, and you're not going to hurt my planet. Maybe that trust is misplaced, but I don't really want to live in a world where I'm wrong about this. About you."

Aaron tightened his arms around Brian's waist, forehead against back of his neck. "Brian Flynn, you are a whole lot of something else. You say things, and I just—do you hear how you sound?"

"Like a traitor?" Brian muttered, body tight against Aaron's, reaching for his hands.

Aaron took them, holding him close and safe. "Like the best person I've met so far," he said, low and sure. "I wish most of the people my people have met were like you."

"I remember what it's like to be trapped. Not able to get where you want to go."

Aaron shrugged. "A lot of people have been caged. That doesn't mean they try and stop anyone else from going through it."

Brian nodded before glancing up at the sky, clouds and sun still obscuring the stars. "Antares, that's in the Scorpio constellation, right?"

Aaron nodded, easing back, palms flat, safe under Brian's pecs and well above his navel.

Brian asked, "It would take one hundred years for us to get there, for you to get back, right?"

Aaron nodded again, dripping hand raising to trace a flight pattern. "We'd be awake the first six months, enough to get the course in, get settled, get caught up on what was happening. Since we left, not much has— Slavery, it—"

He hesitated, and Brian tensed, not sure where he was going with this. "It keeps societies in stasis," Aaron said, voice flat. "When you asked how so many people are enslaved in a world where there's people like me? The powers aren't evenly distributed. The plutonium tends to gather at the poles, caught in our seasonal storms and swept up there. The tribes that evolved and moved up there developed the first radiation resistance and the powers associated with it. The people who lived at the equators have the same aptitude, the same potential, but they're kept away from the radiation that would help them grow the powers. Billions of people, doing work by hand I could accomplish in seconds with my mind. And the powerful have all these excuses, these reasons. Like your noblesse oblige, they think running schools or designing new transport systems for the powerless negates the horror of it. People in the cities keep the plutonium in special buildings only they can access, while people in their houses scrub floors on their knees all day for no pay." He paused. "It's personal. With me."

Brian started, not knowing how to ask. "Were you..."

He gave a harsh laugh. "No, but some of my people on the ship were. They escaped. Courage like you wouldn't believe. I grew up in a nice house with slaves we were supposed to call by their last names." He cleared his throat. "I—" His body shook with tremors.

Brian turned, kneeled up in the tub, and brushed Aaron's hair off his face as he struggled to find the words. "You don't have to tell me."

Aaron's eyes were wide, searching. "But, it's important; it's about me, about this mission. You need to know—"

Brian's mind worked fast, the look on Aaron's face more than enough to convince him whatever Aaron was about to say wasn't worth the pain it would cause him. "Is there anyone else who can tell me? One of your crew?"

Aaron looked relieved, as if he'd been preparing to deadlift the reactor, and Brian had offered a hand. "Yeah. Yeah, I can call when we get back."

"How do you do that? Is it a kind of radio?"

The shadow passed from Aaron's face, his bright smile returning. "Oh, no. You'll love this."

He waved his hand, and his wallet floated up from his jeans pocket. Out slipped a card, like a business card, but stiffer.

"Is that a Diners Club card?" Brian asked, frowning.

"No. It's like a tiny radio. Let's call it a communicator. But instead of bouncing off the ionosphere, it uses a satellite. It encodes and retransmits the signal."

"Okay. So your people use that to communicate?"

Aaron nodded. "So, we can call James, and I think he'll have you talk to Mara. She knows what happened. To me. To us."

"Okay," Brian said, not sure that would work, but certain he didn't want Aaron walking through whatever hell was haunting him. "All right, when we get back, we can do that."

"All right." A small smile drifted up to the surface. "We're a pair, aren't we?"

Brian sat back, legs tangled with Aaron's. "A couple of shell-shocked queers."

"But we look great for our age."

Brian huffed out a laugh. Then he held out his hand. "I'm getting pretty wrinkled in here. How about we dry off and head back for that stew?"

"You just want to see me get out of the bath."

"That is the God's honest truth," he replied with a grinning leer.

Chapter Sixteen: T-28 Days

He tasted till his palate knew their shape
The country's proudest bean, its master grape.
He never talked of fields remembered green,
Or seasons in his land of origin.

And still he felt there lay a bridgeless space
Between himself and natives of the place.
Their laughter came when his had long abated;
He struggled in allusions never stated.

—Adrienne Rich, excerpt from "By No Means Native," 1951

November 22, 1951

The stew was excellent, hot and spicy and filling. They ate it cross-legged in front of the fire, knees touching, communicator on the bed.

"Where's all the wood coming from?" Brian asked, and Aaron smiled.

"I had a bad day. Three summers ago, when I was in the middle of writing my thesis. One of the guys in the lab kept going on and on about the master-slave manipulator; that's what some people call the tools for handling the nuclear material. Wouldn't stop it, had all these awful jokes—" He scowled. "Well, you can guess what word he used. He just went on and on about it, and I—I took the rest of the week, came over here." He looked a little shamefaced. "I took out a hillside of pine saplings with that particular tantrum. I made myself chop them by hand, though, took the whole weekend. It takes a year per inch of wood for them to dry properly to be good firewood, so this is the first winter I've been able to do something good with that particular outburst."

Brian shook his head. "I don't know what you could need me for, with powers like that, in this war you're thinking of starting."

"*Everyone* has powers like mine there if they have access to plutonium. So it's all down to strategy, diplomacy maybe, even." He gave a wry grin. "Things I'm too much of a blunt instrument to handle well. But you—you've survived this place for long enough, survived large organizations who're trying to keep you from taking root. Thrived even." He ran an admiring hand down the muscles of Brian's arm. "So I think you'd be able to plan, to organize us in a way that might work."

Brian frowned. "I'm not some Patton, who can sweep in with the Third Army and retake the Rhine. Militaries are massive organizations;

no one person can replicate them."

Aaron smiled. "I get that. But you'll bring skills no one else in our group of activists, scientists, and refugees has."

"Speaking of," Brian said, surprising Aaron with a kiss before levering himself up. "Before I get knocked out by this hot fire and soup, I should have that conversation with James." Aaron's eyes shuttered a little, and Brian regretted it. He bent down, palm going to the other man's cheek. "I just don't want it hanging between us. I want us to be able to—" He glanced at the rumpled quilts. "—focus on other things the rest of this trip, while we can share our time together. Who knows how long it will be until we can have time like this again."

Aaron's scrambled up. "All right," he said, pulling the communicator out of his pocket. He did something, flipping it open. "The antenna is inside and needs to be at least seven centimeters long to call on the correct frequency."

Brian nodded. That made sense; frequency length was why military vehicles had those long whip antennae.

The screen lit up like someone had placed a bright light behind it, and a grid of circles appeared. Aaron touched one of the red ones and placed the device to his ear.

He pointed to the end of the rectangle near his mouth, whispering, "There's a microphone here."

Brian watched, reaching out to trail his fingers across the buttons of Aaron's shirt idly. Aaron's eyelids fluttered closed, and then he grabbed Brian's fingers with an admonishing look.

"James?" he asked, and Brian heard another voice, tinny, as if on a telephone. "Yeah, I told him. Well, go back one hundred years, and *you* be the captain rather than the chief negotiator, and then *you* can tell me what to do."

And after a pause: "Yes, I know you don't have a time machine. Yes—you think I don't understand the risks? Anyway. Yes. Yes. You can talk to him. No, not now. Because you're like a tub of iced *stissik* to the face when you're like this, and I don't want you to scare him away. *Yes, you would.* Can you put Mara on? Yes. *Yes*, she gets to talk to him first. Yes. On account of your bad personality and worse attitude, James. All right."

He covered the microphone with his palm. "He's getting her."

"What is '*stissik*'?"

Aaron squinted, as if thinking in another language, saying, "Kind of like ice cream. But with berries? Yeah, berries."

Another voice came through, and Aaron returned his attention to the device.

"Hey, Mara," he said, and his entire tone relaxed. "Yeah, I'm doing okay. Yeah, I told him." He hitched a smile, soft like Brian hadn't seen from him except when directed at him. "Thanks. I knew you'd be proud. Tell James I'll talk to him when he's out of this snit."

Another pause. "Okay, fine, I'll tell him myself. Anyway, I was telling Brian about home and about why we left, and I started, you know. Yeah. And he asked if he could hear it from someone else, to spare me going through it."

Aaron glanced up at Brian and then back down again. "Yeah, he's a good guy. I told him you might—" He sighed with relief. "Thanks, Mara."

He said the next words while looking directly at Brian. "Mara Enwine of Antares II, may I introduce to you Captain Brian Flynn of Roswell, New Mexico."

He handed the communicator over.

When Brian held the device up to his ear, it had none of the static and crackle of the radios he used at EBT-I, and even less than the phone lines.

"It's good to meet you," came a woman's deep voice from the top of the device, older, as if she was his mother's age. "Aaron has been shy to share, but what little I've heard about you has been very impressive."

Brian blurted out before he could stop himself, "Shy? *Aaron*? That seems a rather, uh, alien concept."

Her laugh rang out clearly from the microphone, and Aaron's eyebrows shot up. He reached for the device, an argument on his lips, but Brian stood and skipped out of the way. He snagged his heavy coat and headed for the truck. His key jingled against his dog tags, glinting in the warm yellow light flowing through the cabin door before Aaron shut it to keep the warm in. By the time Mara was done chuckling, he was in the cab with the heat going. He looked out at a starlit plain overhung by a crescent moon as she gathered herself to respond.

"I *like* you," Mara said, and Brian's cheeks warmed. He'd never had the chance to meet the family of someone he'd been with before, and he wasn't sure how to respond.

"So." Her voice softened. "Aaron said you were asking about why we left."

"I was."

After a long pause, she said, "He told you he came here to figure out how Gaians ended slavery?"

"He did."

"In the Antares system, like here, it's hard to see what is so cruel about a society when you're inside it. What needs to be changed. But for Aaron, that was never the problem. He could always see a better world. *Just* out of our grasp. Antares IV was brutal and unfair, and Aaron, as soon as he realized it, dove into fixing it. He quit his engineering program. He hid people. Got them free. For years. And one day, he trusted the wrong person. He invited a volunteer in, and she told the trafficker—that's what we call it because they're trafficking in people—and she took them. She convinced them all they were safe to go, and then they were all taken back, taken where Aaron could not get them. He couldn't get them, and he knew they were being hurt, and if he hadn't trusted her, he would have—"

Mara made a sound, soft, so soft it must have hurt. "It—it was bad. What happened to the people he'd meant to help. Who he thinks he failed."

"But what he did—it wasn't him who hurt them. It was this person—"

"Yes, but to Aaron, and to anyone Aaron worked with, these were *his* people. He had a responsibility to them, to others like him. He had that responsibility, and he failed them."

"So he, what, ran away?"

"Maybe? It's hard to explain. He cared so much. And failed so badly and in such a way that people got hurt. And he couldn't live with a world that was like that. That was that cruel. That ridiculous. He needed to be better than that. And he was hurt. Right? He was hurt by not being able to save them, by being too trusting. So it's a lot, for him to tell you. About us. To bring you into our secret when he knows how hurt people can become if trust is shared with the wrong person. But he did what he did. He dealt with that fear of betrayal by just being himself *even louder*. Being himself *even harder*. It was rough for him, for a long time. To be this *kind thing* in this world of grit and torment."

For a long moment, Brian thought he could hear the wind moving across her microphone.

"So, that's what happened," Mara continued. "Aaron lost people.

He lost *himself*. He decided to find the answers outside, to take people, those he could find, so far away no one could take them back. He recruited his sister, got her to use her technical skills to help. Those of us in his crew, who survived and who didn't, some of us were enslaved. Like me. Like James. Some were abolitionists, activists like Aaron and Sara, his sister. All of them want freedom from slavery, for ourselves and everyone on our world."

"And do you think you know how to do it?"

She made a pleased hum. "It's strange how obvious things become from a distance. Aaron had it in his head what a world without slavery would look like. But he didn't know how to get there; politics and diplomacy and movement-building *really* aren't his thing. Now, we've seen what it took—the Underground Railroad, the novels, the war. The ongoing resistance, what still needs doing. And we've got our transmitter stations set up on a dozen reservations, refugees who've integrated into the communities here, who will stay here long after we leave, researching and sending updates."

"He's talking about starting a war."

"It is what worked for you all."

"But not everyone fought in it."

She considered that, then said, "I'm not sure I understand what—"

Brian kept going. "In the Civil War, rich people bought their way out of fighting, paid poor Irish boys to take their place. That's what happened to my great, great grandfather on my father's side and hundreds of thousands of men, women, and—" He tried to remember the word. "—probably nonbinary people too. Though I don't think they're counted the right way in the census." He frowned. "War is hell, and I wouldn't wish it on anyone, not if there is *any* other option."

A long silence followed, and then she said, "I see what he sees in you. Not afraid to argue, quick to pick up new cultural norms, passion informed by history, and a clear sense of justice. I don't know if war will be'the right course of action, but imagine the hell your country would have been *without* the Civil War."

Brian did, thinking of boats and chains and cracking whips.

Her voice was softer when she said, "We've had four years to study and to learn—from Americans, from Haitians, from former colonies and colonizers. Every one of us who was not a scientist has been out, learning all we can, collecting, planning, thinking. I think you can be a part of synthesizing those plans, making them into something real."

There was a rustle on the other end, as if she was moving her device to her shoulder. "We need to get the plutonium to go home first though. Those of us who want to go. For some, this place is the home they've always wanted. The freedom and the safety they've always deserved. They'll stay, keep building the lives they've been living. This world has the kinds of freedoms and the home they'd hoped for. It's not perfect; no world is. But we can protect ourselves from violence, hide ourselves from the laws that so bind and ruin the lives of people outside the mainstream here. And sometimes you find a better home far, far beyond your own borders than the one you grew up hoping for.

"But there are those who wish to return, who want to complete their mission or who simply wish to be buried in their home soil, for their eyes to touch one last time the purple horizon of Antares IV. We're the ones rebuilding the ship; we're the reason Aaron is at EBT-I in the first place."

Brian wondered what it would be like to be trapped on a hostile island, regardless of whether you'd journeyed there for research or a new life. There was a difference between disassembling your ship and turning it into your pioneer village and having the option taken away from you. He imagined what it had been like to spend four years on that kind of island. And he imagined what it would be like to stay.

"All you need is our plutonium."

"Well, I would say *our* plutonium given how many of the US's advances in the past years have been with our covert help," Mara said, a wry smile in her voice." But sure, the plutonium is a missing piece."

"We haven't got it in production yet."

"True. But if Aaron can steal a ship and recruit a crew and survive comets and a crash landing and the bizarre fixation this century has with sexual partners and practices, I think he'll be able to figure the science out."

A small smile moved across his face, and he glanced up at the field of stars he could see through the windshield. "That sounds like Aaron."

"It does," she replied. And after a moment, he considered turning off the truck to head inside, when she continued cautiously, "Aaron hasn't told me any details, hasn't violated your privacy. But he told me your name and where you're from. Captain Brian Flynn of Roswell, New Mexico." Another moment. "Any chance you're related to a Colonel Flynn?"

And Brian was falling, gripping the edge of the seat with his free hand, trying to hold himself upright. "I—yes. That is my father."

Another pause, delicate this time. But when Mara spoke, her voice was clear, hard. "He's been the lead on our case, our crash. We had no idea you would be posted at EBT-I; if we'd known, we would have kept Aaron a thousand miles away from you. We wouldn't have risked him with someone raised in that man's house."

Brian tensed, but her tone stayed calm and open.

"But, like always, he's taken the leap. So I'll take it with him and tell you. Colonel Flynn has been hunting us. Hounding the tribal leaders, ignoring their bans on military access to their lands. He was at the crash site, the first night. He was one of the men with weapons, guns. James modified his memory but, when Flynn saw the press release, it came back. James was just so tired, he wasn't able to do his best. And we've never gotten close enough to fix it." Brian's shoulders were hunching, heart battering against his sternum. "We think he's closing in. We've moved farther into the backcountry, hiding to give Aaron time to finish since EBT-I is further along than any of the other projects."

"How much time do you think you have?"

"A month if we're lucky."

Brian clenched his fist until the blood left his knuckles. "If I knew how to help you, I would."

She made a thoughtful sound. "You know, Brian, I believe you would. I wish we had a chance to get to know each other outside of a time crunch. There's so many better ways to pitch you our culture and society than over a call like this." She continued, voice getting warmer. "We have these dances, this music? You would love it, Brian. I really think you would."

"I hope I get to join you all someday."

"Me too," Mara said.

Brian looked out at the horizon, the impossibly tall mountains, their roots deep into the earth.

"Aaron told you we'll be bringing other humans with us?" Mara asked.

"He did. Something about a serum that shields us from radiation?"

Mara gave a fond snort. "Trust a physicist to misunderstand biologists every day and twice on Sunday. It's an epigenetic converter, using our DNA and yours to modify your genes to provide you the same level of protection as we receive from the radioactive elements we evolved to survive.”

Brian smiled, just a touch, at the excitement in her voice. “Could I eat uranium for breakfast?”

“For—” She chuckled. “Not without replacing your teeth. Why do you ask?”

“It’s something Aaron always says, since the first week I met him. Just trying to see what’s real and what’s not.”

“Nearly everything with him is real,” Mara said, tone sobering. “He’s really the worst liar I’ve ever met. Only the extreme vulnerability of his crew was enough to motivate him to do as much lying as he’s done.”

“Thinking back on it, he *did* try to tell me at least three times that he was an alien.”

“Sounds like him. Any other questions?”

“Will I get powers, like Aaron’s, if I go through with the treatment?”

“No one’s shown powers yet, but who knows, maybe that’s because of a lack of plutonium here. We’ll have to see.” She kept going. “The side effects are minimal, but there’ve been some changes in eyesight since we perceive an increased range of colors from what humans evolved to see. For some reason, Jill’s found she can’t smell blueberries anymore. But it’s possible she’s teasing me.”

“Well, I would hate to trade smelling blueberries for being able to travel to the stars,” Brian said, and Mara laughed.

“And a sense of humor too! Excellent. I can’t wait to meet you.”

“You too.” Brian glanced at the cabin. “But I should head inside. If I had to guess, Aaron is either climbing the walls in anticipation or cooking up a storm, and we need our supplies to last through the end of the weekend.”

"Go check in on him, and give him my love, okay?"

"I will. Thank you, Mara."

"Thank *you*. Oh, wait, let me give you my regular phone number. You can call me anytime, to ask questions about Antares or about our work. It's important you have a safety net, people who know you and who you can go to."

Something ticked over in Brian's chest. It had been worrying him, scaring him about all of this. Something about being alone, about being property.

"I would love that. Let me get a pen." He noted it on a spare bit of paper he found in Aaron's console.

Once they said goodbye, Brian took a moment to think.

Aaron was from another planet. He wanted Brian to come with him. The people he would be with would treat him as an equal; he would have meaningful work and a chance to help correct a major injustice. And if everything went right, he would have Aaron too.

Brian had answered quickly at the hot spring, but it felt right. Real. True. If they could build the plan Aaron had dreamed up, that would be the best future Brian could imagine.

He headed back inside and shut the cabin door behind him carefully.

Aaron sat on the bed, head in his hands. "So she told you?" he asked, voice quiet under the crackle of the fire.

"She did," Brian said, stepping toward him. He wanted to hold him in his arms, but there was distance, a stiffness.

"And?" Aaron prompted, voice rough.

Brian moved closer, fingertips barely brushing Aaron's button-up flannel. He tried to speak as slowly as he could, tone as even and regular as he could make it. "It wasn't your fault, Aaron. It just wasn't. It was something that happened that was terrible—"

Aaron shoved himself to his feet. He began to pace. "You don't understand. I gave them away. I handed them over to the monster I'd told them, *promised* them, I would protect them from—"

"Maybe you did some things wrong. Maybe you know better now. But I *know* you. You've been working to fix the problem, not just for the people you lost but for everyone like them. That's brave and—"

Aaron scoffed, and Brian stepped into him, arms wrapping around him, holding him for a long moment before Aaron sagged into him and muttered, "How can you want to touch me? After—"

Brian slid his hands down to grip Aaron's palms, fingers unwinding his fists. He filled the gaps between his fingers as Aaron's head came to rest on his shoulder. Simply, Brian said, "I'm touching you because I want to. There are things you've done that you would do differently if you had a time machine. But you don't. You are the cause of pain. We all are. Any of us who seek to do good, we can cause pain too. But the only thing we can do to fix that is to try to do better. Over and over and over again. Until we get there. Until we bend the arc back toward justice."

Aaron's eyes were damp when he looked up, startled. "You think we can?"

"I do," Brian said, feeling it in his bones. "We must, so we will."

Aaron gave a little laugh. "I really didn't ask you out here to play Dr. Freud with me. I had a whole plan—hamburgers and stew and hot springs and so much sex. *So* much sex."

Brian laughed, brushing a curl out of Aaron's eyes. "How about we bank the fire and get some rest. Going from working overnights to being awake during the day takes it out of me. After a nap, we can see what else we're up for."

Aaron nodded, not moving from Brian's arms. Brian gathered him close, slowly, and for long minutes, the only sound was the crackle of the fire and the quiet shushing of the winter wind across the white Wyoming plain.

Chapter Seventeen: T-28 Days

My dear Senator:

I read your telegram of February eleventh from Reno, Nevada with a great deal of interest and this is the first time in my experience, and I was ten years in the Senate, that I ever heard of a Senator trying to discredit his own Government before the world. You know that isn't done by honest public officials. Your telegram is not only not true and an insolent approach to a situation that should have been worked out between man and man but it shows conclusively that you are not even fit to have a hand in the operation of the Government of the United States.

I am very sure that the people of Wisconsin are extremely sorry that they are represented by a person who has as little sense of responsibility as you have.

Sincerely yours,

HST

—President Harry S. Truman, drafted response (probably unsent) to a telegram received from Senator Joseph McCarthy on 11 February 1950.

November 22, 1951

They slept for hours under those heaped quilts, wrapped up in each other, bodies soft and warm in the firelight. When Brian woke, Aaron was still easy in his arms, and night had fallen again. Everything in the cabin was hints of shape and flexes of light. Brian wanted to know every curve, every sigh of him. Their bodies had a quiet language, passed messages that could only be carried skin to skin, that only made themselves heard in their own time. It had taken hours for Aaron's body to uncoil, to join Brian's. Even in sleep, he'd been tense. But when he slept, he'd slept deeply, face tucked into Brian's neck, breathing full and even.

Brian hummed and stretched, his body long, curving under the quilts. Brian had slept in fits and starts, trying to think through everything he'd heard, everything he'd learned.

Aaron said, as hushed as the snowfall outside, "So, do your feelings on Thanksgiving extend to Christmas?"

Brian tilted his head against the flat pillow, quirking a smile. "I'm open to the idea of Christmas."

"We don't have Christmas on Antares," Aaron said. "We don't have the kind of weather you do here. A steady wind from the northern hemisphere brings the scents of different seasons—sweet, sharp, spicy, fruity, sour, and foul. That kind of thing. But with our two suns and no planetary tilt, the temperatures stay much the same throughout the year."

Brian frowned, fingers traveling over Aaron's bare chest. "Do you have holidays?"

Aaron squinted, fingers tracing calendars in the air. "We don't have the kind of work schedule you do here."

Brian brushed his lips just above the swell of his pectoral muscle, watching his stomach jump and his dick twitch just after. "That sounds nice."

Aaron shook his head. "Slavery is what gives us our leisure time, slavery and the riches that come from ample energy."

Brian felt a chill, fingers flattening on Aaron's biceps. "When you get back, what are you going to do first?"

Aaron considered the question, face serious. "See if anyone is left from the movement we left behind; it will have been a long time. Maybe the problems of our world will have been solved." He twisted his mouth; even he wasn't that optimistic. "Then find out who is still fighting the fight and see how we can help them, share what we have learned, what you can teach them. Share our hope, the vision Earth provides. Share that we have the chance, the option of finding ways of emancipation, of reparations like your eighteenth century Quakers or during the nineteenth century reconstruction, of all of the things your country tried. With you, with your history, we have a model."

"Not much of one—blue tickets are used by racist commanders who hate Black people as often as they're used against people like us. Jim Crow in the South, segregation in the North, Chinese Exclusion Act aimed at California, internment camps there and elsewhere, and my mother couldn't vote in elections until the year I was born."

"You weren't born in nineteen twenty."

"She's an enrolled tribe member, only allowed to vote after nineteen twenty-four with the Indian Citizenship Act."

Aaron nodded slowly. "It's not that I'm saying this world is perfect. But my sister used to say that 'half a loaf is better than none,' and I find more and more that I agree. You don't need to be perfect to provide us guideposts."

"It's hard to think of a society that's mastered interstellar travel as needing us as a guide for anything."

Aaron shrugged, movement jostling Brian's head, but as he moved to get up, Aaron snagged an arm around him, holding him close and tight.

"Our corner of the galaxy is relatively uninhabited," Aaron said. "Just us, Earth, some small species that live on the spartan moons, and the ancient empires at the edge of things. But we've been traveling the stars for dozens of generations and have touched the outer edges of some much larger, much older societies."

He stroked his hand up and down Brian's arm, voice steady in the cool morning light. "We've seen that societies develop at different paces on different worlds. There's one whose music will make you drunk. Literally drunk. It taps into something in our brains. But they live on a barren wasteland because they've lost the will to farm, eating only things that can be bartered. There's ours, with technological advances that overtake Earth's by a century or more, but where we enslave a full four-fifths of our population."

He swept his hair out of his eyes and sat up, nudging Brian between his legs. Brian let him draw him closer, the entire, wide, flat expanse of his back slotting perfectly into Aaron. All that warm skin tingled across his senses, left him feeling encompassed, protected.

"So it's less about who's ahead in some kind of technological race," Aaron continued, "and more about how far we have to go. If we succeed at EBT-I, Earth will be able to make plutonium at will. That is something that will never go away, no matter what else happens to me. There's so much you can use it for aside from weapons—"

"Like what?"

Aaron's curls moved against Brian's skin, and Brian knew he was giving him a look. But his excitement at being able to speak freely seemed to overwhelm any other worries.

"Cancer treatments," Aaron said, "undersea travel, above sea travel, light, heat. You'll have to figure out where to store the spent fuel, but you'll find there are ways to process it that, while a bit more expensive, mean there's really not much spent fuel left over. Maybe enough to fill a warehouse once every century. And when you find a place where you can store it, you can just—leave it there."

"I expect that will become a sticking point."

"It should be. It's a serious thing for your species since you don't know how to manage the radiation yet. But you can process it down to a tiny physical amount of fuel. And there are places you can store it, where the underlying geology will prevent it from ever touching anyone else."

"On whose land?"

"Hmm?"

"On whose land?" Brian repeated. "Trash heaps, chemical dumps, they always seem to end up hurting the people with the least power to protect themselves."

"Some of my people have been doing research on that. There's a place in Eddy County—"

"Apache land."

"Nearly seven hundred meters of salt *under* Apache land."

Brian frowned. "The plasticity effects of the salt would help seal it?"

"That and thirteen layers of concrete. It's the hottest place in New Mexico, with no traditional hunting, ceremonies, or burials in that area. It's less than a mile square and deep underground. It'll be decades before anyone thinks to start digging, which is enough time for everyone in the tribe and their children to consider if they want it there. It's a ten thousand–year commitment, so it *should* take time to decide. My people have a whole plan, and the tribe would be paid for it."

"That deep underground, and with the salt and the concrete in the way, none of the alpha particles would have a hope of getting out," Brian said, and at Aaron's nod, continued. "There's not an aquifer for fifty miles in any direction. Just miles and miles of sand from ancient, long-dead rivers."

After a moment, Brian went on. "I still have a lot of questions, and I'm not currently on the tribal rolls." He swallowed. "The colonel wouldn't allow it. Mara mentioned something. Something I'm not sure how to ask about."

Aaron looked carefully over at him, giving him space to be.

Brian tried. "When did you know I was related to the man who was hunting your family? When you saw my scars at the gym, when you knew my father's rank, I assumed you'd seen it in my file. But that's not where you knew about him from, was it?" He whispered, "When did you know who I am?"

Aaron shook his head slowly, curls brushing Brian's bare shoulder. "I've known who you were related to since the first night you introduced yourself." He added quietly, "There weren't going to be two Brian Flynns from Roswell, New Mexico."

Brian's heart was going a little faster. "How did you choose to still be around me? I know you changed your schedule to spend more time with me; why would you—"

Aaron tipped his head onto Brian's shoulder, the smooth, warm reality of him softening some of the aching tension that had begun to run through Brian's body. "When I quit my apprenticeship, went to go work in the abolitionist movement, no one but my sister understood. Not my parents, not my brothers, not my aunts or uncles or grandparents. All of them thought I was making trouble, making things harder for the people they'd personally enslaved by causing a ruckus."

His whole body tensed. "When I tried to leave, they locked me up, locked up Sara too. Gave us a drug, forced it on us, that took away our powers. It was our friends, people who had been in chains before, who got us free, got us out." His voice roughened, like remembered hurt. "It's not always the people related to you who love you the best or know how to care for you. Blood can mean less than nothing when it comes down to it. Families of choice, found families, those can and often should be far more permanent than the kind we're born into."

He pressed a kiss to the ball of Brian's shoulder. "All of which is to say, I've known who you're related to since the minute I met you. But I've known who you *are* since I saw you walking from the barracks to the lab. Another commander, *any* other commander, would have demanded his men drive him, would have confiscated one of their vehicles to make his own life easier. But you didn't even think to do that, just like you didn't think to give yourself the choice assignments.

"You didn't meet him, but the last commander was a racist. Always gave Freeman the overnights, dressed him down in front of the others, didn't give him any hope of a promotion or any kind of real support. But you take the power of command seriously. You take your duty of care seriously. You made a fair schedule for the men, gave yourself the worst shifts to give them a real reason to respect you. Not just because they are required to, but because they've seen you looking out for them, protect-ing them, in a way that matters to them day-to-day. A man who thinks about power and fairness in that way, who isn't afraid to literally walk the walk so as to never abuse his own power. That told me everything I needed to know about you."

Brian wasn't sure his cheeks could flush any hotter. "I don't know about all that," he said gruffly.

"Well, I do."

Brian buried his face in Aaron's neck, and Aaron swept his hand up his spine. It was a lot to take in, a lot to think about. He'd never heard himself described that way; the men had hinted in it in their letters, but it was something he didn't know how to think about yet.

He cast around for a new subject and landed on the record box, still carefully filed after Aaron's demonstration the night before. "You want to listen to some music?"

"Sure, we can do that," Aaron said easily. "Any preferences?"

"Did you bring the Lena Horn?"

Aaron lifted a hand, and Brian watched as a record slipped its sleeve and flitted over to the player. The tenor trombone came in, brassy and swooping along with the plucked guitar and sliding violins. Then it was Lena Horn, in all her hopeful sorrow singing about the man she loved.

Brian rolled onto his side to pillow his head on Aaron's chest, bare leg over Aaron's navel, thigh carefully high enough not to encourage anything in particular. Aaron ran a hand down his side, and he eased forward, waking up to the acres of skin in front of him. And Brian could see it, where the rest of the night might go, how it might feel. Brian closed his eyes, letting the music move around him, filling the quiet twilight of the cabin. "I have a request," he said, his words nearly lost in the flare of a trumpet.

"Yeah?" Aaron said, running his palm down Brian's thigh.

"I need you to be soft with me."

"Hmm?"

Brian willed himself to say it, trying to convince himself it would be all right to ask. He let himself whisper, "Before—it was good. You were good. I want it to stay like that. I know men can be hard. Hard with each other, hard with themselves. Men have been hard with me—before. Hard is fine, necessary even, for getting through the fear and sorrow and secrets and pain. We will have to be hard with each other sometimes. But, don't let it be tonight. Tonight, if you can, I need you to be soft with me."

Aaron struggled to sit up, his voice tight, strangled as he said, "Brian, where is this—"

"I shouldn't have—"

Aaron caught his warming face in his two broad hands. "What—why would I ever treat you as anything but precious? Why would I ever touch you as anything but sacred, to my people or yours? When have I ever—" He stopped, trying to figure it out. "You're thinking I might what, hit you?"

And Brian shook his head, feeling the motion in the tense lines down his back. "I never—not that. But some men, with some acts, they like to *teach*." And that word had a cherry-pit sourness about it.

Aaron seemed to be working to keep his tone steady and gentle. "If you can, will you talk to me a little more about what that word means to you?" It barely shook with the effort.

Brian nodded again, this time less jerky. "I want to be an *equal* and sometimes that means—"

"Being able to ask for me to be soft?"

Brian shuddered. The word sounded so weak. But some tiny, stubborn piece of him insisted it wasn't wrong to ask to be given time. That Aaron really meant it when he said they were equals.

Aaron started replying before Brian realized he'd said that out loud. "And these men, they would—"

Brian's replied, tone flat, "They'd say they knew best, and I'd lay down and—"

The music stuttered, Lena's voice crackling.

"Well," Aaron said, carefully controlled. "I'd reasonably expect you to never want to be touched by men ever again after those experiences."

Shame broke over Brian's head about how *fucked up he had to be* that another queer man felt—

But Aaron was still talking, slow and measured. "That means you must be so brave to want to come here, to be how we've been with each other, with this on your mind. Braver than I've ever been in my entire life. And I've done some good things. But you to keep trying to find something, to insist on equality, to come here? God, Brian, I don't know how I could possibly have deserved someone like you. We can just rest here if you want to, or not. Tell me what you want."

Aaron's still hand on his back was light. Gentle. Brian knew he was strong, strong enough to force him, to grab him, to hurt him. But there was a piece of him, some tentative, painfilled, painful piece of them that just *wanted* him, wanted to trust again. He didn't have the words for it. Aaron sat back, and Brian was still, made from unmoving stone, body tight, he felt like he would crack like one of those icicles on the cabin's eaves. But Aaron's touch was gentle. Nothing was being frozen off. So, slow as melting snow, he tucked himself that little bit closer to Aaron, slowly bringing him back to himself, letting his body tick back down.

"Brian, I want to make sure I say it in a way that makes sense," Aaron said quietly, hand still on his skin. "I won't do anything you don't ask me to do. Even if you asked me, I wouldn't push you or call you names or hurt you. I don't *want* hurting. And I want this to be something good. Something safe." Brian counted his heartbeats. "And if I could float every man that treated you as less than you deserve straight up into space, I would happily do it."

Brian buried his face in Aaron's chest. He didn't much care that this obscured his words, the scent and warmth of him helped him stay in this cabin and out of those memories. "Like I said, it was just transactional, back in LA—"

Aaron began to grumble.

"—*and* I can fight my own battles."

"I know you can. But there's something Mara taught me when I first joined her and the other abolitionists. We can't be required to both survive our monsters and slay them. No universe would be that cruel. Sometimes we ask for help. Or our nosy, pushy friends help us when we fail to ask," Aaron said, gently self-mocking. "Over and over, we can fail to ask for help, and those who love us will continue to try to help us. Because we deserve it. Deserve to live without pain, to live inside of ourselves, and outside, in the kind of freedom and peace that all creatures have a right to enjoy. That's what friends are supposed to do."

They let that sit for a long moment, sharing the pine-scented air and the warmth of the quilt.

Finally, Brian said, "I think it has to do with being hidden, with having to keep things secret. I think it poisons something that might have been good, if it had had the normal kind of social supports. Twists people up inside, warps the bones, the foundations of relationships. That's—that's why I needed the books. Proof that other people were doing this, *could* do this, in a way that was good and safe and real; *proof* that there were others out there, social norms and accountability. Not just men alone and whatever they thought they could get." He worked his jaw. "We do seem to have a talent for distracting ourselves from the important business at hand."

Aaron shrugged one shoulder, fingers tracing idly down Brian's arm. "When we get back, we'll have time. The cabin is too far out for anyone to bother us, the lab will be empty—"

"I am *still* not having sex in the lab." He could practically hear Aaron restraining himself.

Then Aaron said, "Fair. I guess. But still. If all we do is talk and eat and listen to music for the rest of this break, it would still be the best Thanksgiving I've ever had."

"You've only been on the planet four years—"

"—And Thanksgiving is a terrible holiday. The best weekend I've ever had? The best weeks of my life? What kind of compliments are we going for here, darling, I'm happy to be obliging."

Something in the teasing tone, the gentle ribbing, made Brian shift his weight and slide his leg over Aaron's hips, straddling his waist, taking in his startled expression with a grin in the flickering light.

"I've got another way you can be obliging," Brian said, low. He dragged his palms over Aaron's shoulders, bracing himself before running a lingering thumb up the side of Aaron's throat, feeling him swallow under his fingertips.

"What would soft look like for you?" Aaron rumbled.

Brian ran his fingers up the curve of the nape of his neck, luxuriating in the spread of curls between them. "We'd touch and kiss, no one in charge, no one barking orders. Like we did before, but when I'm the one going down, I can control that, keep my pants on, pull off when I need to, breathe when I need to. But when it's me being touched it's overwhelming. Intense."

"We don't have to—"

Brian rolled his hips against Aaron's, close enough he caught Aaron's choked off "Fuck."

"I *want* to," Brian continued. "I—it's a lot. For me."

Aaron reached up to cup Brian's cheek. "Then we'll stay right here. Your hand on mine, you stop, I stop. Work for you?"

And something caught in Brian's chest. "Yeah. Yeah, that would work fine."

Aaron gave him a wicked grin, slipping his hand around Brian's and bringing it down to rest on his thigh, a fingertip-length from Brian's slowly filling cock. "So," he said, "Do you like it slow?"

Brian nodded, focused on the sight of their hands together, so close. Aaron was hard, too, tight against his stomach, but aside from adjusting himself to avoid getting caught in the blankets, he was totally focused on Brian.

"Will you show me what you like?" Aaron asked with a rough murmur.

Brian nodded, guiding their hands to his cock, one over the other. He kept his strokes firm and slow and even. Aaron's body almost danced under his with each thrust, but his gaze never left their cocks.

"How about if we—" Aaron started and brought his own palm up to his mouth. Something flipped over in Brian's stomach when, without breaking eye contact, Aaron licked it and slipped it between their bodies, spit-slick and cool against their hot skin.

Brian jerked at the first hard pump, Aaron keeping his pinky tight and his attention fixed on their hands. Brian hissed between his teeth. "Fuck, Aaron, *fuck*."

And Aaron reached up with his other hand, drew Brian into a kiss that was hot with want, tongue sweeping across his lips, and Brian opened with a groan. He found himself thrusting forward but kept still, just for a moment. When Aaron bobbed against him, he reached down with his other hand.

"Let me," Brian said, moving so their cocks aligned on the next thrust.

Aaron lost his rhythm entirely, gasping, "Bri, *fuck*—"

And Brian pressed his lips into Aaron's hair, bodies finding a shared rhythm, hands tight together, with precum and sweat and spit, and harsh breathing. Brian stilled, wanting to take Aaron over the edge with him, and Aaron whined at the pause. Brian whispered, *"Please."*

Aaron's body shuddered, catching and holding Brian's gaze. The sight of him—overwhelmed, hands around their cocks—sent Brian thrusting forward, Aaron losing himself in the motion of it, their bodies coming and making a sticky, ridiculous mess everywhere.

In the quiet stillness after, the first sound either of them made was a laugh, and neither could say for sure who started it, but soon they were in each other's arms, laughing and touching and sticky and whole.

Chapter Eighteen: T-25 Days

"It is the duty of every member of the military service to report to his commanding officer any facts which may come to his attention concerning overt acts of homosexuality. Commanding officers receiving information indicating that a person has homosexual tendencies or has engaged in an act of homosexuality shall inquire thoroughly and comprehensively."

—*US Army, Army Reg. 600-443 ¶ 5 (1950).*

November 25, 1951

The drive back was slow, both men taking turns napping as the other drove. They hadn't gotten much sleep on their last night at the cabin. When Brian saw EBT-I approaching on the horizon, he began rebuilding his captain's mask. Aaron reached over and squeezed his fingers, only to let them go long before the perimeter guard could see into the truck's cab.

*

The first few days back passed in a warm blur for Brian. He was back to working nights with Aaron, then using up his extra energy in the gym before passing out in his single bed. Though he fought hard to appear the same from the outside, on the inside, he was buzzing. He had his books and Aaron's touch to remember and the hope of a future freer than he'd ever imagined. Aaron kept his promise not to start anything in the lab. But if they sat shoulder to shoulder, drafting and redrafting a new design, if Aaron's fingers trailed over his wrist every time he accepted a tool as he worked on the radiation shielding from within the reactor? Brian figured no one would know. A minuscule part of him hoped no one would care.

His coworkers noticed his change in mood. Nurse Kelly had murmured over his weekly blood draw. "You're looking good, Brian. Whatever it is, keep it up."

Dr. Zinn had given him something like an encouraging look, though Brian tried to stop himself from reading too much into it.

But he knew where the lines were. When Hodgins had asked him how Wyoming had been, Brian told him that he and Aaron had barely seen each other.

"I spent most of the time ice fishing while he was working on his reactor sketches in the cabin, but it was beautiful. God's country out there."

Hodgins asked him to go ice fishing with him the next weekend, and they spent a horrifying, frozen morning on a lake up in the mountains. The conversation was pleasant, about his family in New York and Brian's goals as a physicist, but the highlight had been telling Aaron about it after midnight when the lab had long since emptied:

"And then, when we finally caught a single goddamned fish, I had to gut the damn thing! Out there on the ice! I told Hodgins we'd been fishing to get him off my back!"

"Let me guess," Aaron had drawled from under the control panel. "Cleaning fish is rude like snow is rude?"

Brian made a disgusted cat face. "Snow *is* rude. No, I was always given shit duty on family fishing trips to 'make me a better man.' I'm great at cleaning fish. It's just fucking awful. Watching the life leave its fishy eyes, all that gore." He shuddered.

Aaron had hummed a little before sliding out. He flicked his fingers to twist the bolts laid out in a circle around the top of the reactor opening and shrugged off his jacket before leaning against Brian. He wrapped his arm around his shoulder and held him close.

"Well, just imagine," Aaron murmured. "On Antares, you'll never have to clean a fish again."

"Why not?"

"There are no fish."

"Do you have oceans?"

"We do, but we can't eat the fish. It's just a thing, like you can't eat all mushrooms."

Brian nudged him with his shoulder, still grumbling. "Doesn't sound like a problem to me."

Aaron had ducked his head into Brian's shoulder, stifling a yawn. "We're getting closer, now I can work with my powers in here. We're nearly there. Mara just has to hold on."

"I told her I would help if I could."

"Yeah?" Aaron said, focus still on the bolts as a whole ballet line of them moved, twisting themselves into place.

"I have an idea how I can. But I don't think you're going to like it."

Aaron stilled beside him, letting each bolt settle to the platform floor with a *plink, plink, plink.* "What are you going to do?"

Brian took a breath, jaw tense. "I hope the colonel backs off on his own, stops hunting your people, but I don't think he will. I have a way to stall him for one to two weeks if we have to. To take him entirely out of the field, get him put in confinement, tar his name. If we need it."

"Brian, what—"

Brian turned to Aaron. "It's only if we have to, and we can only use it once." Brian blinked, heart stuttering a little, but pressed on. "It's an awful thing to do to someone, and it will blow back on me no matter how we go about it. But if we're close, and if we need to protect your people from the hell he'd bring down on them if he captured them and paraded them in front of the air force to prove his story about aliens, we have the option."

Aaron frowned, hand raising to trace the lines on Brian's forehead, trying to smooth them back down, but they only got deeper. "Brian, what are you planning on doing?" he asked quietly.

Brian twisted his lips into an ugly smile. "You know how I have a file at Vandenburg?"

Aaron froze, holding Brian's gaze for a moment before he nodded.

"If we have to—if we have no other choice—we'll make my father regret ever giving me his name."

*

Whether through luck or coincidence, the colonel backed off enough that Aaron stopped trying to argue Brian out of his intended plan. When Mara said they hadn't seen him on the rez in a week, Aaron decided to let it drop, focusing instead on prying free every spare moment for him and Brian to share time together. The next Saturday, Aaron had pitched they go off and explore Lava Beds National Monument; but after a full Friday night of working, neither was up for it. Instead, they went into Arco, bought some groceries including everything Brian needed to make bread, and headed to Aaron's cabin for the weekend.

The route to the cabin took them along some back country roads. Brian had the sneaking suspicion Aaron used his TK to help keep them clear, the snow piled high on either side but the pathway to the cabin entirely dry and oddly even.

The cabin was more of a house, electric lights running off of a generator and water from a well. Aaron gave him the grand tour: two bedrooms, a living room with a kitchen along the back wall, a bathroom with a massive tub. Diné rugs covered every available surface.

Brian wasn't sure he would ever want to leave.

He started unpacking the grocery bags onto the blue tile counter, saying, "Whenever my mom was anxious or sad, the house would fill with the smell of baking bread."

He glanced up, and Aaron met his gaze before getting out the ingredients: yeast, flour, honey, salt. The honey was from Utah, and clover covered the label.

A small smile crept across Brian's face. "She'd knead it extra hard after a fight and turn the oven up as high as it would go to make a crust my dad could crack a tooth on." He turned the honey around and placed it toward the back of the counter. "But she'd always slice it off for me and my brothers. Always made sure her anger, her fear, didn't touch us in the ways she could help."

"She sounds like a brave woman."

Brian nodded. "She was. Her parents are still on the reservation. Your people have probably met my family there. I haven't made it up to the rez since she passed."

His hands were on automatic, measuring out the flour, checking the water was room temperature with his pinky before dissolving the yeast in it. Aaron came up behind him, telegraphing his movements clearly before easing his arms around Brian's waist. Brian held himself tight and away for one, two, three long breaths before sighing, sagging into Aaron's body.

Aaron's head moved against his as he looked over his work on the counter. "Are you making her bread recipe?"

Brian nodded.

Aaron pulled back. "Are you upset about something?"

Brian frowned for a moment, then turned to bury his head against Aaron's neck, enjoying the prickle of his two-day beard against his cheek. "No, no. I bake when I want to remember her. Remember her strength. And maybe when I want to share her, share that part of my family. But I don't think I can introduce us as a couple."

"You never know—"

Brian looked down. "She might not have raised her fists, but she was raised in missionary schools. So were my grandparents." He frowned, and Aaron's hands tightened on his waist. "I love them, you know?" To his own ears he sounded raw, like a whisper after a scream. "And they love me. I know they do. It's just—they would never—I can't see them as I am, you know?"

Aaron nodded, keeping the quiet of Brian's words between them. "Does—does it hurt to do things like that, to remember her, to remember them?"

Brian stilled, hands deep in the dough. "We're not our worst parts, not the worst things we believe or have done. We're a lot more than that. It would be like me hating Antares IV because there's plutonium there that would probably give me cancer without Mara's wonder drug."

"She's got it ready for us as soon as we're on the reservation. I wouldn't take you anywhere you won't be safe. There are places on Antares, ways to protect you. I want to be able to show you my home without the toxic environment hurting you."

Brian smiled. "I wish I could say the same."

Aaron gave him a sad smile and leaned in, pressing cheek against cheek, voice soft. "So, anything different about this bread recipe?"

Brian drew back to give him a hard look but kept his hands on the dough. "It has a family secret."

Aaron looked torn between dragging the secret out and being hurt he wasn't family, and Brian let it war on his face for a moment before giving in with a smirk.

"We beat the hell out of the dough," he said, and then he cracked up.

Aaron looked up at the ceiling, but then he just rolled his eyes and smiled at Brian's laughter. "I'll get the dessert started, then."

"Dessert?"

Aaron grinned. "What, you think you're the only one who knows how to bake?"

Aaron and Brian traded off using the small counter. Aaron flicked paper airplanes around the room with his powers during the rise time, and Brian roundly critiqued their aerodynamics and general accuracy. The air outside was frosty, but inside the cabin was toasty warm. Brian was down to his undershirt, not thinking about his skin for the first time in a long time. He set the dough on the kitchen counter for its first rise.

"Hey, can I borrow the communicator? I want to chat with Mara about something."

"Are you going to tell her your plan?" Aaron asked, failing miserably at keeping his voice neutral, already handing him the device.

"Not yet, not unless they really need it."

Brian pressed the button and connected to Mara as he wandered back toward the guest bedroom, shutting the door behind him.

"Aaron?" Mara said, sounding tired but still warm.

"No, it's Brian."

"Oh, Brian. I'm glad to hear from you. How's work been?"

Brian smiled a little, sitting on the quilt-heaped twin bed, springs creaking a little. "Good, thanks for asking. I was wondering if Jill is around?"

"Sure, no problem." She got quieter. "Honey? Brian's on the comms." A muffled shout. "She's coming. It's like I have to get her out of the lab with a pry bar most nights."

Brian smiled, hoping it came through over the line. "Same with Aaron."

"Here she is. Give Aaron my love."

"Will do."

"Hey, Brian," a woman's said quietly on the other end. "How're you doing?"

"It's—" He eased himself back onto the small, neatly-made bed. "It's a little rough, thinking about leaving the planet."

Jill chuckled. "You don't say." There came the sound of the door shutting. "So, what's got you this time?"

They'd had a few calls during Aaron's long shifts. First, getting to know each other as fellow humans attached to an Antaran, then as people with Apache family, and finally, as scientists. They'd talked about names, where Aaron and Mara and James had picked theirs from (the phone book) and if Brian and Jill would need Antaran names (probably not). The tiniest details helped to ease Brian's mind. The calls didn't seem to cost Aaron anything, and he gave Brian as much time as he needed with them. Every conversation had circled around to this, the ways in which their lives would change once they left Earth.

Brian flopped onto the bed. "Oh, I don't know. The idea I might never taste my mother's bread again."

"And how's that feeling for you?"

"Kind of crappy."

"Yeah," Jill said easily. "You should have seen the fit I pulled when I realized Mara and James and the rest had no idea what blue corn tacos or pozoles were." Her voice held the sound of a smile. "It's why we've added an entire new section to the garden just for southwestern plants. So we can have a taste of home."

"They let you do that?"

"Yeah, Brian. They want us to be full members of the community. To be happy. It's like when you welcome someone to your family, you buy the spices and the food they like."

"You think they'd let me bring flour and yeast?"

Jill made a teasing sound. "I think if you asked, they'd teach themselves how to grow wheat, how to mill it, and make a whole little yeast culture, kept alive especially for you."

"Oh," he said quietly in the hush of the cabin, listening to Aaron doing the dishes. "I guess I'm not used to the idea that love doesn't come with costs, with consequences."

She gave him time to breathe. "I can see that, from what you've told me of your home life. And the thing is? It does have a cost. The yeast interacts with the wild yeast on our fingers, in the air we breathe. In space, it won't have the yeast from the soil, from the air to work with. Only what you and I and the handful of other humans bring in with us, keep alive in our bodies. Eventually, it will stop tasting like your mother's breath, her home, her bread. They are asking for a sacrifice, for a major change of life."

"But it's something I *want*." Brian put his forearm over his eyes. "I don't understand why I have mixed feelings about it is all."

She sighed softly as if she'd eased herself back onto a comfortable rug. "Well, in my experience of the world, every big decision has a mix of feelings. If you think you only feel one way about something—going to West Point, choosing Vandenburg, being friends with Aaron—then you're probably not thinking hard enough about it."

Jill took a moment. "But, Brian, it's also important not to torture yourself about it. Sometimes, growing up how you did, your brain will try to turn everything good to ash, leave every warm thought cold. Try to see what is real, try to separate real problems and let go of the ones you don't need to solve."

"That's very smart. I don't know if I'll do it, but it's very smart."

"Well, I didn't graduate top of my class at Smith for nothing." Jill said, then let the static on the line fill the space between them before she continued. "No one's seen the colonel on the rez since the last call. I'm hoping he's given up."

"In my experience of the world," Brian said flatly, "he never gives up." He tried to sound more hopeful. "But I hope so too." The water turned off in the kitchen. "Sounds like I've successfully avoided dishes.

I should head back."

"Yeah, I'm pretty sure Mara's already passed out waiting for me to come to bed. I'll see you soon, all right? For Christmas if you all don't get it running before."

"I look forward to it. Stay safe, Jill."

"You too, Brian."

He headed back to the kitchen and lay the communicator on the kitchen table. Aaron didn't ask about the call; he seemed very focused on making sure Brian had as many of his own lines of communication as he needed. They chatted some, about work, about the people Brian would see on the rez, settling on the couch to read by the firelight until they both got sleepy.

Brian was working his way through a new Andre Norton book as Aaron tried out reading Adrienne Rich's debut poetry collection, their legs tangled on the couch. It was—soft. And kind. Knowing this was something he could have. Something he didn't have to earn or hurt for, something real. And lovely. And *his*.

The snow fell thick and deep outside, the layers laying down a kind of quiet, a kind of solitude that had been one of the few things Brian had appreciated about West Point.

But this was so much better. He felt stronger, healthier, more whole. The touch of another person had done it, after those long, ugly months of self-restraint and self-denial. The chance to brush his hand across Aaron's back as he passed him in the small kitchen, the slip of his arm against the other man's side, his rough stubble against his cheek. Things any couple might assume were normal, even forgetting how special it was to be wanted, touched after enough years. But right now, every single one of these touches was precious.

After they ate, they slowly worked their way to bed, falling asleep before they could do more than undress each other and curl up tight beneath the same quilt.

*

Brian awoke with his heart pounding, limbs shaking. It was cold, he was alone. He knew he needed to get up, to get moving. He'd been left outside overnight in winter growing up.

A few times.

He'd been out of doors, the lights off, everyone in the house instructed to not let him in on punishment of joining him. He'd walked for hours and hours to keep himself warm enough to live until morning. He'd gone to school, survived between classes, drunk hot water from the taps in the bathrooms to get warm enough to feel alive again.

But he wasn't in his father's house; these sheets weren't his thin air force-issued blues. Those weren't the sounds of trucks moving outside his window, bringing scientists and materials to the installation. That wasn't the thick curtain blocking out the daylight so he could get enough sleep to make it to his night shift. That was the night sky out of Aaron's window. He sat up, twisting his body, shifting, muscles almost too tight for him to move at all. He forced his feet to the floor, made himself walk into the living room.

He saw a man crouching in the darkness, and he jerked, body moving away from the potential threat long before his mind caught up.

"Fire went out," the man said, and then it resolved; Aaron. They were in Aaron's cabin. Aaron was squatting, naked as the day he was born, shifting logs over the cooling coals. He struck a match, and his features flared to reality.

"Aaron?" Brian croaked, and Aaron dropped the lit match on the unlit logs, then stood and strode toward him.

"Love, what's the matter?"

"Aaron." Brian reached for his hand, feeling pathetic but also trying, for a moment, for now, to let himself seek comfort.

"It's me. I'm here," Aaron said, letting himself be drawn in.

Brian ran his hands over his stomach, down his hips, up his arms and back down to grip his hands. Tracing his body, remembering it was there, it was here, he was here, he wasn't alone, he was warm, he wasn't cold, he was here, he wasn't alone—

"Love," Aaron murmured, sounding worried. "What's going on?"

Brian shook his head, burying his face in Aaron's neck, huddling closer until the soft hair tickled his nose. The deeply masculine scent of Aaron, of their bodies, sharing one quilt, one set of blankets, one space. That grounded him in the moment more than anything else had.

"I'm here," Brian murmured back. "I'm here, and I'm not alone, walking on a country road, waiting to die of frostbite."

Aaron sucked in a breath, and Brian *felt* it against his cheek.

Brian kept talking. "I'm here; I'm not being hurt; I'm here; I'm not being punched or dragged by my hair. I'm cold because the fire went out in this cabin where we can both be, be ourselves, and no one will come in through that door and hurt us. And there is no one we've forced out into the cold, no one watching, waiting for us to let him inside. We've done nothing wrong, and we're here, and we're safe."

Aaron's hands had found the back of Brian's head as he spoke. Once he was finished, he spoke.

"You're here," he agreed quietly. "You're here, and you're safe. We're not hurting anyone, and you're not being hurt."

Brian nodded, squeezing his eyes closed so tightly it hurt. "I *know* that," he said in a cracked whisper. "It's just—sometimes, when I'm sleeping, I forget."

"Yeah," Aaron agreed. "Anything in particular make you forget this time, or just a brain fluke?"

Brian pressed his eyes shut even tighter, little gray shapes moving across his vision. "I think it was the cold? Everyone thinks New Mexico is so hot all the time—"

"But it's cold in the desert. I know." Aaron drew back a little, thumbs working their way across Brian's cheeks, slick with something under his eyes. Brian blinked hard, and more of the stuff came out, tipping over his eyelashes before trickling down his face.

Aaron's face was shadowed in the moonlight coming through the cabin window. "He did that? Made you walk outside all night?"

Brian's nod was so small, he knew Aaron couldn't see it, but he was so close, he knew he had to feel it. "Not often, not as often as other things. But it's a simple enough thing. I never had a key to my own house. So if I went out and didn't come back when he wanted—and it was never clear when he wanted—he would just, not let me in. I'd sit for hours, knocking, waiting. Finally, one of my brothers came to the door, told me he'd said I wasn't permitted in until I learned to come home at the right time."

He tried to force the tremor out of his voice. "It always seemed like something I could do, something I could do right. Something I was just missing. Like wanting women the way he wanted me to. Something I could find in myself, some way to do it right, and I was—I was always wrong."

"You know it wasn't your fault, right?"

"Do I? My brothers didn't get locked out. Just me. Over and over again, just me. I *must* have been wrong, right? Who—what father hates his son? What father hates his *son*? Or—" And here he choked. "—what kind of Mom always said he loved him. Reminded me he loved me. He'd hurt me, and she'd say he loved me. And it—it's rather hard to know what love is, if it's anything good at all, if things are like this. If love means this kind of hurting. If it even can be good."

Aaron leaned down, forehead tight against Brian's. "It is," he whispered. "And she was wrong to say that. And he was wrong to do that. And that you're still you, still capable of love, still capable of dignity and hope, speaks to how strong you are, to still be you in face of all of that."

He took a moment, thinking. Then he said, "For me, sometimes it helps to do something physical when I end up trapped in my head. I turned on the generator, and the water should be hot enough. Do you want to go get a bath ready? Really get warm, down into your bones, while we wait for the fire to heat the rest of the house?"

Brian hugged his arms around Aaron's waist, holding him for a long, sweet moment. Then he nodded. "I'll get it running."

He glanced at the kitchen counter, where he'd left the bread to rise overnight. Fingers careful, he lifted the towel from the thick-sided ceramic bowl. A warm smell of yeast rose. He felt something that might become a smile form. "The bread's okay. The cold just made the yeast work a little slower." He looked over at Aaron, who met his eyes as he built the fire with his power. "It'll taste even better than if it grew quickly, easily."

Aaron gave him a soft smile. "I look forward to tasting it."

Brian started toward the bathroom, calling out over his shoulder. "See you in there?"

"I'll be right behind you, love."

*

The bath was quiet and hot, and Aaron slid in behind him to hold on to him until he stopped shaking, until his eyelids started to droop again as his body decided it was safe.

They went right back to bed as soon as the water began to cool, bodies tangled in the sheets. When Brian awoke next, Aaron was sprawled out next to him, and the cabin was toasty and comfortable again. After a few long minutes of muzzily observing the rafters, Brian felt like something was strange with his body, something unfamiliar. His muscles felt soft and his lips strangely puffed out. He worked his neck for a while and slowly, understanding rose up from the depths for him. He wasn't clenching his jaw. He couldn't remember the last time he'd had a soft jaw; maybe elementary school? Certainly before his mom left.

Brian checked his body; he was *relaxed*, his body quiet, shoulders rounded, back not tight or aching. He didn't know how he'd come to this time and place where this was allowed him, but he appreciated it more than he could say.

Aaron lay beside him, soft and warm, his entire body bare, stretched out in moonlight, soft cock lying between his thighs in a way Brian found frankly satisfying. In Wyoming, they'd been able to take the time to explore, touching, enjoying each other in ways he'd never gotten to do with another person. It wasn't that he hadn't thought about it a lot—he absolutely had. But there was thinking and there was realizing that the stretch of thighs against thighs could be so welcoming, that the tender kiss to a brow in the midst of frantic sex could be as stringing-out-the-soul-sweet as anything else in the world.

He wanted to wake Aaron up, to ask if he was having as star-blurringly good a time as Brian was, if his eyes were tearing over in gratitude for the chance to just be. Be touched, be cared for.

Be loved.

He threw his arm across his face. This was where reading all that poetry had gotten him.

It had only been a few months: how could it be time to talk of love? Aaron called him "love" and "darling," but given that Brian had heard Aaron call the reactor "sweetheart" and uranium "honeybunches," he wasn't sure what to make of it.

But, for himself alone, he wanted to. Oh, Brian wanted to. He wanted to have the chance to say those words and *mean* them and have it be *known* publicly who he was and who he loved. And every single day they got closer to lighting up those four light bulbs at EBT-I, every day they got closer to producing plutonium, was a day he got closer to a world where that was possible. He thought about dancing with Aaron, about holding his hand in front of his people, of spending time with him with no need to make excuses or lie. He wrapped that around himself, letting it settle him to sleep.

Chapter Nineteen: T-13 Days

"'The use of homosexuals as a control mechanism over individuals recruited for espionage is a generally accepted technique which has been used at least on a limited basis for many years.' According to several sources, as soon as the DCI said these words, his aide signaled to take the remainder of the DCI's testimony off the record. Political historian David Barrett uncovered the speaker's notes, which reveal the remainder of the statement: 'While this agency will never employ homosexuals on its rolls, it might conceivably be necessary, and in the past has actually been valuable, to use known homosexuals as agents in the field. I am certain that if Josef Stalin or a member of the Politburo or a high satellite official were known to be a homosexual, no member of this committee or of the Congress would balk against our use of any technique to penetrate their operations [...] after all, intelligence and espionage is, at best, an extremely dirty business.'"

—Director of Central Intelligence (DCI) Roscoe Hillenkoetter when called to Congress to testify on queer people being employed at the CIA. July 14, 1950.

December 7, 1951

Brian checked his uniform again, tugging it around the lap belt. He narrowed his eyes at how the fabric had wrinkled in the hour-long drive to Idaho Falls across the sleeping fields and rocky outcroppings.

"Nurse Kelly has seen you several times a week for months," Aaron said, fondness in his tone. "She's not going to be worried about a few wrinkles." He reached across the bench seat to tangle his fingers with Brian's.

"I've—" Brian bit off what he was going to say, *I've never been invited to dinner by a work friend before*, because it sounded too sad. He just asked, "Have you been there before?"

Aaron shook his head, fingers dancing on the steering wheel as they entered the city limits, craning his neck to read the street signs in the moonlight.

Brian frowned. "Does she invite a lot of folks to meet her family?"

"I think it's only her and her husband. Durbin was over there a few weeks ago. I think, until recently, I wasn't in the regularly scheduled outreach queue."

"'Until recently'?"

He gave Brian a sidelong smile. "Maybe you've had a civilizing influence on me."

Brian huffed but squeezed his fingers back. "Her husband's a professor at the University of Idaho?"

"Yeah, the Idaho Falls branch campus. Teaches poetry, I think?"

Brian tapped his fingers in excitement before stilling them. "I bet he only likes the classics," he grumbled preemptively.

"There's more than enough naughty stuff in the classics—Achilles and Patroclus, anything Suetonius wrote."

Brian laughed. "You can't tell me queer classics in translation was something you studied at UW."

Aaron grinned. "Nope, but it was one of the topics piped through while we were in stasis. I can't recite it from heart the way James can, but I know the strokes of it."

Brian's grin turned wicked for a moment. "Just the strokes?"

Aaron tapped him on the knee. "I can't believe *I'm* telling you this, but *behave*."

Brian chuckled, feeling lighter.

"There we are," Aaron said, pulling a left into a small side street. "Keep a look out for one-oh-seven?"

They pulled up in front of a little blue cottage, grass all dead under scattered snow in the front yard, a prewar Ford sitting under an awning to protect it from snowfall.

They'd swung by the market to get a bottle of wine—two, actually. Brian had been the one to receive the invite with an option of a plus-one, and Aaron's presence was excused by the fact that everyone knew Brian didn't have a car to get around on his own. "Let's see if the mad scientist is house-trained" had been Nurse Kelly's exact words, which Brian had relayed faithfully to Aaron's mock horror and ill-suppressed glee.

As they came around the truck, Aaron murmured, "You look great, Airman."

Brian flicked his eyes up and down Aaron's body: tight jeans, loose hair, shirt properly tucked in for once. "Right back at you, cowboy."

Nurse Kelly opened the door to Aaron, still choking in response. He accepted her hug with grace and gave a firm handshake to her husband as they headed inside out of the chill.

Mr. Nurse Kelly—who gave his name as Dr. Charles Kelly—was a small man with round spectacles and a nearly perfectly bald head. He wore a thick brown tweed jacket, even inside his warm house.

He ushered them into the sitting room where Brian and Aaron took a seat a careful distance apart on the couch, the Kellys taking the chairs beside the fire.

She started them off. "Have an easy drive over?"

Brian let Aaron answer the question as he looked over the bookshelves on either side of the red brick fireplace, subtly angling his knees to catch most of the fire's heat. *All classics,* Brian noted with an internal sigh. A small, dark table sat beside the fireplace, its aesthetic different from anything else in the simple, well-worn house. He squinted, trying to trace the design on the side of it. It looked like writing but not in a Roman script—

Dr. Kelly chuckled, interrupting Brian's thoughts. "I think Captain Flynn is captivated by the side table, my dear."

Brian sat back, trying to look attentive. "It's a distinctive design."

"We've had it since October of forty-five when the camp closed."

Aaron asked, his voice wavering, "The camp?" as he glanced between the table and Nurse Kelly.

Dr. Kelly answered as his wife looked to the side, shoulders tight. "I thought you knew. But you must have been busy with the war effort. There's a camp, just east of here. The Japs, they stayed here for, oh, one, two years, then they got to go right back home. They left all sorts of things."

Aaron stood and crossed the room to kneel next to the side table. He examined it, fingers gentle, careful on the curves of the Japanese characters.

"They left a hand-carved side table with someone's initials in Japanese?" Aaron asked carefully, evenly. Nurse Kelly's hands were between her knees, knuckles white.

"Oh, you know," Dr. Kelly said lightly, "it's part of their religion, letting things go."

The lights flickered for a moment and then held steady.

"Their religion?"

"Hinduism or Buddhism or some such—"

Nurse Kelly stood, her shoulders set. "I'm going to check on the roast." She didn't say anything else as she retreated to the kitchen. Dr. Kelly didn't seem to notice.

Brian tried to restart the conversation. "One of the internment camps, you mean, Dr. Kelly? I thought they were all in Arizona and California."

Kelly shook his head, looking puzzled at his interest. "Oh, no. Over by Hunt, there were, what, ten thousand or fifteen thousand Japs? They were there for three years until they got moved back west. A lot of them volunteered for the service; my brother's school even let their baseball team play in their league. They called it Minidoka."

"These were US citizens?" Aaron asked, clearly struggling to keep his tone even.

Dr. Kelly frowned. "I guess so. They were Japs."

"What—" Aaron started, and Brian broke in.

"Nurse Kelly was in Germany during the war, right?"

Dr. Kelly turned to him. "Yes. Over it mostly though. She was a flight nurse; her family was at the Tule Lake camp in California. Volunteering was how she and her brother got out. After the war, the rest of her family moved as far as they could get away from the west coast. They all live in Boca in Florida now."

He glanced over to Aaron. "Her family that stayed in the camps during the war were treated well, even got to work the harvests while the men were fighting overseas."

"'Got to'? Were they paid?" Aaron asked, voice cracking, hand tightening on edge of the little side table.

Kelly bit her lip, looking into the fire. "I don't know. I'm sure they were, the same as other farmhands."

"Did they—" Aaron started, and then Nurse Kelly called out:

"The roast is ready, dear, can you see them to the dining table?"

Aaron caught Brian's gaze, his expression tense and hurting.

Brian stepped in. Over dinner, he kept Dr. Kelly chattering on about his new translation of Florus's histories. He was working on a section on Spartacus. Aaron stayed quiet, mechanically eating the roast and whatever else Nurse Kelly put in front of him. Brian thought he might actually have eaten plutonium if she'd set it on his scratched china plate, with the mood he was in.

Dr. Kelly was saying, "You know, some sources believe that Spartacus wasn't the leader of the slave rebellion, that it was a spontaneous uprising that later authors imposed their classically Roman, hierarchical beliefs on."

"Is that so?"

Dr. Kelly nodded excitedly. "If so, that would offer whole new potential translation options..." And he was off again.

Dessert was a chiffon cake, which Aaron waved away, face distant. Brian took extra portions. They gave their excuses when Dr. Kelly offered to keep chatting over after-dinner drinks. Brian blamed the roads, and Aaron roused himself to tease about Brian's driving—"California spoiled him for driving in snow—" with a ghost of his usual smile before Brian got them into their coats and out the door with a final wave of thanks.

Brian drew his key out from under his shirt; he didn't want Aaron driving in this state. Aaron wandered over to the passenger side door and stared blankly at the door handle, so Brian scooted over and gently opened it, conscious of Nurse Kelly's eyes through the living room window.

"Come on, Aaron. Let's get you home."

Aaron looked up, eyes showing pain Brian knew he'd barely kept out of them during dinner. "Home?"

"Yeah," Brian said. "I'll drive you to the cabin." Unspoken was: *I don't want you alone right now.*

He nodded slowly and got into the seat, let Brian buckle him in. They were on the road for a moment before he said, "We have to go."

"Go?" Brian asked, merging onto the highway.

"To the camp."

"I—I don't know if that's some place we can just go."

"We should find out."

*

Brian thought Aaron would forget about Minidoka.

He should have known better.

The next evening, when Aaron picked him up for the night shift, there was a packed bag strapped down in the back.

"Going someplace?" Brian asked, tucking the patterned blanket around his knees.

"I was going to head out after your shift, go to see Minidoka. See if I can learn something about why that happened, about why something that close to legalized slavery happened *again* in the US, within your lifetime." Aaron's shoulders were tight, voice low and quiet. "You don't have to come."

"I'll be there." He took a long pause. "Have you heard from Mara lately?"

Aaron accepted the change in subject, updating him on her progress gathering all their people back, getting ready for the launch date coming as soon as EBT-I got fully online.

*

Aaron showed a level of diplomacy and gentleness Brian hadn't seen him use with anyone else when they'd gone to the nurses' station to ask Nurse Kelly if she could draw him and Brian a map to the camp.

She had, with something like steel in her eyes.

Brian had asked if she wanted to come with them, but she'd shook her head.

"I know there's people," she said, "other issei and nisei people, fighting to turn them into national monuments, to make sure the history isn't forgotten." She looked to the side, shoulders tight. "It's important work, but not work I can do. Not right now. Not yet." She lifted her chin. "My job is to remember so everyone will know the details of how people can go so, so wrong. So I can talk when I am ready to talk and not a minute before."

Brian had nodded. He understood being too far inside the fight to be able to carry it on; he thought of people fighting against blood quantum laws, against the Dawes Act, fighting to close the boarding schools. He wondered if he was running away or if saving yourself was a kind of activism too.

The drive to Minidoka the next morning was long and quiet. Brian followed the curve and flow of the snowfields, each rise and crest of volcanic soil, the silver-leafed sagebrush, and snowed-in fields as they rolled across his view.

They wove through fields, each road exactly the length of the property beside it before reaching an unsigned crossroad. The ground had been cleared of the slow-growing sagebrush in the past decade, the land looking almost farmable the closer they got to the camp.

They got out of the truck at the place Nurse Kelly had indicated on the map. The iron gray sky dwarfed the buildings. The pitted gravel parking lot made the truck jerk and twist and when Aaron finally put her in park, Brian could only see a few small outbuildings, a school with a half-fallen-in roof, a one-hundred-yard-long earthworks for cold storage, and a cluster of extremely drafty, empty bunkhouses.

The wind whipped cold and icy around them.

"I'd read about the camps in California," Aaron said, voice tight. "People who'd been forced into these concentration camps had cleared hundreds of high desert acres for farming with no hope or expectation of being allowed to own or work the land once they were freed. Do you know, they made those they imprisoned here build their own buildings? The snows were coming, and they just gave them the supplies and told them to build the best they could. Before being transferred here, a lot of families were forced to stay in stables, on horse tracks. When they were finally let free, they were only allowed to bring what they could fit in a suitcase. None of the furniture they made, none of the crops they harvested, none of the tools of the trades they had to learn to use to survive. That all went to farmers who lived around here. Like that table, sitting there in their fucking living room." He looked down at the cold, frozen earth. "How did this happen?"

Brian kicked the sage-soaked dust, tugging Aaron's jacket tighter around his shoulders. "I don't know. The same way people were forced onto reservations or the Bracero Program was implemented. Just because we ended legal slavery, doesn't mean people don't keep trying to reinstate a world where some people are treated as things."

Aaron looked sick, laying his palm hard and flat against the dented wood. He ran his finger over a bent nail, wood around it cratered by an angry carpenter.

Brian could feel his heart breaking and couldn't stand it, couldn't stand seeing Aaron's brightness dimmed. He placed his hand over Aaron's, pulled it away from the wood, and turned him to look at the fields around them.

"Can you imagine in fifty years, maybe there will be a national monument here, a park to tell people what happened here?"

"No, Americans like to forget," Aaron said.

Brian looked around at the places made by people who had no choice, who had been forced out of their homes by racism and fear. People who had built buildings, buried their dead, educated their children in these camps. He thought of Nurse Kelly's face, the way she'd refused to let the colonel push her around, refused to let him go after Brian just because he was a white man with power. The way she struggled to get that same dignity in her own home but tried to help Brian find his.

He remembered what she'd said about memory.

"Not all Americans," he said quietly. "Not these Americans." He laid his hand on a thin, gray plank. "I think the people who survived these camps and their descendants, those who can, will *make sure* people don't forget. They'll use their rights as Americans and *force* their government to reckon with this history."

Aaron shook his head. "You saw how Nurse Kelly's husband was. The kind of talk she has to live around at home."

Brian nodded, frowning. "I did. It takes a long time to leave. Everything is stacked against leaving bad families, particularly against wives getting free. But working the kind of job she has at EBT-I, maybe it's giving her the stability, the pay she needs to start getting free. Things are changing, and people get out of bad situations all the time." He gave a tight smile. "Just because someone's put up with something for a long time doesn't mean they'll have to do it forever. Just look at you and your family and your culture." He pressed his lips to Aaron's hair, just behind his ear, sure of their privacy in the empty fields behind these forbidding, abandoned barracks. "Or at me and mine."

Aaron sagged, slipping an arm around Brian's side and holding him close. "Still an idealist, Captain."

"Like I said," Brian murmured, tucking his cold fingers into Aaron's jacket pocket. "I have to be."

Chapter Twenty: T-4 Days

"To date, the Department of Commerce has received from the Civil Service Commission the names of 22 alleged perverts in the Department. Of this number: 1 was found not to be an employee; 16 have been or are being separated; 4 cases are pending decision; and in 1 case the evidence developed in the Department's investigation did not substantiate the charge.

[...]

Case D: Arrested on charges of homosexuality. Subject employed in Government service for 31 years. After a thorough investigation by the Department of Commerce and a personal hearing, the allegation was confirmed, whereupon steps were taken to the effect the employee's separated by retirement, to be effective July 12, 1950."

> —"*Perversion Cases - Department of Commerce. Summary, June 15, 1950.*" *An excerpt from the Commerce Department's response to the Senate Hoey Committee. (Records of the U.S. Senate, RG 46)*

December 16, 1951

Brian woke up at 16:30 on December 16th to frantic pounding on his unit door. He stumbled out of bed, pulled on Aaron's jacket and his uniform pants, and cracked it open.

It was Freeman, face lit up with glee. "They did it, Cap! They fucking did it! They got one of the light bulbs to flash on!"

Brian grinned, cheeks aching with it. "That's fucking fantastic, Airman. That is such good fucking news." He looked back at the clock. "Did they say they needed me at the lab?"

Freeman shook his head, tight-buzzed curls barely shifting with the movement. Brian bet he had to cut his own hair; not a lot of Black barbers in Arco. "No, sir, but I knew you'd want to know as soon as I got off shift."

"I did. Thank you for telling me." Brian gave him a tired smile. "I am, however, going to go back to sleep now unless you all need me."

Freeman grinned. "No, sir, we're just fine. I'm going to tell the others."

"Great plan," Brian said.

He lay down in his twin bed, mind buzzing with excitement for long minutes before he eased to sleep.

*

Christmas was on no one's minds on December 18th when the light bulb held on for four seconds before guttering out. On December 19th, at 21:45, with the entire cast of scientists and most of the staff present, all four lights held on for a full minute, enough time for Dr. Antares to sprint from the reactor to the labs and back, whooping the whole way. Brian grinned so hard his cheeks hurt, and his men looked like they were about to burst with pride. After the lights had gone out and backs had been slapped, Dr. Zinn made everyone go home, everyone except for Brian and Aaron.

As soon as the last scientist had left, Aaron tugged Brian into the empty nurses' area. Halo-haired and mad with exhaustion, he was out of his mind with excitement.

"We're going to light up Arco by New Year's; I *know* it."

He pulled out his communicator and called Mara. "I think we're nearly there, Mara. We're close. How are you all faring?"

Brian could hear her tinny voice but none of the words. But watching Aaron's glee dim told him enough.

He said, hushed and worried, "You think he was lulling us into a false sense of security?" He glanced over at Brian, whispering, "The colonel was on the reservation today with a dozen soldiers, searching for the camp. They had a drawing of James."

He turned back to the communicator. "I'm glad you got everyone up the mountain in time, but *shit*. Can you go to the hotel— No, that makes sense; the tribal council wouldn't want you to bring that kind of heat down right in the middle of ski season, not right before Christmas. Could you try farther west, out by White Sands—"

Brian held out his hand. "Can I talk to her?"

Aaron turned to him slowly, face paling. Brian watched him warring with himself, trying to decide if he would let Brian make this sacrifice or try to stop him. Brian reached out his hand, gripped Aaron's free wrist, and held on for a moment, trying to convey: *it's my choice; let me help*.

He saw the moment Aaron gave in, saw the sag of his shoulders.

Into the communicator, Aaron said, "I'm handing you over to Brian. He wants to say something."

"Hi Mara," he said, looking Aaron in the eye. "I think I can help with the colonel."

After a pause, she said, low, serious, "I don't want to put another person in his line of fire."

Brian gave a harsh laugh. "You won't be. There's nothing you can do to make him hate me any more than he already does." He felt it, like a blow to the chest, what he was about to do. "Aaron said that James could change people's minds, change their memories? And it hadn't stuck with the colonel before because James was too exhausted?"

"Yes—but he needs to touch him to do it. But it's still not a sure thing, Brian; the Colonel threw off his influence once, he could do it again—"

Brian spoke over her. "But James has been recovering his strength with the stock of uranium one of the guys from Oak Ridge brought back?" Brian spared a thought for the security director there.

"He has, but it's nowhere near what he would get from a few casks of plutonium."

"We're working on that. You just need a few days grace, right? Long enough for us to produce the plutonium and drive it down to you all?"

Aaron nodded as Mara said, "Yes."

"I can give that to you." Brian stepped into Aaron and tucked his arm around his waist, trying to ground himself in this moment. Then he nodded. "Here's what we're going to do. Do you have something to write this down? The wording is going to be specific."

"All right," she said, tense. "Give me a moment." She called for Jill to bring her a piece of paper.

In the quiet, Aaron whispered, "Brian, you don't have to do this."

Brian gripped his arm tighter, whispering back, "Do you really think you're going to get it working tomorrow?"

"I do."

"And how long do you need to make enough for the ship?"

"About three days, running at the production levels Dr. Zinn has already approved. Faster, if we can double them. Once it's on, we're just going to keep it going."

Brian worked his jaw and looked at what he was about to do. "I trust you."

"Brian?" came Mara's voice.

"I'm here. You're going to have James find someone in the colonel's division who was stationed at Vandenberg. They all like to drink at the same cowboy bar in Roswell."

"I know the one," she said, voice full of disdain. "James is in Roswell tonight; he can go as soon as I call him."

Brian swallowed. "Perfect. It shouldn't be hard to find someone. There's a lot of transfers back and forth. The more highly ranked, the better. James is going to get him to do three things—make his target remember seeing Colonel Flynn's name associated with a blue ticket investigation at Vandenberg—"

Aaron tried to interrupt, but Brian held him tighter as he spoke quickly into the mic.

"Then make him plan to call Vandenberg in the morning and confirm there is a file with the name 'Brian Flynn' and the subject 'Blue Ticket Inquiry.'" He hesitated as Aaron shook his head. "Then James is going to have his contact make a formal report that there is substantive evidence Colonel Flynn engaged in homosexual acts while at Vandenberg Air Force Base last summer and requesting the inquiry be reopened. As soon as that request is made, he'll be yanked from active duty and put under house arrest pending the investigation. Since it's a Friday before the holiday, the MPs won't be able to get the interviews done until after Christmas, maybe even after New Year's, so that will give you all at least a week, maybe two."

There was silence on the line. Then Mara asked, "Is it true?"

Brian coughed. "No. But we'll make the son of a bitch regret naming me after himself. At least long enough for Aaron to get what he needs up here."

"Brian, your career—" Mara started, sounding pained and confused.

He made sure he sounded sure and confident. "My career will be over the instant I leave this lab with the plutonium; I'm not losing anything I haven't already committed to giving up." A vicious smile rose on his face. "And fucking with his career is good in and of itself."

"It is, but they'll figure out it isn't him. And it's not like he'll go quietly, from what we know of him. What if he makes the same claim about you?"

"That's the exact threat he's held over my head since last summer." He set his shoulders. "My whole life, really. As soon as he knows what he's accused of, he'll make the same claim about me."

Brian looked around at the nurses' station, at the record player tucked under the desk, then up through the window, out to the catwalk and the labs, the containment chamber, and the reactor platform. "That will probably make tomorrow my last day at EBT-I." When Aaron shook his head, Brian said quietly, "But it will take them at least until after the holiday to untangle the mess. They'll probably just have me confined to quarters here."

"Brian, that's awful. We can't ask you—" Mara said, her voice tight.

"You're not asking; I'm offering." Brian had no idea how he looked, but from the pain in Aaron's eyes, it wasn't good. "But I can't be handed a blue ticket discharge if I'm not on Earth. And once we have the plutonium and are driving down, we can pick up James in Roswell, then bring him to the colonel's house to properly adjust his memories. Then he won't go after the folks who are staying on Earth." He locked in on Aaron. "I won't let him hurt you or your people any more than he already has."

A long pause followed as Brian traced a pattern on Aaron's back, trying to remember the exact shape of what it looked like in the low light of the cabin.

Then Mara said, "I need to talk to Aaron. And Brian? Thank you."

"You're welcome. Say hi to Jill for me. See you in a week."

"See you."

Aaron took the device, expression intense. "Mara, there has to be—"

Brian buried his face in Aaron's neck, trying to count his heartbeats as his own careened wildly in his chest. He couldn't hear Mara's response, but it took a while.

"No, you don't! He's fought so hard, so long, given up so much. We can't just—"

Another long response. Brian slid his hand under the back of Aaron's shirt, the soft curve of his spine giving him a sense of reality. He thought of his service weapon, carefully cleaned and ready. *At least they're not asking what I'm preparing to do if James can't pull it off.*

After several minutes, Aaron said, "Then I guess I'd better get this reactor online." And then he ended the call.

Aaron drew away just enough to look Brian in the eyes. "You two can have your way, but I think it's too much to ask, Brian. Your career means everything to you."

Brian nodded, heart kicking up again. "It does. But as much as I love this country, I don't see it being a place I can be free in my lifetime. Can you?"

"Anything can happen—" Aaron started, but at Brian's look, glanced down to where they held each other close in the dark of the chief nurse's office. "You're right. Not in the way you can be free with us." He gripped Brian's arms. "Though I hate to say it."

"That's it then," Brian replied, keeping his tone clear and precise. "Going through a blue ticket investigation will distract him for long enough to keep Mara and the others safe, even if we don't get the reactor working until after Christmas. Then we'll get down to where you've stashed the repaired ship on the reservation and be off to Antares before he can return to active duty."

Aaron drew him in again, hands spread wide and protectively over his spine. "I don't know what I could possibly have done to deserve you."

Brian closed his eyes, also holding on tight. "I don't think it's about deserve. It's about doing what's right. For me, for us, and for your people."

"But using the blue ticket process? It's *awful*."

Brian huffed a humorless chuckle. "It's one he was happy to use against me. And I'm just enough of a bastard to think using it is one way of bending the arc toward justice, all on its own."

"I don't think that's what Minister Theodore Parker had in mind with that quote."

"No, probably not." Brian gave the ghost of a wicked smirk. "But he probably never imagined men like us using it to justify our lives, so we'll just have to keep fighting without his approval."

Aaron's expression was pained, but he accepted the lighter tone from Brian. "Sounds like a good plan, Airman. Now, let's see what we can do about that reactor."

Chapter Twenty-One: T-0 Days

"The holder of a blue discharge lands in a predicament not fundamentally different from that of the holder of a yellow or dishonorable discharge received as the result of an open trial in a court-martial under the Articles of War. He finds it very difficult to get a job. The public is warned against the man by the appearance and wording of his discharge certificate in both cases. With an irony perhaps unconscious the same regulation which deals with these discharges on the basis of undesirable habits or traits of character contains a direction that the discharging authority shall maintain close contact with the United States Employment Service and make "every effort" to cause men so discharged to accept employment in industry or agriculture. In addition to the difficulty of getting a job, the holder of a blue discharge does not get mustering-out pay, and finds, too, that he is barred from unemployment compensation. He is ineligible for membership in the American Legion and possibly other veterans' organizations. Some surety companies will not go to his bond. Some colleges will not accept him as a student or a teacher."

—History of the Phrase "Discharged Under Conditions Other Than Dishonorable" and Present Discharge Criteria for Three Services. Investigations of the National War Effort: Blue Discharges. United States Committee on Veterans' Affairs, House of Representatives, 1949.

December 20, 1951

Brian didn't go back to the barracks that night. He stayed to the end of his shift, wanding everyone in. He gave himself a chance to truly see and appreciate every single face.

Then he handed the Geiger counter to Gamgee before heading down to the basement, where he put his back against the wall to watch the experiments in their containment chambers. There were over a dozen pieces of glass in the windows, with mineral oil carefully filling the gaps between them. Without the mineral oil, the glass layers warped the images behind them too much to be useful; but with the mineral oil, they remained clear and nonrefractive. It reminded him of something about things only getting clearer when you added an outside element.

"Hey, Captain," said a voice from the stairs.

"Good morning, Nurse Kelly."

She came over and leaned against the cinder block wall beside him. "I didn't think you took daylight hour shifts."

"I have a feeling they're going to get the lights going today, and I wanted to be here."

She smiled. "Me too. All of the nurses are here, and the maintenance staff."

They watched the experiments.

"It's an incredible thing," she said quietly, "getting to be a part of this. No more belching coal factories, no more cave-ins at the mines. Good, clean energy. Once we get the reactor running, it will be able to keep going, keep producing the materials we need to light up the world. More than enough. What was the calculation I saw? After a month we'll have produced enough plutonium to seed another reactor? They're already talking about an EBR-II once this proof of concept has completed."

Brian nodded, something settling in his chest. "A month or two, yeah, I think so." He let himself smile back at her. "I'm really proud I got a chance to help, even in a small way."

"Me too." She checked her watch. "They said they'd try the next experiment at 09:00. Want to head up with me, get the good seats?"

"Perfect."

They climbed the stairs together after snagging some folding chairs from the spare closet to set them up with a clear view of the reactor platform. At 8:59 a.m., everybody in the lab crowded around the base of the reactor platform, with Dr. Zinn having the honor of running the control panel. Aaron and Dr. Eisenberg were in the upstairs lab, staring at the dials and seventy-two separate color-coded signal lights, ready to note and address any unexpected surges or changes. The four light bulbs were strung in the middle of the lab, empty of light, swaying on a long, thin string.

Dr. Zinn's warm voice echoed through the lab: "Let's get a countdown. T minus thirty seconds."

And, together, airmen and nurses, maintenance men and scientists all counted down, eyes on the light bulbs. Their voices clattered against the cinder block walls and concrete floors, and Brian had never felt more connected, more like he was one piece of a finished, perfect whole than in that moment.

"Ten, nine, eight, seven, six—"

Nurse Kelly reached over and squeezed his hand so tight he was sure he was going to find nail marks on his palm.

"—five, four, three—"

His heart raced, his body tight with anticipation.

"—two, one!"

Dead silence, and then Dr. Zinn flipped the switch, the sound echoing across the installation. There was a low humming sound, a churning moment. Then, bright as day, the four oversized bulbs flared bright and held on, not flickering, not fizzing, not bursting: just steady, clear, even *light.*

The lab erupted.

Nurse Kelly gave him a massive hug before turning to the other nurses and crowding them all into a laughing, crying mass hug. Brian's airmen jumped up and down, tossing their hats like it was graduation. The scientists ran around with clipboards, checking the pipes, racing up to the control panel to note the final calibrations.

Over the noise, Dr. Zinn called, "Mr. Jolley, could I get a ladder, please? And a piece of chalk?"

Brian watched as the head of maintenance pulled a tall ladder from the storage closet and placed it where Dr. Zinn requested against a bare concrete wall.

As the celebrations rushed and eddied around him, Dr. Zinn drew what looked like a mushroom cloud turned on its side. Then Brian realized that wasn't it.

Not a mushroom cloud. It's wind. A turbine being turned.
Power being made.

Under the drawing, Dr. Zinn wrote in a careful block hand, and then, one by one, invited each of the scientists to climb the ladder and sign their names.

*Electricity was first generated here
from Atomic Energy on Dec. 20, 1951.*

Those Present

W.H. Zinn	*H.V. Lichtenberger*
M. Novick	*L.J. Koch*
E.N. Pettitt	*G.K. Whitham*
R. Cameron	*M.L. King*
B.C. Cerutti	*M. Wilkey*
E.J Barrow	
L.E. Loftin	*G.H. Stonehocker*
C.R. Gibson	*K. Johnson*
W.E. Mclen	*F.D. McGinnis*
G. Eisenberg	*J. O'Flanagan*
A. Antares	

*

The rest of the morning was spent checking and rechecking the experiments, testing and monitoring the reactor, checking for radiation leaks, and celebrating in small groups, all while the four light bulbs shone on and on and on. In the afternoon, Dr. Zinn had Brian show the mayor of Arco—a local rancher—in to see it and to give the final approval to begin powering Arco in the new year.

The mayor's awestruck expression filled Brian's chest with hope this would *work.*

Late in the afternoon, Nurse Kelly found Brian, tucked into a corner of the upstairs lab, fourth coffee of the day in his hands, watching the scientists do their final checks.

"Captain Flynn, I have a call for you."

He drew away from the wall, shoulders tight. "Is it my father?"

Her eyes were banked fire. "It is."

"I don't want to put you in the middle, but can you tell him I'm off shift?"

"Brian," she said smoothly, "it would be my genuine pleasure. If he asks, when should I say you're on shift again?"

"'Never' would work well."

"Perfect." She took a hesitating step forward. Then she folded Brian into a brief, tight hug, whispering, "I'm goddamned proud of you, Captain," before drawing back.

"Thank you, Nurse Kelly." Brian took a deep sip of his coffee as she left the room, heels clacking on the polished concrete.

Aaron wandered over and said, keeping his voice low and his hands in his pockets. "Was that your commanding officer?"

Brian shook his head. "The colonel. No other news yet."

Aaron grimaced and nodded. "He hasn't been seen on the rez yet today; everything went fine with James." He gave Brian half of a hopeful smile. "Maybe there'll be no news? It's late enough, and the folks he might have wanted to cause trouble with might have gone home already."

"We can only hope."

Around dinnertime, the reactor was still humming along happily, and all of the scientists and nurses and airmen and most of the maintenance staff left to continue their celebrations in Arco. By 20:00, it was just Brian, Aaron, and Mr. Jolley left in the lab.

In the quiet of the lab, with Aaron running and rerunning yield calculations based off of the live results, Brian wandered downstairs to look at the lights again, still shining brightly on their looping string. He'd heard Aaron propose—and Dr. Zinn approve—tripling the plutonium production goals through the holiday weekend. They would have more than enough for Aaron's people. EBT-I would still be ahead of schedule.

"All that work, just to get these going," he heard from behind him and turned to Mr. Jolley, a fond smile moving across his face.

Brian replied, "I heard Dr. Zinn say they were going to run the building on the reactor tomorrow."

"Is that right?"

"Yep. Then Arco in the new year." Brian looked up, rocking on his heels as he admired the scientists' names on the wall. "This stuff scales quickly."

Mr. Jolley nodded, glancing behind Brian. Pulling his work cart, he stepped up to the massive concrete wall behind the light bulbs. He tilted his head back. "Notice how they didn't ask us to put our names up there? Or any of the nurses?"

"I did notice that," Brian said, moving a little closer.

Jolley looked over at him, considering. "What you think about us fixing that?"

Brian looked at him for a long moment and then nodded. "I think that sounds like a great idea. But won't they just wipe it right off?"

Mr. Jolley huffed a chuckle. "Not if we use grease chalk. It'll smear like nobody's business if they so much as take a rag to it. And Dr. Zinn *hates* that kind of public untidiness." He gave a knowing grin to Brian's expression. "His office is one thing; history is another."

Brian nodded, stepping forward.

*

The next morning, when Brian headed back to the barracks after his shift, the bottom of the wall read:

Kiko Mabuni Kelly

Wilma S. Mangum	*Eleanor B. Barnes*
Gladys Joslin	*Virginia Kruse*
Agnes Williams	*C.H. Jolley*
L. Wilson	*M. K. Martin*
H.R. Ramshead	*J. Hammersley*
R. Woosley	*S. Metzger*
B. Flynn	*L. Gamgee*
J. Hodgins	*R. Durbin*
K. Kingman	*S. Ramirez*
G. Freeman	

*

On Monday morning, Brian was suspended pending a blue ticket inquiry.

It was just after his shift, and Brian was going over the new protocol for visitors with Hodgins since it seemed Argonne Labs would start doing reactor tours in the new year with members of the Congressional oversight committee. Dr. Zinn's steps had been slow and heavy, and for the first time since Brian had met him, he looked his age.

"Captain Flynn, before you head back to the barracks, may I speak with you?"

Brian closed his eyes, and tried to think of arcs bending, of taking a walk in all kinds of weather. Then he looked around, trying to memorize everything again, the feel and smell and sound of it: the containment area, the asbestos-covered tubes, nurse's station, the high catwalk around the central room, the control rooms and labs, the steel spiral staircase leading up to the nuclear reactor platform. Every light in the building powered by the reactor.

And in the heart of the building, four lights, still shining bright.

No more scarcity of light.

Brian set his shoulders. "Of course."

He turned to Hodgins. "I'll update you after this."

"Sure, sir." Hodgins paused at Brian's tight expression. "What's going on?"

Brian forced a smile that felt like it was cracking something. "It'll be all right."

Dr. Zinn's face told him that it would not.

He ushered Brian into his office, shut the door behind him, and gestured for Brian to sit in the flat-backed chair. He did, waiting as Dr. Zinn settled himself heavily into his own chair.

The man's face was pained. He ran his fingers over the edge of his desk, trying to straighten some of the papers there but only lightly disturbing the mess. He glanced up at his books.

"I—" he started, voice cracking, "I was very glad to share my books with you. It's rare to meet an officer, or working scientist, for that matter, with a curiosity as broad as yours." He looked Brian in the eyes. "I've appreciated everything you've brought to this facility. I don't know of someone who could have done your role better and—"

He stood abruptly and paced the tiny space between his desk and the wall, barely making it three steps before he had to about-face. He threw up his hands and said with tamped-down fury, "I don't know how we can go so fast in one direction—splitting the atom to power entire cities—and so *goddamned retrograde* when it comes to people's personal lives. Who in the fuck *cares* what you and Dr. Antares are doing with your spare time as long as you show up to work and do the exemplary job you've been doing?"

He took a shuddering breath, then rubbed his palms on his coat and looked at his desk. "I don't get a choice in the matter. If it was a report from this laboratory, I want you to know Captain Flynn, I would have done everything in my power to quash it." He met his gaze, holding it despite his obvious discomfort. "But it wasn't. It was a report from Vandenberg, and I'm not your commanding officer, and I can't stop the one who calls himself that from doing this."

He flipped over a piece of paper where he'd taken down handwritten notes. "Just a few minutes ago, I got a call on the nurses' line, telling me you were suspended from duties pending inquiry, and I wasn't to allow you into the lab." He frowned, voice turning into a low growl. "I ensured you're not going to be forced to go to the nearest base for confinement. I told them you would stay in the barracks. Nobody wants to send anyone way the hell out here to pick you up on Christmas Eve." He reached for a slip of paper with handwritten notes. "I can tell your men, if you would like, but I can also give you some time to tell them this morning. You know us scientists, terrible at protocol, always forgetting things." He gently slid the notes into the trash can beside his desk. He paused, meeting Brian's gaze again. "You understand I don't have a choice?"

Brian nodded. "I do, sir," he said, keeping his voice steady even as pressure built behind his eyes. "And I would like to tell my men. Thank you for letting me. They can go to rotating eight-hour shifts starting today. Freeman will know how to set it up to make it fair."

Dr. Zinn swallowed and replied, taking some of Brian's even tone. "That sounds like a good idea, Captain. I just wanted to say—" He passed a hand over his face and continued. "This is a goddamned shame of a situation. I am ashamed of our Congress for allowing these blue discharges, and I am ashamed of your commander for seeing it through. They have not respected your service or repaid your loyalty in kind, but you've given it anyway, willingly and with such dedication to our mission as should make anybody proud. You deserve better than this. This entire installation will feel your loss."

Dr. Zinn held his hand out for Brian to shake, and Brian took it. "And if you end up reapplying to UCLA," he said, tone as firm as his grip, "I would be delighted to write you a letter of recommendation."

Brian swallowed, not sure he could muster words at the moment. He nodded his thanks and let himself out of Dr. Zinn's office, closing the door with a careful click.

The walk back to Hodgins was the longest he'd ever taken, body tight and aching. Aaron was lounging next to the door, chatting with the young airman about something. When he looked up and caught Brian's eye, saw his face, he took a step toward him, then visibly forced himself to hold back.

Brian jerked his head to the exit, and Aaron let Hodgins wand him out—still as clean as always—before heading out into the snow. Brian let Hodgins do the same, then put on his cover and held the door open.

"Hodgins," Brian started and then took a quick, hard gasp of the freezing air as the junior airman turned to him.

"Captain?"

Brian swallowed. "My commanding officer at Vandenberg has ordered me confined to quarters pending a blue ticket inquiry based on an accusation from my prior posting."

Hodgins eyes went wide, his mouth opening to say something, but Brian didn't want to know what. He didn't want his men drawn into this inquiry and didn't want to find out from them that they agreed with it.

Brian held up his hand. "Freeman will be creating a new shift schedule, three shifts of eight hours a day, either until the inquiry is dismissed or you are assigned a new commanding officer." He raised his chin. "It has been the greatest honor of my life working with you all to protect EBT-I and ensuring this mission succeeded. If I don't get to say goodbye, I want you to know that."

Hodgins gaped, but he managed to say, "It was an honor to have served with you, sir. I'm proud to have been in your unit." He blinked hard a few times, hands flexing at his sides. "Maybe this will all blow over?"

Brian gave him a hard smile and shook his head. "I don't think so, Airman. But I appreciate the thought."

Then Hodgins pulled himself into a formal salute, holding it until Brian returned it, his heart expanding against his ribs. Brian nodded and went to join Aaron at his truck.

Aaron sat in the passenger seat, and Brian? He could not have been more grateful, at that moment, that Aaron had guessed what he needed most. He slid his key from under his uniform, put it in the ignition, and drove away from EBT-I.

After dropping Brian off at the barracks, Aaron headed back to pack up his cabin for the night. Brian assembled his men and told them exactly what he'd told Hodgins. They were all horrified on his behalf, and he had to caution them not to say or write anything rash, anything that might get them in trouble. Freeman wrote up a new shift chart during the meeting and posted it on the gym door. Then Brian went to his room and took a long, hot shower.

He wouldn't have thought he'd be able to sleep, with all the emotions and pain and anger and hope churning through him. But after a quick breakfast, he dropped off into a deep sleep.

*

That night at 02:00, Brian and Aaron stopped the reactor and watched the four light bulbs dim to dark. Aaron had dropped a pill into the coffee he'd brought for Junior Airman Gamgee, who'd pulled the first overnight duty. It had sent him straight to sleep in minutes while Brian waited in the truck, books and clothes carefully packed in two duffel bags.

Aaron moved all of the plutonium they would need into a half-dozen cat-sized leaded cases as Brian wrote Dr. Zinn and Nurse Kelly goodbye notes. A single cubic foot of plutonium weighed over 1300 pounds; thankfully Aaron's truck had a carrying capacity of over 20,000 pounds. Brian held open the doors as Aaron sweated and floated them through the lab and then out into the Idaho snow. Aaron strapped them down in the bed of his pickup, right at the tailgate so they weren't close to where Brian would be sitting. Then he returned inside to help as Brian got the reactor humming online, the bulbs flashing back on and staying steady and true.

"Ready?" Aaron called from the door. "Gamgee will wake up in a few minutes."

Brian looked around, took a deep breath, and nodded. "I'm ready to go."

Chapter Twenty-Two: T+5 Days

"Nothing could more clearly prove the anomalous and illogical and disingenuous nature of the blue discharge than this policy of the Veterans' Administration. That Administration does not take the discharge at its face value of 'neither honorable nor dishonorable.' It seeks to resolve the questions which the Army has evaded and even assumes the right to separate the sheep from the goats. It says to one holder of a blue discharge, 'Your separation from the service was under conditions which we adjudge to be dishonorable' and to another, 'Your separation was under conditions which we adjudge to be other than dishonorable.'"

> —*History of the Phrase "Discharged Under Conditions Other Than Dishonorable" and Present Discharge Criteria for Three Services. Investigations of the National War Effort: Blue Discharges. United States Committee on Veterans' Affairs, House of Representatives, 1949.*

December 25, 1951

The entire drive south to and through Utah, Brian kept glancing in the rearview mirror. He was waiting to see an air force-issued Jeep on their tail. They listened to the radio, both too caught up in their own thoughts to be much good for conversation. At every gas station, they switched drivers, with Brian keeping his eyes peeled.

But it was always just them and the slowly arcing sun.

At the end of the day was Zion.

Aaron insisted, said it wouldn't take them too far out of their way to see the national park, open and empty on Christmas Day. And it was...Brian couldn't find the words. He'd grown up in a place where the mountains often had more expressive features than the people who lived in their shadows. But the soft alternating blues, the arcing stripes, the cavern walls—it was like nothing he'd ever seen. Like nothing he knew how to find.

And here it was.

Here they were, together.

They pulled over on the side of a dirt road just outside of the border of Zion as the stars came out; they hadn't seen another truck for hours. It was a little warmer than Idaho, probably midforties.

Aaron moved the plutonium into the low pine trees, secured under a tarp, while Brian laid out their sleeping bags in the back of the truck. Aaron hitched himself up onto the tailgate, then crawled toward the cab, lay down, and subtly arced his arm across both pillows, eyes on the stars overhead. Brian joined him after stretching his legs and non-too-subtly making sure they were truly alone. He climbed up into the bed of the truck and lay beside Aaron, letting his head pillow on muscles that let themselves be soft just for him. Brian reached a hand down between them, fingers plucking at the side seam of Aaron's jeans as they breathed together in the quiet twilight, and Aaron floated the unzipped sleeping bag onto them, warm and secure.

Brian inched his foot his way, moving his toes under Aaron's ankle until he got with the program, until Aaron put his leg on his. Something quiet and sure filled Brian's stomach, something easy and ongoing. It was warm, in spite of the chill on their faces, this easy entanglement.

He rolled onto his side, cocking his other leg across Aaron's hip, applying his hand, firmly, definitively in the middle of his chest. And it felt—he felt like a pinup girl, feminine, with Aaron's legs together, his apart, curled up on his *beau*. Just as he was about to get tense about it, Aaron's fingers traced the barest hint of a line down the side of his arm.

"I love how strong you keep yourself."

"Hmm?" Brian said.

Aaron shook his head a little. "You keep your body strong. You don't have to; there's other people in your former line of work who've got some bellies—"

"I like to be able to run away when I want to."

Aaron tensed and then slowly relaxed again under him. "I can see that. But it feels good, too, right? To be strong?"

Brian reached over, felt Aaron's biceps as he wriggled. "You're pretty strong."

"I'm speaking from experience!"

"I like being strong enough to do the things I need to. Not everybody gets the chance." Brian got a little closer and slipped his fingertips between two of the buttons on the front of Aaron's shirt. Aaron shivered at the touch. "All right?" Brian asked.

"I have literally had your dick in my hand," Aaron said with incredulity. "Why would this not be all right?"

Brian hunched his shoulders. "There's fucking, and then there's sex."

"To me, it wasn't fucking—what we were doing in Wyoming or at the cabin," Aaron replied relatively evenly.

"Yeah?" Brian said, soft and unsure.

"Hey, c'mere." Aaron urged Brian off him, and he immediately felt cold. But then Aaron was up and straddling Brian's hips, hands on his face, leaning close and pressing his forehead to Brian's. "Do I need to use more words?"

Brian rolled his head to the side to get away from the intensity, and Aaron let him, still staying close.

Aaron said, "I thought the whole 'you running away with me thing' made it pretty clear what we mean to each other." Brian's heartbeat quickened. "But we should talk about it if it's worrying you."

Brian frowned. "I don't know about *worrying*. I just—" He swallowed. "I don't know any words to describe our 'us,' our relationship, what we're going to call each other to other people, to *your* people." He closed his eyes, trying to see inside himself, to see what was giving him this pebble-in-the-boot feeling of the soul. He clutched Aaron's shirt, the cotton creaking between his fingers. "How do I know?" he said, his voice tiny. "How do I know what this is? What words to use for it, what to call how I feel?"

And Aaron didn't blow him off. He answered, voice quiet and gentle, "What I feel for you—it's special. Different from what I've felt for anyone else I've been with. But I've had other lovers, just like you have. And when I was trying to figure out what I felt for them, I would shut my eyes and think of somebody I knew I loved—any kind of love. Platonic, romantic, familial—any kind of love. The last time I did it, I thought about my sister. And I let myself fill up with that feeling, get a really good sense of where it pushed on the inside of my ribs, how it made me feel. I feel all of that, and then when I think about her or him or them, I think about what it was I was feeling, I think about what I felt—and then I decide if that's love."

"That is the most scientist description of love I've ever heard."

Aaron shrugged. "Physicist!"

"Maybe you could..." Brian drifted his hand up to touch his cheek. "Maybe tell me what you think. What we are."

"Oh." Aaron brushed his lips across Brian's palm. "Well, we're certainly together."

Brian nodded, and he settled.

"We're certainly lovers," Aaron continued and moved his hand back to Brian's side, holding it there for a long, soft second. Brian smiled. "And we're friends."

"Yeah?" Brian said.

"Yeah," Aaron replied.

"But what are we—"

"On my home world, we have words for different kinds of partnerships. Platonic, romantic, sexual, different gradients of each as suits people. Sort of like here you have dates and then boyfriends, fiancés, and husbands, and then..."

"Then? What's after 'husbands'?"

"Things like 'father'—"

"You can be a father without being a husband and a husband without being a father."

"On my world too."

"On Antares, can—are there—"

"My world is flawed in a lot of ways. I came here because— Well, you know why I came here. But we've talked about—and I expect you've talked with Mara and Jill about this too—how on Antares there's a lot of different kinds of gender, different kinds of love. And they all have a place as long as everybody in that relationship is safe, feels safe. Gaians have a higher tolerance for different free members of your community being unsafe than we do. With some very notable exceptions." He rolled his shoulders before stilling. "But you asked what I would call you, and the answer is '*xilla*.'" He started the word with a clicking sound, just like Brian's mother had clicked her tongue at his grandfather's horse.

"You would call me *what*?"

"*Xilla*." Aaron made the sound again.

"What's that mean?"

"More serious than boyfriend, less public than husband. Like, boyfriends don't usually throw away their careers to keep each other safe. And to call you 'husband,' we would have to exchange something in public."

"How do I use it in a sentence?"

Aaron's face lit up as if one of the light bulbs at EBT-I had been installed behind his eyes. He leaned a little closer. "You would say, 'I am *xilla* with him. He is *xilla* with me. We are *xilem*.'"

"Could I say, 'I love you, *xilla*'?"

"Yeah." Aaron breathed. "Yeah, and I would reply, 'I love you *xilla*'."

"Good to know," Brian said before putting his arms behind his head and giving Aaron a unapologetic shit-eating grin. Aaron cracked up, leaning down kiss him sweetly, hand splayed possessively over his chest before rolling to his side and lying beside him again.

Brian looked up into the perfect clarity of the stars, mountains arcing before him, but he had to know. "How many of your people are going to be there? Not just Mara and Jill and James. We'll be there tomorrow, after we deal with the colonel." He bit his lip. "I've been so focused on the plutonium, then on what I would do about the colonel I hadn't thought that far. Is there a formal way to be introduced, or is it more casual?"

"A hundred and eleven of my people decided to stay on Earth, of the two hundred and six who survived the crash. The ship only needs about fifty people to run, and there are twelve Gaians—counting your lovely self and Jill—who have elected to come along. So we'll have one hundred and seven people on the ship. Some of those who are staying will be there tonight to say goodbye; some are so settled in their new lives they're wishing us the best from afar. As for how we'll introduce ourselves, that's equally your choice and mine. You know me. I like to be straightforward. It's pretty much the only straight thing about me." And Brian rolled his eyes. "If you want, when we can, there are rituals, things we can do to formalize being *xilla*. But probably once we're a hundred kilometers up in atmosphere or higher would be a better time."

"I want to be straightforward with them too. Being public, I think it's important, now it won't put us in danger. After we leave the planet works fine for me." Brian loved that that was a sentence he got to say.

"They'll love you. And yeah, on the ship, we can."

Brian settled in closer. "Tell me again about the ship."

And Aaron gestured, bringing up a sheet of sand and glass from the roadside. He traced it out in the air, shining and strange and wonderful, telling Brian about how engines worked with TK, and who filled what roles on the bridge, and a million, billion details. Nearly one for every star arcing above them in the heavenly sky until Brian drifted off to sleep.

*

They came over a rough-cut hillside flecked with half-dead sages, winding and twining down toward Brian's family home. They'd picked up James in Albuquerque, and he'd ridden in the truck bed, warming his hands and buffing up his powers on the plutonium containers. Brian clenched his hands on the wheel until the pain grounded him. He wished he could keep driving right past the house with its cherry tree and the burned out wreck of his truck beside it. But he'd promised Mara he would help. And this was part of it, getting his father where James could change his mind, change his memories; making sure he wasn't in a position to hurt any of the Antarans staying behind to make Earth their home. *Whatever it takes.*

Aaron reached across the bench seat. He slid his palm up Brian's shoulder, fingers gentle on the scruff of Brian's neck. Brian felt as stiff as porcelain and twice as fragile. But they were going to get through this. His father had no idea what Aaron was, where he was from. He had to trust Aaron to protect himself. *To protect me, too*, a tiny voice inside him whispered.

"Ready?" Aaron said as the low house rose over the last ridge.

Brian lifted his foot off of the accelerator to let the gentle slope slow the truck to a halt and perch, rocking in neutral at the top of the hillside. Brian glanced in the rearview mirror, meeting James's eyes as he took in the scene. James's brown face and tightly kinked hair were just visible through the dust-smeared back window. For a moment, Brian wished the truck would roll backward, that they could take the dirt road back to the county road, reverse all the way back to Idaho, to the place where they had to hide but they were safe. Maybe he could beat the blue ticket inquiry this time with Dr. Zinn and his men on his side. He would be out in two years; then he and Aaron could, what? Find a little homestead? Be *gentlemen bachelors*? Raise some fucking sheep?

Let their minds rot in the grooves between the sawtooth mountains, safe as corpses?

No.

No.

He wouldn't let this world limit them. He would get Aaron back to the stars where he belonged. *And where I might belong too.*

Just one more obstacle; just the same one as always.

"All right," he said, voice slow and even. "We can do this."

Aaron's hand slipped down to his knee, gripping it once firmly before letting go.

"Are you sure I can't just stop his heart from outside the house? I could do it, Brian. I could."

Brian felt that, in his bones. It hurt to think of his dad dead; it hurt that the thought was such a relief.

"I want to change him. If the only way to change his mind is to kill him, then fine. But killing him is like firing a neutron into a reactor without any control rods. It's not safe, not for you, not for any of your people who're staying behind. If we don't have to, I don't want to begin us, begin our lives together with a murder. I want us to be free on our own power and not with his ghost following us out to Antares IV."

Aaron nodded; it was a discussion they'd had a few dozen times on the trip down from Idaho. Aaron would respect his wishes, though it was clear he'd prefer a different, more permanent solution. *Respects what I want to do, but not because he understands it.*

Brian pulled up in front of the house and parked beside his father's GMC. His gaze caught and snagged on the crown of the cherry tree as it peaked over the roof. James said the house arrest was still in force and would be through New Year's. Brian let the truck tick down, fingers tight on his key as he slipped it back onto the chain with his dog tags.

He swung himself out of the truck, knowing he could have squeezed Aaron's hand just once more, let the soft, quiet sense of himself wrap around him, gild him, protect him from what was to come.

"Hey," Aaron said, coming around the truck toward him. Brian didn't hear the crunch of the colonel's boots on the gravel, didn't see those old, over-ironed curtains twitch. Yet, still, he shied away.

Understanding and hurt warred in Aaron's eyes. "We don't have to fucking do this, Brian. You're—" Aaron's face crumpled. "You're shaking. This isn't worth it—"

"We need to do this to keep your people safe," Brian said, tight and hard. "And we need to do it now before he finds a way to short-circuit the blue ticket inquiry."

James watched them both, face carefully neutral, hands on top of the containers.

Aaron shook his head, expression holding a world of pain. Brian checked his service pistol was secured at his waist, turned on his heel and walked toward the site of his nightmares. He let the yellow dust of the path swirl up and around his boots, clogging their pores, getting deep and scratchy under the leather, working its way into places where it would blister, between his toes, and at the arch of his foot—in the soft underside of it that his father used to whip with switches from the cherry tree he kept alive in the New Mexico heat out of spite.

"It's not worth it, fighting back," he used to say, *"I'll always win."*

And he always had.

But not this time.

Brian had a plan.

He knocked on the door, Aaron behind him, hanging back on his toes like he was warming up before a boxing match.

The colonel opened the door, and Brian was on him, hand on his throat, throwing him to the floor. Aaron followed at his back as if this had been the plan, though Brian hadn't known it had been until he'd seen his father's rage-red face.

Colonel Brian Flynn, Sr. was smaller than Brian remembered, his mind drifting and quiet as he forced the man into a chokehold. He kept his head ducked so his father couldn't claw his eyes out as Aaron tried to keep the colonel's legs under control with his hands, keep him from getting to his feet.

Choking someone out took a long time and Brian had sweated through his uniform by the time he was certain the colonel was out cold. He counted to 100 and then let go, scrambling to escape the man's limp touch. His back slammed into the wood paneled walls, bruising as he panted. The monster of Brian's childhood lay on the floor, red-faced, with a rising ring of bruises around his neck.

Brian tried to stand, stumbling as he got to his feet, only to feel Aaron's powers catch him and hold him up until Aaron's hand was on his arm.

"See how he fucking likes it," Brian gasped out, hoarse as if he'd been the one who'd been choked. "There's a roll of rope in the shed. If you can get it for me, we can tie him up. James can do his trick while the person is unconscious?"

Aaron nodded, looking like he might be sick, then called out the door. James came to join them, and Aaron waited until he was in the room before leaving to get the rope. Brian couldn't stop staring at the colonel's belt, the well-worn creases in it.

James wore a grim expression, lips tight. When he saw the unconscious man at Brian's feet, he flicked him a wide-eyed look but said nothing.

"Aaron said he didn't need to be conscious for you to do your work?"

"He doesn't. But we'll need to wait for him to come back around to ensure the modifications caught and held. We'll need some reason he'll accept about why he was passed out."

"He drinks," Brian said, smelling the bourbon. "I can find some of his bottles—"

Aaron's voice came from the doorway. "I can get them, Brian. You don't have to."

Brian swallowed and nodded, leaning back against the wall, eyes not leaving the colonel's body.

James knelt and unbuttoned the colonel's shirt. Little wisps of white hair covered his chest, but no muscle, no definition.

Guess beating your sons half to death doesn't build muscle tone, Brian thought, feeling totally untethered.

James laid his hand over the colonel's heart, pressing down *hard* as if he was trying to save him from a heart attack.

A waste of time.

And then it was done. James drew away, looking queasy, and stood. He spoke to Aaron. "We'll need to stay, to wait until he wakes up, to see what he remembers."

Brian choked down a breath. "How do you want to do that?"

James gave him a crooked smile. "I tried to change his memory so he thinks of me as his ally, his spy on the reservation, feeding him information about the visitors. He was expecting a visit from me this afternoon with an update for the raid on our last hideaway we heard he has planned for tomorrow. We'll have a connection, he and I, for the next hour or so." James tapped the side of his head. "So, we can wait until I feel him wake up, then I'll knock on the door and see how we did."

Brian held back a shudder. He'd been hoping to leave right away, but more than anything, he wanted to know his father could never hurt anyone ever again.

"What do you want to do if it doesn't work?" James asked with that same neutral expression he'd had outside.

"I'll take care of it." Brian said shortly.

"Brian—" Aaron said, voice cracking.

Brian shook his head. "I—I can't—"

"Okay," Aaron said. "Okay, Brian. Let's get you out of here, to the fresh air, just for a minute."

Brian let Aaron tighten his grip on his elbow and lead him outside.

They sat on the porch with their backs to the side of the house, leaning on each other. James gave them some space, lying on the porch with his cowboy hat over his face and seeming to take a nap. Aaron's arm never left Brian's shoulders, his fingers never stopping their soft, easy rhythm on his upper arm. They didn't speak as Brian's heart rate finally climbed down from pure panic to something easier, more livable.

After what might have been minutes but was surely less than an hour, James lifted his hat off his face and sat up in a crisp motion. He stood, swiped the dust off his pants, and clapped his hat on his thigh. Then he strode over to the door and knocked.

At the sound of his father's boots on the hardwood, Brian's chest caved in, heart barely able to beat. He pushed his face into Aaron's shoulder and tried to hold back a whine. It was so much worse listening to him, waiting to be found, to be seen.

"Randolph, it's good to see you, boy," the colonel said through the static growing in Brian's ears. "Come in, come in."

"Good to see you too, Colonel. Things are all set for tomorrow—"

And then the door was shut. Through the thin wall, Brian could hear the two men stepping over the bare hardwood and to the couches, a murmur of conversation through the still air of the desert. Silence followed for a long minute until Aaron stiffened beside him.

"Something's wrong—" he said, and then there was a crash, and Aaron was bolting around the corner, Brian right behind him.

Aaron shoved the door open, using his powers on the lock, and then—they froze. The colonel stood over James, gun out and pointed at him; James had his hands up, blood running down the side of his face.

"*Antares*—" the colonel snarled.

Brian tried to force himself to move forward. But Aaron squared his shoulders, raised his hands, and the colonel stopped moving, his body stiff as a statue. His feet rose a few limp inches off the floor, his eyes, wide and terrified. The revolver drifted out of his frozen hand, cylinder popping open, bullets floating free of the chapter, all gliding to opposite corners of the room.

"James?" Aaron said in an undertone. "*What the fuck?*"

James wiped the blood off his cheek with his sleeve. Then he hauled himself to his feet and walked over to stand beside Aaron. He didn't let the hanging man out of his sight. "He must have—thrown it off?" His voice was low, still shaky. "We knew it was a possibility, but—"

"Clinical thick-headedness is a Flynn family tradition," Brian said tightly. "From what I've seen, I don't think a brick to the head would change his mind, so whatever you did probably didn't stand a chance."

He stepped closer to Aaron and put a hand on his arm as he watched his father's face turn purple with rage, bruises like a collar around his pale throat, his belt buckle glinting in the dim light. Brian turned away from his father, to Aaron's face, his gold-flecked gaze softening as soon as they met Brian's.

"Is there anything else you can try to modify his memory?" Brian said to James, not looking away from Aaron. But in the fuzzy space at the edge of his vision, he saw James shake his head.

"This is the strongest I've been in years. Sometimes it just doesn't take. I'm sorry, Brian."

"I'm not."

Brian watched the colonel for a long moment. He knew what he had planned. His service weapon was at his hip. He'd practiced, in his mind, over and over again, what it would be like to look the colonel in the eyes, eyes so like and unlike his own, take aim and fire.

And he found in the moment that he could do it. He *wanted* to do it.

But he knew it would take something from him, something he could not get back.

Walking together in all kinds of weather.

Brian turned to Aaron. "Can you stop his heart from here? I—" He was suddenly just *tired*. He wanted to hold on to Aaron, to leave this place, this *planet*, and never come back. "I don't want to torture him, don't want him in pain. I just want him gone, off my conscience, out of the way of your people. We can burn the body and the cherry tree, make it look like he was drinking away his blue ticket sorrows and fell asleep with a lit cigarette." He shook his head, eyes sweeping around the dry-as-dust yard. "It would make sense. Can you do that?"

"If that's what you need from me, Brian, that's what I will do," Aaron said, and then he took a moment. "Are you sure? I can't undo it once it's done."

Brian cleared his throat and nodded. "Can—can you two take care of the rest of it? There's gas in the GMC that should light the tree up well, and the burned out remains of my Ford are already under the tree. I'm going to take a walk on my own for a bit."

Aaron nodded and leaned toward Brian before stopping himself. Brian stepped into him, pressed a chaste kiss to his mouth, and stepped outside, his father's hate-filled glare on the back of his neck for the last time.

Brian walked for a long time until he couldn't hear the sound of the cherry tree burning, couldn't smell the smoke. He walked until all he heard was the sound of the west wind through the creosote, all he smelled was the desert sage around his knees, so much more tangy and sharp than the sagebrush in Idaho. He fell to his knees, planted his hands in the rusty earth, and let out great, heaving breaths, something like sobs, something like mourning, not for the man who was dead, but for the father he might have been and had never been able to be.

Time passed, the sun got hotter, and Brian pulled himself up. He wandered until he found the shadow of a low hill, where he could have his back against the rock and eyes on the unending horizon.

Eventually, Aaron came to find him, where he sat tracing patterns in the dirt, chest aching but breathing now even, body starting to feel safe and whole in a way he couldn't remember, except for bare, spare moments with Aaron.

Brian blinked up at him, a silhouette in a black cowboy hat.

"Airman?"

"Thanks for doing that. I didn't ever want to hear his voice again. Didn't want to see his face." *Didn't want to see him die, just needed to know that it was done.*

"That's fair," Aaron said, sitting in the dust beside him, leaving a careful distance between their legs. Brian closed it, collapsing against Aaron's side and inhaling the hot, desert smell of him.

After a long moment, Brian shifted to look up at him. "You okay with me driving the rest of the way to the reservation today? I'd rather not spend another night on this land than I need to."

Aaron smiled. "Works for me." He moved to stand, but Brian shook his head, tugging him back down.

Brian nudged him until he was seated again, then swung a leg over his hips, straddling him as Aaron's hands steadied his waist. Brian drank in the calm protectiveness in Aaron's face, the way he didn't smell like smoke or bourbon or cigarettes or cherrywood. He must have used his TK to keep the smells from gathering in his curls or his clothes.

He just smelled like home.

And Aaron just let him look, one hand gliding up his side, up his chest to cup his cheek. Brian leaned in, tightness and pain in his chest finally easing, heart no longer hurting with each panicked beat. He filled his lungs with air. His mind unclenched a little. Then he brushed his lips against Aaron's, and they warmed and parted, giving him space and taste and comfort.

After a long moment, Brian drew back. "Let's get out of here."

*

James joined them in the cab on the drive into the reservation and let Aaron patch him up before they got back on the highway. Aaron watched the horizon as Brian drove the long and dusty road. Stopping for fuel in Glencoe, Brian stepped inside the gas station. On a whim, he bought a five-cent postcard and a stamp, then went back to the truck and unhitched the tarp as Aaron and James stretched their legs amongst the ocotillo and the scrub grass. Inside the W.H. Auden book, inserted at the poem, "Musée des Beaux Arts," Brian found the long bookmark David DuFrois had written his new address on.

He sat in the dust, back against the tire in the shade of Aaron's turquoise truck, and in the light of the fading Boxing Day sun, he wrote:

Dear David,

I cannot express how much you have helped me, changed the course of my life, even. The books you brought opened a new world to me, a world I am now traveling to. I don't think I'll be able to come by for dinner, but I wanted you to know I am going to a good place, a place where I'll be able to hold my love's hand, and no one will sneer or jibe or stalk us like prey. It has evils, too, sicknesses I plan to fight to heal. But I think it will be better for me than here, and I can only hope that you and yours find the peace and purpose I expect to possess soon.

Your friend,

Brian Flynn

Chapter Twenty-Three: T+6 Days

Good-by to you whom I shall see tomorrow,

Next year and when I'm fifty; still good-by.

This is the leave we never really take.

If you were dead or gone to live in China

The event might draw your stature in my mind.

I should be forced to look upon you whole

The way we look upon the things we lose.

We see each other daily and in segments;

Parting might make us meet anew, entire.

You asked me once, and I could give no answer,

How far dare we throw off the daily ruse,

Official treacheries of face and name,

Have out our true identity? I could hazard

An answer now, if you are asking still.

We are a small and lonely human race

Showing no sign of mastering solitude

Out on this stony planet that we farm.

The most that we can do for one another
Is let our blunders and our blind mischances
Argue a certain brusque abrupt compassion.
We might as well be truthful. I should say
They're luckiest who know they're not unique;
But only art or common interchange
Can teach that kindest truth.

—*Adrienne Rich, excerpt from "Stepping Backward," 1951*

December 26, 1951

They drove west into the sunset, the bright southwestern pinks and oranges reflecting lightning stripes down the long, cracked asphalt patches in the road. They were heading to the far side of the rez, to the camp where the Antarans had been hiding to avoid the colonel's prying eyes.

To where they had hidden their repaired ship.

Driving into the camp, it looked like a well-tended Hooverville, circles of mismatched but well cared for tents around campfires, the smell of barbeque and popcorn filling the air. Nearly everyone was at the center of the camp, and Brian caught the flash of silverware, paper plates, and glass bottles before a tent obstructed the view. Over the rumble of the truck, Brian could swear he heard fiddles and guitars and drums.

Aaron grinned. "Trust Mara to throw a good party."

James cut in, "I actually think it's more Jill's doing. She was meeting with the tribal council yesterday, giving them our farewells and thank-yous. They sent her back with a pickup full of fresh meat, corn, squash, beans, and sunflowers."

Brian smiled to himself. "The three sisters."

They drove carefully around the edge of camp, children running out to look at them, then racing back to where their parents were gathered, hollering about "Aaron!" and "his captain!"

Brian pulled the truck into park, and James climbed out of the cab and headed toward the party, giving Aaron and Brian a moment to themselves.

Aaron reached over, putting his hand palm up on the bench seat between them. "Are you ready to meet my family?"

Brian looked at his calloused palm and let the smell of the cool night, the comfort of the truck, and the promise of real, actual welcome fill him up. Then he slid his fingertips across Aaron's palm and gripped his hand tightly. "Yes, *xilla*."

Then Brian popped the door open and tugged Aaron out of the cab with him, laughing as the other man overbalanced on the uneven ground, then used the excuse to wrap his arms around Brian's shoulders, pressing a kiss behind his ear.

Together, hand in hand, they walked toward the crowd.

Brian wasn't sure what he expected. A practiced hush to flow across the crowd, the way it would at a commissioning ceremony or a church? But it wasn't that. It was much louder, warmer, more loving and chaotic than that, people dashing over to hug Aaron as soon as they caught sight of him, then pulling away to let the next person in. With each person, Aaron introduced Brian as: "My *xilla*, US Air Force Captain Bryan Flinn," the full title tripping off his tongue with more pride each time. About the dozenth hug in, when Brian was starting to feel a little frayed, he felt a gentle tug at his elbow. He looked down into the eyes of an Apache woman with long straight black hair worn in the traditional way.

She grinned at him and said, voice crackling over the music, "I'm Jill. This is going to take a while. Want to get some food and some air while Aaron finishes glad-handing?"

"God, yes, thank you, please," Brian muttered. He turned to Aaron, who now crouched beside him as what must have been a half dozen children swarmed him, climbing all over him and wrestling for the best hugging position. Brian said, "Love, I'm going to go get some food with Jill—"

Aaron stood, turning wide eyes to him as children hung and swung off his arms gleefully. "Are you sure, I can—" And he took a breath as he used his TK to gently detach each child and float them in a soft spiral back to the ground as they shrieked and giggled. "I can go with you—"

Brian shook his head, smiling. "No, you're having fun. I'll bring you back a plate, okay?"

"Thank you, love," Aaron said, emphasizing the last word to make sure Brian knew he'd caught it. Then, moving slowly to give Brian a chance to dip away, he made to kiss him goodbye. And Brian leaned into him, grinning against his mouth even as his heart rate cranked into overdrive, certain he'd misunderstood that *something, anything*, bad might happen now he'd shown affection for a man in public, in a massive crowd of strangers. But when he drew back, there wasn't a glare to be seen, no bunched fists, no belts being pulled from their loops. Just happy, smiling people around him.

It buoyed him like helium, like laughing gas, like he'd stepped into another century, another world. It gave him what he needed to raise Aaron's hand to his mouth, kiss the back of it, and then let it go, to shoo him back to his extremely excited miniature fans.

Brian turned to Jill, who was watching him with a knowing eye. She led him in the shortest route out of the mass of bodies to a quiet circle of chairs around a truly astounding feast: ribs and burgers and thick blue-corn soup and sweet squash and colorful beans. She filled a glass with a greenish liquid and handed it to him.

He sniffed it. "Lemonade?" he asked with a smile, expecting something more extraterrestrial.

She smiled back. "Yep, just normal lemonade." She let him fill a heaping plate and settle into one of the chairs. The other folks around them nodded, but left them to talk.

She finished a bite of blue corn before saying, "It's still strange for you, right? Not having to be afraid to touch?"

Brian felt relief like a waterfall on a hot day. "Yeah, and it will sound strange, but I'm grateful to hear you say it."

She raised an eyebrow, taking another big, buttery bite of corn.

He continued, "I was beginning to feel a bit like Ingrid Bergman in *Gaslight*, like I was afraid for no reason, that nothing was wrong."

She shook her head knowingly. "It can get like that, being around them long enough. But if it helps, for the first fifty years of my life, I could never touch a woman in a loving way in public. Not on the rez, not off of it, for fear of what would be done to me by hateful people around us. I was a school teacher, and even if I hadn't been murdered for being queer, I would have lost my job, lost my chance to do anything good to help kids in my tribe."

She rolled her shoulders back, trying to release tension. "Then I met Mara, and slowly, as we got to know each other, things changed. It got easier, having even a weekend every few months where we could just *be*." She gave him a sly smile. "It makes everything else better too. Not having to hide who we are, getting to spend a long day holding hands, sitting next to each other, it improves the sex to no end."

Brian choked on his lemonade, struggling to breathe as Jill cackled.

"Oh, you're going to be fun," she said once he stopped coughing. Then she waved. "Here comes Mara, I think she wants to give you the serum so they can start working with the plutonium without being worried about irradiating you." She spoke quickly as an older woman with white hair and a strong stride approached them. "I got mine a year ago, and there were no side effects. One of the others got hers this afternoon, and it was fine. Are you okay getting it?"

Brian thought for a moment, watching as Mara worked her way

through the crowd toward them. If he had any doubts about going to the stars, about changing his body to make it possible, this was the moment to have them.

But try as he might, all he could feel was giddy excitement. "I appreciate you asking and letting me know it's been safe for you. I'm excited to get it."

She grinned at him before standing to hug Mara in welcome. Brian stood, offering his hand as Mara accepted it with two of hers, her grip strong and sure.

"Captain Flynn, welcome. We are so glad to have you."

"Thank you, Mara. I've felt more welcome here than—" He didn't want to sound bitter, covering it with, "I've felt incredibly welcome."

She twinkled at him. "I am glad to hear it. Has my better half told you about the serum?"

"She has."

"Perfect. Do you have any questions?" She slid her black pack off of her shoulder. Then she removed surgical gloves, a capped needle, and a dark brown bottle of liquid.

"I don't. Jill's told me about it a few times in our conversations."

"I'm glad," Mara said, and they all took a seat. "I can administer it right now if you are comfortable with it."

Brian glanced around. The crowd was beginning to move toward dancing, Aaron's flashing curls still buried amongst hug after hug. The fiddles played something bluesy, something he kept almost recognizing in of the corner of his mind.

"Would you like Aaron with you?" Mara asked, moving to rise; but Brian shook his head.

"He's missed his people, and I'm pretty independent as a person. Even if I'd gotten a chance to get used to having my hand held, I don't know if I'd be the kind of person to want it in a situation like this."

Mara nodded, something like appreciation moving across her face. "That's a good point. He'd mentioned you cared deeply about fairness in relationships; I think that will be good for both of you, starting life on an even footing. Relationships can grow and change, one party taking more of one kind of weight and the other more of another. But just at the start, a perfectly even split is healthy and a good way to practice communication."

"I sure hope so because I don't know any other way to do it," Brian said.

She chuckled and then gestured. "Now, Captain, if you'll roll up your cuff and make a fist for me—ah, good, nice clear veins. This will be easy work."

"Aww," Jill said behind him. "I thought you were going to make him do push-ups to make sure the veins popped clear. We were going to see if Aaron keeled over from the sight!"

Mara huffed her amusement as Brian flushed. "Dear, maybe don't tease the poor man on his first day. He'll be trapped on a ship, lightyears away from escaping your unique sense of humor soon enough."

"*Fine*," Jill said and then took a big bite of stew. "My apologies, Captain. I'll leave you alone."

Brian bit his lips before saying, "I think I may need a few days to adjust. I've never been in a situation where I could talk, much less joke, about being queer without real fear." He looked out at the crowd. "I'll probably lighten up with enough time for my body to realize it's safe."

Mara nodded, then tapped the needle to push the last of the air out. "That's a good way to think of it. It takes most folks, oh, a month to six months. Some of those fears go deeper down, and it can be worth talking to someone for help with unburying and reinterring them in a way that won't cause so much pain." She leaned toward him, voice low. "We'll have lots of time to chat about that kind of thing once we're underway. Are you ready?"

"I am," he said, setting his lemonade down at his feet.

"You'll feel a sharp pinch."

The needle slid into his arm and he gave himself a few long, slow breaths as she carefully depressed the plunger. And then it was done. She pressed down over the needle mark with a cotton ball and put a bandage on his arm. The sounds of the party rose around him again, the hot stew and the cold lemonade gently warming against his ankle. He took a long sip as Mara leaned over him to snag a handful of chips from Jill's plate, making her squawk and gently swat at her.

Mara stood. "I'm going to go and get some good use out of these dancing shoes. Lovely, will you join me?"

"I was keeping Brian company," Jill said as Mara tugged her hand.

Brian waved her off. "I could use a few minutes to myself and to get Aaron a plate. I promise I won't wilt from lack of care."

Jill rolled her eyes but let Mara drag her off to the dancing.

Brian worked his way through a plate that tasted like the best memories of his mother's family before building another for Aaron and then taking his seat again. He tilted his head back and counted to one hundred. He looked straight up into the underbelly of the Milky Way. Even the flickering firelight in his peripheral vision wasn't enough to ruin his night vision as he gazed up and up and up. *In just a few days. In just a few days, I'll see a sky no human had ever seen, see constellations from within them, not just below them.*

He sensed a familiar body coming closer, felt him step between his knees and stand there, following his gaze upward.

"Thinking about the destination?" Aaron asked, voice rough from too much laughing and shouting over the band.

"Imagining the journey," Brian replied, reaching out without looking to trace his fingers up the side of his jeans until he could tuck his finger into Aaron's palm. He squeezed his hand, warm and comforted and held.

Then he met Aaron's eyes, and a flicker of warmth moved in his belly, something slow-burning, closer to an ember than a flame but hotter than skin and just as likely to heat him to his core.

"Want to dance?" Aaron asked.

Brian thought about Arco and about the lab and grinned as he nodded, letting Aaron pull him up and lead him into the heart of the crowd as the music turned slow and soft.

People made way for Aaron, smiling, brushing his shoulders with their hands, giving Brian friendly, soft looks before returning to their own partners. Around them, every variation of couples danced: couples and triads and people dancing happily alone, women and women, men and men, men and women, people Brian might guess were nonbinary with every variation of person. He guessed he would probably have to stop guessing people's genders with so many different kinds accepted around him. He would have to ask Jill for help. And it was *soft*. And safe. And wholesome. And filling, like he'd had a bone-dry vasc in the center of him that was getting its first drips of water in his entire lifetime, just from having these few hours of being himself around people who wouldn't hate or hurt him for it. It felt incredible.

But it was nothing compared to Aaron stopping in the middle of the crowd, draping his arms over Brian's shoulders, and swaying into him. Brian's stomach tightened at the sudden reminder of Aaron's closeness, his careful distance giving Brian the choice, the chance to decide how they would do this, protecting his space even in the crush of the crowd.

But in this moment, Brian didn't *want* space. He didn't *want* separation and careful boundaries. He stepped fully into Aaron, bodies touching in a long line, just to hear the quick gasp between Aaron's teeth, feel his hands tangled in Brian's hair, pulling him until their foreheads were pressing tight and close.

And then it clicked, the song the band was playing. And Brian leaned in, lips moving against the curls around Aaron's ear as he sang along about stormy weather and coming together.

And as the strings faded into the next song, Brian kissed Aaron in the midst of his people, under the loving stars, bodies swaying safe and whole, together.

Chapter Twenty-Four: T+12 Days

Let us return to imperfection's school.

No longer wandering after Plato's ghost,

Seeking the garden where all fruit is flawless,

We must at last renounce that ultimate blue

And take a walk in other kinds of weather.

The sourest apple makes its wry announcement

That imperfection has a certain tang.

Maybe we shouldn't turn our pockets out

To the last crumb or lingering bit of fluff,

But all we can confess of what we are

Has in it the defeat of isolation—

If not our own, then someone's, anyway.

So I come back to saying this good-by,

A sort of ceremony of my own,

This stepping backward for another glance.

Perhaps you'll say we need no ceremony,

Because we know each other, crack and flaw,

Like two irregular stones that fit together.
Yet still good-by, because we live by inches
And only sometimes see the full dimension.
Your stature's one I want to memorize—
Your whole level of being, to impose
On any other comers, man or woman.
I'd ask them that they carry what they are
With your particular bearing, as you wear
The flaws that make you both yourself and human.

—Adrienne Rich, excerpt from "Stepping Backward," 1951

January 1, 1952

In the final hours before the launch on New Year's Day, Aaron kept Brian by his side. Hands held together, shoulders close. And Brian found he mostly felt relieved. He had space inside his mind to think that had always, *always*, since he was a little boy, been dedicated to tracking where his father was.

Now, that space was his again, but he didn't quite know what to do with it yet.

As they sat in the shade of a tent, watching the engineers prepare the fuel, Brian leaned his shoulder against Aaron's. "Tell me about the ship."

Aaron rolled his eyes. "I *told* you about the ship already."

"Aaron," Brian said, low and sure, "if you think I will ever get tired of hearing about the *spaceship* we are *escaping Earth* on, you really don't know me at all."

Aaron chuckled and wrapped his arm around Brian's shoulder. "All right, love."

He described the propulsion system and how the body of the craft was still folded up in a massive natural crack in the mountainside, and they would reattach the engine soon, do the safety checks throughout the afternoon. He told about how they were taking Aaron's truck and how he'd convert her engine to run on solar, how big the captain's quarters were, how Brian would have his own rooms, and—

"And at sunset, we'll take off?"

"At sunset, we'll be off to the stars."

"Perfect," Brian said, feeling it in his bones. "That is perfect."

Brian had grown up in these mountains. Climbed them on orders only to get left behind on them by his brothers as "pranks." Drank from their waters, ran in their winds. The sweet-sour smell of the sage had been the closest thing to home he'd ever loved. And it was in these mountains of his childhood that they'd hidden Aaron's ship.

One of his instructors had come back from the battle of Okinawa with a habit of folding paper cranes. He'd been in a camp there, had nothing to say about it one way or another. But while he taught, his hands were always folding cranes. He'd take a piece of paper the size of a fist and fold it into a crane the length of his thumb. He had a tall glass vase he would toss them into every time he was done. Over and over and over again. Brian figured it was better than smoking or picking at his nails or his face or any other ticks that people who needed to move might have.

Brian would watch him make a crane, trying to guess which sides of the paper would touch which in the final version. He'd tried his hand at it but found the precision of the folds hard to grasp.

That afternoon, Brian stood where the ship had been folded up, slipped between two cantilevered crevices and the desert floor, and watched as it folded and unfolded. Mara, eyes closed, hand outstretched, guided each piece into place, face serene as the material chimed like sweet music as its pieces slotted. The ship's purple-orange glow filled the sky as its repaired engine hummed to life: a nuclear sunrise.

The repetitive motion reminded him of his instructor's cranes; the slide and slickness of it reminded him he'd never seen the inside of space. That the things and shapes that would survive there had absolutely nothing to do with what was needed on Earth.

Brian asked, "How does it break the atmosphere without cracking?"

Aaron raised his eyebrows. "We can lift anything with our powers we could lift with our bodies, so it needs to be light. We can lift it up and up, slowly. But after that, when we need to go into cryosleep, we will need slow-burning, hard-pushing fuel."

"The plutonium."

Aaron nodded.

They watched as Mara loaded the plutonium canisters, Argonne Labs stickers still shining bright on them.

Mara kitted everyone out with some skintight clothes. Close-knit, closer knit that anything Brian had seen before. Something like the pantyhose Nurse Kelly liked. Mara had said it had something to do with helping the blood flow when he was weightless, but he rather suspected Aaron just wanted to see him in tight pants. He certainly didn't mind the view going the other way. The ship shuddered down a final time, the last fold bending and rebending until it was a simple shape. A smooth, gliding shape.

*

The launch was nothing like the exploding and screaming rockets Brian had expected, sitting beside the captain's chair on the bridge.

The ship lifted from the desert floor with a lightness that belied the weight of the people filling it. The bridge wavered and shook as they fought their way up and up through the desert winds that Brian knew only got stronger the higher you flew.

The delta-riven hills and arroyos became like veins, like great, green spreading hands across the landscape as they rose. Then there was Aaron's hand, wrapped around Brian's, fingers fitted between his before the main hatch was even shut. Aaron gave orders to his crew like he'd been the one who'd gone to West Point, and all the time, Brian's hand was in his.

No one did anything, said anything. A few smiled, like it was sweet, like it was *normal.* Something deep and abiding was beginning to unhitch under Brian's breastbone with each passing minute they rose into the sky.

"You ready to see something wonderful?" Aaron murmured, and Brian grinned, his shoulders loosening further as the reservation disappeared into the checkerboard clouds below them.

"Sure," he said.

Aaron looked out the window and closed his eyes, raising his other hand. He frowned a little, his face working as if he was lifting a weight, moving something heavy. Then he sighed, easing back in his captain's chair a little.

He nodded toward the window to where one of those high clouds was rising, rising with them. Then it began to break apart, to spread, and spread, and spread, until it was all filaments and dust, the crane-wing shadow of their ship hard and black across it. And then, just as they turned, the sun broke over the ship, slipping through the cloud, lighting it up until—

"You going to keep showing off or get us into the ionosphere, Captain Antares?" came Mara's wry voice from the science officer's station.

Aaron's gaze never left Brian's as he said, "I intend to do both."

And Brian leaned in to give his smirking mouth a kiss, knowing the rainbow Aaron had made him would keep outside the window for a few moments more.

Acknowledgements

Thank you to author Eric Bell (Mescalero Apache). Thank you to Mescalero Apache Reservation Cultural Center Director Joey Padilla for welcoming me to your Cultural Center, reviewing the manuscript, and providing incredibly helpful feedback.

Thank you also to Brycea Pacheco for providing a cultural sensitivity read as an enrolled member of the Quechan tribe.

Thank you to Elizabetta McKay for the thoughtful, funny, astute, and impactful editing.

Thank you to Argonne National Laboratory for confirming the use of the excerpt from the *Argonne News*.

Thank you to the anonymous Congressional staffer who wrote so sympathetically and passionately in support of queer, disabled, Black, and other marginalized services members who were subject to blue discharges during and after WWII in your report, *Investigations of the National War Effort: Blue Discharges. United States Committee on Veterans Affairs, House of Representatives* (1949). Though even the superheroic librarians at the Library of Congress couldn't find your name, someday I hope to honor you more fully.

Thank you to the Jess Collins Trust for granting permission for the use of Robert Duncan's exquisite poetry, which is copyrighted by the Trust. Excerpts are from: "Under Ground," "Passage Over Water," and "A Pair of Uranian Garters for Aurora Bligh."

Thank you to W.W. Norton & Company and Adrienne Rich's estate. The lines from "By No Means Native," "For the Conjunction of Two Planets," "The Kursaal at Interlaken," "Stepping Backward," and "Vertigo." Copyright © 2016 by the Adrienne Rich Literary Trust. Copyright (c) 1951 by Adrienne Rich, from Collected Poems: 1950—2012 by Adrienne Rich. Used by permission of W. W. Norton & Company, Inc.

Thank you to the Harry S. Truman Library and Museum for confirming the use of the two quotes.

Thank you to Mark Mitchell and David Leavitt for producing the exceptional volume *Pages Passed from Hand to Hand: The Hidden Traditional of Homosexual Literature in English from 1748 to 1914*, Houghton Mifflin, NY (1997).

We have always been here.

About Jo Carthage

Jo Carthage is a bi, cis woman living in Silicon Valley. In her career, Jo has worked with survivors of labor and sex trafficking in DC, helped get incredible women and queer folks elected to state and national office in three states, and thinks politics and science fiction go together beautifully. Jo's grandfather worked as a nuclear physicist at Oak Ridge in the 1950s, but it wasn't until a 2019 family road trip veered off course and she spent an afternoon at EBT-I that she started to write Atomic Age fiction.

Jo was honored to have *Nuclear Sunrise* favorably reviewed by the Director of the Mescalero Apache Cultural Center and intends to donate a portion of proceeds to their important work. As a writer, Jo loves slow burn, hurt/comfort, queer history, enemies-to-lovers, and happy endings.

Email

jocarthage@proton.me

Facebook

www.facebook.com/jocarthage

Twitter

@jocarthage

Website

www.jocarthage.com

Instagram

www.Instagram.com/jocarthage

Tumblr

www.Jocarthage.tumblr.com

www.ninestarpress.com

www.facebook.com/ninestarpress

www.facebook.com/groups/NineStarNiche

www.twitter.com/ninestarpress

www.instagram.com/ninestarpress